Adrienne Chinn was born in Grand Falls, Newfoundland, grew up in Quebec, and eventually made her way to London, England after a career as a journalist. In England she worked as a TV and film researcher before embarking on a career as an interior designer, lecturer, and writer. When not up a ladder or at the computer, she can usually be found rummaging through flea markets or haggling in the Marrakech souk.

🐦 @adriennechinn

f @AdrienneChinnAuthor

# Also by Adrienne Chinn

*The English Wife*
*The Lost Letter from Morocco*

# The English Wife

## Adrienne Chinn

**OneMoreChapter**

One More Chapter
a division of HarperCollins*Publishers*
The News Building
1 London Bridge Street
London SE1 9GF

www.harpercollins.co.uk

This paperback edition 2020

First published in Great Britain in ebook format by
HarperCollins*Publishers* 2020

A catalogue record for this book
is available from the British Library

TPB ISBN: 9780008387006
PB ISBN: 9780008314583

This novel is entirely a work of fiction.
The names, characters and incidents portrayed in it are
the work of the author's imagination. Any resemblance to
actual persons, living or dead, events or localities is
entirely coincidental.

Set in Birka by Palimpsest Book Production Ltd, Falkirk
Stirlingshire

Printed and bound in Great Britain by
CPI Group (UK) Ltd, Croydon CR0 4YY

*For my mother, Charlotte Mary (Mae) Edwards Chinn*

*Always a Newfoundlander*

*'The huge island ... stands, with its sheer, beetling cliffs, out of the ocean, a monstrous mass of rock and gravel, almost without soil, like a strange thing from the bottom of the great deep, lifted up, suddenly, into sunshine and storm, but belonging to the watery darkness out of which it has been reared; the eye, accustomed to richer and softer scenes, finds something of a strange and almost startling beauty in its bold, hard outlines, cut out on every side, against the sky.'*

*– Robert Traill Spence Lowell, nineteenth-century American missionary*

# PART ONE

PART ONE

# *Chapter 1*

## Liverpool – 5 February 1946

The grey bulk of the RMS *Mauritania* sits like a warehouse alongside the Liverpool dock. Black smoke belches from its two large funnels. Ellie bounces Emmett, swaddled in a thick wool blanket and the garments she'd spent the winter knitting by the fireplace, and coos into his shell-like ear. He fixes her with his impassive blue/brown gaze. Such an odd little man with his one blue eye and his one brown eye, and the fine blond eyebrows he'd taken to arching when unimpressed. The ship melds with the lowering clouds and the rumbling sea, but, at least for now, the incessant rain has let up, though Ellie's face is damp with the humid threat of an imminent deluge.

'It would take a huge iceberg to sink that thing,' Ellie's sister, Dottie, says, blowing into her mitts. 'There's lots of icebergs around Newfoundland. I read about it in the library.'

'Thanks, Dottie. You're a harbinger of doom, as always.'

Henry Burgess lifts his glasses and squints at the ship. 'I shouldn't worry, Ellie Mae. I've been reading about the *Mauritania*. She's been doing runs all over the world since the war began. She's a tough old thing.'

Ellie scans the pier, crowded with thousands of young women, many with infants and toddlers, with faces as blank and terrified as her own. 'There are so many of us.' She looks at her father.

'What are we all doing, Poppy?' She bites down on her lip and blinks back the tears that salt her eyes. 'I can't even remember what Thomas looks like.'

Henry lifts a gloved hand as if to pet Ellie's arm, but hesitates and shoves it into his coat pocket. 'I don't expect he's changed all that much.'

'I never even knew about the prisoner exchange until I received the telegram from Canada. I still can't believe he was in hospital in London for four months and I didn't even know. He was too sick to get a message to me.'

'Quite. But he's recovered now, I understand. Didn't you say he's back fishing with his father?'

'That's what he said in his letter. In a place called Tippy's Tickle on the north coast of Newfoundland. I couldn't find it on the map in the school library.'

Dottie shifts Ellie's suitcase from one hand to the other with a grunt. 'You'll be off feasting on bananas and white bread instead of having to eat Woolton pie and that horrible National Loaf that everyone knows they put cinema sweepings into.' Dottie pouts, her lips reddened with what Ellie suspects to be one of her stolen lipsticks. 'You'll forget all about me and Poppy once you're over in Canada, just like you forgot about George.'

'Don't be ridiculous. You're family, though I don't know what happened to the lovely little girl you used to be. Hopefully, by the time I see you again, you'll have matured.'

'I'm mature. I'm sixteen. I'm not a child, Ellie. Just ask George.'

'It's not Canada, pet,' Henry corrects Dottie. 'It's Newfoundland. Newfoundland is a British dominion, similar to Canada and Australia.'

'What do you mean, just ask George?'

The ship's horn blows out an ear-splitting bellow. The crowd surges forward like a wave, knocking Ellie off balance. Henry grabs her arm. 'You should be going, pet.' He removes a ticket from his coat pocket and places it in her gloved hand. 'I've paid a porter to take your trunk to your room. It's first class, so you and Emmett should have some privacy.'

Ellie's eyes widen. 'First class? Poppy! You didn't have to do that. It's far too dear.'

'It's the least I can do, pet.' He tweaks Emmett's chubby cheek. 'Take care, Ellie Mae. He kisses her awkwardly on her cheek. 'You know you can always come home if things ...' His voice catches and he clears his throat. 'Right, Dottie, we'd best be off before it starts raining again. They're threatening gales from Iceland and we've got a long journey home.'

Dottie kisses the baby on his cheek. 'Bye, little one.' She holds out the suitcase. 'Goodbye, Ellie.'

'That's no way to say goodbye, Dottie. I don't know when I'll see you again.'

Dottie stares at Ellie. 'What do you expect? You're off to a big new country where everything will be lovely and easy. They weren't bombed, were they? They don't have rationing, do they? Thousands of people weren't killed there, were they? I think you married Thomas just to get away from this horrible place. To get away from Poppy and me.'

'Dottie, how can you say that? I've been crying every night wondering when I'll see you and Poppy again. It's crushing me to leave you, and Norwich, and ... and everything. You have no idea. It's my home. I'm going to miss you and Poppy awfully.'

'If you really cared about us, you'd stay. You promised you'd stay. You promised! You're a liar, Ellie!'

'Now, pet, you don't really mean that. Ellie's your sister. Blood is thicker than water and all that.'

*Adrienne Chinn*

Dottie tucks her hand around her father's elbow. 'Let's go, Poppy. It's cold, and I'm hungry. Let's get some fish and chips. Just the two of us. I saw a place just around the corner.'

Ellie stumbles into her cabin with Emmett and the suitcase. Four double bunk beds crowd the floor space and someone has deposited her trunk behind the door. A young woman in an ill-fitting suit leans up on her elbow from the top of one of the beds. 'Bloody 'ell. A baby? It isn't a crier, is it?'

Ellie looks down at her ticket and back at the young woman. 'I'm sorry. I think I'm in the wrong room. I'm meant to be in first class.'

A whoop of laugher. 'This is it, angel.' The young woman rises and swings her legs over the side of the bunk, the skin stained with gravy browning to look like tights. Thank goodness for Thomas and his 'in' with the American GIs. She'd never been short of nylons.

Ellie takes a deep breath and sets the suitcase down beside the bunk by the small porthole window. 'Is there anyone here?'

'Be my guest.' The rasping of a match against grit. 'I'm Mona. Had to haul my ass all the way up 'ere from Lewisham. Bloody nightmare.' She holds the match against a cigarette and inhales until the tip glows red. She blows on the match and drops it on the linoleum floor. 'Still, I'm off to Toronto. Can't be worse than Lewisham. They bombed the shit outta that place.' She sucks on the cigarette as she watches Ellie set Emmett on a bed and free him of the blanket and knitted cap and mitts. 'Where you off to, luv?'

'Newfoundland.'

'Holy shit. I heard about that place. Dated a bloke from there before I met Dave. Better you than me.'

'Boat,' Emmett says, fixing Ellie with his serious gaze.

'Yes, darling. We're on a boat. And now you're on a bed. You'll sleep with me while we're on the boat and then we'll go live with Daddy, like I told you.'

She leans over and gives him a kiss on his chubby cheek. Sniffing, she wrinkles her nose. Taking off her coat and her feathered fedora, Ellie lays them neatly on the bed and fishes a cloth nappy out of her suitcase.

"Old on, luv! What're you doing?'

'Changing his nappy.'

'Give us a flippin' break.' Mona climbs down from her perch and shoves her feet into a pair of sturdy shoes.

The cabin door swings open. A young red-haired woman in a net snood and camel-hair coat stands in the entrance, cradling an infant. She glances around the room in confusion. 'Is this first class?'

Mona rolls her eyes as she pushes past the new arrival. 'Bloody Nora. Dave bloody better be worth five days of this or I'll be straight back to Blighty on a troop ship.'

**Five days later**

Halifax harbour is drab and grey. A flurry of snow swirls over a rocky shoreline and wooden houses like upturned apple crates. Ellie edges her way past the others onto the deck, Emmett clutching her hand as he toddles along beside her.

The crossing had been awful, the waves a seascape of mountains and valleys, the ship like a cork bouncing and tipping its way across the Atlantic. She'd given up trying to eat after the first day, and would have stayed prone on her bed if the stench of vomit and drying nappies hadn't driven her out to sit on the stairs to the deck where she at least could breathe in the fresh, salty air.

As the grey bulk of the *Mauritania* steams into the harbour, the juddering black line on the harbour front transforms into a mass of shouting, waving people. Ellie clutches Emmett closer. Thomas is out there somewhere. Waiting to take her and the baby on the train up through Nova Scotia and onto the ferry across to Newfoundland. They'll be a family in this new land of hers. She can make this work. It will be fine.

She picks up Emmett. Resting his weight against her hip, she points at the wooden buildings clustered along the harbour. 'Look, Emmy. Houses. Daddy's there to meet us.'

Emmett fixes his mother with a serious gaze. 'Boat.'

When she finally disembarks, Thomas is there waiting for them in a dark brown wool coat and a felt fedora. He leans on a crutch and holds up a bag of oranges. His face is lean and lines fan out from the corners of his eyes as he smiles. A thin scar like a sickle loops around his left eye and cheek. He leans forward and kisses her.

'Ellie Mae.'

Her eyes sweep over the pinned-up trouser leg; at the space where his lower right leg and foot should have been. Setting her jaw in a firm line, she smiles at him. At this stranger. Her husband.

# *Chapter 2*

## New York City – 9 September 2011

A movement outside the window catches Sophie's eye. The hawk turns its head, fixing her in its yellow eye as it glides past the shining glass, its orange-red tail feathers a stark contrast to the blue summer sky above the city's skyscrapers.

'Sophie? Can I have Jackie book your flight to Newfoundland? You're clear what the consortium needs you to do?'

Sophie looks across the vast Italian glass desk at Richard Niven, the man whose award-winning architecture practice had drawn her over from London to New York ten years before. His thinning grey hair is cropped close to his bull-like head, and round, black-rimmed glasses frame his piercing hazel eyes. *You look like a buzzard.* She imagines him in twenty years' time, jowls dropping from his square jawline, his eyes drooping and watery. By then he'd look like a vulture. Turning into his spirit creature.

'I understand, Richard.'

'Those photos you took up on the Newfoundland coast ten years ago, well, that coastline is just what the consortium has been looking for. Luxury travellers love nothing more than a place in an exotic, "eco"—' he tweaks his fingers to indicate quotation marks '—location. Especially one that's virtually impossible to access. Keeps out the riffraff. We're talking about absolute exclusivity here, Sophie. They love the idea of Newfoundland. No one's even heard of the place.'

'Richard, the photos weren't really meant ... I mean, they were basically holiday snaps. The local community ... I'm not sure how the consortium's vision is going to go down with them. The hotel's going to be a hard enough sell, but, seriously, Richard, a golf course? It's winter there for eight months of the year, and it's all moss and wonky trees. You have no idea. Those cliffs are a death trap. You know the locals call it The Rock? There's a reason for that.'

Her boss waves his hand as if he's swatting an annoying fly. 'They play golf in Scotland, don't they? My God, they haven't seen the sun there for centuries. I got dragged around St Andrews last June with that obnoxious TV guy, pitching for his hotel job in a bloody parka. Couldn't feel my fingers for hours. Bloody June! I could see my breath! Newfoundland can't be any worse than that.'

'Yes, but, you know, the locals in Tippy's Tickle ... I mean, don't you think it's better to get the locals on board rather than buying them out? It could be a wonderful employment opportunity for them. They've been having a hard time up there since the cod fishery shut down. There are a lot of talented people—'

Richard's fleshy face folds into in a frown. 'That's another thing. Tippy's Tickle? What kind of a name is that? That'll have to go.' He pushes his glasses down his large nose and peers at her over the top of the frames. 'All you need to do is secure the land, Sophie. Everyone has a price and the treasure chest is full. We need hotel staff with experience, not some local yokels. Get them to sell up, and I'll make you the lead architect on the project.'

Sophie sits back in the black leather chair. 'The lead architect?'

'Absolutely.'

This was a turn-up for the books. No matter the awards she'd brought to the practice, the front-cover features in *Architectural Digest*, the hard graft on the front line as the project architect, she'd never been made lead architect. That was a job for the big boys. Richard Niven, Tony Mason and Baxter T. Randall. The Triumvirate.

She frowns. 'I'm not sure, Richard.'

A thick black eyebrow twitches above his glasses. 'You're not sure?'

'I want you to make me a partner in the firm.'

Richard's eyebrows shoot upwards like two birds taking flight. 'Partner? You know I can't promise that. I have to speak to the other partners. It has to be a unanimous decision, which is ... well. I'm sure you understand.'

*Yeah, sure I understand.* She could almost feel the glass ceiling bang against her head. 'You're the controlling partner. I'm sure you can sway the others.' She stands and straightens the jacket of her Armani suit. 'Think of the consortium, Richard. Think of all the awards the firm will win. Think of the publicity. Richard Niven & Associates Architects will be up there with Corbusier and Frank Lloyd Wright.'

Richard fixes her with a stare, his eyes like two green marbles flecked with orange. 'Fine. A partner, then.' He presses the intercom on his desk. 'Jackie, get Sophie on the next flight to Newfoundland.' He glances over at Sophie. 'Book economy.'

# *Chapter 3*

## Over the Atlantic Ocean – 11 September 2011

Sophie leans over the armrest and squints through the greasy fingerprints streaking the aeroplane's window. The late summer sky is vivid blue above the clouds drifting like wads of tissue over the inky water far below. The afternoon sun throws a sharp streak of light across her lap. Pulling down the shutter, she glances at her watch. Three forty-five. She could have done without the 4am dash to LaGuardia and the tedious layovers in Toronto and Halifax. Halifax airport, the most boring airport in the world. Not even a Starbucks. Almost eight bloody hours to Gander since she stepped on the plane in New York. Getting Jackie to book her on the milk run had to be Richard's idea of a joke.

Sophie rubs her temples. The aeroplane rattles with the excited chatter of "plane people" heading back to Newfoundland for a ten-year reunion. Ten years already since those thirty-eight international planes had been diverted to Newfoundland on 9/11. She is a plane person too. But she isn't here for a reunion party. A party is the last thing on her mind.

She squints as a face materialises in the murk of her mind's eye. *Will he still be in Tippy's Tickle? No, no, no. It's over, Sophie! It's been ten years. Get a life, woman.* She erases the face, like she's wiping away a chalk image on a blackboard.

She stuffs in her iPod earbuds and switches on her chill-out playlist, slumping back into the lumpy seat with a yawn. Her body feels so heavy, like she's wrapped in a duvet. If only she could just do that – burrow under a duvet and block out the phone calls and the emails and the meetings, meetings, meetings. She swore her skin had looked grey this morning when she'd staggered into the bathroom at three-thirty, drenched in sweat. Bloody New York humidity. She had to do something about that fluorescent light, though. No woman over twenty-five, let alone a forty-eight-year-old, should have to deal with fluorescent light. It was the light of the devil.

Still, this time the prize is worth it. Partner in Richard Niven's architecture practice. Everything she's ever wanted. Everything her late mother, Dottie, had always wanted for her. Success. Independence. Freedom. Queen of the hill. Top of the heap. New York. New York.

Well done her. She'd held her nerve with Richard. Refused to back down. Just like her mother had taught her. Dottie would be so proud.

She rubs her eyes. So why has she been feeling so bloody ... empty? If only she didn't feel like the air was constantly pressing her into the ground, like she was a lump of mozzarella having the water pressed out. If she could wake up for once without the empty-stomached anxiety that had been plaguing her for months. Everything was just so ... just so nothing.

She shakes her head impatiently and closes her eyes as Adele's 'Someone Like You' wafts into her ears. She's just tired. The break from the office will do her good.

It'd been ten years since she'd stepped foot on The Rock. Stranded there for five days in the middle of nowhere after all the air traffic was grounded, while the world fell apart on 9/11.

At least this time she was coming to Newfoundland voluntarily. Well, almost voluntarily. She never should have shown Richard the photos she'd taken in the outport village of Tippy's Tickle back in September 2001. Of Ellie and Florie's general store, of the whales spouting off the coast, of her aunt Ellie's handsome Victorian merchant house, Kittiwake, standing like a colourful sentinel on the cliff above the village. On the same cliff where the consortium wanted to build the hotel.

What would her mother have said about turfing Ellie off her property? Sophie grunts. That wasn't hard. *'Keep your eye on the prize, Sophie. Don't let anyone keep you from fulfilling your potential, least of all your aunt. She squandered everything God gave her on a man. She made her bed, now she has to lie in it. You don't owe Ellie anything.'*

She could hear her mother's clipped English accent over Adele's honeyed voice. *'Do your best, Sophie. Get up early. Stay up late. Work those weekends and holidays. Show everyone that you're somebody. Show them. Show them all. Don't let anyone stand in your way or distract you. Don't make my mistake, Sophie. Don't regret the person you could have been.'*

Oh, she'd been a good student. She'd worked hard and now had everything she'd ever wanted – an imminent partnership at an international architectural firm in New York, a gorgeous rent-controlled apartment in Gramercy Park, a pension plan, designer clothes, money in the bank. No plants, pets, partners or children to distract her. It was better not to get too attached to living things. They only ended up leaving. Or dying. First her father, George, over twenty years ago of a heart attack as he inspected the Cherry Cobblers production line at Mcklintock's, then Dottie back in 2000. Lung cancer. Cigarettes will get you every time.

It was okay. She was okay. She didn't need anyone.

Sophie hadn't even known her aunt Ellie existed until she'd opened an envelope addressed to *The Parry Family* one Christmas back in the late 70s. The card had a cartoon moose surrounded by tinsel-strewn Christmas trees on the front. Inside, in a fine, confident hand: *To all of you at Christmas, from your loving sister and aunt, Ellie.* She'd copied the address into the small green leather address book her father had given her for her fifteenth birthday. Then she'd placed the Christmas card beside the mahogany clock on the black marble mantelpiece, with the ones from her father's colleagues at Mcklintock's Chocolates, and the ones from the Women's Institute and the Norfolk and Norwich University Hospital Auxiliary. It was gone the next day.

Sophie shakes her head to jolt away the image that threatens to materialise again in the blackness behind her eyelids. She can't let him into her head. His brown eyes, quizzical and teasing. Her mother had been right. Men only confuse you. Best to keep them at arm's length. At least the ones who could matter. The ones like Sam.

Maybe that's why her mother had married George Parry. Because he never really mattered to her. She didn't do much to hide that fact. Poor Daddy was a means to an end. A means for her mother to become top of the social elite of Norwich.

George did everything he could to make Dottie happy. Join the Lions Club. *Tick.* Suck up to the owner of Mcklintock's Chocolates. *Tick.* Become a patron of the Norwich Philharmonic Orchestra. *Tick.* Buy bigger, more expensive houses in better neighbourhoods as he worked his way up to managing director of Mcklintock's. *Tick. Tick. Tick.* But her mother was never a happy woman. Sophie had grown up in Norwich in a beautiful house heavy with unspoken words. She'd escaped to university in London as soon as she turned eighteen, Frank Lloyd Wright's *The Natural House* and a sketchbook under her arm. It'd been a relief. Like throwing off a thick wool coat in an overheated room. She'd never get married. Ever.

Sophie opens her eyes and examines her hands, moving her fingers the way she'd been taught at the Sign Language Centre. *'Hello, Becca. How are you?'* Becca must be eighteen now. Sophie didn't really know what had prompted her to learn sign language, when she'd never intended to go back to Newfoundland. She'd been curious, she supposed. And it was something else to put on her CV. Chances were Becca and Sam didn't even live in Tippy's Tickle anymore. People move on. It will be better if they've moved on.

Sophie loosens her seatbelt and rubs at the stiffness in her neck. She'd meant to keep in touch with her aunt. But after posting out the first couple of Christmas cards, bought in a hurry at Browne's between client meetings, time just got away from her, even as Ellie's annual Christmas and birthday cards, full of the chatty goings-on of Tippy's Tickle, sat on Sophie's mantelpiece like a reproach, until they'd end up in the 'To Do' pile on her desk, begging for a response that she'd never get around to writing.

She'd thought of Sam often, at first, and an ache would form that would roll into a ball and sit in her stomach like an anchor. He'd left messages, which she hadn't returned, even though her heart had buzzed with pleasure when she'd found his messages on her phone. She'd meant to call, to text at the very least. She'd stood in the kitchen of her apartment with her finger hovering over the numbers on her mobile phone at least a half dozen times. But, she hadn't called him. Or texted him. She'd wanted to so much. But, it would never work. He knew that. He'd said as much himself the last time she'd seen him. That had hurt. Especially after ... No. She wasn't going to let herself be hurt.

She shakes her head, catching a sideways glance from the over-tanned Florida retiree beside her as she grabs for an earbud that pops out of her ear. Bloody Sam. What is he doing in her head like this?

Sophie turns off the music and stares out the window at the sky. They say time heals all wounds, but they're wrong. Time buries all wounds. Dig them out, and the wounds still bleed. Better to keep them buried. The words from a pop song spring into her mind. *Absolutely no regrets.* She has absolutely no regrets. There'd been a crazy moment when the idea of living an artist's life on the north coast of Newfoundland with a widowed lover and his deaf daughter, not to mention that ridiculous beast of a dog, had brought her up short on the path that had always been so clear and straight. Then Sam had rejected her. The phone messages he'd left her in New York couldn't erase that fact. If he'd done it once, he could do it again.

No, she has absolutely no regrets. Her path is clear, her focus laser-sharp, as long as she stays on course. The prize is everything: partner in the firm now; then, in a few years, when Richard retires, managing director of Richard Niven & Associates Architects. A long-distance relationship with Sam would have complicated everything. Some things were better left alone.

All she needs to do now is convince Ellie and Florie and some of the villagers with places along the tickle to sell up. The consortium wanted to build a restaurant down on the shore too, and put in a marina for the multi-millionaires' yachts sailing up from Massachusetts and Rhode Island. The financial package the consortium was offering to the villagers was generous. It shouldn't be that hard. She'll keep telling herself that. But she has a bad feeling. Her stomach flutters and beads of sweat break out on her forehead. She brushes the sweat away with the back of her hand. *Why's it so bloody hot everywhere?*

The plane veers right. Sophie flips up the window blind. The sun, bright in the western sky, burns out the blueness until all that's left is throbbing white light. She leans her forehead against the warm glass and closes her eyes. Willing the heat to erase the face that threatens to form again in her mind. Wondering if coming back is a huge mistake.

# Chapter 4

## Norwich, England – 26 July 1940

Ellie steps back from the easel and squints at the dimpled peel of the orange on the canvas, looking, she thinks, like the spitting image of the dents and pores on the face of Mr Pilch, the greengrocer. She picks up a small, fine-tipped paintbrush and dabs at the titanium white paint on the palette she balances in her left hand. Leaning closer, she brushes delicate strokes of white onto the dimpled skin, copying the effects of the light filtering through the branches of the elm tree outside the large arched window as it gleams on the fruit.

'Cracking job, there, Miss Burgess. You've caught the feeling of that orange extremely well. Can you see when you paint, that you must put aside your notions of what you're observing, and become like a child observing an object for the first time?' The woman points a blunt-tipped finger at Ellie's artwork, dragging the sleeve of her embroidered white muslin blouse across the rainbow of wet paint on Ellie's palette. 'Can you see the green cast to the orange? The way the shadow at its edges is almost violet? Can you see how the orange is telling you its story?'

Ellie's heart jumps. Four weeks into the advanced oil-painting class and this is the first time the celebrated guest tutor, Dame Edith Spink RA, has singled her out for praise.

'Thank you, Dame Edith. I do think I understand. I'd always

thought an orange was round and smooth ... and orange. But, it's not at all. My brain was telling me one thing, but my eyes are telling me another.'

The great woman stands upright and rests her hands on the yellow canvas skirt covering her generous hips. 'Indeed, Miss Burgess. Now you begin to be an artist, rather than simply a renderer.'

Ellie's face burns, the compliment almost too much to process. She catches a blue-eyed glare aimed at her by Susan Perry-Gore. 'Thank you, Dame Edith.'

'You've heard that I've been commissioned to do some work for the War Artists' Advisory Committee?'

Ellie nods at the other students dabbing earnestly at their canvases. 'We ... we've all heard.'

'Indeed. I'm working on a portrait of Corporal Deirdre Cross. Very brave young woman. Saved one of our pilots by pulling him out of his burning plane and throwing herself on top of him when the plane's bomb went off.'

Ellie shakes her head. 'I hadn't heard of that.'

The older woman huffs and runs her hand over the neat central parting of her greying brown hair. 'The war isn't just about men, Miss Burgess. There are many brave and capable young women out there doing their part. Their stories must be heard.'

'Yes, Dame Edith.'

'I find that I'll be requiring an assistant. I have another commission to start as soon as I finish Corporal Cross's portrait.' The woman frowns, a deep line creasing the still-smooth skin of her broad forehead. 'Just to mix the paints and clean the studio, of course. Would you be interested, Miss Burgess? I couldn't pay you, of course, but you could watch and learn.'

Ellie sucks in her breath. Had she just heard right? Had Dame Edith Spink, the first woman to be elected as a full member to the Royal Academy, asked her if she'd like to help in her studio?

'Oh, yes! I'll do my absolute best for you.'

'Right. See me after class on Monday. We'll make arrangements. You're not worried about travelling around town, are you, what with this bombing nonsense going on?'

Ellie shakes her head, the net snood holding her ash-blonde hair bouncing on the shoulders of her blue cotton dress. 'Not at all. My father said the Germans are mainly after the factories down by the riverside, so I don't go anywhere near there. In fact, I'm meeting my friend Ruthie to see a film after class. We're not going to let any Jerry keep us away from Tyrone Power in *Jesse James*. We've been waiting ages for it to reach Norwich.'

'Good show. *Nil illegitimi carborundum.* We'll speak after class on Monday.'

Ellie spins out the door of the imposing Victorian red-brick edifice of the Norwich School of Art and Design, her heart beating so fast that she's sure it will fly out of her chest. This is the day her life starts. She'll be an artist, just like the wonderful Dame Edith. No, no, that's not quite right. I AM an artist. I AM an artist. Dame Edith has chosen her over everyone else in the class. Over that swot Graham Simmons and his aggressive Cubism, over Grace Adamson and her neo-Impressionist dots and splashes, over even Susan Perry-Gore and her precise Constable landscapes.

She hurries up the road, skirting around the cobbles filled with muddy water from the morning showers, past the knapped flint walls of the medieval Halls, and up St Andrews Hill towards the shops in London Street. She glances at her watch as she rushes past the outdoor market and weaves her way through the busy shopping streets to All Saints Green. When she reaches the soaring Art Deco exterior of the Carlton Cinema, she stops under the canopy and leans her flushed face into the cool, light breeze.

She can't wait to tell Ruthie the news. And George too, of course. She'll ring him tomorrow before he heads off to work at the chocolate factory, though she already knows what her fiancé will say: 'Well done, old girl. I always knew you had it in you. You're as good as that French fellow, Money, in my eyes, you know that.'

Sweet, faithful, reliable George, who'd once got Picasso confused with a piccolo. He was nothing like Tyrone Power, but maybe that was all for the best.

A poke in the ribs. 'C'mon, Sleepy. We're home.'

Ellie blinks and rubs her eyes with her gloved fingers. The bus lurches to a stop. She yawns and rises from her seat.

'Sorry. I wasn't snoring, was I?'

'Fit to beat the band. You must've been dreaming about divine Tyrone. He's absolutely gravy, don't you think? I just love his little moustache.'

Ellie looks over at her friend's broad, friendly face, the cheeks flushed bright pink from the warm summer air. Under her navy felt beret, Ruthie's carefully rolled brown hair sits unravelling on the collar of the summer dress she's remade out of her mother's old floral dressing gown.

'Last week it was all about Clark Gable. You're as fickle as they come, Ruthie.'

Ruthie Huggins prods Ellie down the bus' stairs. 'Hurry up,

Ellie. It's late and I'm starving. Mum said she'd save me some shepherd's pie.'

'Shepherd's pie? Where'd she get the lamb?'

'Uncle Jack's old ewe kicked the bucket last week. He's been divvying it up. Dad's taking the train up to Fakenham tomorrow to get some more.' She presses her forefinger against her lips. 'All strictly hush-hush.'

They jump off the platform onto the pavement. Ruthie grabs Ellie's arm and pulls her back sharply as a bicycle whips by in front of them.

'Crumbs!' Ellie exclaims. 'That was close.'

Ruthie tucks her hand into the crook of Ellie's arm. 'You'd think they'd be more careful in this blackout. Margery Roberts's cousin got run over by a bicycle in London last week.' She reaches into her sleeve and pulls out a white handkerchief, waving it into the inky night as they pick their way across the road.

They hurry past the boarded-up windows of Mr Pilch's greengrocer's and down the road, stopping at an iron gate in the cobbled flint wall of St Bartholomew's Catholic School for Boys. Ellie jangles her key in the lock. The gate swings open, screeching like a gull. Ruthie reaches over and gives Ellie a hug. Their arms intertwined, the girls gaze up at the sliver of moon in the sky. A lone cricket chirps from somewhere in the school's new vegetable garden.

'Do you suppose they'll come back, Ellie?'

'I hope not. But they probably will.'

'It's been quiet since the nineteenth. And that was only one plane. They'll probably go after London before us. There's nothing much here but mustard and chocolate.'

'There's the munitions works down by the riverside, Ruthie. They shot that up the other day.'

'I know.' Ruthie sighs and leans her head on Ellie's shoulder. 'I like to think they'd ignore us. I don't want things to change.'

Ellie brushes her hand against Ruthie's soft hair. 'Everything changes.' The night air, humid with the promise of rain, is like a velvet cloak around them.

'That's such great news about working for Dame Edith, Ellie. Your dad's going to be so chuffed.'

'I'm over the moon. But it'll probably mean I won't see much of George.'

'You barely see much of him now!'

'I know. The Home Guard takes up all his time when he's not at Mcklintock's. He takes it very seriously. I think he feels bad about being rejected because of his eye.'

'No one wants a half-blind pilot.'

'No one wants a half-blind anything. He's not even allowed to man the ack-ack guns by the castle. He keeps the shells stacked and ready for the gunners.'

'At least he'll be safe in Norwich, Ellie. I doubt they'll target Mcklintock's any time soon. I don't expect chocolate factories are high on their list. Why don't you just get married? Then you'd see plenty of him.' Ruthie giggles and pokes Ellie in the ribs. 'At least at night.'

'Ruthie! Honestly! I think Tyrone Power has addled your brain. Anyway, George is meeting me at the dance at the Samson tomorrow night. You're coming, aren't you? You know he hates to jitterbug and you're the best.'

'Wouldn't miss it for the world. I'm going to keep my eyes peeled for a handsome Newfoundlander. My cousin Sheila in Yarmouth said she's seen Newfoundlanders all around town. They've just been stationed somewhere near Filby.'

'To protect the coast, I imagine. Pops says the Germans would have a clean sweep into England if they landed up on Holkham Beach. It's as flat as a pancake up there for miles.'

'I wouldn't be surprised if they start showing up in Norwich. Filby's not far.'

'Well, I hope they can dance.' Ellie disentangles herself from their embrace. 'George stomps about like an ox.'

'George is solid. When you're married you won't have to worry about him running off with a barmaid.'

Ellie gives her friend a quick peck on the cheek. 'I'm only turning eighteen in September. I'm in no rush to marry. Besides, I'm too busy. I've got art classes and the painting to work on for the summer exhibition next month, and now I've got the job with Dame Edith. George'll just have to wait.'

'Oh, he'll wait. George adores you. The way he looks at you ... it makes me jealous.'

Ellie shuts the gate behind her and wraps her fingers around two of the black iron rails. 'Don't be silly, Ruthie. He's just a boy. You're my best friend.' She slides her hand through the gate and extends her little finger. 'Friends forever?'

Ruthie slides her little finger around Ellie's, then grasps Ellie's hand. 'Friends forever, Ellie.'

# Chapter 5

### En Route to New York From London –
### 11 September 2001

Sophie ducks under a luggage strap hanging like a noose from an overhead storage compartment and dodges an elbow as she inches her way past the other passengers. She eyes her window seat and spots two barrel-chested men in crumpled navy suits in her row. Their faces are flushed a sticky red and their voices cut through the din of the embarking passengers.

'Gary's gotta do something about the way he holds his club. We lost it on the eleventh hole, I tell you. Downhill from there.'

'Yeah. 'Least the boss was happy. You don't wanna be too good, if you know what I mean. Gotta keep the main man and his clients happy. We got a good deal outta that day.'

Sophie shifts her Longchamp shoulder bag to her opposite shoulder, careful not to dent the thick pad of her new green Escada crushed-velvet jacket, and rests her new carry-on case on the aisle. Checking her ticket, she groans inwardly. *Fabulous. Eight bloody hours on the London flight to New York beside an overweight, drunken salesman who'll hog the armrest and manspread into my leg space.*

Shifting aside her new digital camera, she tugs a stack of blueprints out of a pocket of her case. Someone behind her pokes her in her shoulder. She turns around and smiles apologetically at the impatient woman. Tucking the drawings under her armpit, she wedges her case into the overhead locker and shuffles past the two salesmen. As she slumps into her seat, several blueprints fall into her neighbour's broad lap.

'Here you go, hon,' the man says as he hands her the drawings, his fingers like stout red sausages.

Sophie smiles politely. 'Thanks.'

'No problem, sweetheart. You don't wanna get your boss's drawings messed up.'

Her smile stiffens. 'They're my drawings.'

The man jabs his colleague with his elbow. 'Hear that, Bob? You never would'a thought that, would you?' He thrusts out his meaty hand to Sophie. 'Mike O'Brien.' He jabs a thumb at his companion. 'This is Bob Roberts.' He digs into his jacket pocket and pulls out a business card. 'We're in garbage. Biggest garbage contractors in Queens. Been talking to London. They like our methods.' He rubs his sausage fingers together. 'Very lucrative. Let me tell you, everybody makes garbage. The twenty-first century is gonna be the garbage century.'

Sophie hands the flight attendant her breakfast tray across Mike O'Brien's head and rolls out a blueprint across the flip-down table. She scans the plans of London's Millennium Pavilion, remembering inking every line, every vertical, diagonal and horizontal. A Point One pen for the glass and the finer details, Point Three for the interior structure, and the heftier Point Five for the concrete exterior structure.

She has to get this job. The teenage summers given up to advanced calculus courses at the expense of the art courses she'd preferred, the seven years of study and internships, the slog jobs making coffees and photocopies, then the better jobs, then winning the commission to design the Millennium Pavilion, and – she still can't believe it'd actually happened – the call from Richard Niven's New York office to come for an interview. Everything she'd ever done had led to this moment. Her life was about to change. She could feel it. All she had to do was ace the interview and the presentation. No pressure.

The plane drops suddenly and veers sharply to the right before levelling out. Sophie looks out the window. Blue sky, clouds and miles of white-tipped water. Just another ordinary day.

The intercom bell dings.

*'This is your captain. Sorry about that, ladies and gentlemen. An, um, an instrument problem has arisen and I'm afraid we need to divert to the nearest airport, in Gander, Newfoundland, to have it checked. It's nothing serious, but regulations state we must have it looked at before continuing on our onward journey. We'll give you more information once we land. The seatbelt signs have been switched on, so please buckle up. Apologies for the inconvenience. We'll have you on your way as quickly as possible.'*

*An instrument problem? Seriously?* Sophie glances at her watch. Nine forty-five. The interview wasn't until tomorrow, but still. She'd planned everything so carefully to get there early so she'd have time to practise her presentation and get a good sleep.

'Don't worry, hon,' Mike says, patting her on her knee. 'These kinda things happen all the time. Nothin' to worry about.'

'It's not that. I have an important meeting to get to.'

Bob leans across Mike's girth. 'Don't worry, sweetheart. You'll make it. We'll be outta here in a shot. Like Mikey here says, nothin' to worry about. We'll be in New York by lunch, you can bet on it.'

'Right. Thanks.' She shuts her eyes, willing the butterflies bashing around her stomach to settle. *Just a minor hiccup, Soph. Nothing to worry about. Take a chill pill.*

Half an hour later the aeroplane begins its descent. Sophie peers out the window. The flat, grey roof of an airport building a fraction of the size of Heathrow comes into view below, a grey island in an ocean of trees. About twenty aeroplanes, parked in an orderly row, gleam like silver arrows on the tarmac.

The plane bounces onto the runway and breaks to a gradual stop. Sophie watches out the window as it taxis towards the queue of aeroplanes. Her eyes travel over the bright logos. British Airways, Alitalia, Delta, Virgin, United, Northwest, and others she can't identify. Another plane, a Lufthansa, glides in to land, while far above, the sun glints on the silver wings of an airliner circling in the September sky.

She glances at Mike who is straining to look over her shoulder. 'There are over twenty planes out there.'

The intercom bell dings again.

*'Ladies and gentlemen, you must be wondering if all these aeroplanes around us have the same instrument problem as we have. The reality is that we're here for another reason. We have received a report through our communication lines that there is an armed threat at the World Trade Center in New York. We've been advised that international airspace over North America has been shut down and all flights diverted to the nearest airports. We're to stay on the plane until further notice.'*

The World Trade Center? Richard Niven's office was only a few blocks away. Sophie pulls her phone out of her bag and taps out the number for the office. Nothing. She tries again. Not even a dial tone. She looks out the window. A faint breeze rustles through the green-black evergreens in the distance. The metallic aeroplanes waver under the bright sun like a mirage in a desert oasis. A blackbird lands on an aeroplane wing. It opens its beak, but the song is silent through the thick glass.

# *Chapter 6*

## Norwich, England – 27 July 1940

Dottie Burgess leans her elbows on the vanity table, watching her sister pucker her lips into the mirror and slick on red lipstick.

'Can I try?'

Ellie laughs at the reflection of her sister's inquisitive face in the mirror. Sharp-chinned and curious, just like their cat, Berkeley Square. 'You're not even twelve yet.'

Dottie reaches out for the lipstick. 'Please?'

Ellie twists the tube closed and slides on the brass cap. 'No. It's my last lipstick and Buntings hasn't got any more in stock right now.' She waves the brass tube at her sister. 'This might have to last me till the end of the war.'

'Milly's mum's started using beet juice. Her fingers are all stained red from it.'

'Well, that's just silly, isn't it?'

'Milly's mum says "Needs must".'

Ellie taps Dottie on her nose with her powder puff. 'Here, have a go with this. Powder your nose.'

Dottie leans into the mirror and dabs the powder puff over the three freckles on her nose. 'I thought that meant you had to go to the loo.'

'It does. It's a euphemism.'

'A eupha—eupha—'

'Euphemism. You say it so you don't have to say "toilet" or "loo". It's more polite.'

'But it's a fib. Father McAuley says fibs are a sin.'

'Well, it's only a little sin. Say two Hail Marys and you'll be fine.'

Dottie hands back the powder puff and picks up the large white-bristled brush with its gleaming mother-of-pearl handle. Edging onto the stool beside Ellie, she unclips her pink plastic hair buckle and drags the brush through her long brown hair.

Ellie watches her sister in the mirror. Dark hair and eyes. So like their mother. Wilful like their mother too. Ellie had loved watching their mother, Winnifred, brush her long, chestnut-coloured hair with the same brush in the evenings. One hundred strokes. Always one hundred exactly. They'd count together.

'Here, Dottie. Let me do it.' She stands behind Dottie and runs the brush through the fine brown strands until her sister's hair gleams.

'Is George picking you up?'

'If he's finished his shift at the ack-ack guns in time. Otherwise I'll meet him and Ruthie at the hall.'

Dottie frowns into the mirror. 'I don't like this war.'

'Nobody does, honey.'

'Don't you worry about George being by the guns? He's awfully brave, isn't he?'

'George is very brave indeed. There's no need to worry about him. He's very careful. He's lucky he didn't have to go over to Europe with the others. I feel much safer knowing he's here, don't you?'

'I always feel safe if George is around. He's my guardian angel.'

Ellie chuckles as she snaps the pink hair buckle back into Dottie's hair. 'Is he now? How's that?'

'Well, Sister Marguerite Mercy said we all have guardian angels who've been sent to protect us. Nothing bad will ever happen when your guardian angel is nearby.' She shrugs. 'So, George is my guardian angel. I decided.'

'I'll be sure to tell him. He'll get a kick out of that.'

Dottie spins around on the stool and grabs the sleeve of Ellie's pastel blue dress. 'No! Please, don't! It's a secret.'

'How can he be your guardian angel if it's a secret?'

'Oh, he knows it in his heart. He just doesn't know it in his head.' Dottie yanks on the thin blue cotton. 'Please don't say anything, Ellie. Promise.'

Ellie kisses the locket around her neck and holds it in the air. 'On Mummy's locket, I promise I won't tell George. My lips are sealed.'

Dottie's face breaks into a beaming smile. 'Now can I try some lipstick?'

'Ellie! Over here!'

Ellie cranes her neck over the heads of the dancers shuffling around the glossy wooden floor of the Samson and Hercules dance hall. She spies Ruthie waving at her from in front of the stage, where a band of men in white dinner jackets plays a seductive version of 'Begin the Beguine'. A short, ginger-haired man in a khaki green uniform stands next to Ruthie, clutching a glass of beer in one hand and flapping the other around like a broken sail as he yells into Ruthie's ear. Ellie dodges past the dancers' thrusting elbows and squeezes through a bottleneck of sweaty bodies.

'Hi, Ruthie. Crumbs, that's a crush.'

Grabbing Ellie's elbow, Ruthie shouts into her ear. 'This is Charlie. He's from the 57th Newfoundland Heavy Regiment.' She smiles over at Charlie. 'Did I get that right?'

'That's it exactly, duck.' The young soldier thrusts out his hand. Ellie extends her hand and he pumps it like he's jiggling a stubborn bottle of brown sauce. 'Charlie Murphy from Ship Harbour, Newfoundland,' he says, drawing out the last syllable. 'Newf'nland like understand.'

Ellie raises her eyebrows as she rescues her hand. 'I'm sorry?'

'That's how you pronounce it. Like "understand". I tells you, it's like chalk on a blackboard whenever I hears people say NewFOUNDland.'

Ellie grins at Ruthie. 'That's us told then.'

'Oh, don't you worry, duck,' Charlie says, his green eyes twinkling under his ginger eyebrows. 'I wasn't havin' a go at you. Ruthie's told me all about you. Says you're an artist.'

'Just starting out, really.' She smiles weakly and glances at Ruthie. 'Have you seen George?'

Ruthie shakes her head. 'Not yet. I'm sure he'll be here soon.'

'All right. I'll go get some Cokes.'

'Now, don't you be doing that, maid,' Charlie says. 'Where's my manners? My mudder'd give me some smack. Two Cokes is it? I'll be right back. Least I can do for campin' out in your backyard.' Gulping down the rest of his beer, he heads into the crowd.

'You've got yourself a live one, there, Ruthie.'

'I think he's a doll. He looks like Mickey Rooney.'

Looking towards the crowded entrance, Ellie frowns. 'I wonder what's taking George so long?'

'Oh, Ellie. I wouldn't worry. The sirens haven't gone off.'

'They didn't go off last week when they dropped the bombs on Heartsease Lane.'

'That was just one aeroplane. The pilot was probably lost and thought he'd take a pot shot at poor old Norwich on his way home.'

Ellie sighs. 'I don't know why I'm so wound up. It's probably all Dottie's talk about guardian angels tonight. It made me think of Mummy. How people can just ...' Ellie's voice catches.

Ruthie slides her arm around Ellie and gives her a squeeze. 'Accidents happen, Ellie. That's not to say George's been in an accident ... Oh, Ellie, you know what I mean. George is probably drinking tea and playing cards with the other Home Guard chaps over by the castle. I hear they've all gone mad for Whist.'

Ellie presses her lips together and nods. 'I suppose you're right. I'm just being silly. I'm all nerves about starting at Dame Edith's studio on Monday. I wasn't able to sleep a wink last night. I must look a wreck.'

'You look fine. You could wear my grandfather's pyjamas and you'd look amazing. If I wore my grandfather's pyjamas I'd look like my grandfather.'

Ellie laughs. 'That's absolute rubbish, Ruthie, and you know it.'

'Here we go, duckies.' Charlie holds out two tall glasses of Coke.

'Thanks, Charlie,' Ruthie says as she takes the warm glass. 'What about your beer?'

'T's got that all sorted out. There he is now.' Charlie waves at a tall, slender soldier in the same khaki green uniform holding two glasses of beer aloft as he weaves through the dancers towards them. 'Tom, b'y! Over here!'

The soldier breaks through the crowd. 'There you goes,

Charlie,' he says, handing Charlie a beer. He smiles at the two young women, his pale grey eyes lighting up. 'Looks like you found us the best spot in the house.' He extends a hand to Ruthie. 'Thomas Parsons. Call me Tom. Everyone does but my mam.'

Charlie takes a swig of beer. 'I'd say the sun's shinin' on us tonight, wouldn't you, Tommy?'

Ruthie's cheeks dimple and she holds out her hand. 'Ruth Huggins. Call me Ruthie.'

Charlie taps Thomas on the shoulder. 'This here is Ruthie's friend, Milly.'

Thomas spins around, his hand outstretched for a handshake. Ellie's glass goes flying, Coke splashing a brown deluge over her blue dress.

Ruthie gasps. 'Oh, Ellie, your dress! It's your favourite!'

'Oh, Jaysus, Mary and Joseph,' Charlie swears. 'What has you done, b'y?'

Thomas tugs a white handkerchief out of his trouser pocket and offers it to Ellie. 'I'm so sorry, Milly.'

Glaring at the abashed soldier, she takes the handkerchief and rubs at the spreading stain. 'It's Ellie. Not Milly. Ellie.'

A hand presses onto her shoulder. 'Sorry I'm late, Ellie. Good grief, what happened to you?'

Ellie nods at the tall Newfoundlander, whose long, handsome face is drawn into an expression of deep remorse. 'George, this is Thomas Parsons. Thomas, this is my fiancé, George Parry. Now, if you don't mind, I'm going to powder my nose.'

# *Chapter 7*

Gander International Airport,
Newfoundland – 12 September 2001

The school buses inch along the tarmac. They look like a line of fat orange and black caterpillars, Sophie muses, as she clutches the handrail of the metal staircase they've rolled up to the aeroplane. She blinks at the morning sun. The autumn grass is yellow around the runways, and a forest of trees so dark that they appear almost black ring the patchy fields and the nondescript grey buildings of Gander International Airport. Yawning, she rolls her head from side to side. Her calf muscles spasm. She could've done without the night in her economy seat, cramped between the window and Mike's spreading bulk. It's added a year to her age, she's sure, and at thirty-eight, that's something she absolutely can't afford.

She follows the other passengers onto a bus, pulling her carry-on case behind her. All around her, thousands of other travellers – their expressions disoriented, upset, puzzled, worried – climb down the staircases from their aeroplanes and file into the waiting buses.

Inside the terminal building, the yellow vinyl airport seating has been shoved into clusters against the beige walls of the cavernous 60s interior. Under a stylised Mid-Century mural, Canadian immigration officers in short-sleeved white shirts sit at rows of tables, processing the exhausted arrivals. High up on another wall, above a portrait of the Queen, large brown letters spell out CANADA, flanked by flags of Canada, the UK and an odd, multi-coloured flag that looks like a modernist Union Jack.

After an hour in the immigration queue, Sophie finds a space by a pillar. She tries her mobile phone again, but the signal is still blocked. Slipping her phone into her shoulder bag, she scans the terminal. Its brown and beige terrazzo floor is virtually obliterated by the passengers sitting, standing and lying down wherever they've found space. She wanders aimlessly into the crowd. At a large sculpture, she reaches out and grasps the head of a bronze bird, the touch of the cold metal grounding her. She spots a queue in front of tables staffed by local women handing out plastic bags of provisions. Pulling her case across the terrazzo floor, she joins the queue.

A middle-aged woman with a tight brunette perm drops an *Oh Henry!* chocolate bar and a bag of ketchup-flavoured potato chips into a plastic Foodland bag. 'It's not much, duckie, but I hopes it'll take the edge off till we can gets you sorted out with a hot supper and a bed for tonight. You gots yourself all sorted out over there in Customs and the Red Cross? Janie Brinks at the Salvation Army's sorting out beds over at the legion hall. We've gots the colleges and schools chippin' in too. I hears a bunch of you'll be off to some of the other local towns. We're only nine thousand, give or take, here in Gander, and it looks like we've doubled the population today, so we had to call round for more places for everyone to stay.'

'What do you mean you're looking for places for us to stay? Aren't we leaving later today? I've got to get to New York. I've got an important meeting tomorrow.'

The woman drops a bottle of water into the bag. 'Oh, no, not today, duckie. The planes are all grounded. They're sayin' it'll be two, three days most likely. Could be more. Don't you worry. You're all welcome here, duck. I'd have you at my place, but I's already got some newlyweds stayin'. They were off on their honeymoon to Las Vegas. I'm chuckin' my husband onto the couch and I'm bunkin' in with my daughter to give them some privacy, if you knows what I mean.'

She holds out the Foodland bag to Sophie. 'They're sortin' all the buses out there now. Who's goin' where, when, all that stuff. Logistics, y'know? God help us. We had a bus strike goin' but they cancelled it today. It'll probably start up again once you're all gone, but thank heaven for small mercies, is what I says. Mavis over there can set up you up with a hot coffee or tea, if you likes.'

Sophie's heart thumps around her chest like a loose spring. 'Is there anywhere I can make a phone call? I've got to call New York. My phone's not working.'

'Nobody's phones is workin' just now, pet. There's just the payphones over there by the stairs. There's only one workin', but it looks like half the country is waitin' for it. And I hears you can only make local calls. They should'a fixed the phones ages ago, but they're talking of tearin' down this place, so there didn't seem much point, did there?'

Sophie steps away from the table, clutching the plastic bag against her chest like a protective pillow as she stands in the middle of the crowded terminal. *Okay, okay. One thing at a time. One thing at a time. Bloody hell. Frig.*

*I'll have a cup of tea and find a phone. I'll get to New York somehow. I have to get to New York.*

She joins the line at the tea tables behind a group of agitated

Italians, and has to duck several times to avoid their gesticulating limbs.

'Your turn.' A tap on her shoulder. 'Your turn.'

She turns to see a tall man in leather biker gear behind her. His lean face is shadowed with stubble, and his black hair looks like it could use a comb. He gestures towards the tea table with his bike helmet. 'Your turn. You must be thirsty or you wouldn't be here.'

'I am thirsty, but I'd actually very much prefer not to be here—' she waves her hand at the heaving terminal '—wherever here bloody is.'

A line creases the man's forehead as he grins. His face is brown from the sun, and the fine lines at the corners of his brown eyes deepen. 'Oh, you've come to the best place on earth. You don't know how lucky you are.'

'Yes, m'love, I'm Mavis,' a woman in a purple tracksuit and pink-rimmed bifocals says from behind the table. 'What's your fancy?'

Frowning at the biker, Sophie turns to Mavis, who's now tugging at the cellophane covering a bag of cookies.

'Tea, please.'

'We've gots a shedload of teabags in from Foodland,' Mavis says as she dumps the cookies onto a yellow plastic tray. 'Runnin' thin on the ground with the Nescafé. Those Americans all loves their coffee.'

'Tea's fine. Thanks.'

Mavis holds up a can of Carnation Evaporated Milk, her fingernails the same bright pink as her glasses. 'Milk, duck?'

Sophie stares at the canned milk. She shakes her head. 'No. Just black. Thanks.'

Mavis pushes the plate of cookies towards her. 'Have a cookie, duck, while I pours your tea.'

'No, thanks all the same.'

'Oh, no, no, no. You've got to have a Jam Jam.'

Sophie turns around and glares at the biker. 'What?'

He points to a tray of beige, jam-filled cookies. 'A Jam Jam.' Leaning past her, he grabs one and stuffs it into his mouth. 'Thanks, Mavis,' he says, wiping crumbs off his face with his fingers. 'Anything else you need? I've got the *Warriors* on standby out in the parking lot.'

'Thanks, Sam. Hold on a minute. I'll go ask Mudge. I thinks she was looking for some Cheezies for the kids.'

Sophie waves at Mavis's retreating back. 'But ... but ... Great. So much for my tea.'

'Stay right there.' The biker squeezes around the end of table and drops a teabag into a Styrofoam cup. Holding the cup under a hot water dispenser, he turns on the tap, releasing a stream of steaming water. He presents the steaming cup to Sophie with a flourish. 'There you go, Princess Grace. Best tea in Newfoundland. Or, at least ... here.'

'Princess Grace? Seriously?' Sophie screws up her nose as she sips the bitter tea. *Who is this guy?* Sophie grimaces at the queue for the payphone. 'You don't happen to know where I could find a phone, do you?'

'There's one over at the library. I can give you a ride over there if you don't mind hopping on the back of a bike.'

*A bike? In this Escada suit?* Sophie eyes the man's dusty leather trousers and battered jacket with a *CHROME WARRIORS* badge in yellow embroidery, and a smaller one with DAD in white letters. *There's no bloody way.*

'Thanks. I'll get back to you on that.' Adjusting her shoulder bag, she loops the Foodland bag over her arm and picks up the handle of her case.

'Sam Byrne.'

She jerks her head towards the biker. 'What?'

'You'll need to know my name if you're going to get back to me.'

'Right. Thanks.' She turns and heads towards the phone queue.

'And you are?' he shouts after her.

'It doesn't matter who I am,' she says over her shoulder. 'I'm leaving here as soon as I can.'

'Delta! All passengers from Delta Flight Fifteen from Frankfurt travelling to Atlanta!'

A beefy man in a short-sleeved check shirt and sleeveless red woollen vest stands by the front doors waving at the crowd with one hand while he holds up a megaphone with the other.

'Please make your way out the front doors here, folks. We've gots a bus ready to take you to Lewisporte. It's a lovely spot on the coast. We're puttin' you up at the high school there. It may not be the Ritz Carlton, but you'll have beds and blankets and all the tea in China. Delta Flight Fifteen, off you goes.'

Sophie pushes through the surging bodies. 'Excuse me!'

'Hello, m'dear.' The man points at the doors with the megaphone. 'Are you Delta? Just follow the crowd through the doors there.'

'What's happening? Why are we getting moved? I've got to get to New York. I've got an important meeting first thing in the morning.'

The man clucks his tongue. 'I'm afraid that won't be happenin', m'dear. The planes are all stayin' here till further notice.'

'You don't understand. I've got to get to New York. I've just got to.'

The man shakes his head, setting his jowls wobbling. 'Don't

you worry, m'love. We'll gets you there as soon as we can. The last I heard it's goin' to be a few days yet. Things aren't lookin' too good in New York right now.'

'What's happened? Someone said something about the World Trade Center. I tried to call New York, but none of the phones are working. They said one of the payphones was working, but it's not anymore.'

The man's fleshy red face clouds over. 'You haven't heard?'

'Heard what?'

The crowd surges forward, knocking Sophie into the stocky man. 'I'm sorry, m'dear. I've gots to get this bunch back under control.' He presses the megaphone to his mouth. 'C'mon, now, behave nice or I'll be asking you to do this single file like the nuns makes them do down at Notre Dame Academy. Orderly fashion, please! Delta Fifteen. Is that all of you?'

Sophie squeezes through the crowd back to the bird statue. She sets the Foodland bag on the floor beside her case. Her heart pounds against her ribcage like a mallet. It's like her future is on a raft that's drifting out to sea. One more wave and it'll be gone forever.

She reaches into her shoulder bag and fumbles for her change purse. Her fingers rub against the edges of her old green leather address book, wedged into an inner pocket. Slipping it out of her bag, she flips through the flimsy blue pages full of scribbles and crossings-out. D, E, F, G, H. There it is. Parsons. *Ellie Parsons. 1 Tizzard's Point, Tippy's Tickle, Newfoundland.* No phone number.

She tucks the address book into her bag and heads back to Mavis.

*There's no bloody way I'm bunking down with hundreds of strangers on a gym floor. Aunt Ellie, you're about to meet your niece. Surprise!*

'Hello, my love.' Mavis greets her, picking up a plastic cup. 'Tea?'

'No thanks. I was just wondering, have you heard of a place called Tippy's Tickle?'

'Tippy's Tickle? Well, sure. It's up the coast past Gambo. Back of beyond, and that's sayin' a lot in these parts.'

'I have an aunt there. I'd like to try to get in touch with her but I don't have a phone number.'

'Well, duckie, today's your lucky day.' Mavis drops a teabag into the styrofoam cup. 'Sure you don't want some tea?'

Sophie shakes her head. 'What do you mean, today's my lucky day?'

'We've gots somebody here from Tippy's Tickle.'

Sophie's heart leaps. 'You do?'

'We sure does, duck. I'll go give them a holler.'

Sophie watches Mavis disappear through a door. Her stomach rumbles. The last thing she'd eaten was half a stale cheese sandwich the night before. Eyeing the tray stacked with beige cookies oozing red jam, she grabs one and takes a tentative bite.

'I told you you had to try a Jam Jam.'

She looks up to see the biker grinning at her. 'You?'

Mavis smiles, displaying a set of bright white dentures. 'Here you goes, duckie. This is Sam Byrne. He lives in Tippy's Tickle. Didn't I say it was your lucky day?'

Sam sweeps an arm towards the front doors of the terminal. '*Miss Julie* awaits.'

'*Miss Julie?*'

'My bike. Named her after Julie Christie. Saw *Doctor Zhivago* at least ten times over at the Popular Theatre in Grand Falls when I was a kid. My uncle Jerry at the candy counter used to sneak me a *Cherry Blossom* if I promised to behave. Well, he wasn't really my uncle. We all just called him uncle.'

'I imagine that was hard for you.' Sophie looks over at Mavis. 'Maybe there's a taxi I can take?'

'A taxi to Tippy's Tickle?' Mavis laughs. 'Did you hear that, Sam? No, m'dear. It's too far for that. Sam's your best bet unless you hires a car. Only they're all out getting' folks to Gambo and Lewisporte.'

'Well, Princess Grace, it looks like I'm your man.'

Sophie rolls her eyes. 'Bloody hell.'

'You could always bunk up in the legion hall with a thousand others.'

Sophie fixes Sam with a glare that could freeze the Sahara. 'I'm only going with you because Mavis knows you.'

'Oh, you'll be all right with Sam, duckie,' Mavis says, patting Sophie's arm. 'Sweetest fellow you'd ever meet. Even all those years he was down in Boston didn't rub it out of him. That's as long as you don't gets on his bad side. Now that's another story. Whatever you do, you don't wants to do that.'

# Chapter 8

## Norwich, England – 27 July 1940

The late afternoon sun slides into Dame Edith's attic art studio through a window filmed with a fine layer of dust. The light casts a halo around the helmet worn by the young woman perched on a stool in front of the artist. She holds a gas mask as she looks past the artist's shoulder at Dame Edith's parrot, Sir Ralph, who sits preening his rainbow plumage on his perch by the door.

Dame Edith thrusts her paintbrush at Ellie and wipes her hands on her beige gaberdine smock, smearing it with streaks of the cadmium yellow, raw sienna and chromium oxide green paints Ellie had had to rush out to Jarrolds to buy during her lunchtime.

'That will do for today, Corporal Cross. When can you come by again? We'll only need a couple more sittings. I'll fill in the background scenery afterwards.'

The young woman yawns and stretches. 'I'll check my rota and ring you tomorrow, if that's all right. Things have been pretty quiet since that chap popped a few blighters down on us on the nineteenth. We're working on getting a barrage balloon up over by Fairfield Road, and they've got me doing recruitment now.' Handing the gas mask and helmet to Ellie, she sweeps her eyes over the younger woman. 'Have you thought about joining up with the WAAF? We could use capable young women like you.'

Ellie smiles politely as she glances over at Dame Edith. 'Thank you very much, but I'm rather taken up with my art studies right now.'

The young corporal adjusts her cap. 'Of course. Well, things look like they may hot up, so do have a think about it. If not the Air Force, there's always the Red Cross or the fire service. We all must do our bit.'

Ellie nods. Corporal Cross had no idea how busy her schedule was. She'd been up till midnight last night working on sketches for her submission to the college's summer exhibition. Then she'd overslept this morning, missing Ruthie at the bus stop on her way into town to the college, and earned a reprimand from the principal, Mr Harris, for being late.

'Yes, of course, Corporal Cross. I'll think about it.'

Ruthie drags the blackout curtains across the cottage window and switches on the ceiling light in the tiny front room.

'Mum's out at her knitting club, Dad's gone up to Uncle Jack's in Fakenham, and Richie's staying over at Bobby's tonight. Do you want to stay for tea? We've got some tinned salmon. I can make a salmon loaf.'

Ellie kicks her shoes onto the blue carpet and flops onto the overstuffed green sofa. 'Can't tonight, Ruthie. I promised Pops I'd babysit Dottie. It's Boy Scout night. He's teaching knots.'

'He's the Scout Master now as well as the headmaster? He's rather a glutton for punishment, don't you think?'

Ellie shrugs as she thumbs through an issue of *Woman's Own*. 'He's starting up a marching band too. He says it's good for the boys' morale.'

'Righto. Two hundred Catholic boys running around, day in and day out, would do my head in.' Ruthie heads towards the kitchen. 'You'll want bickies? Mum's made her orange drop cookies. I'll put the kettle on and we can have a quick cuppa. Turn on the wireless, would you, Ellie? See if there's any music on the Forces Programme.'

Tossing aside the magazine, Ellie wanders over to the large wooden wireless on a table beside the gas fire and fiddles the knob until the strains of 'I'll Never Smile Again' filter into the room. She sways around the sofa and the two armchairs with their chintz slipcovers and lacy antimacassars, careful not to knock Ruthie's mother's china budgie collection off the display table.

Ruthie enters the sitting room carrying a pink plastic tray laden with a brown teapot, a small jug of milk, a dish with a couple of teaspoons of sugar, flowery china mugs and a plate of round cookies flecked with orange rind. She sets it down on the coffee table and pours out the tea, adding dollops of milk and a sprinkling of sugar. She hands Ellie a mug of the milky tea and sits on the sofa, tucking her legs beneath her.

'So, what do you think of Charlie?'

Ellie blows on the hot tea and sits on the sofa. She peers at Ruthie over the rim of her mug. 'The Newfoundland chap? Really?'

Ruthie dunks a cookie into her tea. 'I think he's a doll. He's invited me out to the cinema next Saturday. We're going to see *Gone with the Wind* at the Electric.'

'You've seen that a half a dozen times already. I should know. You dragged me with you.'

Ruthie giggles. 'All the more reason to see it again. I can concentrate on Charlie instead of Rhett!'

'Oh, Ruthie. You're incorrigible.'

Ruthie smiles slyly at Ellie as she chews her cookie. 'What about Tom Parsons? He seems nice. Clumsy, but nice.'

Ellie shrugs. 'I suppose so. George liked him. He's going to give George the Newfoundland stamps from his letters for George's stamp collection.'

'So, George liked him, but you ... didn't?'

'I honestly didn't think anything of him one way or another.'

'That's a shame. I thought he was dreamy. A Gary Cooper type, except friendlier.' She makes a face. 'Oh well, I'll have to find someone else to double date with me and Charlie.'

'Ruthie, I'm engaged, remember? I couldn't date the fellow even if I wanted to. Which I don't.'

Ruthie bites into another cookie, catching the crumbs in her tea. 'He's a good one, that George. He never gives you any bother. You're so lucky to have a fellow like that.'

Ellie settles back into the spongy cushions. She is lucky to have George. She's just never really thought about it. He's always been there, ever since they were children at St Augustine's Catholic School. She just wishes he was a bit more ... No, she's being silly. Ruthie can have her Tyrone Powers and Clark Gables and Charlie Murphys. Maybe George isn't a dish, exactly, but he's certainly presentable. George is all she needs. And her art, of course.

Why everyone thinks life is so complicated, she'll never understand. Life is incredibly simple. Only people make it complicated.

# *Chapter 9*

## Northern Newfoundland Coast –
## 12 September 2001

S am takes off his helmet and looks over his shoulder at Sophie.
'There's a payphone around the back by the toilet. Didn't
know they'd closed the library today. You hungry? I'm getting
myself a Coke.'

'I'm fine.' Sophie winches the helmet off and runs her fingers
through her brown fringe. She squirms off the motorbike seat
and straightens her velvet skirt. What was she thinking, accepting
the ride to Tippy's Tickle on the back of a stranger's motorcycle
to see an aunt who might not even know she existed? She
probably should have stayed in Gander with the others. This
was quite likely a huge mistake.

She tugs at her jacket and readjusts her shoulder pads. 'So
much for my interview suit.'

Sam swings his leg over the bike and kicks the stand into
place. He points at her scuffed patent leather shoes, the shine
obscured by a thick film of dirt. 'Looks like your shoes are done
for, too.'

Sophie glares at him as she rubs a dusty shoe against her leg.
'I didn't exactly plan to be in the bloody middle of nowhere
today.'

A short, burly man wearing grease-stained blue overalls and

a Boston Bruins baseball hat ambles over to them from the garage, the stub of a yellow pencil tucked behind his left ear.

Sam slaps the man on his shoulder. 'Life's like that sometimes, isn't it, Wince?'

'Sure is, b'y. How's she cuttin', there?' Wince grabs the handle of the petrol pump and unscrews the cap on the bike's petrol tank.

'Best kind, b'y.'

Sophie runs her hands over the wrinkles in her skirt. 'I have no idea what you're saying. I expect there's toilet paper?'

Wince peers at Sophie with eyes that pierce her with their blueness, and raises a thick brown eyebrow. 'Sure thing, maid. You hasn't fallen off the end of the world yet. You gotta go up to Brimstone Head on Fogo to do that. We've gots plenty of toilet paper in Newfoundland.'

'Sam said you have a phone?'

Wince jabs his thumb towards the weather-beaten clapboard garage. 'On the wall behind the garage. The dial sticks. You gotta press hard. Make sure you got some loonies.'

'Loonies?'

'A Canadian dollar.' Sam reaches into the back pocket of his leather trousers and fishes out a handful of coins. He flips a coin to Sophie.

She turns the brass coin over in her hand. The Queen's head on one side, a swimming bird on the other. 'Thank you.'

'You'll need two if you're calling your aunt and New York.'

'I don't have Ellie's number.'

'Give us your pencil, Wince.' Sam takes a wrinkled receipt out of his jacket pocket and scribbles on the back. He hands the receipt to Sophie with another loonie. 'Tell her I'll get you there in half an hour.'

'You know her number? And you didn't tell me?'

'How was I to know you didn't have her number?'

Wince shakes his head as he and Sam watch Sophie stumble over the gravel in her high heels to the toilet. 'That's some maid, Sam, b'y. Fancy askin' 'bout toilet paper.'

'I'd say she's what you call "high maintenance". Don't let her get to you, b'y. She'll be gone before you know it. Back to the big city doing whatever it is she does.'

'Suppose you're right, b'y. Can't let these Come From Aways get up my nose.' He looks up at the blue sky, a solitary cloud hanging overhead. 'You seen the news, Sam? Terrible, terrible thing. I was shitbaked when I saw the TV last night. I felt like I was watching some kind of disaster film.'

Sam shakes his head. 'Just awful. There were thousands at the airport. Mayor Elliott over in Gander told me he figures there's almost ten thousand people who've just landed from all over the place.'

'Jaysus God. That's a lots of people.'

'They're bussing some out to Gambo and Lewisporte. Putting them up in schools and churches and legion halls. The bus drivers cancelled their strike to help out. I was down there with the *Warriors* helping out. We jumped on our bikes as soon as we heard the call out on the radio.'

'Well, you gots to, don't you?' Wince squats down to check the pressure on the bike's tyres. 'I hears some of the locals are puttin' the plane people up in their own houses. Government told them not to, but you know you can't tell Newfoundlanders not to be hospitable. We all gots to stick together at a time like this.' Wince nods towards the garage. 'What's she doin' up all this way?'

'She's got relatives in Tippy's Tickle. Ellie Parsons is her aunt.'

'Ellie's her aunt?' Wince grunts as he rises. 'What's that make you, then? Her cousin?'

'No relation. Ellie's my mother-in-law.'

'How'd you get roped into drivin' her up all this way?'

'Mavis Hennessy insisted, and you know you can't say no to Mavis.'

'Oh, God, yes. I knows Mavis. I plays cards at theirs when I'm in Gander visiting Uncle Garland at the home. There's no sayin' no to Mavis.'

Sam nods towards the garage. 'Your TV in the garage working? She doesn't know what happened in New York. They didn't want to tell them at the airport. There was only one payphone working and they had Joyce Fudge on the other line down at BT answering the calls, telling everyone they couldn't redirect. They didn't want people panicking. She had to get back home when her kids got home from school, so they put an "Out of Service" sign on the phone.'

'Sure, b'y. It's on every channel. Saddest thing. Still can't believe it.'

'Hello? Ellie speaking.'

Sophie bites her lip at the sound of the woman's voice, the English accent lightly tinged with the local lilt.

'Aunt Ellie? It's Sophie Parry. Dottie and George's daughter.'

The line goes silent for a moment. 'Sophie?'

Sophie coils the payphone's rusty cord around her finger. 'I'm ... I'm sorry. I know this is unexpected. I was flying over to New York from London and my plane was diverted to Gander. In fact, a lot of planes were diverted there for some reason. I still don't know why. Something was going on in New York and they shut down the airspace. That's all I know.'

'You're in Gander? With the plane people?'

'Well, no. I was. I'm at the Irving petrol station on the way to Tippy's Tickle. I got a lift with someone called Sam Byrne on his motorcycle. I ... I had your address from an old Christmas card, but I only just got your number from Sam. I couldn't get to a phone earlier anyway. The payphones were out of order at the airport and our mobile phones weren't working. They're bussing everyone to schools and gyms. There are thousands of us.'

Another silence. 'My goodness, Sophie. You're really here? In Newfoundland?'

Sophie glances at the scrubby spruce trees behind the garage. 'Yes, I'm really here.'

'You haven't heard what happened?'

'Well, I heard something about an incident at the World Trade Center, but I don't know anything else.' Sophie swallows down the lump that is forming in her throat. She licks her dry lips. 'I'm so sorry, Aunt Ellie. Perhaps I should've stayed with the others. You don't know me from Adam. I'm sorry I bothered you.'

'Good heavens! Don't be silly, Sophie. Get back on that bike, and tell that Sam to drive carefully. We'll talk as soon as you get here. Florie's got a stew on, and there's plenty of room here. You're family, my dear. You can stay as long as you like.'

'It's only for a few days. I don't want to impose.'

'You're not imposing. You're welcome for as long as you want.'

'Thanks so much, Aunt Ellie.'

She hangs the receiver back on its hook, blowing her fringe out of her eyes as she fishes her address book out of her

Longchamp bag. Taking a deep breath, she dials the New York number.

Sophie presses the receiver to her ear. 'Oh, my God. I had no idea. Is everyone okay?'

'We're fine here.' The receptionist's voice wavers. 'But we had clients in the North Tower. We just, we just—'

Sophie holds her hand to her mouth. 'Oh, no. I'm so sorry ... Excuse me, what's your name?'

'Jackie.'

'I'm so sorry, Jackie. They didn't tell us anything.'

'It's like a war zone down where the Towers were. There's smoke and dust everywhere. The whole financial district is under a black cloud.'

'Good Lord.'

'Look, don't worry about the meeting, Ms Parry. It's the last thing we're thinking about right now. We'll sort something out whenever you get here. Just call me.'

Sophie expels a puff of air as relief floods over her. 'Oh, thank goodness. Thanks very much.'

The receptionist sucks in a breath. 'My brother-in-law's a fireman. He had the day off. It was my nephew's birthday. Frank was called in. We haven't heard from him since yesterday. His boy's only four.'

Sophie leans her forehead against the payphone. *The world's fallen apart and all I've been worried about is getting to a bloody job interview.* She runs her tongue over her lips. 'I'm sure he'll be all right, Jackie. Don't worry. Just let Mr Niven know my plane was diverted to a place called Gander in Newfoundland. They'll fly us out as soon as they can. They're saying two or three days. I'll call you as soon as I know more.'

'I'll let him know.'

'I'm sure everything will work out for your family.'

Jackie's voice catches in a swallowed sob. 'Thanks, Ms Parry. I hope so.'

Sophie stares up at the television in Wince Moss's garage. A silver plane, the sun glinting off its wings as it banks, spears into the tower. A cloud of grey smoke, growing like a cancer, obliterates the blue summer sky. Orange flames devour the metal structure. She raises her hand to her mouth in the only possible response.

Silence.

# *Chapter 10*

## Norwich, England – 30 July 1940

The bombs woke her. She didn't know they were bombs at the time, of course. But what she remembers is that she was so solidly asleep, she was in that place of blackness between dreams and wakefulness. Then her eyes opened, and, for a moment, the blackness of unconsciousness and the blackness of the lightless room melded together so that she wasn't sure whether she was dreaming.

A thrumming. Outside the window. Growing louder.

Ellie kneels up in her bed, glancing over to Dottie who is still asleep under her covers. She peeks behind the blackout curtain. The sky is clear blue, with a few puffs of clouds hovering around the early morning sun. Then she sees it. A flash of sunlight on a metal wing as it banks and heads back towards the city centre. Growing larger as it approaches. The bomb falling through the blueness, past the oak trees on Victoria Terrace. An enormous crash. A cloud blowing up skywards, pink with brick dust. The black cross on the bottom of the wing as the Heinkel powers over the house.

Dottie bolts upright in her bed. 'What's that?'

'Get out of bed, Dottie. Hurry. They're bombing. We've got to get to the cellar.'

Throwing back the covers, Dottie jumps out of bed. Ellie

tosses her the dressing gown her sister had left in a heap on the old Persian rug and shrugs into her own. She grabs Dottie's hand and pulls her sister towards the bedroom door.

'Ellie, wait! I can't find one of my slippers.'

Another crash, near the city centre.

'It doesn't matter. Come on.'

Ellie flings open the bedroom door. Their father is on the landing, his thin brown hair dishevelled, his round glasses sitting crookedly on his face. He has pulled on his white cricket jumper over his striped pyjamas and stuffed his feet into green wellies.

'Hurry up, girls, hup hup.'

Dottie runs over and clings to her father. 'Poppy. We didn't hear a siren.'

'No, dove. There wasn't one.'

Ellie hurries down the stairs after her father and sister. 'I saw a bomb come down. It looked like it was near Ruthie's house.'

'Don't worry, Ellie Mae. They've got the Anderson shelter. They'll be fine.'

Ellie runs past the red-brick church at the bottom of the road and rushes around the thick hornbeam hedge into Victoria Terrace. The cobbled street and neat rows of terraced Victorian cottages she knows so well are coated in a thick sheet of grey dust. A smoking mountain of rafters, smashed roofing slates and charred furniture sits in the space where Numbers 43 to 51 once stood. The once proud oak trees behind the cottages are nothing but skeletons, their leaves blasted off by the force of the bomb. The acrid smell of burning sap seeps up her nose and scrapes against her throat as she swallows.

She hurries towards the empty space where Ruthie's cottage should have been, her feet crunching on broken glass hidden by the dust. She coughs as the brick dust settles in her throat. A team of men in the tin helmets and navy overalls of the Auxiliary Fire Service sift through the debris, pulling at pieces of rubble as they lean into the pile, listening. A frazzled-looking young woman in a navy AFS uniform is unloading a tea urn from the back of a staff car by the kerb.

Ellie stumbles over to her, leaving a trail in the grey dust. 'Excuse me. Do you know where the people living here are? I'm looking for my friend Ruthie. She lives here with her brother and her parents. They have an Anderson shelter.'

The young woman's pale blue eyes sweep over Ellie. She has a round, friendly face under her tin helmet. She shifts her gaze back to the tea urn and shakes her head. 'They didn't find anyone in the shelter.'

'But if they weren't in the shelter ...'

The young woman looks back at Ellie. 'I'm so sorry.' She reaches out and squeezes Ellie's arm. 'They wouldn't have known what was happening.'

Ellie's heart jumps in her chest. 'What do you mean by that?' She can hear her voice rise. 'What do you mean? Maybe they went to a neighbour's—'

'There wasn't any siren. There was only one plane. It took everyone off guard. They would have been sleeping. I'm so very sorry.'

# Chapter 11

## Tippy's Tickle, Newfoundland –
## 12 September 2001

The motorcycle bumps down a potholed road running along-side a narrow inlet, which pokes into the rocky landscape like a giant finger. On a spit of rocky land to the left, a white clapboard church with an aluminium steeple sits with its back to the churning ocean. They round a hill and pass the chain-link fence and steel gates of a cemetery. St Stephen's is spelled out in black letters across the two curved gates, and a wooden bench, bleached grey, sits just inside the gate, with a view over the weather-battered headstones to the puffing ocean.

'What are those?' Sophie shouts into Sam's ear, pointing at the water spouts.

'Whales.'

'Whales?'

'Humpbacks. Minkes. Finbacks – they're the second largest after the blue whale. We've got those too, down off the southwest coast. Sperm whales, of course. Orcas. Lots of dolphins. It's whale paradise around here.'

Sam steers the bike through a village with box-like houses painted white, dark red and vivid blue. Ropes of bright orange buoys the size of bowling balls hang over peeling picket fences like necklaces. As they approach a small general store, a long-haired black dog the size of a small bear rushes out the door and down the white wooden steps, barking huskily.

'Good grief!' Sophie pulls her elbows into her body and huddles against Sam's back.

Sam slows the bike to a stop and reaches out to the panting dog. 'Hey there, Rupert. Did you miss me? Where's Becca? Come on, let's go find her and Ellie.' He undoes the chinstrap of his helmet and winches it off his head. 'Welcome to Tippy's Tickle.'

Sophie takes off her helmet and slides her leg over the seat, her velvet skirt riding up her thighs despite her best efforts. Stumbling onto the gravel drive, she thrusts the helmet at Sam. 'Why on earth is it called that?'

'Tippy's Tickle? Well, legend has it an old fisherman named Tippy saw a mermaid in the tickle here years ago.'

'What's a tickle?'

Sam points to the narrow inlet. 'That is. Narrow inlets. We call them tickles here. They're like fingers of water tickling the rock. Usually between islands or an island and the mainland. The church isn't on an island, but the spit it's on is close enough to an island. The church gets cut off sometimes in the spring. Then it really is an island and the only way to Sunday Mass is by boat.'

She tugs her skirt back into place. She looks up to catch Sam grinning at her. 'What?'

'I don't think Tippy's Tickle has seen quite the likes of you since old Tippy saw that mermaid.'

'I'll take that as a compliment.' She squints at the single-storey wooden building perching on a raised concrete foundation. Two large white-framed sash windows frame the white-screened door, and an odd octagonal bay clings onto the left side of the modest dark red clapboard building like the afterthought of a builder harbouring delusions of grandeur. A sign above the door reads *F. Quick and E. Parsons, Props.* in bright yellow letters.

'What's this place?'

'It's your aunt's store.' Sam dismounts and adjusts the bike's kickstand. 'It's the heart and soul of the town. Ellie prints her art over in the room with the bay window when she's not schooling Becca, and Florie sells it to any tourists who manage to find their way here, along with basic provisions. We get the tourists here for the icebergs in the spring and the whales in the summer. Ellie'll probably be at the printing press with Becca this time of day.'

'Who's Florie?'

'Ellie's partner.'

'Her partner?'

'Yes. They've been together for years.'

'Florie's a ...?'

'Woman. Yes.'

Sam climbs the steps, Rupert at his heels, and calls out to the screen door. 'Ellie! Florie! Becca! Roll out the red carpet. We've got company.'

Sophie follows Sam up the steps, clutching at the white-painted railing as the steps judder under his footsteps. 'Who's Becca?'

'She's my daughter.'

The door swings open and a small girl of about eight, her blonde hair tied into a messy braid and her face painted with bright pink and green dots and hearts, throws herself into Sam's arms, gesticulating wildly with her fingers.

'Florie painted your face? Yes, I can see that, Becca. What? She did? Let's go see.'

Becca catches Sophie's eye and pokes Sam on his shoulder, opening her hands in a question.

Sam glances at Sophie. 'That's Sophie. She's come all the way from England. Remember that poem about the cat who went to London to visit the Queen? That's where Sophie's from.'

Sophie follows Sam and Becca through the screen door. Inside, long white-painted wooden counters stacked with boxes of art cards, homemade jams, rolls of colourful ribbon, plates of fat muffins, tempting cookies and red paper bags of something labelled hard tack flank the narrow walls in front of the sage green shelves displaying handmade glazed pottery and framed art prints.

Four lively dachshunds clatter through the doorway from a back room, followed by a sturdily built woman of about fifty, in paint-spattered jeans and a Joni Mitchell T-shirt.

'C'mon in, c'mon in. You wants a cup of tea? I'll get that sorted. How was it down in Gander, Sam? We've been watching the news and listening to the radio all day. Planes have been landing in St John's and Stephenville too.'

Sam sets Becca down amongst the excited dogs. 'It's a bit crazy down there, Florie, but lots of people have been showing up to help. I was down there with the *Warriors*.'

Florie nods at Sophie. 'Who's this waif and stray, then?'

Sophie reaches out her hand. 'Sophie Parry. I'm Ellie's niece from London.'

'You're Dottie's daughter, then? Thought you'd all forgotten about us out here. Wonders will never cease. You sounds right like the Queen.' Florie pushes past Sam and gives Sophie a hearty hug. 'Ellie said you'd be coming. I gots a good old Jiggs dinner cooking up for supper. We'll feed you up some good here.'

Standing back, she sweeps her eyes over Sophie's wrinkled

velvet suit, dusty shoes and dishevelled hair. 'I gots to say, girl, you looks like something the cat dragged in. We'll get you in a shower so you can feel human again.'

'Florie, are you giving our guest a hard time?'

Sophie glances towards the back room. A slender woman in her seventies, wearing a green bibbed apron over rolled-up jeans and a pink T-shirt, stands in the doorway. Her white hair is cut into a neat bob, and the toenails on her bare feet are polished bright pink. A pair of turquoise cat's-eye glasses hangs from a cord around the woman's neck. She smiles, and a web of fine lines fan out from her blue-grey eyes. 'Sophie?'

'Aunt Ellie?'

'Well, I never thought I'd live to see the day.' Holding out her arms, she pads across the polished wooden floor, enfolding Sophie in a hug and kissing her robustly on the cheeks.

'Oh, don't be so dramatic, Ellie,' Florie says as she winks at Sophie. 'Your aunt's an artsy-fartsy type.' Florie regards Sophie with a critical eye. 'You must takes after the other side of the family.'

'How are your parents?' Ellie asks as she stands back and surveys her niece.

*She doesn't know! Mum didn't even bother to write Ellie to let her know that George had died. And now I have to tell her they're both dead.*

Sophie swallows and runs her tongue over her dry lips. 'I'm sorry, Aunt Ellie. Dad … he passed away. Ten … no eleven years ago now. He had a heart attack at work. Mum didn't write to you?'

Ellie presses her hand to her mouth. Sophie notices her aunt's fingers trembling against her lips.

Ellie takes a deep breath and shakes her head. 'No. No, she

didn't. Poor George. I'm so sorry, Sophie. He was a lovely man. I knew him since I was six – did you know that? We were at school together. Right from kindergarten. Dottie must miss him terribly. How is she?'

Sophie bites her lower lip. 'I'm sorry, Aunt Ellie. Mum's gone too. Last year. Lung cancer. She was a smoker.'

'Oh, Sophie.' Ellie reaches out and pulls Sophie to her in a hug. 'I'm so sorry. Your poor mother.'

Sophie leans awkwardly into the embrace as her aunt's warm, bird-like body presses against her. *Weren't Ellie and Mum sworn enemies? Mum was never able to mention Ellie's name without getting into a rant about her sister's selfishness and cold-heartedness. This woman doesn't seem anything like that.*

Ellie steps back and shakes her head, her fine white hair swinging against her cheeks. 'Poor Dottie. I'd always hoped to see her again. To see them both. She was so upset with me, and I never really understood why. Everything was fine until I met Thomas. Then she changed.' She sighs. 'I wanted to work things out with her. Florie and I were just talking about a trip to England next year, weren't we, honey?'

Florie wipes a cookie crumb from her lip. 'God's truth. Got the travel brochures in the desk up in the house.'

'I'm sorry that didn't happen, Aunt Ellie. Mum would have loved that.' *She wouldn't have. Not at all. Mum wouldn't have opened the door to Ellie. And Ellie and Florie would have been too much for her to handle. It's a good thing they never made it to England.*

'Well, you're with family here, Sophie. There'll always be room for you at Kittiwake. Oh, it'll be so lovely having you here, won't it, Florie?'

'Oh, Lord, yes, duck,' Florie says as she hands Sophie a mug of steaming chocolate. 'We's got more rooms in that big old house than I can find. We'll set you up right good. Stay as long as you likes.'

Sam waves his hand at Becca, who is on the floor, giggling soundlessly as the dogs jump over her. *'Come on, Becca-bug,'* he says as he signs to her. *'Time to go. Let's get some supper.'*

Becca springs to her feet and signs something back. Sam glances over at Sophie. 'Becca wants to teach you something.'

'Teach me something? I'm ... I'm not sure ...'

'Just watch her and do what she does.'

Becca takes Sophie's hand and tugs her towards a battered wooden table in front of the bay window. She pulls out a wooden chair and gestures for Sophie to sit.

Sam drags a chair from under the table and straddles it like a bike. 'Do you know the old nursery rhyme about the cat who visits the Queen?'

'Yes,' Sophie says as she sets her mug of hot chocolate on the table. 'I think I can remember it.'

'Just say it, and Becca will sign. Then do what she does.'

Sophie glances over at Ellie and Florie who are standing beside a counter, Florie's arm draped casually across Ellie's shoulders. Ellie nods encouragingly. 'Go on, Sophie. It's easy.'

Sophie takes a breath. *'Pussy cat, pussy cat, where have you been?'* She watches Becca's hands closely as she clumsily mirrors the signs.

*'I've been to London to visit the Queen.'* She glances at Sam. 'I'm afraid I'm not very good at this.'

Ellie sits down in a chair on the opposite side of the table. 'Nonsense. You're doing very well. Go on.'

*'Pussy cat, pussy cat, what did you there?'* Sophie continues, copying Becca's finger movements as Ellie and Florie join in.

*'I frightened a little mouse under her chair.'*

Beaming brightly at Sophie, Becca wraps her arms around her in a hug. Ellie smiles at them across the table. 'It looks like you've made a friend.'

Sam rises abruptly and frowns at Sophie. He pushes his chair under the table. 'Becca has plenty of friends.' He taps Becca on nose. *'C'mon, Becca-bug. Supper time,'* he signs.

Becca kisses Sophie on her cheek and takes hold of Sam's hand. Sophie watches them walk towards the screen door, spying Sam sneak a chocolate chip cookie from a plate on the counter to give his daughter, as Rupert drools.

'It'll ruin her supper,' Florie calls after them as the screen door slams shut.

Sophie picks up the mug of hot chocolate and takes a sip. 'What happened there?'

'Don't mind him, duck,' Florie says. 'He's all right. He's just overprotective of Becca since Winny passed.'

'Winny?'

'My daughter.' Ellie rises from the table and walks over to the bay window, folding her arms as she looks out to the inlet beyond. 'She died three years ago.' Turning back to Sophie, she smiles sadly. 'She would have been your cousin. It's such a shame you never had a chance to meet.'

'She was a beauty, was Winny,' Florie says as she heads towards the back room. 'Blonde like Ellie. You don't look much like her. C'mon, let's go have a scoff. I'm gut-foundered.'

# *Chapter 12*

## Norwich, England – 7 August 1940

Ellie walks over to a wooden bench under an overgrown cedar and sits down, the tree's branches sweeping out above her like the wings of a giant crow. She crosses her ankles and tucks her feet under the bench, steadying herself by pressing her hands into the rough grey wood. The mourners melt away, slipping back to their lives, far away from the eerie quiet of the cemetery.

Beside the graves, George talks to the priest. Ruthie, Richie, and their parents, Bryan and Peggy – the whole Huggins family – never waking up to see these trees and the sky, or eat fish and chips on the pier in Yarmouth on a hot August day. The raider had been back the next day, bombing Boulton and Paul's Riverside Works and machine-gunning King Street on his way home. More deaths. More freshly dug graves under the leafy canopy of elms and oaks in the cemetery. And more to come – she is sure of that now.

George shakes the priest's hand. Ellie watches him stride towards her, the vibrancy of the green grass under his feet somehow at odds with the mood that has settled over the ancient city. He's lost weight; his dark grey suit hangs loosely on his body. He sits beside her and places his hand over hers. His is warm, reassuring, and she feels the tension in her fingers slowly dissolve.

'Are you okay, Ellie?'

She bites her lip and looks at him, willing the tears not to come. Amazed that there are any tears left inside her.

'No. No, I'm not.' She dabs at her eyes with a white hand-kerchief. 'I remember when I met Ruthie on our first day in Brownies, in the basement hall at St George's. She'd tied her tie all wrong. I showed her how to do it. Pops had taught me. She shared some rock candy she'd saved from her summer holiday in Yarmouth. It was fuzzy from her pocket, but I didn't mind.' She blinks hard, balling her hands into fists. 'It's not fair.'

George squeezes her hand. 'No, it's not fair. But there's nothing for it but to keep on going. Ruthie would want that.'

Ellie nods. 'I know.' She smiles sadly. 'She knew every dance hall and picture house show going on in Norwich. She wasn't one to sit at home waiting for things to happen.'

'Then the best thing you can do for Ruthie is live your life, Ellie. Become an artist. I'll always support you in that – you know that. I'm awfully proud of you, you know. You're talented. Dame Edith wouldn't have hired you if you weren't.'

Ellie sighs, the air rushing out of her lungs like bellows deflating. 'That's the thing, George. I've been standing at the easel in art class painting oranges and apples, and running all over Norwich searching for Prussian Blue, or Cobalt Violet or whatever tube of oil paint Dame Edith's decided she needs urgently, and it just seems so pointless.'

She looks at George's kind face, at his concerned brown-eyed gaze behind his glasses. 'I couldn't find the Cobalt Violet paint anywhere. I'd been to Buntings and I was on my way to Jarrolds, but when I got to Bethel Street my stomach was growling so I thought I'd nip into a tea shop to pick up a sandwich. There was a sign outside the fire station asking for women to join the Auxiliary Fire Service. I went in and I signed up.'

'You signed up? In the fire service? Are you sure, Ellie?'

'Yes, absolutely. I have my uniform and I'm to work as a clerk in a room above the fire engines. I start on Thursday.'

'But what about your art classes? And Dame Edith?'

'I'm cutting down the classes and I'm afraid I'm just going to have to tell Dame Edith I can't help her anymore. It's fine, George. I've decided. Susan Perry-Gore will be over the moon for a chance to work with Dame Edith.'

'It's dangerous work, Ellie.'

'No more dangerous than sleeping in your bed when the air raid siren doesn't go off.'

'What did your father say?'

Ellie grimaces. 'I haven't told him yet. But, it doesn't matter. I've made up my mind. We're in the war now, George. The Germans are flying over here more regularly. And the War Office has the Newfoundlanders building pillboxes and fortifications all along the coast. Ruthie's Uncle Jack in Fakenham heard some of them talking about it at the Limes. Swanning around being an art student is just selfish right now. I have to do something real. I have to do it for Ruthie. And for me.'

# *Chapter 13*

## Tippy's Tickle – 12 September 2001

'Emmy! There you are.'

A warm, yeasty fragrance fills the room, and Ellie pushes a plate of freshly baked tea-buns and the butter dish across the mahogany dining table. 'Sit down and have a bun. We've got your dinner heating in the oven. Florie'll get it for you.'

Florie raises her eyebrows. 'Oh, she will, will she?'

'Yes, please, Florie. I have to make the introductions.'

Dropping her napkin beside her plate, Florie pushes her chair away from the table. 'Florie do this, and Florie do that. I only stays with you because of your blueberry pudding, Ellie, you gots to know that.'

'Just the blueberry pudding?'

'Well, I'll gives you your Yorkshire pudding too,' Florie says as she pushes through the swing door to the kitchen.

Emmett Parsons slides his tall, thin frame onto the chair and lays a napkin neatly over his lap. His greying hair springs from his head in unruly waves, but otherwise his appearance is neat and orderly; his checked flannel shirt buttoned to the neck, his grey trousers neatly ironed, his brown shoes polished to a high gleam. Bowing his head, he presses his hands together and mumbles a prayer of thanksgiving.

'Emmy, this is your cousin, Sophie. She's come from England, where I was born.'

Emmett looks over at Sophie. He nods. 'Pleased to meet you. Pass the jam, please.'

'Oh, of course,' Sophie says, momentarily disarmed by his unusual eyes, one the same blue-grey as Ellie's, the other as brown as the mahogany table. 'I'm very pleased to meet you too. You know, you're my only cousin. My father didn't have any brothers or sisters.'

Emmett scrapes butter and a dollop of blueberry jam onto a tea bun and takes a bite. 'Pass the water, please.'

Sophie pushes the water jug over to him. 'What do you do, Emmett?'

'I builds boats. I fixes them too.'

'That sounds interesting.'

'Yes.'

'Good. That's very good.'

Ellie pours out a cup of steaming tea. 'Emmy works with Sam down by the tickle.'

'Sam works for me.'

'Yes, of course, darling. Emmy's got Rod Fizzard's old store – that's a shed they used to gut the fish in – down on a wharf by the shore. What are you working on now, Emmy?'

'Boat from Salvage.' Emmett reaches for another tea bun. 'A 1996 Sea Ray 330 Sundancer. Hull's leaking.'

The door from the kitchen swings open and Florie ploughs into the dining room, her hand encased in a thick oven glove, carrying a plate of pink corned beef, cabbage and boiled vegetables swimming in gravy. She sets it down in front of Emmett. 'There you goes, Emmy, b'y. Jiggs dinner, just how you likes.'

Emmett regards the steaming plate of food. Picking up his fork and knife, he addresses no one in particular.

'Mustard, please.'

Sophie pushes the curtain – a cotton chintz printed with blue roses and pink ribbons, the colours long since softened by bleach and laundering – to one side, and raises the sash window. Leaning her elbows on the sill, she gazes across the edge of the stony cliff to the ocean beyond. The waning crescent of the moon throws a faint silver glow over the black landscape, its pale light catching the waves as they crest. As Sophie's eyes adjust to the darkness, the sky comes alive with thousands of stars, shining like diamonds someone has scattered across a swathe of black velvet.

She'd expected to be in New York tonight. Eating a room service dinner as she flipped through the TV channels, the interview behind her. Debating with herself whether to spend money for the porn channel, but deciding against it when the last vestiges of Catholic guilt would prick her conscience. She might have ordered a small bottle of champagne, if the interview and her presentation had gone well. Picked up her mobile phone, and thumbed through the contacts, looking for someone to call, to let them know her good news. But there wouldn't be anyone to tell. Not anyone who'd care.

She surveys the glittering sky and thinks of the thousands of people who'd been lost in the attacks in the United States the day before. Seeing the stars they would never again see, hearing the waves crash against the rocks below the cliff. Closing her eyes, Sophie sends them the sight of the stars and the sounds of the waves and the feeling of the cool breeze on her skin.

She doesn't know what she is doing here, in this odd little place called Tippy's Tickle. And why had her mother hated Ellie so much, Ellie who seems so perfectly lovely? And then there's Florie. She's what Poppy would've called a "character". Emmett is a strange one. He doesn't seem all that bothered about her, but, then, why should he be? She might share DNA with Ellie and Emmett and Becca, too, but they are all still strangers. Then there is Winny, the cousin she's never heard of; Sam Byrne's dead wife and Becca's mother. What were the chances that she'd meet her late cousin's widower in Gander Airport? How small *is* this place? And why is Sam working for Emmett? That seems like an odd set-up.

Didn't Mavis at the airport say Sam had spent time in Boston? That's why he sounded so different from the others, though she'd noticed the Newfoundland lilt slip in when he spoke to Wince at the garage. Such an irritating man. Calling her Princess Grace. What did he mean by that? Winny must've had the patience of a saint.

Why on earth had she thought seeking Ellie out was a good idea? Was it because, after years of devoting herself to her work at the expense of relationships, she was feeling ... lonely? Sophie grunts. That's ridiculous. She's surrounded by people; her colleagues at the London practice, clients, builders, engineers, quantity surveyors, suppliers. There are a lot of people around her life, just no one in it.

She'd been curious to meet Ellie, that's all. What's wrong with that? Her parents were dead, and, as far as she'd been aware when she stepped off the plane, Ellie had been her only living relative. Now there were three: Ellie, Emmett and Becca.

Fate had conspired to put her down in Newfoundland. The

least she could do was follow the thread, and find the answer to the question she'd wondered about all her life. What had happened between her mother and her aunt all those years ago, before Ellie left for Newfoundland? What did Ellie do to make Dottie hate her so much?

# Chapter 14

## Norwich, England – 21 December 1940

Ellie jumps off the bus in front of the portico of the Samson and Hercules dance hall, where two chunky white-painted statues of the mythical figures hold up the porch roof. George waves at her from the top step, and she runs up to meet him and gives him a quick kiss on his cheek.

'You look like a soldier in that outfit, Ellie.'

Ellie glances down at her navy uniform. 'I'm sorry, George. It was busy over at the station. Fire over in Pegg's Opening. It doesn't take much for those old cottages to go up. It was just a cigarette this time that did it. I hope you don't mind dancing with a girl in uniform.'

'No, it's nice. I just wish I'd known. I would have put on mine. It would have evened the balance.'

'Don't be silly, George. You look just fine.' She smooths the white handkerchief that he's tucked into the breast pocket of his brown wool suit jacket. 'I can't believe you managed to get us tickets. Everyone in town wanted to come to see The Squadronaires.'

'Just lucky, Ellie. My boss was sent some tickets and his wife didn't want to come.'

They push through the doors and through the crowd into the ballroom, the party dresses and suits of the recent past outnumbered by the khaki, Air Force blue and navy of uniforms. Paper-loop streamers hang from the ceiling and the Air Force dance band, The Squadronaires, handsome in their Air Force uniforms, are in full swing on the stage.

George squints at the room through his glasses. 'Looks like all the tables are taken. We should've arrived before the interval.'

'Oh, George, no one gets here before the interval,' Ellie says as she bounces to the music. 'Girls need time to get ready. Anyway, I've been at my desk all day. I want to dance, not sit.'

'Fine, but I need a beer first. I'll meet up with you over there by the stage. What would you like?'

'Beer, please. Just a half.' Ellie makes her way around the perimeter of the dancers until her way is blocked by the backs of a group of tall Newfoundlanders. 'Excuse me.' She clears her throat and shouts. 'Excuse me!' She pokes a broad shoulder.

The man turns around. 'Well, there she is, after all this time.' The smile lighting up his grey eyes. The long, handsome face. The name slips out of Ellie's mouth before she has a chance to think. 'Thomas Parsons.'

The smile turns into a grin. 'You and my mam. The only two people who calls me Thomas.' He hands his beer to one of his friends. 'C'mon, maid. Let's have a dance.'

George sweeps his gaze around the crowded dance floor and spies Ellie's blonde head, topped by the neat navy AFS cap, bouncing to the rhythm of the swing band with a tall Newfoundlander. The soldier looks vaguely familiar, and George rakes through his brain to remember where he's seen him before.

'Well, what do you figure?' A hand pats George's shoulder. A soldier's moon-shaped face, with a dusting of freckles across his nose, grins at him. 'Charlie Murphy from the 57th Newfoundlanders over in Filby. You remember? I met you here with my friend Tom back in the summer. He spilt Coke all over your girlfriend's dress. Oh, she was some vexed, wasn't she? Could have frozen the North Atlantic with that face. I've been lookin' out for you lot. Where've you been?' He scans the crowd past George's shoulder. 'Is Ruthie with you? I'd be up for a dance or twenty with her.'

George looks at the boyish face and shakes his head. 'Ruthie ... Ruthie's not here.'

Charlie's face falls. 'Don't tell me another fella's cut in?'

'No. I'm terribly sorry, Charlie. There was a bomb. Her whole family ... they were sleeping. They didn't make it, I'm afraid.'

'Oh, Jaysus.' Charlie rubs his fingers over his eyes. 'You knows, b'y, when you joins up you knows there's a chance ... there's a chance you might not come back. But you never figure a pretty girl you meet at a dance, in her own home ...'

George looks at the young soldier. It's like all the joy stored in Charlie's compact, exuberant body has melted away, like the ice lolly from Mr Suckling's newsagent's that he'd once left out on the garden table. He pats Charlie's shoulder. 'How about I get us a couple of beers?'

'Nah, b'y. If it's all the same to you, I'm gonna call it a night.' Charlie nods towards the dance floor. 'I sees Tommy's off dancin' with your girlfriend. Let him know I've caught the early train back to Great Yarmouth. I'll gets myself a lift to Filby from there. I don't much feels in the mood anymore.'

'Of course.'

Charlie gives George a thumbs up. He nods in Thomas's direction. His friend is swinging Ellie around the floor in an energetic jitterbug. 'I'd be watching out for old Tommy, there. All the girls loves him back home. He's as smooth as the ice on an inland pond, that one.'

George looks over at the two dancers. Ellie throws back her head and giggles as she loops under Thomas's arms.

'Thanks, but I don't need to worry. Ellie's my girl. We're getting married as soon as the war's over.'

'Well, that's all right, then. Nothin' to worry about.' Charlie adjusts his beret. 'All the same, I'd keep my eyes peeled, if I was you. There's nothin' on earth like the charm of a Newfoundlander. And, I knows what I'm sayin' 'cause I am one.'

The music segues into a leisurely foxtrot. Thomas draws Ellie closer and she smiles at him nervously, though she's in no particular rush to leave the dance floor. 'I'm getting rather thirsty after all that jitterbugging, Thomas. George was getting us some beer. He'll wonder what's happened to me.'

'I'm pretty sure he knows where you're at.' Thomas nods towards the stage, where George leans against a pillar sipping a beer as he watches the dance floor. 'Can't say as I blame him.'

Ellie glances over at the stage and gives her fiancé a wave. 'George has nothing to worry about. We've been engaged for ages.'

Thomas taps Ellie's ring finger. 'Why haven't you got an engagement ring on your finger, then, maid?'

'Oh, well, you know, the war and all that. He needs to save up some money. He works over at Mcklintock's Chocolates. He's in administration. He's making his way up the ladder.'

'Sounds like a clever fella.'

'Oh, he is.'

'I've saved up some stamps for him. Why anyone'd want to collect stamps is a mystery to me. Just pieces of paper as far as

I can tell. My mam writes to beat the band. Every week I gets seven letters from her. She must be usin' up all the ink in Newfoundland. I'll bring the stamps next week.'

'Next week?' Was he expecting to see her next week?

'Sure thing. We all wants to get away from barracks come Saturday. They're puttin' on trucks to bring us into town from next week. We won't need to squeeze onto the two carriages on the train. Some fellas always get left behind. They were goin' to have a riot on their hands if they didn't sort it out.'

'Well, George will appreciate that. The stamps, I mean.'

Thomas raises an ash-blond eyebrow. 'How about you? Would you be happy to have a go on the dance floor again with a fella with two left feet?'

'Two left feet?' Ellie laughs. 'You must be joking. You jitterbug better than any of the boys around here.'

'That's because a lot of us have family down in Boston. They brings us American records when they visits. Newfoundland's a right crossroads of the world. All the aeroplanes heading to Europe has to refuel in Gander. They'd drop like a brick into the ocean on their way over if they didn't. We had Carole Lombard over there in St John's just before I signed up. The girls were all out in force hopin' to see Clark Gable, but he didn't show up. That's her husband, you know. I read it in the *Telegram*.'

'Ruthie would have loved to see Clark Gable.'

'You never knows. Maybe she'll see him here in Norwich some day.'

Ellie shakes her head. 'Ruthie ... Ruthie's gone. Her house was hit by a bomb in July.'

Thomas squeezes Ellie's hand. 'I'm sorry. That's hard.'

'Thanks. Yes. It's very hard.' Ellie leans her head against the rough khaki wool of Thomas's uniform. 'It doesn't seem fair.'

'No, it's not. We just has to keep going. That's the choice we got.'

'It's why I decided to join the fire service. I couldn't not do something.' Ellie sighs against the khaki wool and looks up at Thomas. 'I was studying art. I had a job helping a famous artist.' She shrugs. 'I gave it up. I still take an art class a couple of times a week, but it's getting busier at the fire station. The Germans have already been over twice this month. One just missed bombing the Cathedral by a whisker.'

'He must have been blind. A boy with a slingshot could hit that with his eyes closed.'

Ellie laughs and looks at Thomas. Ruthie was right. He has the same sandy blond hair and strong-boned face as Gary Cooper. The nose a little too long but fitting just right in his angular face. Not that it mattered, of course. It was just nice to dance with someone who knew how to, for a change. What was wrong with that?

A crash outside the building thunders through the music and the chatter, setting the paper streamers swaying. The band judders to a stop and a silence as thick as a winter quilt falls over the room. Then, a crush as the crowd suddenly surges towards the exit. Another crash outside, further up the road, followed by the whine of the air raid sirens.

Thomas grabs Ellie's hand. 'Not that way. There's a cellar. The door's at the back.'

'No, I need to find George.' Ellie pulls away and fights her way towards the stage. 'George!'

A pair of arms enfold her. The familiar brown wool suit. 'I'm here, Ellie.'

Thomas taps George's shoulder. 'C'mon, b'y. There's a cellar. We'll be safe there.'

Ellie sits on a wooden crate packed with wine bottles beside a large beer cask. The cellar windows are blacked out and reinforced with a crisscross of masking tape, and a single electric bulb hangs from the ceiling, throwing an eerie yellow light over the round-bellied beer casks and wooden crates of wine and soft drinks. Others have found their way to the cellar as well, and they sit together in an uneasy silence, waiting for the all-clear.

Thomas nods at the crates. 'We're not goin' to go thirsty, that's for sure.'

George squints through his glasses at Thomas's face, lit pale yellow by the electric light. 'How did you know there was a cellar?'

'I always makes it my business to check these things out. Just in case.'

'Well, I'm very glad you did.' Ellie shifts on the crate, away from a splinter pushing through her navy skirt. 'I wouldn't have wanted to be squeezing into the shelter up the road with everyone else.'

George removes his glasses and tugs the handkerchief out of his breast pocket. 'I saw your friend Charlie,' he says as he wipes a film of dust off his glasses. 'He said to tell you he'd gone back to Filby early on the train.' He tucks the handkerchief back in his pocket and pushes the glasses over his nose.

'That's not like Charlie. He's one for a party.'

'He asked about Ruthie.'

Thomas nods. 'All right, then. I see.' He looks at Ellie. 'He liked your friend. He talked my ear off all about her for months. He kept looking for her at the dance halls every time we came to Norwich.'

Ellie presses her lips together, willing the sob that's forming in her throat not to spring into life. If it does, she can't trust herself not to stop crying. She'd thought she'd cried all the tears allotted to her body, but she was wrong. They were like a perpetual spring with a source that never dried up.

The ear-splitting wail of the all-clear slices through the heavy stillness of the December night. They rise and stretch, unfolding into the pale yellow light illuminating the cellar. The revellers pick their way over the crates and beer casks and make their way up the cellar steps.

Outside, a half-moon hangs like a Christmas bauble in the twinkling sky. George holds out his hand to Thomas. 'Thanks for your help tonight.' His breath forms into a cloud that sits on the cold air. 'Will you get back to Filby okay?'

Thomas shakes George's hand. 'No problem, George, b'y. There's always someone happy to give a soldier a lift.' He looks at Ellie and touches his forehead in a mini-salute. 'See you anon. Thanks for the dance.'

Ellie watches as Thomas walks down the street, his tall figure growing smaller, his outline growing fainter, until he melds into the black winter night.

# *Chapter 15*

## Tippy's Tickle – 13 September 2001

The screen door from the yard into Ellie's kitchen swings open and Becca bounds into the room, the great black bulk of Rupert at her heels. She runs over to Florie, who is drying the breakfast dishes at the sink, and gives her a hug. Scampering over to the table where Ellie and Sophie are drinking coffee, she hugs them both. She pulls out a chair and sits down beside Ellie.

'Sam!' Florie calls out. 'Sam! Get that dog outta here! This place isn't big enough for all of us!'

The door springs open and Sam strides in holding a bright pink school bag, his leather jacket replaced by a plaid flannel shirt and a jean jacket. 'Rupert! Get out here, b'y!' The dog lumbers across the linoleum floor, pausing for a pet on the head from Sam, then pads out of the door.

'Jaysus God, Sam. I don't even let my doxies in here,' Florie says as she wipes the breakfast dishes dry by the sink. 'They've got a right nice kennel behind the shop. Don't know why you don't do the same for that bear.'

'Rupert'll go into a kennel the day palm trees grow in Tippy's Tickle, Florie. You might be all spit and vinegar, but Rupert knows you're a soft touch. I found date-square crumbs on him the other day and Becca swore it wasn't her.'

'Well, one date square won't hurt him. Look at the size of him.'

Sam hands the school bag to Becca and takes the cup of coffee Ellie offers him. Nodding at Sophie, he sets the mug on the table and bends to give Becca a kiss on her blonde head. *Be a good girl, honey,* he says, signing to her. *Listen to Nanny, and show me what you learned at supper tonight, okay?*

'You down at the store today, Sam?' Ellie asks as he heads to the door.

'No. Heading down to Gander to see what's going on with the planes. Meeting up with Thor and Ace to move some supplies around to the legion hall and the gym for the CFAs. I'll be back by supper.'

'Could you ask about my flight, please?' Sophie asks as she spreads thick purple blueberry jam on a warm scone. 'BA101 going to JFK in New York.'

'Can't wait to get out of here, can you?'

Sophie blinks at Sam, the scone halfway to her mouth. 'Well, I need to know when to get back to Gander. I've got a meeting—'

Sam jerks his head in an impatient nod. 'Yes. You're a high-flyer, we all know that.'

'Come over here for supper, why don't you, Sam?' Florie says as she slides the final plate into the plate rack over the sink. 'Doing macaroni and cheese tonight. There'll be plenty.'

'I'll see how I go, Florie.' The door slams shut behind him. 'Don't wait if I'm late. I'll be back in time to put Becca to bed.'

'That's enough studying for today,' Florie says as she stomps into the kitchen and drops several wicker baskets onto the old wooden table. 'Grab yourself a basket, girls. We're going out berry picking. I've closed up the shop. Anyone needs anything, they'll just have to wait till tomorrow. I'll makes a pie for supper tonight when we gets back. Nothing like Newfoundland wild blueberry pie. You'll think you've died and gone to heaven, Sophie. Becca'll teach you what to look for.'

Sophie looks up from her mobile phone. 'Berry picking? I don't have anything to wear for that. My suitcase is still in the plane.'

'Don't worry about that,' Ellie says as she corrects Becca's spelling test. 'I'll lend you some clothes while you're here.' She runs her eyes over Sophie. 'They won't be fancy, mind you.'

Sophie glances down as her crumpled velvet skirt and the white silk blouse now webbed with creases and spots of maple syrup from the morning's pancake breakfast. 'They kept our suitcases on the plane. I only dress like this for work.'

'Which I understands you does all the time,' Florie says as she folds tea towels into the baskets. 'Sam said.'

'Sam doesn't know anything about me.'

'Oh, right.' Florie raises an eyebrow. 'Didn't mean to hit a nerve there, duck.'

*'Show Sophie your lettering, Becca,'* Ellie says, signing to Becca.

Becca passes a large piece of cardboard covered in crooked green-crayoned letters to Sophie. 'B-E-C-C-A B-R-Y-N-E,' she signs as Ellie says the letters.

Sophie looks over at Ellie. 'What do I do if I want to say something? I don't know how to sign.'

'Just face her so she can read your lips.'

Sophie nods. 'That's very good, Becca. But isn't it supposed to be …?' Sophie frowns as she concentrates on the green letters. 'Isn't it supposed to be B-Y-R-N-E?'

Becca rolls her eyes and nods. 'B-Y-R-N-E,' she corrects herself.

'Well done, Sophie.' Ellie rolls up the cardboard, securing it with an elastic. 'You've been paying attention.'

Sophie slides her phone into the pocket of her velvet jacket, which she's slung over the back of her chair. 'Well, the London office has my work there under control, and there's nothing I can do about the New York interview right now, so, consider me a student of berry picking.'

Sophie follows Florie, Ellie and Becca up a rocky path in a pair of Ellie's jeans, a large striped sweater pilfered from Florie's closet, and an ancient pair of Adidas trainers, wading through knee-high bushes and over fallen logs as they pass clumps of fat blueberries sprouting from the rocky scree. Every now and then, she stops to take pictures with her small digital camera.

'What about these ones?' she asks as they trek by a large clump.

'Nah, maid. These ones has been picked over,' Florie calls back to her. 'There are better up higher. The berries likes the slopes, and there was a forest fire up there a few years ago. It stimulates the berries. There's lots more up there.'

They stop on a slope near the top of the hill where the mash of grey rocks sprout masses of thick bushes heavy with ripe blueberries. Beyond the tops of the fir trees, the inky blue water of the ocean glimmers in the sun, and down the coast, a red-roofed lighthouse and a tall white house can just be made out on a protruding cliff.

Ellie hands her basket to Sophie. 'Pick some for me, too, Sophie. I'm going to draw.'

'I don't really know what I'm doing.'

Florie waves at Sophie. 'Come on over here, duck. We'll shows you how it's done.'

Sophie joins Florie and Becca beside a carpet of blueberry bushes. Squatting beside a bush, Becca cups a clump of plump berries with her hand. She pries them away from their stalks with her thumb and lets them roll off her palm into her basket.

'Just do what Becca's doing, maid,' Florie says. 'You'll knows if they're ripe if they just falls into your hand. If they resists you, best to leave them be. Your hands are going to get purple. You don't minds that, do you? They stains like the devil.'

'That's all right. I'll wash them later.'

Florie chuckles as she bends over a blueberry bush. 'Yes, sure, duck. You do that.'

Sophie wanders over to a clump of berries and tests out Becca's technique, abandoning it when she finds herself pulling off huge stalks of unripe berries. Sitting on a warm rock, she settles on a one-berry-at-a-time method.

Ellie wanders over, her drawing pad under her arm. She sits on a rock near Sophie and flips open the pad. 'Do you mind if I draw you?' she asks, a pencil poised over the paper.

'Me? Are you sure you wouldn't rather draw Becca or Florie? I'm pretty slow at this.'

'Don't worry about the berries. Those two can pick for England, and I draw them all the time. I'd love to have a drawing of my niece.'

Sophie tucks a strand of hair that has escaped her ponytail behind her ear. 'I look like a wreck.'

'You look lovely.'

Sophie smiles. 'I think you need to put your glasses on, Aunt Ellie.'

Ellie looks down at the turquoise glasses hanging around her neck and slides them onto her nose. She peers at Sophie. 'Ah, you're right. My mistake.'

'Aunt Ellie!' Sophie says, laughing.

Ellie giggles. 'I'm teasing, Sophie. Just relax and pick your berries. Ignore me.'

A companionable silence settles over the berry pickers and the artist, overlaid by the buzz of insects and the hammering of a woodpecker deep in the woods. After about half an hour, Sophie stretches and sits beside Ellie on a velvety cushion of green moss. She looks at the drawing, her eyes widening. 'Oh, you've made me look quite nice.'

Ellie laughs. 'You're very nice-looking, Sophie. You've got your parents' dark hair, but the blue-grey Burgess eyes. Becca has the same eyes. Winny did too.'

Sophie smiles at Ellie. 'You have them too. Mum had dark eyes though.'

'Yes. Like our mother, Winnifred. She was half French. I named Winny after her.'

'Really? I didn't know that.' Sophie sweeps her eyes over the drawing – the confident outlines of her own face and her body bending over the berry bushes, the fine feathering of her hair where strands are caught by the wind, and the craggy stones and fat, shaded ripeness of the berries.

Her mother had never told her anything about the family, shutting her down with a sharp *'That's all in the past!'* whenever she'd asked. And all her father would say was that her grandparents had been 'lovely'. She'd given up asking, in the end.

'I used to draw, too, a long time ago. Mum thought it was a waste of time. She said I'd never be able to make a living that way.' Sophie shrugs. 'I became an architect instead. Mum didn't have a problem with me learning technical drawing. Everything had to have a purpose for her. She didn't believe in art for art's sake.'

'Really?' Ellie flips closed the cover of her drawing pad. 'She didn't used to be like that. She was an excellent pianist, you know.'

'Yes, Dad told me. She played in concert halls and everything. I never heard her play. We had a piano, but she never touched it.'

Ellie shakes her head. 'That's a shame.' She slides her glasses off her nose and lets them fall against her chest. 'You should take up drawing again.'

'Oh, I don't know. I'd be awfully rusty, and I don't have much free time.'

'You have plenty of free time here. Let's go out tomorrow. We'll go drawing together. I'll teach you some techniques.'

'Um ... sure, why not?' Sophie glances over to the others who are scrambling over the rocks in a competition to pick the most berries. 'Will Becca and Florie come too?

'No, Florie's starting Becca on her multiplication tables tomorrow.'

'Sam mentioned you teach Becca at home.'

'For now, anyway. Sam thinks she's too young to be sent off to board at the school for the deaf in St John's, and, since the primary school in Tippy's Tickle closed a few years ago, the closest public school is an hour bus ride away in Wesleyville. I used to teach Emmy at home before the old school reopened back in the Fifties. I taught art at the high school in Wesleyville for years, too, before I retired. Becca's in good hands.'

'How did Winny meet Sam?'

'They met at Memorial University in St John's. He'd come back from Boston to study mathematics there and be closer to his mother in Grand Falls. She wasn't well, poor thing. Ovarian cancer. His father died in a car accident down in Boston when

Sam was sixteen and she'd moved back to her hometown. He stayed in Boston until he finished high school.'

'What were they doing down in Boston?'

'Sam's parents moved down there when he was a boy. Looking for more opportunities, I suppose. They had relatives down there. A lot of Irish Newfoundlanders do.

'Sam and Winny got married at St Stephen's here after she graduated with her Master's in Psychology. They moved back to Boston and Sam had a very successful property development company there. They tried for years to have a baby. They'd almost given up when Becca finally came along.' Ellie sets the drawing pad and the pencil in her lap. 'Then ...' Ellie sighs as she looks out over the grey-blue ocean. 'Then, she died. There was an accident.' She shakes her head. 'She was only forty-five.'

'I'm so sorry.'

'Yes.' Ellie clears her throat and picks up the drawing pad and pencil. Flipping open the cover, she bends over the pad and draws sweeping strokes onto the paper. 'Poor Sam was beside himself. He was here with Becca for the funeral. We buried Winny's ashes in St Stephen's Cemetery. This was her home, after all.'

'Why didn't he stay in Boston if his business was there?'

'Things became ... difficult for him in Boston.' She opens her mouth as if to say something, but presses her lips together.

'What do you mean?'

'Well, Becca needed special attention and ... Sam took Winny's death hard. Florie and I were worried. There were ... problems with his business. He had to close it. We persuaded him to come to Tippy's Tickle. So, three years ago he came and started helping Emmy in his boat-building business.' She smiles at Sophie. 'I had to twist Emmy's arm. He's never been one to like working with others. He fished for years up in Fogo, saved every penny he could. When Rod Fizzard's boat-building business came up for sale twenty years ago he bought it. He's been working there ever since.'

'So, Emmett owns the business?'

'Yes.'

'And Sam's his employee?'

'Well, part-time. It was always meant to be a temporary arrangement until Sam got back on his feet financially. Sam's started his own business working on the houses around here and he's making furniture as well; Emmy showed him how to turn wood, and he's really taken to it. He's got a real talent for it.' She looks over at Sophie. 'I doubt Sam'll stay for long. Becca loves it here. We love having them, but people move on. Tippy's Tickle is a small place for someone like Sam.'

'It can't be easy for him, after running a big business in Boston.'

'I suppose.' Ellie smiles at Sophie. 'Things change. Life never stays the same. I hear people say they don't like change. That's just ridiculous. If you don't make choices, you can be sure choices will be made for you. I've always thought that it's better to be the agent of your own destiny. Though sometimes you'll wonder if you've made a huge mistake.' She smiles at Sophie. 'There were times I certainly did.'

'You did?' What kind of mistakes? What had happened between Ellie and her mother? Was that one of the mistakes?

'Oh, yes. Yes, indeed. Never mind. We all make mistakes, don't we?' Ellie gestures to the expanse of sea glinting in the late summer sunlight below. 'Anyway, my decisions have brought me here, and that's just fine with me.'

'So Sam didn't choose to be here.'

'No. That's why I expect he'll move on, unless he finds a

reason to stay. I think he's getting restless.' Ellie holds the drawing up to Sophie. 'There, all done. What do you think?'

Sophie runs her finger over the pencil lines, over the loose ponytail with the strands flying about her face; at the light eyes narrowed with laughter, at the rolled-up jeans and Florie's too-large striped sweater, and the greyed shading on her fingers where the berry juice has seeped into her skin. 'I don't recognise myself.'

Ellie tears the drawing out of the pad and hands it to Sophie. 'Well, you should. It's you.'

Sophie stares at the drawing. *This isn't me. I don't know this person.*

'Are you sure?'

Ellie laughs. 'Of course I'm sure! One for each of us. My niece who dropped out of the sky.'

# Chapter 16

## Norwich, England – 14 February 1941

Ellie taps her pencil on the desk blotter. She watches the minute hand on the wall clock click to four-forty. Just one more hour before she signs off. Another Valentine's on her own. Well, not exactly on her own. She'd be with her father and Dottie, but family wasn't the same thing. George probably hadn't even remembered it was Valentine's. Romance wasn't something he was terribly good at.

What did Valentine's matter now, anyway? George was needed on the searchlights over at the castle tonight. Two more people killed over on Plumstead Road in last week's raid, and more injured. Everything had settled down now, people going about their daily business, but it was a veneer of normality. She was on edge, just like everyone else. Plymouth had received a bashing just a month ago, and she'd listened to Churchill's speech with her father and Dottie on the wireless just a few nights ago when he'd asked the Americans to 'give us the tools'. *That'll fall on deaf ears,* her father had said.

She gazes around the cluttered room. Manila files disgorging paper spill out of the wooden shelves, and a cricket bat sits across the one spare chair. Her attempts at order in the fire station's Stores Department seem destined to failure in any office shared with Fire Officer Williams. She tucks the pencil behind her ear.

'Would you like some tea, sir?'

Fire Officer Francis Williams peers at her over the top of the requisition list, twitching his broad nose over his grey moustache. 'That'd do the trick, Burgess. Milk, two sugars.'

She pushes her wheeled office chair away from her desk and heads over to the hot plate. After picking up the kettle, she holds it under the cold-water tap in the tiny kitchen. Milk, two sugars. Every time. *Yes, Burgess. Milk, two sugars.*

'Burgess, would you check the store and count how many oranges came in? This list says twenty-four, but I'm sure there were only meant to be eighteen.'

'Some oranges came in, sir?' Ellie sets the kettle onto the hot plate and switches the knob to high. She hadn't seen an orange since last summer. Nor a banana since the war began. It was Poppy's birthday next week and he was going to miss out on his favourite banana cake for a second year running.

'Commander Barrett brought them in from Filby. One of the Newfoundlanders got hold of some. Don't ask me how. Those chaps could find a diamond in a glass mountain. Barrett said the chap insisted he give them to us here in the fire station. Said they were a thank you for all the work we did. Very nice gesture, don't you agree?'

'Very nice, sir. Yes.'

Leaning over the hot plate, Ellie unhooks the clipboard from a hook on the wall. She tugs the pencil out from behind her ear as she enters the store room. Oranges for the Norwich Fire Station? From a Newfoundlander at Filby? She'd told Thomas at the New Year's Eve dance at the Lido that the thing she missed most about Christmas was not getting the orange in the toe of her Christmas stocking. She shakes her head. She's being silly. Thomas wouldn't remember a thing like that.

She heads past the shelves of blankets and steel helmets to the shelves stacked with boxes of canned goods. She rummages through the canned evaporated milk, salmon, and baked beans, and is about to give up when she spots a net bag full of fat oranges on the floor, hidden behind a box of powdered eggs.

She sets the bag down on her desk with a loud thunk. 'Found them!'

'Good show, Burgess. Have a count.'

Ellie is halfway through her second count when the kettle whistles. She hurries over to the hot plate and pours the boiling water through the tea strainer into the fire officer's china cup. She adds a dollop of evaporated milk and two meagre teaspoons of sugar to the cup.

She shifts aside a stack of papers and sets the china cup of steaming tea and its saucer onto a clear spot on the fire officer's desk. 'There are definitely twenty-four oranges, sir.' Who'd ever told him there were eighteen was very much mistaken.

Fire Officer Williams looks up from the requisition order and frowns, his thick grey eyebrows drawing together like two fat slugs. 'I'm afraid that's impossible, Burgess. Commander Barrett told me very clearly there were eighteen.'

Ellie stifles a frustrated sigh. 'Yes, sir. I'll count them again.'

She begins counting them out on her desk again. One, two, three ... She is about to reach for the nineteenth when Fire Officer Williams's thick-fingered hand picks it up.

'There, eighteen. Correct?'

'But—' Ellie stares up at the fire officer's florid face. He reaches for three of the oranges and sets them on the desk in front of her, then he chooses three of the fattest oranges and scoops them into his large hands.

'Eighteen. Correct, Burgess?'

Ellie eyes the three oranges lined up in a neat row on her green desk blotter.

'Bake your father an orange cake. He'll enjoy that.'

'An orange cake, sir?'

'For his birthday. You said it's his birthday next week.'

'Yes. Yes, of course. Thank you very much, sir.'

The fire officer drops the oranges into his desk drawer. Closing the drawer, he peers over at Ellie. 'You said you drove, I believe?'

It hadn't entirely been a lie. Her father had let her practise on the farm lanes around Holkham Hall during their summer holiday. 'Yes, sir.'

He gestures to the bag of eighteen oranges. 'Take the staff car and share them around the chaps on the guns over at the castle. Can't let them go to waste.'

She'd see George for Valentine's after all! 'Yes, sir. Thank you very much, sir.' She grabs her coat and umbrella from the coat stand, and pulls her AFS satchel over her shoulder as she heads for the door.

'Burgess!'

'Yes, sir?'

'You'll be needing these.' Fire Officer Williams tosses Ellie a set of keys. 'I've not known an automobile to work without them.'

The fender of the staff car scrapes along the edge of the pavement stones as Ellie shifts gears and parks under the trees of Chapelfield Gardens. She scoops an orange out of the net bag and tucks it into her satchel. Across the street, the red-brick mass of Mcklintock's Chocolates sprawls across the block. Opening the car door, she gets out and heads towards the entrance.

Ellie hurries down the green linoleum corridors and spies George, neat as always in a dark green V-necked jumper over his white shirt, at his desk behind the glass partition of the staff offices that overlook the production floor. His short, brilliantined black hair is carefully combed, and his tortoiseshell glasses perch on the end of his nose where his nostrils have arrested their downward slide. She taps on the window and waves at him when he looks up.

George meets her in the corridor and gives her hand a squeeze. 'Ellie, what are you doing here?'

Ellie digs into her satchel and pulls out the orange. 'Happy Valentine's Day, George.'

'An orange?' He stares at the fruit. 'Where'd you get an orange?' He frowns as he pushes his glasses up his nose. 'You didn't steal it, did you?'

'Good grief, George. Don't be silly. The Newfoundlanders sent them to the fire station. I'm to deliver them to the fellows on the guns by the castle. Since you're one of the fellows, I thought I'd give you the pick of the bunch.'

George sniffs the orange. 'Oh, that's lovely. I've missed that smell.' He gives Ellie a peck on her cheek. 'Thanks for that, El.'

'Don't thank me. Thank the Newfoundlanders.'

George's forehead wrinkles as his eyebrows draw together. '*The* Newfoundlanders or *a* Newfoundlander?'

Ellie laughs. 'Do you mean Thomas Parsons? Honestly, George, you're being beyond silly today. I doubt he even remembers my name. I haven't seen him since the New Year's dance.'

'Right. Okay, then.' He pockets the orange and holds up a finger. 'Wait here. I've got something for you too.'

'You do?'

'Of course I do.'

Ellie watches him through the glass partition as he rifles through his desk drawers. He takes out something small, hiding it in his hand as he enters the corridor.

'Oh, George. You remembered Valentine's!'

'I work in a chocolate factory. How can I possibly forget?'

'If it's a box of chocolates, it's awfully small.'

'It's much better than that.' He opens up his hand.

Ellie stares at the lump of pink, heart-shaped rubber. 'What's that?'

'It's a pencil rubber. It's shaped like a heart. Isn't that clever? I saw it the other day at Jarrolds and thought of you. You can use it at the fire station. Every time you use it you'll think of me. If you don't press too hard, it should last a year.'

'A pencil rubber?'

George presses the pencil rubber into Ellie's hand. 'I've got to get back to work or I'll get a ticking off. Meet you at eight tomorrow at the Samson?'

Ellie folds her fingers over the lump of rubber. 'Sure. Fine. See you at the Samson.'

She walks down the green linoleum corridor towards the entrance doors. A metal bin is wedged beside a fire extinguisher in the corner of the entrance lobby. She tosses the pencil rubber into the bin and walks back to the car.

### One week later

'Poppy, I have a question for you.'

Henry Burgess looks up from the second slice he's cutting from the orange cake. 'What's that, Ellie Mae?'

'Is it really the thought that counts rather than the gift itself?'

'I would say that's right. Not everyone can afford expensive gifts. A thoughtful gift should be appreciated even if it's something simple.'

Ellie screws up her lips. 'I thought you'd say that.'

Dottie scrapes the icing off her plate with her fork and reaches over to pull the cake stand towards her. 'Ellie's cross with George.'

Ellie taps Dottie's hand with the back of her fork. 'You don't need any more cake. You've already had two slices.'

'Why's Ellie cross with George, then?'

Dottie slouches back in her chair and crosses her arms. 'He gave her a pencil rubber for Valentine's and she threw it away.'

Henry Burgess's eyebrows rise over the frames of his round glasses. 'George gave you a pencil rubber?'

'Yes. Honestly, Poppy, what kind of gift is that?'

'You should've given it to me if you didn't like it, Ellie.' Dottie runs a finger over her plate, catching the last drops of icing. 'I would've used it. I'd pretend George gave it to me.'

'No one asked you, Dottie.'

Dottie licks her finger. 'You're just being selfish.'

'Stop licking your finger – it's rude.'

Henry clears his throat. 'That's enough, girls. Go practise your piano, Dottie. I want to hear Beethoven's 'Moonlight Sonata' before you go to bed.'

Dottie groans. 'Again? I played that yesterday, Poppy.'

'Practise makes perfect, pet. Mrs Banister says that with a little effort you'll be ready to sit your Grade Five exams this summer. The Easter recital is coming up soon. Don't you want us to be proud?'

Dottie looks at Ellie. 'Is George coming to the recital?'

'I expect so.'

Dottie expels a sigh as heavy as a farm labourer's. 'All right, then.' Pushing away from the table, she slumps towards the dining room door.

'Dottie? You didn't happen to borrow my lipstick, did you? I can't find it anywhere. I've torn up my room looking for it. There was still a bit left in the bottom.'

Dottie shrugs. 'Why would I have seen it? You never even let me try it.'

'Oh, crumbs.'

'Ellie Mae. Your language.'

'Sorry, Poppy,' Ellie apologises as she watches her sister slope off into the sitting room. 'It's just that they're not selling lipsticks anywhere anymore. All the metal has to go to the war. How am I supposed to keep up my morale without lipstick?'

'You don't need it, pet.'

'Poppy, every young woman needs lipstick. I just read in the paper last week that the Ministry of Supply says that make-up is as important for women and tobacco is for men. The British government, Poppy!'

'Well, you have me there, pet.'

'I'll just have to pray that Jarrolds or Buntings gets a delivery of refills soon. Otherwise it's beet juice until the end of this wretched war.'

Henry scoops up the last bite of his birthday cake. 'That was a lovely treat, Ellie Mae. I must write a letter to the Newfoundland regiment to thank them for the oranges.'

'Oh, no, don't do that. I—I mean, I'll do it. It was my surprise for you. I'll send them a thank you note tomorrow.' Her father must never know she'd nicked the oranges for the cake. She'd have to do at least fifty Hail Marys at confession if he ever found out.

'Well done, then. Do tell them how much I enjoyed my

birthday cake.' Rolling up his napkin, he pokes it through his napkin ring. 'Don't be too hard on George, Ellie Mae. It was a very nice gesture. You should be grateful he remembered.'

'I suppose so. I just wish it'd been more romantic.'

'It's wartime, pet. It's not easy to buy gifts.'

'Poppy, he works at a chocolate factory.'

Pushing out his chair, he nods. 'That's a good point. You might drop him a hint next year or you're likely to receive a stapler. George is nothing if not practical.'

### Five days later:

Thomas stops abruptly and turns in the direction of the woman's voice.

'Yes, I'll take the navy fedora, one of the pheasant feathers, half a yard of the back grosgrain ribbon and half a yard of the black netting, please.'

The stout woman stallholder squints at the wide-brimmed fedora on display on a home-made mannequin's head. 'Are you sure about the hat, miss?' she says in a broad Norfolk twang. 'It's a man's hat.'

'Yes, I'm aware of that, Mrs Goodrum. I'm going to dress it up. I'll come and show it to you when I'm done.'

Thomas edges past the noonday shoppers to the market stall. He points at the navy fedora. 'Could I have a look at that hat, please?'

'Thomas?'

Mrs Goodrum shifts her gaze between Thomas and Ellie. 'I believe this young lady was 'bout to buy it.'

'The young lady hasn't bought it yet, has she?'

The woman shakes her head, setting her double chin waggling. 'It's twelve bob.'

Thomas lets out a whistle. 'Twelve bob! That's highway robbery.'

Mrs Goodrum purses her lips. 'You'd pay over three quid for this brand new. Just have a feel of this. Best felt. Christy's of London. The king has one just like it. He was in the papers wearing it just the other day.'

'Ol' George's gots a hat like this, does he?' Thomas says as he runs his fingers along the soft brim. 'Then I've gots to try it—' he grins at Ellie '—if it's all the same to you.'

Ellie grabs Thomas's arm. 'Excuse me! That's my hat. I was just about to pay for it.'

Thomas shoves his army beret into Ellie's hand and sets the navy felt fedora on his head. 'How's it look?'

'That was my hat. I've been saving for it for weeks.' Ellie turns to the stallholder. 'I'm sorry, Mrs Goodrum, I have to cancel my order. I have no use for ribbon, feather and netting if I can't have my hat.' She thrusts Thomas's beret at him. 'Here, I'm not your coat hook.'

Thomas watches Ellie storm through the heaving waves of shoppers. He pulls out a crisp blue-orange one-pound note and presses it into Mrs Goodrum's plump hand. 'Don't bother with the change, duck.'

Tucking the fedora under his arm, he elbows his way through the shoppers as he readjusts his beret. He follows Ellie thought the maze of market stalls to the corner of Exchange Street where he spies her disappearing though the white pillars of Jarrolds department store. Inside, he finds her in the cosmetics department, frowning as she reads a notice stuck to the front of the display case.

Taking a deep breath, he presents the fedora to Ellie with a flourish. 'I thinks you might be needin' this.'

She looks up at him, her blue-grey eyes startled. 'You again?'

'You'd freeze a swimmin' cod with that welcome.'

'Well, what do you expect after stealing my new hat? I wanted to have something nice for Easter Sunday.'

He waves the hat at Ellie. 'Please, maid. Take the hat. Consider it an early Easter present. Spend the money on somethin' nice for your mam. If she's anythin' like mine, she'll dance a jig with a few extra bob in her pocket.'

'My mother died in a car accident when I was ten.'

Thomas's face falls. 'I'm sorry. That's a hard thing.' He offers the hat to her again. 'Please, the least you can do is take the hat. I bought it for you. I saw you in the market and I had to do something. It's the first time I've seen you without your shadow.'

'George is my boyfriend. Of course he'd be at the dances with me.'

'Well, that's just made my day.'

Ellie frowns. 'What do you mean?'

'Last time I heard, he was your fiancé. Now that he's been demoted, maybe I've gots half a chance.'

'George *is* my fiancé. I just don't have a ring yet.'

'He's asked you, then? Got down on one knee and all that?'

'No, not exactly. Not yet.'

'He better get his skates on.'

'What do you mean by that?'

'It means "all's fair in love and war".' He holds out the fedora. 'Please, take the hat. One of the other fellas will only steal it if I takes it back to the barracks.'

Ellie runs her fingers over the indent in the crown. 'All right. But I must pay you back.'

'Don't be stunned. I won't have a penny off you. I'd only go spend it on beer.'

Ellie smiles, and to Thomas it's like the sun breaking through a storm cloud. 'Well, then, thank you very much.' She fixes her blue-grey eyes on him. 'I was just about to post a thank you letter to your captain.'

'What's that for then?'

Ellie digs into her AFS satchel and pulls out an envelope. 'For the oranges he sent over to the fire station with Commander Barrett. It was a real treat. Fire Officer Williams and I couldn't for the life of us figure out how'd they'd got all the way to England. We haven't seen an orange in a year.'

'You told me at the New Year's dance. You said you missed getting an orange in your Christmas stockin'.'

Ellie arches a fine eyebrow. 'You didn't have anything to do with the oranges, did you?'

Thomas sucks his breath in through his teeth. 'You never asks a Newfoundlander where they gets things.'

'Good grief, you didn't steal them, did you?'

'Now, where'd I find oranges to steal them?'

Ellie leans towards his ear. 'Don't tell anyone but I stole three to make an orange cake for my father's birthday last week.'

Thomas grins. 'Did you?'

'Well, Dottie and I shared one while we were making the cake. We couldn't resist.'

'Then I'm pleased as punch.'

'So it was you!'

'That would be sayin'.'

Smiling, Ellie looks down at the fedora in her hands. 'I haven't seen you around since the New Year's dance. I thought you might've been moved out.'

'You've been lookin' for me, then, maid?'

Ellie shakes her head, her blonde rolled hair bouncing on her shoulders. 'No, no. I mean ... well, you know.'

Thomas smiles. All this time he'd thought Ellie was off limits. It had been torture to watch her dancing with George. He'd drag poor Charlie off to one of the other dance halls if he spotted them. But no matter what pretty girl he danced with – and there had been plenty – the only girl who'd stayed in his mind was Ellie. All's fair in love and war. It wasn't his problem if George was slow off the mark.

'See you at the Samson on Saturday? I'll bring some stamps for your boyfriend.'

Ellie laughs, and to Thomas it's like the sound of ice dripping off the stage roof after a long winter. It was the sound of hope.

She glances at her watch. 'Oh, good grief. I must get back to the fire station. You've made me late.'

Thomas calls after her as she hurries towards the exit. 'Was it worth it, Ellie Mae Burgess?'

Turning around, she waves the fedora at him. He watches her until she disappears through the glass doors.

# *Chapter 17*

## Tippy's Tickle – 13 September 2001

Rod Fizzard's boat shed – or 'store' as Florie had corrected her – perches on a base of stilts on the edge of the tickle, its red paint faded to a pinkish rust by the assault of the salty North Atlantic wind. 'It's what we calls a stage, duck. The shed's the store, and the wharf and the shed together are the stage. You'll has to get used to that. People here'll think you're some stunned if you calls it a shed.'

The frames of four small square windows – two facing the tickle and two facing the shore – gleam with a coat of fresh white paint, and a wharf, its wood as grey as a winter sky, and stacked with lobster traps and crab pots, leads down from the rocky shore and wraps around the side of the store. A small motorboat is moored to the wharf, and a larger boat – a shiny white streamlined cruiser – is beached on the shore, propped up by three-legged metal stands.

Sophie snaps several photos, then she slides her camera into the back pocket of Ellie's borrowed jeans. She pushes the sleeves of Florie's striped cotton sweater up her arms and heads down the hill. As she descends the wooden steps from Kittiwake, the sound of an electric tool filters over to her from the cruiser. 'Hello?' she calls out as she approaches the boat. She raises her voice. 'Hello?'

Rounding the prow of the boat, she spots Emmett on his knees pressing a sander against the boat's hull. She taps him on his shoulder and he jerks to his feet. Switching off the sander, he pushes his safety glasses up onto his forehead.

'Hi, Emmett. I'm sorry, I didn't mean to interrupt. I was wondering if Sam was here.'

Emmett points at the store. 'He's in there.'

'Thanks very much.'

Nodding, Emmett slides the safety glasses over his eyes.

'That's a lovely boat,' she says, but Emmett is back on his knees, her words swallowed by the whir of the sander.

She heads down the wharf and finds Sam inside the store, frowning over a piece of wood he's turning on an old electric lathe. She knocks on the doorframe.

Sam looks up. He turns off the lathe and pushes his safety glasses to the top of his head. 'Well, if it isn't Princess Grace. I thought you were out picking berries.'

Sophie holds up her purple-stained fingers. 'We've just got back. Becca's helping Florie make a blueberry pie. You don't have any white spirit, do you?'

'You're definitely a CFA, aren't you? Just use some salt and lemon juice. That'll get the stains off your skin.'

'A what?'

'A Come From Away. CFA for short. Not from around here.'

'Well, that's for sure,' she says as she wanders into the room. 'That's quite a boat out there Emmett's working on.'

'We're fixing it up for an American client over in Salvage. He hit a rock in the harbour and she sprung a leak.'

'Emmett's full on with the sanding. It'll be smooth as a baby's bottom when it's done.'

'You know what they say. If a job's worth doing, it's worth doing right.'

Sophie strolls over to the lathe. 'Did you find out anything about my flight?'

Sam shakes his head. 'Nothing yet. The airspace reopened today, but Gander hasn't been told when the planes can leave yet. Best guess is a couple of days, but it could be as long as a week, with the backlog. Don't worry, I've got a fellow in air traffic control on speed dial.'

'Thanks.' She peers out a window to the view of the steeple of St Stephen's Church glinting in the morning sunshine. 'I can't believe I'll be in New York in a few days. I like the quiet out here. It makes for a change.'

'It'd bore the socks off someone like you.'

Sophie grunts. *Who's he to judge me? He doesn't even know me. But what do I care? I don't care. I really don't. I'll be done soon and we'll be out of each other's hair.*

'What would I do without Harvey Nichols or Neiman Marcus, right?' She runs her hand over the smooth curves and valleys of the wood on the lathe. 'This doesn't look like it's for a boat.'

'It's not.' Sam fills a mug with coffee from a coffee machine set up on a table under one of the windows. 'Coffee? Only black here. No fridge.'

'No arsenic in it?'

Sam grins. 'No. It's safe. Promise.'

He pours out a second mug and hands it to Sophie. She takes a sip, grimacing at its bitterness. She nods at the lathe. 'What are you making?'

Setting down his mug, Sam strides over to a bulky mound covered by a large Hudson's Bay point blanket. He pulls off the blanket. Underneath, two chairs, contemporary in design but with intricate turned-wood spindles supporting their fanned backs, sit on the battered, wooden-planked floor.

'Oh, wow. They're beautiful, Sam. Can I sit?'

'That's what they're for.'

She sits on one of the chairs, tracing the subtle curves of the arms with her fingertips. 'Aunt Ellie said you made furniture, but I had no idea. These are stunning.'

'Emmett works on them too, sometimes. He's the one who got me started.'

'Where do you sell them?'

'Tourists in from St John's mostly. I've sent a few pieces off to Toronto and Montreal. Florie puts the pieces in her shop when they're finished.' He shrugs. 'It's just furniture.'

'Are you kidding? You could sell pieces like these in New York. Boston. Anywhere. Interior designers and architects would go crazy for this kind of handmade quality.'

'Sure.'

'Yes, really, Sam. I'm an architect. I'd love to commission pieces like this for my projects.'

'You're an architect?'

'It's why I need to get to New York. I have an interview at Richard Niven Architects.'

Sam whistles. 'Richard Niven? That's a big name.'

'You've heard of him?'

Sam laughs. 'You know, we've even heard of this band from England called the Beatles out here.'

'Very funny.'

'I was a building contractor in Boston before I moved back here with Becca. I've heard of Richard Niven.'

Sophie looks over at Sam. 'Ellie told me you'd been living in

Boston. She told me about the accident. About Winny. I'm sorry, Sam. That must have been ... that must have been awful.'

Sam rubs his forehead. 'Yes.' He nods. 'Yes, it was. I moved here for Becca. It seemed the right thing to do. She loves it here with her grandmother and Florie.'

'How about you? It can't be that easy after living in Boston.'

'Away from the bright lights of the big city, you mean? It was tough at first, but this place ... it grows on you. There's nothing like living up here on the coast, by the sea. It's, I don't know, it's pure. Unspoiled. You get to understand what nature's all about up here.'

Sophie shrugs. 'I guess. It seems pretty isolated to me. I mean, it's a nice place to visit, but, you know, where am I going to get my grande skinny latte?'

Sam laughs. 'I don't think being away from a city is bad thing, Princess Grace. It gives a person space to think.'

'Aunt Ellie said she thought you might be getting restless.'

'Oh, she did, did she?' He grunts. 'Well, I'm not. It's why I bought the bike. If I need to get away, I just get on it and go out for a ride with the other Chrome Warriors, or head out along the coast on my own.' He looks at her for a long moment. Picking up the mug, he takes a sip of coffee. 'You should come out with me. Before you go.'

*What! Where did that come from? After the cold shoulder he's been giving her?*

Sophie's mobile phone buzzes. Setting down her mug, she pulls the phone out of the back pocket of Ellie's jeans. 'Sorry, Sam. It's New York. I'll just be a minute.'

'Sure.'

Turning her back on Sam, Sophie ambles over to the window, nodding as she listens to the caller.

'Yes, fine. Yes, absolutely, Jackie. I understand. He's leaving for Tokyo when? The nineteenth? Right. He can see me on the eighteenth. Okay. I'll find a way. Put me in. Two o'clock is perfect. Yes, I understand. I'll find a way. Thanks for calling.'

She slides the phone back into her pocket and looks at Sam. 'That was Richard Niven's office. I've got to get back for the interview on the eighteenth or I'm out of the running. I've got to get to New York, Sam. My future depends on it.'

# *Chapter 18*

## Holkham Beach, Norfolk – 21 June 1941

Setting down her sketchbook and charcoal pencil, Ellie leans back into the yielding warmth of the sand dune. She waves at Dottie who shouts at her as she splashes through the sea with George, Charlie and Thomas. If she tilts her head and squints, she can just manage to obscure the rolls of barbed wire massed along the sands of Holkham Beach.

She closes her eyes and raises her face to the sun. The unseasonal heat beats into her wet skin, evaporating the salty drops, and turns the blackness behind her eyelids a deep crimson with the heat. Somewhere in the tufts of marsh grass between the pine woods and the dunes, a cricket saws out a buzz into the still air.

A shower of droplets, cold like rain, jolts her from her drowsy torpor. Thomas flops onto the sand beside her and picks up the sketchbook.

She struggles to her elbows in the shifting sand and attempts to snatch the sketchbook as he flips through the pages.

'Give that back.'

'Hold on a minute. These are good.'

'They're nothing. Just some scribbles.' She grasps the sketchbook, but he jerks it out of her reach.

'Why can't I have a look?'

'I'm not an artist. I was at art school, but I quit after Ruthie ... after Ruthie ...'

Thomas closes the cover and hands back the sketchbook. 'I'm sorry. You're right. It's none of my business. I wish it was.'

Ellie squints at Thomas through the sun's glare and holds her hand up to shade her eyes. 'Why do you wish that?'

He leans on his elbow in the dune, sand clinging to his wet arm like a sleeve. His grey eyes sweep over her face. His skin is tanned and his ash-blond hair has turned the colour of wheat from the long days in the sun he's told her about, laying out barbed wire and wooden fortifications on the Norfolk beaches. Her fingers itch to touch that wheat hair. She folds her fingers into balls and buries them in the sand.

'Draw me.'

She looks at him. 'What?'

He picks up the charcoal pencil and holds it out to her. 'Draw me. I want something of yours. Something just for me.'

'Really?'

'If I could draw, I'd draw a hundred pictures of you. But I'm just a fisherman with a rifle and a shovel.'

Opening the sketchbook to a blank page, Ellie takes the pencil from Thomas. Sucking in a deep breath, she wills her hand not to shake. She looks over at him.

'The sun's in my eyes.'

'That's no good.' Thomas rises to his feet and holds out his hand. 'Let's go around to the shady side of the dune.'

Ellie looks at him. 'All right.' She slides her hand into his and he pulls her to her feet.

'I don't think the fellows have laid the mines there yet.'

Ellie pulls her hand away. 'Mines?' She gapes at the sand and lifts up a bare foot. 'There are mines on the beach?'

Laughing, Thomas slaps his sand-covered leg. 'I'm just teasing, maid. Not yet, anyway.' He waves towards the east. 'Further down. Near Cromer. There's lots of beaches closer to Germany than Holkham.' He grabs hold of Ellie's hand. 'C'mon.'

They plod through the soft sand and into the shade of the dune. Across the marsh grass, the towering pines line the shore like a dark green wall, and coils of barbed wire curl along the base of the green line.

Ellie lies against the cool dune and burrows her toes into the sand. 'It's a shame about the barbed wire. It's easier to pretend that life is back to normal when you're looking at the sea.'

Thomas flops into the sand beside her. 'I likes it better here. I prefers the view.'

She runs her tongue over her dry lips as she feels the colour rise in her cheeks. 'Right. So, sit back and just talk. You're good at that.'

'What do you want to know, Ellie Mae?'

Ellie raises her eyebrows. 'My father calls me that. How did you know my middle name is Mary?'

'You're a good Catholic girl, aren't you? I've never known a Catholic girl who didn't have Mary in her name somewhere.'

'I guess there's some truth in that.' Holding the pencil poised over the sketchpad, she peers at Thomas's lean face and draws a line. Another glance and another line. 'Tell me about Newfoundland. Do you have any brothers or sisters?'

'I had two brothers and a sister. They died from the Spanish flu the winter of 1918. One after the other. I got sick too, but God must'a taken one look at me and said, *Not on your life. You're not ready to come through the Pearly Gates yet.*'

'I'm sorry, Thomas.'

'I was only three. I only knows about them because of the

three little crosses with their names in St Stephen's Cemetery and what my mam told me once when I asked her about them.' He holds up three fingers and counts them off. 'Elizabeth Mary, Ephraim Paul and Alphonsus William.'

Ellie flicks her eyes over Thomas's face as he stares at the line of trees. A gust ruffles his hair.

'What about your parents? How did they feel about you joining the army?'

'They didn't like it one bit, and that's the truth.' Thomas clears his throat. 'Did you ever hear about the Battle of the Somme?'

'Of course. It was a horrible battle in the last war. Thousands were killed.'

'Seven hundred and eighty fellas from the Newfoundland Regiment went over the top at Beaumont Hamel on July 1st 1916. In the middle of No Man's Land there was a burnt-out tree they called the Danger Tree. Most of the fellas fell at the tree.'

Thomas clears his throat and presses his fingers over his eyes. 'Three of my uncles died there that day. The next day only sixty-eight men answered the roll call. Dad was one of them.' Thomas looks over at Ellie. 'Mam says he turned to drink after that.'

Ellie sets down her pencil and takes hold of Thomas's hand.

He gives her hand a gentle squeeze. 'The king renamed the regiment the Royal Newfoundland Regiment after Beaumont Hamel.' He shrugs. 'I guess that's supposed to be some kind of compensation.'

'I'm so sorry, Thomas.'

'When I signed up, Dad went out in his boat. Said he wouldn't come back till I was gone.'

Ellie looks at Thomas, at his strong, angular profile outlined against the blue sky. 'My father was in the Royal Horse Artillery.

He was gassed somewhere. Mustard gas. He won't talk about it. His lungs have never been the same.'

'Ruddy wars.'

Ruthie's cheerful face flashes into Ellie's mind. She puts down her pencil and leans her head against Thomas's shoulder, and they lie together in the shadow of the dune as the sounds of the crashing waves, the keening gulls and the crickets buzzing in the marsh grass wash over them, until the war is like a disturbing dream that dissipates with the warmth of the summer day. The kind of day when it seems wishes could possibly come true.

Thomas sits up, pointing to Ellie's sketchbook. 'Let's have a look, then, maid.'

She sits up and hands him the sketchbook, watching him as he runs his fingers along the lines of the portrait. She's managed to capture something of him, she thinks. The lines are right. The nose fine and long. The cheekbones sharp over his strong jaw. But, the eyes. Something isn't quite right. The eyes have eluded her.

'Best kind, Ellie Mae. You're a talent.' He rips out the page.

'What are you doing?'

'I'm keepin' this,' he says as he folds the drawing into a square. 'It'll remind me of you.'

'Be careful. The charcoal will smudge.'

'I don't care.'

When he kisses her she doesn't know whether he's heard her wish through the thundering waves and the buzz of the crickets. All she knows is that he is here and she is here, alone in the shadow of a sand dune on a summer day that's been offered to them like a gift. She reaches her arms around his neck. She'll take the gift. Come what may.

# Chapter 19

## Tippy's Tickle – 13 September 2001

Ellie throws the covers aside and slips out of the four-poster bed, leaving Florie snoring gently under the thick duvet. She slides her feet into her slippers and pads across the braided rag rug to the turreted bay window. A thin crescent moon hovers in the sky, casting a faint silver light into the room. Picking up the drawing from a small wooden table nestled in the curve of the turret, she lifts it up to catch the light.

So, this is Sophie. Her sister's daughter. And George's daughter, too, of course. She'd often wondered about her; even more since Winny's death. What she looked like. What she liked to do. What she'd done with her life. Dottie had never written, but there'd been a scribbled note on the odd Christmas card from George over the years. And, in 1968, one small photo tucked inside the card.

Fingering the gold locket around her neck, she opens it and looks down at the two tiny photos. Winny's sunny face under a halo of blonde hair on one side; Sophie on her fifth birthday, her fine brown hair cut into a blunt bob on the other. And now here she was. Just like she'd dropped out of the sky.

*Oh, Dottie. Whatever happened to us? I know you felt I treated George badly. Maybe I did. Maybe I wasn't as honest with him as I should have been. But Thomas … how can I make you under-*

stand that Thomas and I were … fated? I know you don't believe
in fate – you were always a better Catholic than me – but it's true.
We tried to keep away from each other, but it was impossible. I
had to leave. Don't you understand that? I loved Thomas. He was
my husband. But leaving you and Poppy was so hard. You must
know that. But I had to follow my life, and my life was with
Thomas. Why did you cut me off? We could have worked things
out. I know I upset you, but you upset me too, with some of the
things you did. Awful things. But I forgave you. What did I do that
was so unforgiveable? Why did you hate me so much?

There's another thing, Dottie. Why did you ever marry George?
Was it to get back at me? You ruined him, you know. He was a
good man and he deserved a wife who loved him. Why did you
make George so miserable? It was there in his letters, the ones
after Thomas's death. It was there if you knew how to read between
the lines. Then the letters dried up. You did that, too. George told
me. That time he came here. You made him stop. He'd been my
friend, Dottie, long before we were engaged. Did you make him
stop writing to punish me?

Ellie closes the locket. Well, Sophie, it's just you and me and
Emmy and Becca now. It's time for the wounds to heal. Thomas,
George, Dottie and my poor Winny are all dead, and I'm not young.
Seventy-nine in three days. I know what harm secrets and misun-
derstandings can do to people, Sophie. That's why I'll never tell
you mine.

# *Chapter 20*

## Norwich, England – 20 September 1941

'I wasn't sure you'd come.'

Ellie steps through the Gothic archway and into the shadowed interior of the medieval tower. 'George stopped by for tea on his way to the guns.'

Thomas reaches through the shadows and pulls Ellie to him. Pressing into him, she reaches her arms around his neck as he bends his head to her mouth. She closes her eyes and abandons herself to his kisses, meeting them with her own, their bodies embraced by the curved brick wall of the tower. His hand searches for the buttons of her uniform and slides beneath the thin wool, resting on the soft cotton blouse covering her left breast. Sucking in the air between his teeth, he pushes away from her abruptly.

'I'm sorry. I shouldn't have done that.'

Ellie presses her lips together and readjusts her jacket. 'No, Thomas. I wanted you to. I wanted you to so much.' She looks up at the open sky above them, willing her heart to stop its wild beating. The first stars push through the orange-streaked greyness of the approaching night.

'You've got to do somethin' about George, Ellie Mae.'

'Yes. I know.'

'Why haven't you told him about us?'

Ellie takes a deep breath and lets it blow through her lips like the cigarette puffs she's seen in the movies. 'I don't want to hurt him. He's a good man.'

'He's a good man and I'm not? You're worried about his feelings? You've got to be jokin' me. What about my feelings?'

She closes her eyes. Why is she such a coward? What's stopping her from telling George that she's fallen in love with Thomas? What's she afraid of? That George will hate her? No, he'd never hate her. He's too kind. They've known each other forever. Maybe that's it. They're too familiar. It's like having a faithful dog by her side. No surprises. Maybe she wants surprises.

She'd once had to walk along the narrow tread of a balance beam in a PE class. She'd wobbled, but it hadn't been so hard once she'd adjusted her balance. By the end of the class she was doing it with her eyes closed. That had been her life until Thomas had crashed into it with the spilt Coke. Like a balance beam she could walk on with her eyes closed. What will happen if she lets Thomas push her off balance? Where will she land?

Thomas reaches through the darkness and takes her hand. 'It's best we leave, maid. I don't trust myself.'

He leads her out onto the riverside path to a bench under the twisted branches of a silver birch. They sit down and he rests his arm across Ellie's shoulders. She leans her head against the rough wool of his uniform jacket and watches the multiplying stars glint in the river's mirror-like reflection.

'No moon tonight.'

'No.'

'Do you think they'll be over?'

'Might be.'

'They haven't been over for six weeks. We've been quiet at the fire station. Fire Officer Williams is teaching me Honeymoon Bridge.'

'They've probably gots their hands full in Russia.'

'Do you suppose the world will ever return to normal, Thomas?'

'Maybe a different kind of normal. I doubts it'll ever be the same.'

They sit together for several minutes in silence, with just the ripple of the Wensum River and the occasional clatter of a vehicle over a nearby bridge filtering through the stillness.

Ellie feels Thomas's chest rise under her cheek as he sighs. 'I never in all my life imagined myself over here in England, Ellie Mae. When you're bobbin' along the sea in a fishin' boat halfway to Greenland, you feels like the rest of the world is on another planet.'

'Tell me more about Newfoundland.'

'Oh, it's a magical place, Ellie Mae. They calls the eastern part Avalon, did you know that?'

'Avalon? The place they took King Arthur?'

'The very same.'

'That's very romantic.'

'Newfoundlanders are hard cases with soft hearts. We've gots places called Heart's Content and Conception Bay and Happy Adventure. And then there's the fairies.'

Ellie giggles. 'The fairies?'

'Are you laughin' at me, maid?' Thomas bumps her shoulder with his. 'Well, I don't believes in them myself, but plenty does. They says the fairies are the angels that fell from Heaven but were shut out of Hell. When they fell on The Rock – that's what we calls Newfoundland – they liked the look of it. So, you've gots to watch out for the fairies when you're out pickin' berries or walkin' in the woods. You've gots to wear a piece of clothin' inside out. That confuses them. And never anythin' green. That's just askin' for trouble.'

'You're not serious.'

'Oh, yes, I am. You'll see some of the older folks about with their hat or their jacket inside out. That's the reason. And they never goes out without a bun or a piece of bread in their pocket. That's to appease the fairies if they comes upon them.'

'A superstitious lot.'

'Well, we gots our reasons. I don't imagine there's another place on earth like it. There's a fog rolls in off the sea sometimes that sits on the land like a cloud. We calls it a mauzy day when that happens. Everythin' goes quiet. Not quiet like this. Quiet like you're in the middle of a bag of cotton wool. It's soft and it's quiet and the damp sits on your skin. Then you might hear somethin' out on the sea beyond the fog. Like a fountain bursting out of the water. And you wonders what kind of creature could'a made that sound.'

'What is it?'

'Well, some says mermaids.'

Ellie rolls her eyes. 'Mermaids?'

'That's what some says. But they're really whales.'

'They're that close to shore?'

'Oh, yes. They loves to dance off the shore. I once saw about fifty of them when I was out in the boat with my dad. I tells you, you feels small when fifty humpbacks are spoutin' and breachin' all around you. It's a sight to behold.'

'That sounds terribly frightening.'

'Oh, no, Ellie Mae. They're just dancin'.'

Ellie rubs her chin against the wool serge of Thomas's uniform. 'What are we going to do, Thomas?'

Thomas leans his chin on Ellie's AFS cap. 'That depends on you, maid.'

Ellie shifts away and he drops his arm. She looks at him in the dim night light. 'What do you mean by that?

'I never thought I'd meet you, Ellie Mae. I don't mean someone like you. I mean *you*. I dreams about you at night. I wants to wake up with you beside me.'

Ellie's heart jumps, battering against her ribs. 'We can't, Thomas. It would be a sin.'

'I wants to marry you, Ellie Mae.'

'You w-what?'

'Wait, I'm an idiot. Hold on a minute.'

Thomas kneels on the grass in front of Ellie. 'Will you be the face I wakes up to in the mornin', and the face I falls asleep to at night? Will you marry me, Ellie Mae Burgess? I might not have a ring, so don't hold that against me. I'll get you the finest ring in England, maid, and that's a promise.' He draws an X across his chest and kisses the side of his thumb. 'Cross my heart and hopes to die.'

Her heart drums so quickly she can barely breathe. She looks at Thomas, his face outlined by the soft light of the starry sky. Every cell in her body screams at her: *Say yes, Ellie! Say yes!* But, what about her father? Her sister? She'd found a map of North America in the library and looked up Newfoundland. It wasn't even a part of Canada. An island the size of Ireland on the other side of the Atlantic. Miles away. Another world. How could she leave her family behind? Never see Poppy again? Never get cross at Dottie again for stealing her lipsticks? She wouldn't know a soul there but Thomas. What had she been thinking?

She drops her head into her heads. 'I can't marry you, Thomas. I'm so sorry. I just can't.'

# Chapter 21

Tippy's Tickle – 14 September 2001

The gate of St Stephen's Cemetery, once black but now seemingly held together by rust, screeches as Sophie tugs it open. It jerks to a stop, refusing to budge any further.

Handing the patchwork bag she's filled with drawing materials to Sophie, Ellie squeezes through the opening. Sophie follows, wrenching the protesting gate closed behind her. Tufts of yellowing grass splay against the weather-beaten headstones and crosses on the gentle slope below. Beyond the hill, on its spit of land the other side of the tickle, the aluminium steeple of St Stephen's Church points its glinting finger up into the blue sky. They stand for a moment on the hill, looking out to the sea below, which shines like new-polished silver in the morning sun, its stillness broken only by the occasional whale spout blasting through the surface and the tickle-ace gulls ducking and diving along the shore.

'It's lovely here, Aunt Ellie,' Sophie says as she snaps several photos.

'I've always thought so. I've been coming here for years, since before Thomas died. It was a good place to hide from my mother-in-law, Agnes. She wouldn't come near the place. Said it was full of fairies who'd reach up from the graves and pull you down to Hell for disturbing the dead.'

Sophie laughs. 'They don't sound like any kind of fairies I've ever heard of.'

'Oh, yes. They all believed in fairies back then. Emmett still does. Agnes infected him with that when he was a boy, I'm afraid. They weren't the nice fairies of England or Walt Disney, like Tinker Bell. These ones played tricks, and led little children into the woods with their fairy music, or hit you with a fairy blast when you were out in the woods or fields on your own.'

'A fairy blast?'

'Yes. Agnes swore she'd seen a boy with a fairy blast once. All sorts of nasty stuff came out of the wound – fish bones and sticks and insects.'

Sophie shudders. 'That's awful.'

'I loved those fairies. I always had the cemetery all to myself.' She points to an old wooden bench peeking out from behind a stunted cedar near the gate. 'Come on. It's where I always sit.'

They sit together on the bench and Ellie reaches into the bag, dispensing charcoal pencils, pastels the colours of ice cream and a drawing pad to each of them. 'Let's have a go at drawing the church.'

Sophie picks up a charcoal pencil and squints at the gleaming steeple. 'I don't know if I can remember how to do this. I only draw construction drawings now.'

'Just trust your eyes and your hand. Don't overthink it.'

'All right. Here goes nothing.'

After a few tentative lines, and the conviction that any latent artistic talent has deserted her, Sophie turns over a fresh page. The sun kisses her face with a soft warmth, and a light breeze dances up the hill from the ocean, rustling the tufts of grass like a mother tousling her child's hair. Taking a deep breath, she begins to draw, letting the pencil find its way across the rough white paper. She feels her way, increasing the pressure on the pencil for the thick line of the church's walls, and lifting the pencil to a fine point for the window frames and the door. She shakes out the tension in her hand and leans over the drawing, shading in the shadows with a fine cross-hatching, frowning as she attempts to transfer the white puffs of clouds to the drawing.

As she draws, she finds her mind settling into a calmness she hasn't felt since she was a teenager drawing their cat, Sopwith Pusskins, a puff of fur curled up in front of the fire, for her final art-class assignment. The memory settles into her mind as she draws the lines of the rocky spit of land where it meets the tickle. It had been a chilly December Sunday afternoon. Her face warm from the gas fire, and the radio was on, probably *Sing Something Simple*, which her father liked. Rattling sounds from the kitchen – her mother baking something for some Women's Institute do. It had been ... perfect. A moment of truce in her parents' fractious relationship.

She flips over the page and starts another version of the church. Stronger lines this time as she draws the clapboard building. Softer on the waves slapping up against the rocks, looser on the tufts of long grass sprouting around the old headstones. Changing pressure on the charcoal pencil for the different effects. Remembering something she'd lost, something she hadn't even realised she'd forgotten: the Sophie she once was, before she'd packed her away like an old coat. The Sophie who loved something.

'What do you think?' Sophie holds up her drawing to Ellie.

'That's lovely, Sophie. You have a wonderful sense of perspective. Why ever did you give up drawing?'

Sophie sighs as she closes the drawing pad, and rests it on her lap. 'My mother wanted me to focus on a career. I think she resented having to give up her musical career when she married my father. Poor Dad ... They used to argue. Or, she would argue, and he would just take it.' Sophie looks at her aunt. 'You know she was pregnant when they got married?'

Ellie nods. 'Yes, I knew. You father wrote to me.'

'She miscarried and then she was trapped. That's the word she'd use with my father. Trapped. She wouldn't divorce, being a Catholic. So, she decided to make Dad her project. Push him up the Norwich social ladder, but that only went so far. Then, out of the blue, after ten years of marriage, she gets pregnant. Shaking her head, Sophie smiles. 'It must have happened during one of their truces. That was me, and I became her project.'

'And, what about you? You never married?'

'No. Why would I want to do that, after seeing how miserable Mum and Dad were? I wanted to be able to stand on my own two feet. Art, well, it wasn't really a solid career choice. Dad thought I could give it a go, but Mum was dead against it. She wanted me to be financially secure. She said a "proper"—' she tweaks her fingers to indicate quotation marks '—career would give me freedom. She was right.'

Ellie nods. 'Marriage isn't for everyone, I suppose. With Thomas there was never any question, once I'd got my head around leaving Britain. He proposed to me in a medieval tower in Norwich, did you know that? He gave me a lovely Art Deco ring. I don't know whatever happened to it. I lost it years ago with my wedding band.'

'That's a shame.'

'Yes. I would have loved to have given them to Becca.' Ellie flips over the page in her drawing pad and begins on a view out to sea. 'You could have made an art career, Sophie. Many people do.'

Sophie shrugs. 'Maybe. The idea just faded away. I didn't want to be a doctor or a solicitor, but since I could draw, Mum and I agreed on architecture. The only problem was that I was terrible at calculus, and I needed it to study architecture. Poor Dad. I think I drained his bank account with all the summer calculus courses and tutors Mum made him pay for. I finally scraped through and got accepted to the University of Manchester to study architecture.'

'Did that work for you? Did you enjoy it?'

'It was fine. I worked hard and I did like parts of it quite a lot. The more creative elements. I graduated with first-class honours, found a good entry-level job in London and made my way up to senior architect at the firm. I went out on my own when I turned thirty. Six years ago I won the tender to design the Millennium Pavilion. It received a lot of publicity, and I had a call from a headhunting firm about a position at a leading architecture practice in New York. That's where I was headed for an interview when my plane was diverted to Gander.' She opens up her arms. 'And, now, here I am.'

'My heavens, Sophie! You've been busy. And you're happy?'

'I can't complain.'

Ellie raises an eyebrow. 'You can't complain?'

'No, I mean. Yes. I'm happy.'

Ellie nods. 'Good. It's important to be happy. Or, content, at least. I'm not sure I ever found out what happiness is.'

'But weren't you happy when you came to Newfoundland? Mum seemed to think you'd run off to dance through daisy fields here with your husband and your baby.'

Ellie laughs, the sound warm and husky. 'Dancing through daisy fields? I certainly can't imagine Emmy doing that!'

'I heard her say that to Dad once when she was having a turn.'

Ellie sighs as she tucks a strand of hair the wind has caught behind her ear. 'If Dottie only knew. It was very hard. There were times when I wanted to run away and take the first boat back home with Emmy. Thomas's mother and I didn't get on. She made my life a misery. But, I had no money to return to England even if I'd wanted to. And I loved Thomas. He was a good man.'

Ellie turns over another page and shifts on the bench to face a view of the village houses clustered along the coast. 'I fell pregnant with Winny, and I knew then that I'd never leave. After Thomas died ...' She looks out to the sea and sighs. 'After Thomas died, life just went on. One day after another, one year after another. And, me, always wishing I could go home. Then, when I was forty-four, Florie careered into my life, and I realised that this place, this rock of an island, *is* my home. And I've been content.'

She smiles at Sophie, her blue-grey eyes the colour of the ocean beyond her. 'Now that you're here, Sophie, my family's complete. I might even say I'm happy.'

'There, Becca, duckie,' Florie says as she sets a loaf of bread and a grater on the wooden table, 'climb on a chair and start grating some breadcrumbs for the meatballs.'

'What are you making?' Sophie asks as she pockets her mobile phone. 'Can I help?'

'Sure, thing, duck. Spaghetti and meatballs tonight. Meat's in the fridge. Everythin' else's in the pantry.'

'Righto' Sophie heads through the door into the small pantry. *Spaghetti and meatballs. How hard can it be? Boil up some spaghetti, heat up some sauce and fry up some meatballs.*

She returns to the kitchen with a package of spaghetti. 'I've found the spaghetti but there doesn't seem to be any sauce.'

Florie laughs as she spoons blueberry pudding batter into a ceramic pudding bowl. 'There won't be, maid. We makes it from scratch here.'

Sophie's face falls. 'From scratch?'

Florie peers over at Sophie and grins. 'Don't get in a hobble about it, duck.'

The screen door swings open and Sam strolls into the kitchen, Rupert at his heels. He heads over to Becca and kisses her on her head. 'What's Princess Grace in a hobble about?'

'I'm supposed to make spaghetti and meatballs and I haven't got a clue how.'

Sam's eyebrows shoot up. 'You don't know how to make spaghetti and meatballs?'

'No, I don't. I don't cook. I usually pick up something at Marks and Spencer or grab a pizza at Pizza Express.'

*'Did you hear that, Becca-bug?'* Sam signs. *'I think we need to teach Sophie how to make spaghetti and meatballs, don't you think?'*

*'Yes! Yes!'*

Florie secures a piece of wax paper over the pudding bowl with a large elastic band and sets the bowl in a pot of boiling water. 'Right. Hopes you like blueberry duff, Sophie. Was my Auntie Gladys's recipe from down on the Burin Peninsula.' She wipes her hands on a tea towel and heads to the door. 'Ellie's havin' her nap, Sam. I'm off to feed the dogs. I'll leave you to it. I'll call by Emmy on the way back, tell him supper's ready.'

Sam hangs his jean jacket over the back of a chair and rubs his hands. 'Right, Princess Grace. Come with me.'

She follows him into the pantry. 'I didn't even know people still made their own spaghetti sauce. Why would you want to do that when you can just buy it in a jar and heat it up?'

'Once you taste Becca's and mine, you'll never buy store-bought again.'

'I never actually buy store-bought sauce. There's a brilliant little Italian place on the King's Road where I can call in an order from work and pick it up on the way home.'

Sam tosses a large onion and a head of garlic at Sophie. 'I'm warning you, Princess Grace. Once you eat ours, you'll never want to eat anyone else's spaghetti and meatballs.' He grabs a punnet of tomatoes off the shelf and several jars of dried herbs. 'Grab that olive oil, will you?'

Sophie takes a bottle of extra-virgin olive oil off the shelf and follows Sam back into the kitchen. 'What now?'

Sam hands her a wooden cutting board. 'Chop up the onion and three cloves of garlic nice and fine. I'll get the ground meat and an egg and we'll mix it all together with Becca's breadcrumbs.' He pats Becca's head. *'That's enough breadcrumbs, honey,'* he signs. *'We'll soon have enough to stuff the Thanksgiving turkey. Find Florie's big bowl and dump them in there.'*

Sophie looks up from the lumpy bits of chopped onion and wipes at the tears welling up in her eyes. She watches Sam boil an electric kettle and pour the boiling water into a large pot on the stove with a handful of salt, then move around the kitchen and Rupert's panting body, gathering, mixing and chopping ingredients for the spaghetti sauce with his daughter. She's never had a boyfriend who'd cooked. She's never had a boyfriend who'd had a child, either. She likes it.

*Hold on, Sophie. Why are you thinking about boyfriends? You don't even like this guy. He's bloody irritating.*

Sam sets a plate down on the table. 'Right, Princess Grace. Meatball time. Let's show her how it's done, Becca.'

Becca pushes the large bowl into the centre of the table and dumps the breadcrumbs over the ground meat. She holds up an egg to Sophie and cracks it perfectly in two on the rim of the bowl.

'Add the garlic and the onion,' Sam instructs Sophie, gesturing to the bowl. He sprinkles in dried sage, basil, thyme and marjoram. 'Salt and pepper, Becca.' She grinds in the pepper and salt from two shakers shaped like sailors.

*'What next, Becca-bug?'*

Becca holds up a spoon and, scooping out a spoonful of meatball mix, she rolls it into a perfect ball and drops it onto the plate.

Sophie smiles. 'Well, Bob's your uncle, Becca!'

Becca looks up at her father and signs, *'What?'*

'She wants to know what Bob's your uncle means,' Sam says.

'Oh, right. Uh. It means, "There you go".'

Sam nods. 'Bob's your uncle. You learn something every day. Wait till I tell Florie that one.' He hands Sophie a spoon. 'I need two dozen perfect meatballs. Bob's your uncle.'

Sophie watches Sam skirt around Rupert and head back to the stove.

Yes, she likes it. She likes it a lot.

# Chapter 22

## Norwich, England – 7 December 1941

'Come in here, George. Ellie's still getting ready.'

George shucks off his shoe rubbers and hangs his coat and scarf on the hallway coat stand. A melody of something vaguely familiar tinkles from the piano in the drawing room. Entering the room, he heads over to Dottie, who is frowning over the piano keyboard as her fingers fly over the keys. She shifts over on the bench without looking up and he sits down beside her, turning the pages of the sheet music when she nods at it with her chin.

Dottie taps out the final notes, as pure as crystal, and sits back on the bench.

'That was lovely, Dottie,' George says. 'What was that?'

Dottie rolls her eyes. 'Debussy, of course. 'Clair de Lune'. I'm practising it for my Grade 6 piano exam. I'm going to be a concert pianist.'

'I thought you were going to be an actress? You told me you wanted to be the next Gene Tierney just this summer.'

Dottie shakes her head impatiently, her brown curls bouncing on her shoulders. 'That was ages ago. I mean, I still like acting. I'm auditioning for the role of Cecily in *The Importance of Being Earnest* for the Easter play at school. Did Ellie tell you? I'm up against Beatrice McCormack.' She makes a face. 'I'm sure I'll get it. I'm much more talented than she is.'

A cough and a clearing of a throat. 'That's not a very charitable attitude, Dottie.' Picking up the *Eastern Evening News*, Henry Burgess settles into his favourite overstuffed armchair with a sigh and rests his feet on the matching ottoman.

'I'm sorry, Poppy.' Dottie shrugs, the lace collar of her blouse rising and falling. 'But it's true.' She looks sideways at George and smiles. 'You think I'm a good actress, George, don't you?'

'You are indeed, Dottie. Your Viola was the best I've ever seen.'

A slender tortoiseshell cat pads into the room and leaps onto Henry's corduroy-clad legs, settling in the groove between his knees. 'I hadn't taken you for an expert on *Twelfth Night*, George.'

'No, sir. I'm not. I've only seen it the once at the school.'

'Flattery corrupts both the receiver and the giver, George.'

'Yes, sir. I'm sorry, sir.'

'That wasn't me, by the way. That was Edmund Burke.'

'Edmund Burke, sir?'

Henry coughs. 'Never mind, George.'

George turns back to Dottie. 'I'm sorry, Dottie. I shouldn't have flattered you. Though your Viola was really very good.'

'I know I was very good.' Dottie spins around and wiggles her fingers in the air over the piano keys. 'What would you like me to play? Ellie told me you like 'Tangerine'. I've been practising. I found the sheet music at Bonds.'

The newspaper rustles. 'Thank you for the shilling, Poppy,' Henry says behind the paper.

Dottie looks at George and rolls her eyes again. 'Thank you for the shilling, Poppy.'

Henry surveys his daughter over the top of his glasses. 'Don't play it just now, Dottie. I'm late for the news. Turn on the wireless, will you?'

Dottie expels a dramatic sigh as she slumps off the bench. She fiddles with the wireless knob until Alvar Liddell's authoritative voice transmits into the room.

'… *with air attacks on United States naval bases in the Pacific. Fresh reports are coming in every minute.*'

Ellie flies into the room, shrugging into her tweed winter coat. 'I'm so sorry I'm late, George. There wasn't much hot water—'

'*Sssh.*' Henry holds up his hand.

'What is it?'

He points to the wireless.

'… *Japan has announced a formal declaration of war against both the United States and Britain.*'

Ellie stares at the wireless as the newsreader reports on the bombing in the Hawaiian Islands. When the announcement is over, Ellie looks at her father. 'What's going to happen now, Poppy?'

'The Americans are going to join in.' Henry grunts as he rustles his newspaper. 'About time.'

'But that's a good thing, isn't it, sir?'

'It's a very good thing, George.' Henry clears his throat and suppresses a cough. 'I only wish they'd offered the hand of help two years ago. Then this bloody war might be over by now.'

'Poppy!' Dottie and Ellie look at each other wide-eyed at their father's uncharacteristic expletive.

'Sorry, girls.' Henry buries himself behind the paper. 'If they'd joined in earlier, this blasted war might be over by now.'

Ellie wipes at the foggy window of the bus with her gloved hand. Outside, rain spatters the window with a persistent drizzle as the bus rumbles past the Victorian mass of Mcklintock's Chocolates and the air raid shelter that has been dug into the lawn of Chapelfield Gardens. As the bus sweeps around the roundabout, the black bulk of St John's Cathedral rises into the lowering grey night sky, not a chink of light seeping from the stained-glass windows.

'Do you think Americans will be stationed in Norfolk, George?'

'No doubt, Ellie. We have a lot of air bases here.'

'When do you think they'll be over?'

'I expect they'll start coming over in a couple of months.'

The bus turns right, through the ruins of the medieval city wall, onto St Benedict's Street. 'We'll probably get bombed more once they're here,' Ellie says.

'Possibly.'

'It's been awfully quiet since the summer. It's eerie. It's like waiting for a storm to hit.'

George rests his hand over hers. 'Don't worry, Ellie. The sirens are working properly now, and there are plenty of shelters around the city.' He shifts in his seat, frowning at her behind his tortoise-shell glasses. 'You really must speak to your father about building an Anderson shelter behind the headmaster's house. I don't like that you have to run across the quad to get to the shelter with all the boys.'

'I have, George.' She slides her gloved hand out from underneath George's. The window has fogged up again, and Ellie idly draws a heart in the film. 'He feels it's his duty to be with the boys when there's a raid. Most of the time Dottie and I go down to the cellar. I've set us up some cots down there.' She draws an arrow through the heart and an 'E +', hovering over the empty space where she should write 'G'. She wipes her hand through the heart.

'I haven't seen Thomas or Charlie at Samson's or the Lido for a while.'

'I bumped into Charlie at the Coach and Horses at lunchtime the other day,' George says. 'He was having a pint with a few of his mates. They were in town picking up some supplies.'

'Was Thomas with them?' Ellie asks, trying to sound casual.

'No, now that you mention it.' George grins and nudges Ellie's shoulder. 'You're not soft on him are you?'

Ellie looks sharply at George. 'No, of course not. Don't be silly.'

'Don't be cross, Ellie. I'm only teasing. I know you're my girl.'

Ellie sweeps her eyes over George's benign face, the warm brown eyes like those of a faithful dog, the round cheeks and neatly combed black hair slick with brilliantine. Not handsome exactly, but presentable. He'd make any girl a perfectly fine husband.

'When are we going to get married, George?'

George's eyebrows shoot up above his glasses. 'What?'

Ellie drums her wool-clad fingers on the window. 'When are we going to get married? I don't see why we need to wait.'

'After the war is over. That's what we've always said. When things are back to normal.' George squints at Ellie through his glasses. 'Why do you want to get married all of a sudden?'

Ellie fiddles with a loose thread of wool on her glove. 'This war could go on for years. And who's to say we're going to win?'

George sits back against the seat. 'Of course we're going to win.'

A silence descends between them, broken only by the thrum of the bus's engine and the murmuring of the other passengers.

Ellie reaches across George and pulls the cord. The bell dings.

George rises and stomps down the aisle to the exit. Ellie hurries after him as he steps off the bus.

'Aren't you going to wait for me?'

Pausing on the pavement, he offers his arm to Ellie. She loops her hand around his elbow, quickening her pace to keep up with him as he strides towards the Electric Cinema. They join the queue for tickets for *That Hamilton Woman*.

'I'm sorry, George. I shouldn't have said that. It was silly. Of course we're going to win.'

# *Chapter 23*

## Tippy's Tickle – 15 September 2001

Sophie sets down the jug of maple syrup and slices into the stack of blueberry pancakes. She takes a bite and nods appreciatively at Florie, who is busy stacking several pancakes onto Becca's plate.

'These are amazing, Florie. I've never tasted anything like them. And those blueberries—' she licks a drop of maple syrup off her lip '—I never knew blueberries tasted like purple heaven until I came here. If I stay much longer, I'll be as fat as a house.'

'Newfoundland blueberries is the best in the world, duck. We gots chefs all the way from Toronto sendin' folks up here for blueberries for their fancy restaurants. They gots to buy them from middlemen in St John's. No one'll tell them where to find them. Everyone here's got their secret places.'

'Quite right,' Ellie says as she fills in another word in the *Telegram*'s crossword puzzle. 'Sometimes secrets are necessary.'

Outside, a dog barks as the whine of a motorcycle's engine grows louder. It shuts off abruptly.

'That'll be Sam,' Florie says.

On cue, Sam pushes through the screen door in his motorcycle leathers, Rupert bumping past his legs.

'Get that dog out of here, Sam,' Florie protests. 'He'll have the pancakes down him as sure as today's Saturday.' The huge black dog pushes past Florie and settles beside Becca, resting its immense head on Becca's lap.

'He's just had Emmett's salmon sandwich down at the store,' Sam says as he tosses his leather jacket onto a chair. He accepts a mug of coffee from Ellie. 'He's full.'

'That dog can eat for Britain,' Ellie says. 'I swear he gets bigger every day. Where are you off to?'

'Wesleyville to pick up some supplies. Going to meet up with Ace and Thor and have a ride up along the coast up to Musgrave Harbour. We'll grab some lunch at the Rocky Ridge. Got to take advantage of this weather.' He looks over at Sophie. 'So, Princess Grace, do you want to come?'

Sophie swallows down the pancake she's been chewing. 'What? Me?'

'You're not going anywhere else today, are you?'

'I haven't got a jacket.'

'Well, I thought of that. I brought you Winny's old jacket. Should fit.'

'Oh, I don't know. I'm not much of a biker chick.'

'Oh, go on with you, duckie,' Florie says as she scrapes Becca's leftover pancake into a bowl and sets it on the floor by the fridge. 'We'll be over in the shop all day today. Ellie's doing art with the Brownies.'

'We're making a banner protesting the closure of the Heart's Wish fish processing plant,' Ellie says. 'Florie and I've organised a protest down there next week when Grimes is in town for the public inquiry.'

'Not that the government'll do a thing,' Florie grumbles.

'That may be so, Florie, but we have to try.'

Sophie watches the great dog lumber over to the bowl and wolf down the pancake. She looks over at Sam. *Why does he have to look so bloody … male? It's like he's stepped out of* Mad Max 2: The Road Warrior. *But then, Mel Gibson was pretty hot in that. Must be the leathers.*

'I guess it won't hurt to see something of this place. Who are Ace and Thor?'

Sophie leans into the curve of the road as *Miss Julie* shoots along the road to Wesleyville. Sam's warmth filters though their leather jackets and she's conscious of her thighs pressing against his as she clings to his waist. She closes her eyes to the wind, and a lightness fills her as she feels the layers of the old Sophie peel away and fly into the September sky.

*Who is this person? This isn't me. Riding on the back of a strange man's motorbike in the back of beyond in borrowed clothes? Mum would be appalled. But Mum's not here. It's me. Sophie. It feels good. Better than good. It feels amazing.*

Sam veers the bike into the parking lot of the long, squat Home Hardware store in Wesleyville and pulls up beside two large motorcycles parked near the goods-in door. Two bearded men in sunglasses and Chrome Warriors leather jackets straddle the bikes, dismounting as Sam parks.

One of the men, with shoulders as wide as a door and a body hefty enough to support them, embraces Sam in a bear hug. 'Sam, b'y. Thought ol' Mavis had swallowed you up down in Gander the other day. Where you been?' He turns his sun-glassed eyes towards Sophie and extends a hand the size of a small plate. 'We hasn't had the pleasure,' he says, pumping her hand vigorously. 'I'm Ace Dunphy. This here's my brother, Thor.'

Thor, only slightly smaller than his brother, and sporting a neat ginger goatee, shakes her hand. 'Nice to meet ya. Where 'bouts ya from, b'y?'

'Uh, London,' Sophie says, wiggling her fingers. 'I was on my way to New York. My plane got diverted.'

Thor turns to his brother. 'That's odd, isn't it, b'y? Why'd they send a plane from Ontario all the way up here when they'd just have to turn right back round again to gets to New York?'

Ace shakes his head. 'Doesn't make any sense, b'y.'

Sophie raises her eyebrows. 'Ontario? No, I came from England. London, England.'

'Oh, well, then,' Thor says. 'We thought ya were comin' from London, Ontario.'

'That's not so far,' Ace says.

'No, not far at all,' his brother agrees, nodding. 'Not when ya compares it to London, England. Didn't Uncle Lance's wife's sister Eunice marry someone from London?'

'London, England?'

'No, b'y. London, Ontario.'

'No, b'y. That was Regina. Married a fellow in Waterloo.'

Sam slaps Thor on his shoulder. 'You've got us all confused there now, b'ys. I've got to go pick up some stuff in the hardware.' He glances at Sophie. 'Do you want to come in, or stay here with the boys?'

'Oh, I'll come in. Definitely. Hardware is absolutely my thing.'

'That's fine, b'y,' Ace says. 'We'll stay where we're at till ya comes where we're to.'

Sophie steers the trolley along a wide aisle lined with vats of nails and screws, and sheets of MDF.

'What exactly are the Chrome Warriors, anyway? Are you outlaws or something?'

Sam laughs as he examines a package of 4mm flathead screws. 'No, we're just guys who like to ride bikes. We're a Riding Club.'

He taps his shoulder. 'You see the "RC" patch on the back of my jacket? That's what it means. Riding Club. We're not a motor-cycle gang. We get together whenever we can and go for rides.' He hands two boxes of screws to Sophie. 'I used to bike down in Boston. It clears my head. We do a lot of charity events too. Ace's wife died from breast cancer last year, so we're doing a ride for that at the end of the month.'

'Oh. I'm sorry to hear that. How do you know them?'

Sam picks a nail out of a plastic bin and measures it against his thumb. 'Ace is my dentist.'

'Ace is a dentist? Seriously?'

'Yep. His name's actually Adrian.' Sam counts out a dozen nails and drops them into Sophie's free hand. 'Thor's Rupert's vet. His name is Thornton. Any wonder he calls himself Thor?'

'He's a veterinarian?'

Sam grins at her. 'What? They don't look like a dentist and a vet?'

'Not like any I've ever met.'

'One thing I've learned here is that it's best not to judge a book by its cover.' He points down the aisle and to the left. 'I need to find the sandpaper.'

'And you're all ... bikers?'

'Something wrong with that?'

'Uh, no. Not really, I guess.'

Sam laughs. 'People get the wrong idea about bikers. We're not all Hells Angels. There's nine of us in all, from Gander all the way to Musgrave Harbour. A couple of ex-military guys, a doctor, a couple of fishermen, a teacher ... We just like bikes.'

'Right,' Sophie says as she juggles the boxes and screws. 'Where did you say we're going now?'

'To a lighthouse up the coast. The one you can see from

Kittiwake on a good day. There's a great beach out there. You'll think you're in Florida.'

Sam's bike bumps along behind the two other motorcycles, following them along the narrow road that snakes through a carpet of purple heather along the crest of a cliff. In the distance a white lighthouse topped with a red beacon squats on a headland beside a small white house.

They park in front of the lighthouse and dismount. Sophie is about to follow Ace and Thor into the lighthouse when Sam takes her hand and pulls her towards a narrow footpath that follows the cliff edge. 'C'mon, Princess Grace. Nothing to see there, just a lot of stairs up to the beacon. There's a great view this way. You can see the beach down towards the west.'

Sophie tugs her hand free. Holding up his hands in surrender, Sam grins. 'Sorry, I just don't want you to blow over the edge.'

'I'll be fine.' She peers at the path. 'It's not that close to the edge.'

'Fine. Suit yourself.' He heads out along the path, following it as it meanders through the heather towards a headland where the cliff thrusts like a blunt thumb into the sea. A curtain of lacy clouds hovers on the horizon, and the sea, under the warm blue sky, is almost turquoise where it puddles into bays at the foot of the cliff.

Sam points to the gulls swooping along the cliff's edge. 'See those? The ones with the black tips on their wings? Those are kittiwakes, but they call them tickle-aces here. You know why?'

'No.'

'Because they chase after other birds and peck at their tail feathers to make them drop their food. Then they swoop in and steal it. Tickle-ace is the politer version of tickle-ass, which some prefer to call them.'

'Trust Newfoundlanders to say it like it is.'

When they reach the headland, Sophie joins Sam at the end of the path. A curving stretch of beige sand stretches out along the coast to the west, just as Sam had said. Ahead of them, the long line of the horizon divides the ocean and the sky. Shutting her eyes, she lifts her face towards the sun.

'You look better.'

She opens her eyes and peers over at Sam. 'I look better?'

'Better than you did when I saw you in Gander.'

Sophie grunts. 'That wasn't hard. I'd been on the plane for over twenty-four hours.'

'That's not what I mean.'

'What do you mean?'

Sam looks at her, his brown eyes giving nothing away. Bending forward, he kisses her.

Sophie pulls away. *Oh shit.*

They look at each other, the silence that engulfs them pierced only by the cries of the tickle-aces swooping below the cliff. Then her arms are around his neck, tugging his head down to hers. He wraps his arms around her, pulling her against his body. They kiss, the wind wrapping them in the salt-tinged air. Sweet, hot kisses, as delicious as the blueberries in Florie's pancakes. Kisses like purple heaven.

# Chapter 24

## Norwich, England – 14 February 1942

Ellie pulls her wool scarf up over her nose and hurries down Earlham Road past the Gothic spires and turrets of St John's Cathedral. Glancing behind her, she veers left down a narrow gravel path, past the shuttered gatekeeper's hut, and down a steep hill lined with neatly trimmed bushes and artfully placed specimen trees. Clumps of fresh green vegetation spring through the earth on the terraced hill, and thrushes swoop amongst the tree branches, oblivious to the cold. At the bottom of the hill, Ellie follows the winding path along the edge of the lawn and awakening flower beds to the Gothic fountain, with its struts and arches dressed in velvet moss.

A figure steps out of the shadows behind the fountain.

Ellie hesitates, crossing her arms and tucking her hands against the warmth of her body. 'I got your note. I told Fire Officer Williams I had to run over to Curls to get a new type-writer ribbon. I have to get back soon.'

Thomas walks towards her, tall and slender in his khaki wool great coat. He reaches out a gloved hand. 'I'm glad you came, Ellie Mae.'

Ellie looks at the black leather glove and back at Thomas. 'What is it, Thomas?'

Thomas drops his arm and sits on the fountain's low stone

wall. Reaching into his coat pocket, he takes out an envelope. 'I haven't been able to stop thinkin' about you, Ellie Mae,' he says as he holds out the envelope to her.

Ellie frowns at her name in spidery blue handwriting on the envelope. 'What's this?'

'What day is today, maid?'

'February fourteenth. Oh, it's Valentine's. I've been so busy I actually forgot.'

Thomas gestures to the envelope. 'Well, then, have a look.'

Running her finger under the flap, Ellie tears open the envelope and draws out a postcard. On the front is a picture of a blonde woman kissing a soldier in front of a large red heart. She holds up the card and reads. *'Cupid is the victor o'er many a heart today. He's made me love you, sweetest, far more than words can say. One little kiss would be such bliss, oh, don't refuse me, pray!'*

She smiles. 'That's very sweet of you. He's an airman, though.'

'What do you mean?'

Ellie taps the picture of the soldier. 'He's wearing a blue uniform. RAF.'

Thomas frowns at the postcard. 'Oh, no. Am I stunned, or what?'

Ellie slips the card back into the envelope and tucks it into her coat pocket. She'll have to hide that from Dottie or she'll never hear the end of it.

'I thought you'd forgotten about me. I wouldn't have blamed you if you had, after ... after the last time.'

Thomas peers up at a raven cawing and flapping at a red squirrel in the spreading branches of a beech tree. 'I've tried to forget about you, Ellie Mae. I threw myself into buildin' those pillboxes along the coast. They've probably gots twice as many as they wanted. Good luck to any German who lands on the Norfolk coast is all I says. I figured if I tired myself out, I wouldn't be able to think about you. But as soon as I closed my eyes, you were there, smilin' at me with your lovely eyes the colour of a stormy sea, and that yellow hair of yours.'

Ellie looks down at her booted feet and knocks her toes together, flexing them in her boots to jolt the sluggish blood back to life. 'I haven't seen you for months.'

'I've seen you, though.'

She jerks her head up. 'What do you mean, you've seen me?'

'At Samson's a few times. The Lido once.'

'You did? Why didn't you ask me to dance?'

'Because I couldn't trust myself with you. With George either.'

Ellie runs her tongue over her dry lips. 'George is a good man.'

'So you've told me a hundred times.'

'Not a hundred times.'

'More times than I wished to hear.'

Ellie sits on the ledge beside Thomas. She's never been to the Plantation Garden in the winter. Not a soul here but the two of them. 'How did you know about this place? It's off the beaten track.'

The corner of Thomas's mouth twitches. 'I likes to find the hidden corners of places. If you ever come to St John's, I'll show you all the secret places there.'

'Secret places? To entertain the ladies?'

He chuckles. 'Well, now, that would be sayin'.'

'So, what am I? Just another girl to chat up?'

Thomas frowns at her, his grey eyes as stormy as the winter

sky. 'Do you wants to know the truth of it, Ellie Mae? You were just that, at the beginning.'

Ellie bolts to her feet. 'Well, thank you very much! That's the most insulting thing I've ever heard.'

Thomas grabs hold of Ellie's arm. 'Please. Sit down. Let me have my say. Then if you wants to send me packin', I'll go and I'll not bother you again.'

Ellie sits down. 'Fine.'

'The first time I saw you at Samson's with your friend Ruthie I thought, now there's the best-lookin' girl in Norfolk by a long shot. Just like Betty Grable.'

'Then you spilt your Coke all over me.'

Thomas scratches his cheek. 'I was a right idiot. I thought that was the end before I'd even started.'

'Well, you made up for it at the Christmas dance. I think George was jealous of your jitterbugging. He's not much of a dancer.'

Thomas taps at the thin film of ice on the surface of the fountain. 'What is it about George?' He looks back at her, and his gaze, naked with love, pierces her heart. 'Because if you loves him, Ellie ... well, if you loves him, I'll just have to work a lot harder to make you love me more.'

Ellie's heart batters against her chest. 'George is ... George is ...'

'Do you love him, Ellie Mae? Tell me you love him.'

Ellie stares at Thomas, knowing that this is the end. The end of the life she's known. The end of the life she thought she was heading for.

'I—I ...'

Then they are kissing, and Thomas's warm mouth tells her everything she needs to know, everything she wants to know.

'Does George kiss you like this?' Thomas says as he covers her face with kisses. 'Does he see the woman you are? Tell me you love him, Ellie Mae. Tell me.'

Ellie gasps for breath. 'I love you, Thomas. I love you. Not George. I love you.'

# *Chapter 25*

## Tippy's Tickle – 15 September 2001

'Sam! Oh, thank God you're here,' Ellie calls out to them from the porch at the top of the steps to Kittiwake. 'Becca's missing.'

Sam flies up the steps two at a time, Sophie following behind. 'What do you mean, she's missing?'

Ellie stands on the porch, rubbing her arms. 'We were over in the shop with the other Brownies this morning painting that banner. Then Emmy came in looking for lunch.' Ellie steadies herself against the railing. 'He suggested he take Becca out to look for partridgeberries since it's such a lovely day. He took Rupert with them. He came back an hour ago. He was in a terrible state. He said the fairies must have taken her.'

'What! Good God. Why didn't you call me?'

'We've been trying. Your phone was off.'

He runs his hand through his hair as he paces the porch. 'Where's Emmett?'

'He's gone back out past the marshes near the woods looking for her.' Ellie clears her throat. 'They were near the brook where we had the picnic on Canada Day. Oh, Sam, he's beside himself.'

'Becca! Becca, girl! Where you at, maid?'

Emmett stamps through the brush, heedless of the jabbing

needles of the twisted larches that scratch at his hands and face. The great black dog gallops ahead, like a bear on the hunt for honey. Emmett flops onto a large moss-covered rock and, taking a handkerchief out of his back pocket, wipes the sweat dripping down his face.

*Where you at, Becca? Didn't I tell you to watch out for those little people? They goes after children like you. They wants you as their own, you see. You wouldn't've heard them singin', so they must'a showed themselves to you. I told you not to follows them, didn't I, Becca? Why'd you follow them? You didn't even takes the bun with you to keep them away. You has to keep some bread on you, maid, or they'll come after you.*

Dropping to his knees, Emmett clasps his hands and looks up through the branches to the patch of blue sky above. *Holy God, I knows the fairies are your angels fell from Heaven. Can you have a word in their ear, God? Tells the little people not to hurt Becca? Keep her safe, will you, God? Help us find her. Please, Holy God. Please.*

When Sophie and Sam reach the clearing in the woods, they find Emmett sitting on a fallen log by the brook, his head in his hands, Rupert curled on the moss by his feet. Sam stomps through the long, dry grass towards him. Emmett looks up as they approach, his cheeks wet under his dishevelled grey hair. His faded blue gaberdine jacket is turned inside out and he holds one of Florie's currant buns, the crumbs dusting the grass at his feet. The dog lumbers to its feet and saunters though the meadow grass towards Sam.

'I'm so sorry, Sam, b'y.' Emmett shakes his head. 'I found me a good patch of partridgeberries over there.' He points to a stand of bushes dotted with crimson berries. 'I thought Becca was right behind me. Then Rupert starts barkin' and fussin', and then the next thing I knows she's gone.'

Sam grasps the collar of Emmett's jacket and hauls him to his feet. 'Where was she the last time you saw her?'

Emmett points towards a clump of orange hawkweed near a stand of silver birches that border a dense wall of larches and thick-branched conifers. 'Just there. She said she was pickin' some flowers for her.' Emmett jabs his finger at Sophie. 'I's looked everywhere, Sam. Been through the woods, alls the way down to Joe Gill's field where he keeps that old horse.'

'You couldn't have looked everywhere or you'd have found her.' Sam pulls his phone out of his back pocket and taps out a number. 'Ace? Becca's gone missing out by Pickersgill's Woods. Get the boys together. Get here as soon as you can.'

'It's the fairies, Sam,' Emmett says as he wipes at his wet face with his handkerchief. 'The fairies musta taken her, just like they took that child down in Colinet all those years ago.'

Sophie picks her way through the bushes under the grasping branches of the larches. She calls out Becca's name, even though she knows it's fruitless. Becca could be just out of sight, around the next rock or fir tree, but she'd never hear the call.

Rupert lumbers past her, his muscular body and giant webbed feet smashing a path through the undergrowth. 'Good boy, Rupert. Find Becca. You can do it.'

She follows Rupert through the scrub. How is it possible that she's only been in Tippy's Tickle for three days? The place has taken hold of her. She already feels closer to these islanders than any of the people she's worked with for years. A fear grows inside of her. Bad things can't possibly happen here. Not in this place. Not with these people. Her people.

'Becca! Becca!' she screams into the forest. She can't stop herself.

After a few minutes the scrubby larches thin out and give way to a carpet of moss and green rootless liverworts where the branches of the firs and the spruce trees form an umbrella over the forest floor. A silence as thick as the moss engulfs her, broken only by the panting of the dog and the thud of its feet as it lopes deeper into the forest. The firs close around her like an enemy army. She squints into the shadows.

'Rupert! Wait! Come back!' She turns her ear in the direction Rupert has disappeared, but the forest has swallowed him just as it has swallowed Becca. 'Rupert! Come here!' But the dog is gone.

She stands on the moss, peering into the darkening forest. If she continues, she'll get lost too. *Becca. Becca. Where are you?* She presses her hands to the top of her head and yells.

'Becca! Rupert!'

The forest swallows her cries, smothering them in its velvet darkness. Her shoulders dropping in defeat, she turns and stumbles back to the clearing, following the path the dog's huge paws have forged through the underbrush.

Florie enters the kitchen from the hall. 'Any news yet?'

'No, Florie,' Ace says. 'Sam's still out with Zeb and Lloyd. Thor and I's gotta get back to Wesleyville. We'll come back tomorrow if we needs to. Just get Sam to call me.' He pokes his brother on his shoulder. 'C'mon, b'y. Sooner we go, sooner we can come back.'

Sophie watches the screen door slam behind them. Florie plods over to the coffee pot and pours herself a cup of coffee and joins Sophie at the kitchen table. Out by the tickle the motorcycles roar to life.

'Finally gots Ellie asleep,' Florie says as she yawns and rubs her eyes. 'She's right upset. Blames herself. Said it was a school day and she should never have let Emmy take Becca out.'

Sophie sets down her mug. 'Emmett's inconsolable. He's locked himself in the store.'

'That's no place for him. He should be out there with the others lookin' for her.'

Sophie sits back in her chair. She hadn't wanted to say anything, but she couldn't hold it any longer. The thought had been niggling at her all evening.

'Florie, Emmett's ... okay, isn't he?'

Florie jerks her head up. 'What do you means by that?'

Sophie shifts in the chair. 'I ... I'm sorry, Florie. I just ... He'd never do anything, would he?'

'Are you saying he did something to Becca?'

'No. Of course not. I just ...' Sophie presses her fingers against her temples. *Bloody hell. Bloody hell.* 'I'm sorry. I shouldn't have said anything. I was out of line. It's just that—'

Florie pushes her chair away from the table with a loud scrape. She picks up four empty mugs and takes them over to the sink. 'Those kinds of things might happen in the cities, but not out in these parts. Becca's just wandered off, mark my words.'

Sophie nods. 'Right. No doubt you're absolutely right.' *Please God. Let her be right.*

# Chapter 26

## Norwich, England – 14 March 1942

'I hardly recognised you, maid. I was startin' to think you slept in your uniform.'

Flashing Thomas a winning smile, Ellie brushes her hands against the full skirt of her jade-green tea dress. 'I wasn't working today, so I had a chance to wear something pretty for a change. Do you like it?' She glances over at George, who is leaning against the bandstand beside her, rubbing his glasses with a handkerchief. 'George hasn't said a word.'

'Well, then, George is blind as a bat.' He holds out a hand. 'You can't pass up the chance of dance for St Patrick's Day.'

'I'm going to have a dance with Thomas, George.'

Thomas extends his hand. 'Good to see you, b'y. Better put those glasses on before someone steals Ellie away while you're not lookin'.'

George smiles lamely and shakes Thomas's hand. 'Hello, Tom. Ellie can dance with anyone she likes.' He pats her clumsily on her shoulder. 'She's my girl.'

Charlie Murphy breaks through the crowd, ale sloshing over the tops of the two pint glasses he's carrying. 'Here you goes, b'y,' he says as he thrusts a glass at Thomas.

'Give it to George, b'y. I'm busy.' He leads Ellie into the heaving sea of party-goers swinging to the band's rendition of the latest Glenn Miller hit, 'A String of Pearls'.

Charlie hands George the ale. 'Down the hatch, b'y. Your shout next.'

George readjusts his glasses. 'Thanks, Charlie.' Taking a swig of the ale, he considers Ellie and Thomas swinging along to the bouncy tune. 'Tom's a good dancer.'

Charlie focuses on the laughing couple. 'They gets on, those two.' He gulps down half his beer and wipes his mouth with the back of his uniform sleeve. 'You don't suppose anythin's goin' on with them, does you?'

George's head snaps around. 'Why should I think that?'

Charlie pats the padded shoulder of George's brown tweed jacket. 'Calm down, b'y. You gots a face on you like a hen's arse in the northwest winds. All's I'm sayin' is I'd keeps my eye on them, if I was in your shoes. I told you before that Tom's a charmer.' He leans closer to George. 'He's been comin' up to Norwich every chance he gets. He's got himself on the supply run with the QM every Thursday.' Charlie takes another swig of beer. 'He's a sly one, is our Tommy. Gets him outta a day of trainin' or diggin' fortifications up on the coast. Since we got changed to the 166th Newfoundland Field Regiment in November, they've kept us as busy as a bayman with two chainsaws.'

George eyes Charlie's flushed face. Come to think of it, Ellie had been a bit off this past month, he thinks. Even the chocolates he'd brought her for Valentine's hadn't done much to thaw out her mood. He'd put it down to her extra workload at the fire station. She was there all hours now, though he couldn't for the life of him figure out what kept her so busy. There hadn't been an air raid for months. They hadn't been to their Friday night film in weeks except for once, and even then she'd wanted to get home early instead of stopping at the Coach and Horses for a glass.

Charlie downs the last of this beer. 'G'wan, b'y. I'll be three down before you finishes yours.'

George eyes Thomas and Ellie, bouncing amongst the GIs and local girls to 'Chattanooga Choo Choo'. He gulps the beer and hands the empty glass to Charlie. Fishing a handful of coins out of his pocket, he drops them into Charlie's hand. 'My shout.'

Charlie tips a salute and ducks into the crowd. George sweeps his eyes around the bobbing heads of the dancers, but Ellie's shining blonde head and the tall Newfoundlander are nowhere to be seen.

George shoves his empty beer glass at Charlie.

'Hold on, b'y,' Charlie says. 'Where you off to?'

'I'm going to find Ellie.'

'She's probably just gone to the Ladies'.'

George squints at Charlie through his glasses. 'With Tom?'

Charlie chuckles over the top of his beer glass. 'I expect we would'a heard screams in that case.'

'Where do you think he is, then?' George's tongue is thick in his mouth, and the words come out fat and slurred. 'They've been gone for the past half hour.' George taps on his watch. 'Since ten twenty-three. I've been keeping an eye out, like you said.'

Charlie pats George on his shoulder. 'Me and my big mouth. C'mon, b'y, They probably just went to get some air. It's hotter'n the insides of a bibby in here. I'm used to choppin' ice off the privy round St Paddy's Day back home.'

George thrusts away Charlie's hand. 'I'm going to go and find them.'

Charlie watches George barrel through the jitterbugging dancers. 'Jaysus, Mary and Joseph.' Gulping down his beer, he sets the glass down on the bandstand and heads after him.

'I've missed you, Ellie Mae.' Thomas wraps his arms around Ellie in the alley behind the Samson and Hercules.

'It's only been two days, Thomas.'

'Half an hour in Plantation Garden is enough to be a torture, maid.'

Ellie loops her hand around his neck and pulls his mouth to her lips, pressing her body into his.

Sighing happily, she looks up at him, cupping his face with her hands. 'Where did you come from, Thomas Parsons?'

'From your dreams, Ellie Mae Burgess.'

'I never imagined anyone like you in my wildest dreams.'

Thomas traces the contours of her face with his fingertip. 'You never drew a picture of your true love? With lots of hearts and cupids, like I've seen the girls back home do? You're an artist, aren't you?'

'I wasn't a silly girl like that. But, Ruthie, now she was always in love with the latest movie star. Tyrone Power was her favourite. Anyway, I can't draw from my imagination. I need to see what I'm drawing.' She shrugs, her naked shoulders a soft white in the dull night light. 'Sister Mary Geraldine told me once that I'm just a copyist. You never forget the people who tell you things like that.'

Thomas rubs his chin, drawing his eyebrows together in a frown.

'Thomas? What's the matter?'

'You're Catholic, Ellie Mae. Most everyone up on my part of the coast is Protestant. The Irish are all down around the south coast of Newfoundland, and from places like Ship Harbour where Charlie's from and up on Fogo. My mam—' Smiling, he pulls her closer. 'My mam always warned me about Catholic girls.'

'Your mother needs to broaden her point of view. Anyway, I'm just an adequate artist. I'm nothing special.'

Thomas's eyes narrow. 'Don't you be talkin' yourself down, Ellie Mae. You've got a fine talent. That Sister Mary Geraldine was full of baloney. Why haven't I seen you draw anythin' since we were at Holkham?'

Ellie rests her head against the khaki wool of Thomas's uniform. His heart beats steadily under her ear. 'It just seemed ... frivolous, I suppose. Art was everything to me once. Then after Ruthie ...' She sighs, her breath puffing into the cool air like a small cloud.

Thomas rubs her back and whispers into her ear. 'Promise me you'll keep drawin', m' love. It's part of you. Don't you forget it.'

A clatter of tin as a rubbish bin crashes onto the cobbled alley. 'Ellie!' A slurred voice. 'Ellie! What's going on?'

Ellie and Thomas jolt apart. 'George?'

'You remember me, don't you?' George thumps his chest, throwing himself off balance. 'I'm your fiancé.'

Charlie takes hold of George's arm. 'Steady on, b'y. Jaysus, you only had two beers. You definitely don't have any Newfoundland blood in you.'

Shoving Charlie away, George walks unsteadily up the hill towards the couple. 'Let's go, Ellie. Charlie warned me about Tom. I won't blame you.'

Ellie crosses her arms, shivering as the winter chill settles into her body. 'Blame me for what, George? For wanting to be with someone who makes me feel special? Who treats me like a woman, instead of like some ... some schoolmate? I'll be twenty in September. I'm a woman, George, not that you've noticed.'

'That's not true, Ellie. I've noticed.'

'You've a funny way of showing it.'

George flicks his gaze between Ellie and Thomas. 'I gave you chocolates for Valentine's. They were a week's wages.'

'Only after Dottie reminded you. And what about last year? You gave me a heart-shaped pencil rubber. What was I supposed to do with that?'

Charlie chuckles. 'Oh, Georgie, b'y.'

George reaches out and tugs Ellie's hand. 'Come on, Ellie. I'll bring you home. I've had enough of tonight.'

'I'd let her go, if I were you, b'y.' A nerve ticks in Thomas's cheek.

George releases Ellie's hand. 'I'm sorry, Ellie,' he says, pressing his fingertips against his forehead. 'I love you. I've always loved you.'

'You never said it, George. I waited for it. I waited for it for years. Now, it's too late. Love is a hungry thing. If you don't feed it, it withers and dies. Ours died.'

# Chapter 27

## Tippy's Tickle – 15 September 2001

Sophie raises the collar of Florie's yellow raincoat and pulls it close around her neck. The rain pelts steadily onto the umbrella she's pulled out of Ellie's umbrella stand, the printed scene of Montmartre and the Moulin Rouge a feeble barrier against the downpour. She strains to listen for voices, or footsteps, anything, from her vigil on Ellie's porch.

Then, a dog's bark, and Rupert's dark bulk emerges from the black night. Then Sam, and, in his arms, Becca.

Sam climbs the steps with the sleeping girl, the dog pounding up the steps behind him. He stops before Sophie. 'You waited.'

'Yes, of course. Is she okay?'

'She's fine. I found her hiding under a rock outcrop at the bottom of the cliff. Rupert brought me to her. She was about a half mile away from the clearing.'

Sophie opens the screen door and follows Sam and the dog into the kitchen. 'A half mile away? How did she get there?'

'Fairies.'

'What?'

'She said she followed a beautiful fairy on a red pony.'

'She has a lively imagination.'

Sam grunts. 'Emmett's been feeding her nonsense. I'm going to put a stop to it tomorrow.'

'She's okay otherwise?'

'Yes, she's fine. But all she could tell me about were fairies.'

'Sam, it might be my fault.'

Sam stops in the doorway to the hall, Becca curled against his leather jacket. 'What do you mean?'

'I read her a fairy story from an old Enid Blyton book I found in the living room the other day. She ... she seemed to love it. The Fairy Queen especially.'

Sam shakes his head and smiles. 'Thanks for reading her the story, Princess Grace. You're obviously a good storyteller. She said the fairy looked like you.'

Sophie grunts. 'You said she followed a beautiful fairy.'

Sam grins, his dark eyes warm. 'Like I said, Princess Grace. She said the fairy looked just like you.'

Sam brushes the hair from Becca's forehead and leans over the bed to give the sleeping girl a kiss. So much like her mother. So much like Winny.

*You gave me a real fright tonight, Becca-bug. There was a moment there when I thought ...* No, he isn't going to go there. He can't go there again.

He sits on the end of the bed and closes his eyes. Weariness drags at his body. Pressing his fingers against his eyes, he yawns. *I wish you were here, Winny. This would never have happened if you'd been here.*

Another face floats into his mind. Sophie. She's nothing like Winny. Nothing like Winny at all. But, she makes him laugh with her odd, uptight ways. That only irritates her more. Which amuses him even more. It's like being on a carousel. She keeps him on his toes.

He rubs his head. *Why'd you have to go, Winny? And now*

*there's Sophie, and I just don't know. I just don't know. It wasn't supposed to be like this.*

He looks down at his sleeping daughter. *I'm sorry Winny. I'm so sorry.*

# *Chapter 28*

## Norwich, England – 27 April 1942

The sound took her by surprise. It'd been so quiet since August, almost like the war had decided to pass them by. Now, the roar of the plane, like a zipper through the sky, coming on suddenly, then, in an instant, so loud it's shaking the bed. Her mirror falls off the wall over her dresser and crashes onto the Persian rug, imbedding slivers of glass into the faded tufts.

The siren screams awake, and another plane thunders over the house. Heading west. *They're ours. Something's coming.*

She drops her new Daphne du Maurier novel onto the bedcovers and jumps out of the bed. Throwing back the blackout curtain, she sees the sky ablaze with searchlights. The ack-ack guns come to life, throwing black flak into the moonlit sky. Then she sees them, the silhouettes like insects in the angry sky. Growing larger, louder. Then the whistling and the explosions as the bombs fall over the unsuspecting city.

'Dottie!' Stumbling over her discarded pumps, she pulls open her door. 'Dottie!'

Dottie stands, pale and shaking in the doorway of the old nursery that she'd reclaimed as her bedroom the previous year. She hugs the struggling cat against her flannel nightgown. 'Where's Poppy?'

'He has his Red Cross meeting tonight. He was meant to be back by ten. He'll find a shelter, don't worry.'

A bomb screams through the air nearby then goes silent. The sisters freeze. Then, an enormous explosion as the bomb ploughs into the back garden, shaking the house and blowing out the fanlight over the staircase. Glass showers the carpeted steps like silver confetti. A second bomb whistles through the air. A dull thud as it lands in the garden. Silence.

'It didn't explode, Ellie.'

Ellie grabs her sister's arm. 'Hurry, Dottie. We've got to get to the cellar.'

The sisters huddle together on one of the cots in the cellar. The cat is curled up beside them, seemingly oblivious to the devastation raining down on the city. The room is narrow, with a brick ceiling only just high enough for them to stand under. A faint mustiness sits in the cool, damp air, tinged with the tang of drying onions. Ellie draws the grey blanket around them, tugging the folds around their heads to muffle the cacophony of the aerial battles being waged overhead.

'It's dark, Ellie.'

Ellie squeezes her sister's quivering body. 'I know. But we can't put on the light till this is over.'

'I wish Poppy were here.'

'He'll be fine. He got through the last war in one piece, didn't he? He's indestructible.'

'Do you suppose George is on one of the ack-ack guns tonight?'

'I expect so. Helping at least. They won't let him be a gunner because of his eye.'

'How did he hurt his eye, Ellie? It doesn't look any different from his good one.'

'Conkers.'

'What?'

'He was playing conkers with Joey Fisher at school recess when he was nine. George's conker was a six-er so he was pretty confident. But when it hit Joey's conker it smashed apart and a long splinter flew into George's eye. Nurse got the splinter out and wrapped a bandage around his head. The next day half his eye jelly had leaked out. They patched him up at the hospital but his eye was blind after that.'

'Poor George.'

'They found out Joey had baked his conker. It was hard as a rock.'

'That's cheating.'

'People cheat sometimes, Dottie. They do it to get ahead, I suppose. Life isn't always fair.'

'You mean sometimes cheaters win?'

Ellie shrugs. 'Sometimes they do.'

Dottie's dark eyebrows draw together. 'But isn't winning what we're meant to do?'

'Yes, but ... you shouldn't be selfish about it. It's not nice.'

'Ellie? Do you think Mr Churchill cheats sometimes? To help us win?'

'Oh, Dottie. I don't know. Maybe. Winning the war is important. You don't want that nasty awful Hitler over here, do you?'

'No. Of course not.'

'So, there. Needs must.'

'Like Milly's mum and the beet juice lipstick.'

'Milly's mum didn't steal the beet juice, did she, Dottie?'

'I didn't steal your lipstick that time! I don't know how it got in my drawer. Honestly, Ellie. Maybe you put it there by accident. You've gotten all dreamy lately.'

'I haven't.'

'You have.'

They fall silent as the bombs whistle and crash and the anti-aircraft guns shoot their flak into the sky. Dottie thrusts her hands over her ears. 'I hate the whistling. I hate it.'

Ellie clutches the blanket under her chin. 'Me too.'

'I wish George were here.'

'Why?'

Dottie leans her head on Ellie's shoulder. 'I'd feel safer. Like nothing could happen to us.' She squints at Ellie through the cellar's gloom. 'Why didn't he come here for Easter supper? He's always come before. He didn't even come to the Easter concert, and I really wanted him to hear 'Clair de Lune' I've been practising for months.'

Ellie chews her bottom lip. 'Dottie, George and I aren't seeing each other anymore.'

Dottie pulls away from her sister, the blanket dropping around their knees. 'What? Why?'

'It just wasn't working out.'

'But why?'

'Dottie, sometimes people just ... sometimes people just fall out of love.'

'You don't love George anymore?'

'Of course I do, but just not that way. I met someone else, and I've fallen in love.'

'You've fallen in love with someone else? Who?'

'Thomas Parsons. You met him last summer.'

'The one who went to Holkham with us last summer with his friend?'

'Yes. That Thomas.'

Dottie winds the memory of the day at Holkham Beach

through her mind. It had been so much fun. She peers over at her sister, at her hair glowing silver under a thin finger of moonlight that has slipped past the cellar window's blackout fabric. She'd had George and Charlie all to herself that day at Holkham Beach because Ellie had gone off with Thomas. It had been wonderful.

'How could you do that, Ellie? George's only ever been lovely to all of us. You were supposed to get married. I was going to be the bridesmaid.'

'You can't help it when you fall in love. I loved George, but I wasn't *in love* with him. I didn't know that there was a difference until I met Thomas.' Ellie grabs the blanket and pulls it up over their knees. 'It just happened, Dottie. I didn't expect it. I didn't even want it to happen.'

'So, stop it.'

'I can't. I don't want to.'

'Are you going to marry him?'

'I don't know.'

Dottie slaps the blanket. 'But you're engaged to George!'

'We were never really engaged. We just assumed we'd get married someday. But he never asked me, Dottie. He never gave me a ring.'

Dottie reaches over and picks up the cat, nestling it against her. She pulls the blanket up over the cat, tucking it in like a swaddled baby. A soft purr wafts into the room, barely audible amongst the noise from the bombing assault outside.

'Dottie, Thomas asked me to marry him last autumn.'

Dottie's eyes widen. 'He did?'

'I said no.' Ellie looks over at her sister who is clutching the cat against her chest like a doll. 'I said no because I couldn't bear leaving you and Poppy. That would be an awful thing for me to do. Imagine us never seeing each other ever again. I couldn't do that to you and Poppy, not ever.'

'I'd never forgive you if you went, Ellie.'

'Don't say things like that.'

'I don't care. I hate Thomas. I hope he dies.'

'Stop it, Dottie. That's no way to talk.'

The wooden stairs creak. The girls look up as their father steps down into the cellar.

'Poppy!' Dottie throws off the blanket and shoves the cat into Ellie's arms. Running over to her father, she flings her arms around him. A cloud of silvery dust rises from his jacket. 'Ellie's broken up with George and she loves Thomas and I thought we were going to die!'

Henry coughs, his shoulders shaking as he gasps for breath. He wipes his mouth with a handkerchief and clears his throat. 'Well, I can see you're both in one piece.'

'But, Poppy! What about George?'

Henry runs his hand over Dottie's smooth brown hair. *'Love looks not with the eyes, but with the mind, and therefore is wing'd Cupid painted blind.'*

'What?'

*'A Midsummer Night's Dream*, pet. It's not for us to interfere with Ellie's romantic life. She's a grown woman and she can make her own decisions. Now, let's light a candle and play Whist.'

# *Chapter* 29

## Tippy's Tickle – 16 September 2001

'*D*addy!'

Sam looks up from the wooden chair he's sanding as his daughter runs over to him. She throws her arms around his neck, and he gives her a hug and a kiss on her cheek.

'Hi, Becca-bug. What are you doing here?'

A young woman in a loose cotton dress printed with pink rosebuds follows the girl into the store and sets a small paper bag on the workbench. The scent of warm pastry and dates wafts into the room.

'We've been helping Nanny make date squares,' the woman says as she pulls her long, blond hair into a ponytail. 'I think Becca ate half the filling before it made it into the squares, isn't that right, honey?'

Becca reaches into the bag and lifts out a date square, the crumbly oat topping spilling out onto the planked floor as she bites into the treat. 'They still taste good, Daddy,' she says as she wipes the crumbs around her mouth.

The woman walks over to Sam and gives him a quick kiss on his lips. He pulls her closer and kisses her. Pulling away, she laughs and ruffles his hair. 'You'd think we were just married.'

'That's wrong, Mommy,' Becca says as she chews. 'I'm eight, so you married Daddy before that.'

'You're right, Becca-bug.' Sam reaches into the paper bag. 'Daddy married Mommy ten years ago, then we moved to a big city called Boston. That's where you were born.'

'Why did we move here, Daddy?'

'Well, because ... Because ...' Sam looks at the woman and frowns. 'What are you doing here, Winny?'

The woman laughs, the sound floating on the air like petals. 'Of course I'm okay, silly. I'm healthy as a horse. In fact, I'm so hungry I could eat one.' She plucks the date square from Sam's hand and takes a big bite.

Becca giggles, her laughter as light as the trills of the puffins on the cliffs up the coast. 'You can't eat a horse, Mommy. That's impossible.'

Sam presses his fingers into his forehead. 'But, Becca and I came here after—' He jerks his head around to his daughter. 'You're talking, Becca.'

Becca rolls her eyes behind her glasses. 'Of course I'm talking, Daddy.'

'You can hear me, sweetie?'

'Daddy, you're being very silly.'

A rap on the store door. It swings open, the rusty hinges protesting with a ragged squeak. 'Sam? Ellie sent over some scones and blueberry jam for you since you missed breakfast.'

Sam looks over at the woman in the green velvet suit that looks like it has been dusted with a fine coating of sand. 'Sophie?'

Sophie smiles at Winny and sets the basket of scones on the workbench beside the paper bag of date squares. 'There you are, Becca. Did Florie give you those squares? Ellie was wondering what happened to them. We need them for her birthday party tonight. You might have to help me make some more.'

*Becca claps her hands. 'Oh good! I know how. I can make chocolate chip cookies too. Mama taught me.'*

*Sophie extends her hand to Winny. 'You must be Winny. Ellie's told me all about you. It's nice to meet another cousin. I've got you and Emmett now, and Becca. Only a few days ago I thought I didn't have any!'*

*Waving aside Sophie's hand, Winny gives her a hug. 'I was hoping to meet you, Sophie. It's why I came.' She smiles at Sam. 'I have to go, now, darling.'*

*'Where are you going?'*

*'For a walk.'*

*'A walk? Wait and I'll come with you.'*

*'No, not right now, darling.' Kissing Becca on the top of her head, she heads to the door, pausing with her hand on the doorknob. 'Why don't you have one of those scones with Sophie? They smell delicious. Ellie makes the best on the island. Have them with some of Florie's blueberry jam. That was my favourite.'*

Sam opens his eyes. The room is heavy with the black night. He turns to look at the empty pillow on his right. Four years next May. An age and a moment.

# *Chapter 30*

## Norwich, England – 11 September 1942

Rampant Horse Street is a shadow of the bustling shopping street that had been part of the beating heart of Norwich just a few months ago, before the Baedeker air raids of the spring and summer. The elegant frontages of Bonds department store on the south side of the street and Curls on the north have been reduced to mounds of rubble and mangled iron, though Mr Bond has entrepreneurially set up shop in three damaged buses in the parking lot.

Ellie picks her way over the bomb-pitted roads and up Timberhill. She hesitates in front of the nondescript red-brick façade of The Gardeners Arms – known locally as The Murderers owing to the unfortunate death of a previous resident. Surely no one will know her in there. It was far enough away from the fire station and Mcklintock's, in a part of town that she'd usually only hurry through to get to the bus station. The Murderers was known as a drinkers' pub, and the newly arrived American soldiers and airmen had adopted it as their own. It wasn't the kind of place she'd ever been, nor had ever been curious to enter. It wasn't the kind of place she'd bump into George. Which made it perfect.

She pushes the door open and finds herself amongst a mass of broad, khaki-uniformed shoulders. She presses past the soldiers, who answer her apologies with offers of a drink, a dance, and less salubrious suggestions. She spies Thomas at a table hidden in a niche under a medieval brick arch. He waves at her and she pushes through the last phalanx of soldiers.

Thomas gives her a quick kiss on the cheek. 'Good thing you made it when you did, m'love. I've had to buy six Yanks a round to keep them from chucking me off the table.'

Ellie lifts the strap of her satchel over her head and sits on the bench beside Thomas. 'I'm sorry, darling. It's been a madhouse at the fire station. They've been over at Magdalen Street knocking down the walls of the shops that were bombed last week. I've been back and forth all day with tea and sandwiches.'

Thomas pushes a glass across the table. 'I gots you a gin and tonic. No ice though. The bartender looked at me like I'd asked for milk and cookies when I asked for ice.'

Ellie reaches for the glass and takes a sip. The tonic bubbles rasp down her throat. 'Thank you, Thomas.' Setting down the warm glass, she gazes into his grey eyes as he smiles.

'How is it you get more lovely every time I sees you, Ellie Mae?'

'Is everyone in Newfoundland as full of baloney as you are?'

Thomas chuckles. 'Newfoundlanders are made of baloney. That doesn't mean that what I says isn't true.' He leans in and kisses her on the lips. A catcall from the bar. Ellie sits back against the brick wall, heat flashing into her cheeks.

'We probably shouldn't do that here.'

'You'd be a test for the Angel Gabriel himself.' Thomas reaches for his pint glass and takes a long draught of the dark ale. Setting down the glass, he looks at her, his eyes clouding. 'There's some news.'

'News? What kind of news?'

Sitting back, Thomas examines Ellie's face. 'They're movin' us out.'

Ellie intakes a sharp breath. 'They're moving you out? Where?'

'Don't know. They won't say.'

'But, when? Not before Christmas, surely?'

Thomas reaches over and cups his hand over Ellie's. 'They're sendin' us down to London next week and shippin' us to the show sometime in October, far as I knows.'

'You're leaving next week?'

'Next Thursday. Ellie, m'love. It's a war and I'm a soldier. It's what I signed up to do.'

She pulls her hand away and folds her arms against her body. 'Yes, of course.' What had she thought? That nothing would change? That Thomas would be here, safely and happily in reach until this horrible war was over?

'Ellie, marry me. Come down to London and marry me before I go. I loves you, maid. You know I loves you.'

Ellie stares at Thomas's long, handsome face, at his grey eyes stormy with emotion. 'Oh, Thomas. How can we? We haven't time. We have to post the banns a month in advance.'

'We don't need to marry in a church.'

'But I'm Catholic, Thomas.'

'We can marry in a registry office and have a church weddin' later. Here, or in Newfoundland. Wherever you like.'

'Are you suggesting we ... elope?'

'Why not? We could go now. Tonight.'

Ellie shakes her head. 'You have to apply for a wedding licence a month in advance, too. I ... I've looked it up.'

'You've looked it up?' Thomas frowns. 'For me or for George?'

'For you. Of course, for you.'

Thomas looks at Ellie as he drains the last of his ale. He sets down the glass. 'Why haven't you told your family about us? I'm tired of sneakin' around like I'm some sort'a thief.'

Ellie bites her lip. 'I know. I'm sorry. I haven't been ready.'

'Will you ever be ready, Ellie Mae? That's the question I've gots for you.' He pushes away from the table. 'Maybe we should say our goodbyes now. Give George my regards.'

Ellie grabs his arm. 'No, wait. Please.'

'I can't takes much more of this dancin' around the mulberry bush, Ellie Mae.'

'I know.'

Ellie looks at Thomas, her heart pounding the way it does when she's run all the way from Jarrolds back to the fire station at lunchtime.

*I love him. I love him. I'm sorry Dottie. I'm sorry Poppy. Thomas is the one.*

She places her hand over Thomas's. 'I will.'

'You will what?'

'I'll marry you. There, I said it. I'll marry you, Thomas Parsons. We can apply for the marriage licence before you leave Norwich and we can marry in London before they ship you out. All you need to do is send me a telegram and I'll take the first train down to London.'

'Are you serious, Ellie Mae?'

Ellie stands up and wraps her arms around Thomas, to the hoots and hollers of the soldiers. 'The question is, will you marry me, Thomas Parsons?'

'I will, Ellie Mae Burgess. I will.'

Thomas hugs Ellie so tightly that she can feel the buttons of his uniform pressing into her. Her heart flutters in her chest like a butterfly set free and her body buzzes with joy. She's marrying the man she loves. That's all that matters. Everything will be fine.

Poppy and Dottie will understand. Of course they will.

# *Chapter 31*

## Tippy's Tickle – 16 September 2001

Becca runs over to the stern of the white cruiser that is bouncing in the water by the wharf, waving at Sophie, Ellie and Florie as they make their way down to the tickle over the rocky path from Kittiwake. Rupert's bear-like head pops up beside her and the dog barks out a deep woof.

'Sam, b'y!' Florie calls out as they approach. 'Whoooo, Sammy! We're all here to see Ellie's birthday whales, b'y. Holy God, it's hotter than a sauna today. Never had a September like it.'

Sam joins Becca on the boat, leaning over to pat Rupert's head. His jean jacket is topped by a windbreaker, and a Boston Bruins baseball cap perches on his head, the brim shading his eyes.

Ellie holds up a basket stuffed with food. 'Hope you're hungry. We've got provisions.'

'C'mon, then,' Sam says, beckoning to the women. 'We're ready to go. Thor and Ace saw a pair of humps over in the cape yesterday feeding on capelin. Looks like a female and her calf. With any luck, they'll still be there.'

Sophie follows Ellie and Florie onto the boat, reaching out to grasp Sam's hand as she clambers aboard. His fingers close over hers. *Warm. Nice.*

Sophie pulls her hand away to brush at an invisible strand

of hair. She nods at Becca, who is standing at the steering wheel, signing animatedly to Ellie and Florie. 'How's Becca?'

'She's fine. But she's had a talking-to about wandering off.'

'Good. I'm glad she's okay.'

He reaches out and squeezes her arm. 'Thanks for staying up last night.'

She shrugs. 'I only wish I could have done something more. I felt pretty helpless.'

Sam smiles, fine lines fanning out from the corners of his brown eyes. 'You did great.'

'Sam,' Ellie calls over. 'Becca wants to know if she can have a date square now.'

He heads towards the bridge. 'Don't you let her wrap you around her finger, Ellie. Let's wait till we're moored in the cape.' He turns on the engine and rests his hands on top of Becca's, helping her steer the cruiser out of the tickle into the ocean.

Sophie catches her breath. A buzz zips around her body, settling in a swirl of warmth in her solar plexus. Pressing a hand to her stomach, she takes a deep breath as she watches Sam and his daughter laughing as they motor past the clapboard houses in their candy-box colours toward the ocean.

*Bloody hell.*

Sam scans the water for signs of whales. Behind him, the women's laughter floats in the air, prompted by Sophie's inept attempts at sign language and Florie's literal translations. He glances into the boat mirror. Becca is doubled over on a seat clutching her stomach in silent laughter at Sophie's efforts to copy Florie's signed descriptions of the coastal scenery. Notice the grudges by the leech. Aren't the turds lovely?

The wind has brought colour to Sophie's cheeks, he notices,

and her fine brown hair flies around her head where it's escaped her ponytail. She's nothing like the uptight, short-tempered woman who'd stepped off the plane just four days ago. Who'd have thought she'd get on so well with Becca? Or that Becca would like her? Who is this Sophie Parry?

A memory of Winny laughing on a sailboat off Nantucket wafts into his mind, her skin tanned and her hair bleached almost white from the summer sun. The summer she was pregnant with Becca.

He looks back at Sophie. *There's no point. She's leaving tomorrow. She'll get on that plane to New York and that'll be the end of that. Back to her busy, big-city life. It's probably for the best. There you go. Bob's your uncle.*

# *Chapter 32*

## Norwich, England – 16 September 1942

A shape moves out of the darkness towards her.

'Ellie Mae?'

'Thomas.'

His arms fold around her and she leans into his kiss. When she opens her eyes, she traces her fingers along his face, following the outline drawn by the faint moonlight shining through the open top of the medieval tower.

'Oh, Thomas, I can't believe you're leaving tomorrow.'

'I knows, maid.' Thomas looks down at the woman in his arms, trying to take in every detail, how her nose turns up slightly at its tip, how her beautiful eyes shine so seriously at him beneath eyebrows the colour of wheat at harvest time, at the set of her determined chin. *Oh, Ellie Mae, how have I been so lucky to find you?*

'I can't stay long, Thomas. Dottie's baked a birthday cake for me.'

'Oh, Jaysus, I totally forgot it's your birthday. I'm a terrible one for dates.'

Ellie shakes her head. 'Don't worry. It's the last thing I'm thinking about. Dottie ... she's invited George over.'

'She did, did she? She's a little tinker.'

'He's just a friend.'

'You may thinks that, maid, but has he got the message?'

'Yes, yes, of course. I've barely seen him since that time at the Samson on St Patrick's Day.'

'Thomas reaches into the pocket of his khaki uniform. 'It might not be a birthday present, Ellie Mae, but I has a little somethin' for you. For you to remember me by.'

'Oh, Thomas. You don't have to worry about that.'

Stepping out of their embrace, he drops to one knee. He opens the small navy velvet box and takes out a ring and holds it out to her. The silver moonlight catches the large square-cut stone, setting it glinting in the shadowy darkness of the tower. 'Didn't I say I'd find you the most beautiful ring in England, maid? I always keeps my promises.'

Ellie's face breaks into a wide smile. 'You did say that. I remember.'

'Ellie Mae Burgess, will you do me the honour of being my wife and making me the happiest man who walks this earth?'

'Oh, Thomas. Yes. Yes.'

He takes hold of her left and hand slides the ring over her ring finger. 'Perfect fit. It's like the ring was made for you, Ellie Mae.' He looks up at Ellie's face, lit a soft silver in the moonlight. He presses his fingers to his eyes and blinks.

'Thomas Parsons, is that a tear in your eye?'

Thomas smiles. 'I'm not ashamed to say it is.' He turns her hand over and kisses her palm. 'How did I get so lucky? You looks like an angel, maid. My angel.'

# *Chapter 33*

## Tippy's Tickle – 16 September 2001

S am steers the cruiser past the grey cliffs that press their jagged forms against the blue sky in a jigsaw of abutting and diverging diagonal slabs. Around the boat, tickle-aces, turrs and noddies keen and swoop, skimming the ocean's surface for their next meal.

The lighthouse comes into view on the edge of a cliff about ten kilometres away, the white house crowding against it, as if seeking reassurance on their precarious perch above the ocean. Leaving Ellie and Florie playing cribbage, Sophie joins Sam and Becca on the bridge.

Sam glances over at her as he steers the boat through the waves. 'Is that flight information phone number I gave you any good? Any word about your flight?'

'Not yet, Sam. There's only a few more planes to leave, including mine. I tried to get on another flight to New York, but they're not allowing it. I have to go on the plane I came in on.' She shakes her head. 'I've got to get to this interview Tuesday morning, or ... or, I don't know what. Back to London with my tail between my legs, I suppose.'

'Back to the big city where you belong.'

'What do you mean by that? I don't have to live in a city. I spent a lot of time in the countryside in Norfolk growing up.'

She juts out her chin. 'I could live here if I wanted to. I'd have to change my entire life, but anything's possible.'

Sophie looks out to the ocean. How was he to know that she'd sat on the rock under the old spruce beside Kittiwake sketching the view while she imagined herself with a cottage by the tickle, making a life here as an artist? Picking blueberries and partridgeberries with Florie and Becca from secret places she'd find? Maybe designing a few holiday homes to pay her way? Never having to wear a designer suit again. It was a fantasy, of course. She knew that, even as she let the daydreams drift through her mind. Lovely dreams. But dreams weren't reality.

Sam grins. 'You might look like one of us in Ellie's clothes, Princess Grace, but underneath beats the heart of a career woman. I've seen you checking your phone at breakfast.'

'A lot of people check their phone messages in the morning. I need to see if I have to call anyone back.'

'And at dinner.'

She shrugs. 'I have a lot of responsibilities back in London.'

'I'm sure you do. Just be careful you don't miss the important things while you're being so busy.'

'What's more important than work?'

'Life, Princess Grace.'

Sophie presses her lips together. 'Spoken by a man who seems to have given up on it.'

Sam whistles. 'That's harsh.'

Ellie joins them, tucking her arm around Sam's waist. 'This is a lovely birthday treat, Sam. It's so nice of your client to let us go out in the boat today.'

Sam laughs and hugs Ellie against him. 'Do you think I told him, Ellie?'

'Sam! You mean he doesn't know?'

'Oh, he knows we have to take the boat out to check it's running right. That's all he needs to know.'

Picking up a pair of binoculars, Sophie scans the water for a waterspout. 'Emmett didn't want to come?'

'No,' Ellie says as she roots around the icebox. She pulls out two bottles of Coke. 'He's still upset about yesterday. He just needs some time. He'll come around.'

Sophie sets down the binoculars. 'I'm afraid I owe him an apology.'

'Why's that, Sophie?' Ellie asks.

'I ... I asked Florie if he was trustworthy. I'm so sorry, Aunt Ellie. You hear stories ...'

'Sophie! Emmy would never! He's my son. How could you think that?'

Sophie feels the blood rise in her cheeks. 'Of course, of course. I know. I'm so sorry. I was out of line.'

Becca taps Sophie on the arm, signing excitedly. In front of the boat, at the foot of the lighthouse, the glistening grey back of a whale curves amongst the waves and slides into the blue-grey depths.

'Oh my God. That was a whale.'

Sam nods. 'It sure was. A humpback.' He steers the cruiser into the cove below the lighthouse. A spray of water shoots up through the waves, dissipating into a cloud of fine mist.

Becca jumps up and down in front of the window. Folding her right arm across her body, she raises the thumb and pinkie of her left hand, waving it up and down behind her right arm.

'What are you saying, Becca?' Sophie asks as she signs.

'She's saying *whales*,' Ellie says, offering Sophie a Coke. 'I'm sorry I was sharp.'

Sophie accepts the offering. 'It's okay. I'm sorry I upset you.' She sets the Coke on a ledge and signs to Becca. 'Teach me.'

Sophie copies the movements of Becca's arms and fingers. 'How was that?'

Becca places the fingers of her right hand against her mouth, then rests her right hand in the palm of her left.

'Good,' Sam says, cutting the engine and releasing the anchor. He smiles at Sophie. 'Really good.'

Becca signs something at Sam.

'Yes, honey. Me too.'

Sophie looks at Sam. 'What did she say?'

He takes off his cap and rubs his forehead. 'She said she wishes her mother were here, too.' He peers through the window, scanning the top of the rippling water. 'This is as good a place as any to stop. We're far enough away not to bother them. We should be able to see plenty from here.'

As if on cue, the great grey-black body of a humpback soars out of the water. Its white belly and flippers glisten in the sunlight as it thrusts its bulk backwards onto the surface, throwing up a storm of foaming waves as it crashes back into the ocean.

Florie staggers across the juddering boat and joins them on the bridge. 'My God, b'y. This is as bad as the Port aux Basques ferry in January.'

A second whale, even larger than the first, breaches and slams back into the cove, sending a spray of water splashing across the cruiser's window.

'How's that for a birthday present, Ellie, my girl,' Florie says as she squints into the binoculars. 'Ordered specially for the day.'

One of the whales arches through the water and slides back into the waves until only its black and white flukes hover above the surface, before they, too, disappear into the sea.

A bright smile breaks across Ellie's face. 'You know, Sam, this is the first time I've been this close to the whales.'

Sophie reaches for the Coke and flips off the cap on the edge of the ledge. 'Really, Aunt Ellie? Uncle Thomas never brought you out to see them?'

Ellie laughs. 'Oh, no. You didn't do that kind of thing back then. But Thomas loved the whales. He had lots of stories about seeing them when he was out fishing. He said they were a good omen.'

Florie pulls the basket of food out of the store cupboard. 'Right, so. Anybody as gut-foundered as me? We've gots egg salad and ham and mustard, not forgetting Becca's date squares, of course. Don't eat too much, though. We've got baked cod, brewis and scrunchions and my special recipe birthday cake for supper, and I expects everyone to have a piece of that.'

# *Chapter 34*

## Norwich, England – 4 October 1942

Dottie is reaching the crescendo of 'Ode to Joy' when she hears someone knocking loudly on the door.

'Hello? Hello? Anybody home?'

Huffing, she slides off the piano bench and stomps across the sitting room carpet and out into the hallway. She opens the door. A telegraph boy in a navy-blue uniform and pillbox hat edged in red piping fidgets on the stoop. He thrusts out his hand.

'Telegram.'

'Telegram?'

'For, uh, Ellie Burgess. Any reply?'

'I'll take that.' Dottie tears open the envelope before the boy has a chance to object.

3.45 LONDON

DEAR ELLIE MAE – REGISTRY OFFICE SORTED – OCT 11 2PM – MEET YOU LIVERPOOL ST IN MORNING – BRING MARRIAGE LICENCE – I LOVE YOU – THOMAS

Dottie gasps. She glances at the telegram boy and shakes her head. 'No reply.'

Clutching the telegram, Dottie steps back into the hallway and shuts the door. She wanders into the kitchen and spies Ellie through the open window, bent over a flower bed, humming as she pulls weeds from between the parsnips.

Dottie sits on a chair by the table. She fingers the telegram and a thought grows in her mind. Ellie opens the kitchen door and Dottie slides the telegram into the pocket of her skirt.

'Can you believe this weather, Dottie? It's like summer out there today.' She turns on the tap at the sink and washes the dirt off her hands. 'Was there someone at the door? I thought I heard a bicycle bell. We really must get the doorbell fixed.'

'You must have heard me on the piano. I'm practising Beethoven's 'Ode to Joy'.'

Ellie picks up the kettle. 'Would you like some tea? I'm about to put the kettle on.'

'Yes, please, but I'll have to run out to the Co-op for some milk. Poppy had the last of it this morning.'

'All right. Be sure to shut the gate. You haven't found the key, have you? Poppy's misplaced it somewhere.'

Dottie shakes her head as she rushes out of the kitchen.

'And pick up some Robertson's! Poppy's eaten it all. Marmalade if they have it.'

Dottie slams the front gate shut and turns right down the road. Her mind is a whirl. Should she run across the quad and meet up with Poppy when lessons were finished and show him the telegram? Or should she just ... tear it up? Poppy would be so upset if he read it. Ellie would get into so much trouble. That would be good to see. Saint Ellie could do no wrong in Poppy's eyes.

The thought that had planted itself in her mind like a seed

grows, as strong as a weed. If Ellie thinks Thomas has gone off and forgotten about her, maybe she'll start thinking about George again. She'll forget all about Thomas and stay here in Norwich with her and Poppy and George. They'll be a family together, the way it's supposed to be.

She didn't like Thomas at all. Sure, he was handsome, and he could be funny, though his friend Charlie was much funnier. But, he wasn't George. She could get George to do anything she wanted. So what if it was just because he wanted to make Ellie happy? She didn't care. George was sweet. A bit dull – even she could see that – but sweet. Thomas was, well, he never paid her any notice, and that just wouldn't do at all.

Dottie stops on the corner by the church and unfolds the telegram. Why did Thomas have to come to Norfolk and make a mess of everything? She takes a deep breath and tears the telegram in two. She's about to tear it again when she stops.

*No, Dottie. No, you never know when it might come in handy. Ellie would never want Poppy to see it. Trying to keep everything a secret, weren't you, Ellie?*

She folds the two pieces of paper together and slides them back into her pocket. She'll keep the telegram. Put it in a safe place. You never know when it might come in handy.

# Chapter 35

## Tippy's Tickle – 16 September 2001

Emmett grasps the jagged rock at the face of the cave and pulls himself up the cliff face until he secures a foothold on the cave floor. He clambers into the cool dampness, the safe place.

He'd had to come the long way today, and hide the boat behind some rocks on the far side of the headland at Seal Point, what with Sam coming out this way on the cruiser with the others later. Tricky manoeuvring that, what with the waves, but luckily the wind wasn't up too much. Another couple of weeks and the waves would make getting to the cave impossible. Winter was hard. No place to escape to. No place to go where he couldn't be bothered by anyone. Eight months before he could get back to his cave.

Everybody's a busybody in a small place like Tippy's Tickle. Sam'd said once you could disappear in a big city like Boston. People keeps to themselves. That'd suit him just fine.

Unlooping his brown leather satchel, he takes out a paper bag and two of his mother's white linen napkins. Spreading one of the napkins out over a flat rock at the mouth of the cave, he unloads the paper bag: a chicken sandwich, a dill pickle, a piece of blueberry duff, a bottle of Molson's Canadian. He tucks the other napkin into his shirt collar and settles back to eat.

Emmett wipes his face with his handkerchief and rolls up the paper bag and the two napkins and stuffs them back into his satchel. Reaching into the bag, he removes a stack of papers. He slides out one of the papers and reads.

Something out on the water below the cliff catches his eye. The cruiser. He shrinks back against the cave wall. He can just make them out. Sam at the wheel with Becca, his mother and that Englishwoman. The boat comes to a stop. Florie totters from the stern to join the others just as a humpback breaches near the boat. Becca jumps around, clapping her hands.

Relief floods over him, like the warmth of the sun breaking through a thundercloud. *Becca seems all right for all she went through yesterday. The fairies must'a just wanted to play.*

He takes a swig of beer and slides out another piece of paper. Wiping his mouth with the back of his hand, he settles down to read.

# Chapter 36

## Norwich, England – 13 November 1942

Ellie reaches into the drawer and lifts out the folded pink nylon negligee. She sits on the bed and runs he hands over the silky fabric. It had been dear, a week's wages and eleven clothing coupons from the ration book, but she'd wanted to look special on her wedding night. The wedding night that hadn't happened.

*Thomas, why didn't you telegram me like we'd agreed? I was ready to jump on the train to London. What happened? Did you change your mind? Are we still engaged? What am I to think, Thomas?*

She carefully unfolds the negligee. Her heart jumps in her chest. She drops to her knees, searching under the bed and the chest of drawers. Nothing.

Where's her engagement ring?

She roots through the underwear and nighties in the drawer. She'd put the velvet box in here, folded inside her negligee. She knows she did.

She closes the drawer and stands up. She looks into the mirror sitting on top the chest of drawers. Drumming her fingers on the lace doily, she draws her eyebrows together in a frown.

Dottie.

* * *

'Ellie? What are you doing in my room?'

Ellie looks up at her sister from the window bench, the navy velvet jewellery box in her lap. She holds out the telegram. 'What's this?'

'You shouldn't have been looking in my room!'

'This is my telegram. What are you doing with it?'

Dottie rushes forward and snatches for the sheet of yellow paper. Ellie jerks it away. 'It's *my* telegram, Dottie! I was supposed to go to London to marry Thomas. He'll think I ... he'll think I—' She presses her hand against her mouth. 'Oh, Dottie, how could you? This is an evil thing you've done.'

Dottie stamps around the room, her arms wrapped around her body. 'I'm going to tell Poppy you went through my things.'

'Dottie! What's got into you? You stole my engagement ring *and* you hid a telegram meant for me. A very important telegram. Poppy would be appalled! Poor Mummy must be spinning in her grave.'

'Don't you talk about Mummy like that!'

'Well, it's true, Dottie! It's shocking what you did. It's theft, pure and simple. It's a sin.'

Dottie throws herself onto the bed and bursts into tears. 'You're awful, Ellie! You're awful! You were going to just run away!'

'I wasn't going to just run away. I was coming back. I was only going to be gone a few days.'

'You were! You were running away! You were leaving me and Poppy behind!'

'I wasn't, Dottie!'

'Wait till I tell Poppy!'

'No, don't do that. Don't tell Poppy. Promise me. This whole thing will only upset him. I'm still here. Nothing's changed.'

'You were going to leave! Just like Mummy did.'

'What do you mean?'

Dottie sits up and wipes at her tear-streaked face. 'Mummy left us, didn't she?'

'It was an accident, Dottie. You know that. You were there.'

A sob escapes from Dottie's mouth. 'Don't leave me, Ellie. Please don't leave me.'

Ellie sets down the telegram and walks over to the bed. Sitting down, she hugs Dottie. 'I won't leave you, Dottie. I promise. We're sisters, aren't we? If you promise not to tell Poppy about the engagement, I won't tell him that you've turned into a little thief.'

Dottie sniffs and nods. She doesn't need to tell Ellie that Thomas rang from the train station. That she'd promised him to tell Ellie he'd rung. Ellie doesn't need to know that. Maybe Thomas would never come back. That would be the best thing. Everything was fine now. Everything would be fine.

# *Chapter 37*

## Tippy's Tickle – 16 September 2001

Florie sets three cake tins on the kitchen table with a piece of oily paper covered with blue-inked scribbles. 'Right. Are you sure you knows what you're doin'? You have baked a cake before?'

'Well, I used to help my mother occasionally,' Sophie says as she fishes two wooden spoons out of the cutlery drawer. 'I'm sure Becca and I can figure it out, can't we, Becca?'

Becca nods and signs, 'Yes!'

'Off you go, Florie. Go spend some time with Ellie. Just show me how to turn on the oven.'

'You don't knows how to turn on the oven? This is gonna go well.' Florie twists a knob and sets the temperature. 'Don't put the cake into the oven until that red light – you see that little light there? – until that light goes off or the cake'll come out flat as a pancake.'

'Got it.'

'Right. I'm thinkin' I'm makin' a big mistake here.'

'Go, Florie.' Sophie marches her towards the door to the hallway. 'We'll do you proud, won't we, Becca?'

Becca signs to Florie.

'*Oh, is that right, maid?*' Florie signs back. '*The best birthday cake Ellie's ever had? Better than my cakes? We'll see about that.*'

Sophie ties on a pink-flowered apron and gestures for Becca to turn around as she ties a yellow apron with bee pockets around the girl's tiny waist. 'Okay, Becca. Do you know where Florie keeps the flour?'

Becca takes Sophie's hand and leads her into the pantry. Sophie holds up Florie's scribbled recipe. Pointing at the paper, Becca signs to Sophie.

Sophie shakes her head. 'I'm sorry, Becca. I don't understand.'

Becca lets out a loud huff. She points at the word *flour* and signs it. Sophie copies her, the recipe fluttering through the air with her movements. *'Flour. Right, I get it.'*

Becca points to a top shelf and Sophie reaches for the large yellow bag of Robin Hood flour and sets it on the floor. 'Okay, boss, what's next?'

Becca points to the next ingredient on the list and signs *cocoa*.

'Got it.' Sophie signs *cocoa*. She scans the shelves until she finds the can of Fry's Cocoa. She points at a bag of sugar. 'We need sugar, right?'

Becca nods and signs *sugar*.

Sophie tosses Becca the bag of sugar. 'We make a great team, Becca. This cake is going to be awesome.'

Sam jabs his finger into the bowl of chocolate icing and sticks it in his mouth. Becca slaps his hand and signs at her father.

'Oh, really, Becca-bug? I'm naughty, am I?'

'Get your hand out of there, Sam,' Sophie says as she sets a china cake stand on the yellow checked oilcloth she's draped over the mahogany table. 'We have a lot of cake to frost. Just look at them. They turned out great.'

Sam leans over one of the rounds of chocolate cake cooling

on racks on the table. 'Smells fantastic.' He looks over at Becca. 'Maybe I can have just a little piece now.'

Becca shakes her head, her blonde ponytails bouncing either side of her face. *'No, no, no, Daddy. It's for Gramma's birthday,'* she signs.

*'If you don't tell Gramma, I won't.'* Sam takes a fork off the table and makes to stab at the cake.

Sophie dives at the fork. 'Oh, no you don't! Give me that fork, Sam.'

Sam hides the fork behind his back. 'I'm having that cake, Princess Grace.'

Becca giggles soundlessly, clapping her hands and stamping her feet as Sophie grabs for the fork.

'Give me that fork!'

Sam holds the fork above his head. 'I don't think so. Rupert! Get away from that cake!'

The dog barks out several loud *woofs*.

The screen door flies open and Florie enters the kitchen carrying packages of birthday candles. 'Jaysus Murphy, you could wake the dead with all this racket. Look at the state of this place. Did you use every bowl in the kitchen? I thought you said you knew how to bake.'

'We do know how to bake now, don't we, Becca?'

Becca runs over to Sophie and gives her a hug. She smiles at her father, signing.

Sam looks at Sophie and nods. *'Yes, Becca. I think you make a great team, too.'*

# Chapter 38

## Letters – Winter 1942–1943

166th (Newfoundland) Field Regiment
c/o APS Algiers, Tunisia
December 11th, 1942

My darling Ellie Mae,

Here I am in Africa. Not a place I ever thought I'd set foot in. You probably heard what's going on here on the wireless. The Newfoundlanders have been in the thick of it. Can't say more than that, as I know they'll take their black pen and XXXXXXXXXXXXX.

What happened, maid? I waited for you at Liverpool Station. Sent the telegram out to you a week before to let you know where and when. I stood there all day. Must have smoked three packets of cigarettes, and I don't normally smoke! I tried calling the fire station, but the phone just rang on. I called your house and got hold of Dottie. She said you were out with George. I told her to tell you that I love you. I made her swear. They shipped us out shortly after that. My heart's down in my shoes, Ellie Mae, and that's not a good place for it at all.

Write to me, maid, please? Send it to the Army Postal Service in Algiers. The office has just been opened or I'd have written sooner.

*It's awful not hearing from you. It's a feeling worse than pulling up your squid jigs and finding them empty. That's a terrible thing, let me tell you.*

*I miss you, maid. Even more than I miss my mam's cod and brewis, and that's saying a lot. Once you taste it, you'll know what I'm saying.*

*My darling, I think about you from the moment I wake up to the moment I fall asleep – did you know it's as cold as a turr on a ballycatter here at night? Never thought the desert would be cold. You learn something every day.*

*Tell me about the fire station and your sister and your dad. Tell me everything you're doing. I want to imagine it all. You don't know how much thinking about you gets me through these days.*

*If I don't hear back from you, I'll guess that you've had some sense talked at you and you've decided to give me the heave-ho. It'll break my heart, maid. I expect George is buzzing around you like a nipper in August. I'll bet he danced a jig when I was gone.*

*I love you, Ellie Mae. You know I do.*
*Thomas*

*PS: I've just looked. My heart's still in my shoes.*

*Headmaster's House*
*St Bartholomew's Catholic School for Boys*
*Norwich, Norfolk*
*February 5th, 1943*

*My dearest Thomas,*
*I can't tell you how happy I was to receive your letter! Yes, my darling, I'm here in Norwich, working at the fire station*

as I ever was, missing you every day. Poppy and Dottie are well, though Dottie has taken to moping about and being cross with me when I tell her I'm not interested in getting back with George since you left, except as a friend, of course.

I waited for your telegram. After you left, I listened for the telegram boy every day when I was home. It was the first question I'd ask Poppy and Dottie when I arrived home from work. But it never came. I thought you'd changed your mind. I thought, once you'd got to London, you'd realised how impossible it was for us to even think of a life together. We're from different parts of the world, you're Protestant and I'm Catholic, and you said your mother warned you about Catholic girls!

I was so upset. I'd sit in Chapelfield Gardens in my lunchtime and cry. I walked in Plantation Garden and cried. I cried all over Norwich! I'd take my engagement ring out of the box and put it on when I was alone in my room. I'd pretend you were about to arrive. I'd dress up in the green dress you like and even put on the lipstick you got me from the GIs. I'd imagine us dancing at the Samson. Then, of course, I'd cry.

Then, a couple of months after you left Norwich, I found your telegram in a drawer in Dottie's room. I went quite mad with her, you can imagine! And after I read in your letter that you'd rung the house and spoken to Dottie, well, I was very, very cross indeed! And she said she'd forgotten you'd rung! I honestly don't know what's got into her. She's become a right little madam. I've barely spoken to her since. I'm still very cross with her.

Here's me running on about my sister problems. Darling

*Thomas, my heart is soaring and I'm happy as I've ever been. I'm waiting for you, my darling. Come back to me. I'll be here.*

*Your loving fiancée,*
*Ellie Mae*

# *Chapter 39*

## Tippy's Tickle – 16 September 2001

Emmett heads further into the cave and steps onto a calcified ledge, reaching around a stalactite for the cloth bag. He unties the drawstring and lifts out a package the size of a basket-ball wrapped in one of Florie's red bandanas. Unwrapping the bandana, he runs his hands over the gift he's been working on for the past few months.

He doesn't know where he got the idea from. It just came to him, as things often do, out of the blue. Just pieces of driftwood and old lobster traps he's carved up and slotted together, like putting one of his mother's puzzles together, until it has formed into a vase the shape of the earth. A flat-bottomed earth, open on top.

She probably didn't even have a gift for his mam, seeing how she'd just showed up out of nowhere. His cousin, Mam had said. He didn't need a cousin. They'd all been just fine without her. People complicated things, like when Sam came.

He'd been happy doing his boat work. He'd saved hard to buy Rod Fizzard's old store. No one bothered him there. Home for noon dinner and supper, prayers and bed. Church on Sunday. Going out in the boat whenever he wanted. Now he's got Sam there down at the store. He did that for his mam; took Sam on as a favour. And even though they got through more work, it wasn't the same. It wasn't the same as being on his own.

Sooner they both left, the better.

He wraps the vase back up in the bandana and tucks it into the cloth bag. Time to get back to the house. He can't wait to see his mam's face when she sees his gift. Nothing is too good for his mam.

*I'll set things right for you, Mam, don't you worry. Don't you worry at all.*

# *Chapter 40*

## Norwich, England – 24 December 1943

The large red bauble sits like a newborn in its swaddling of newspaper. Ellie lifts it carefully out of its wrapping and holds it up to the ceiling light, smiling at her distorted reflection in the round ball. It had always been her favourite, and it had somehow managed to escape unscathed through twenty-one years of curious cats and Christmas trees pulled down by grasping toddlers. She rests it back in its newspaper nest and picks up the string of coloured light bulbs, wrapping the string around her arm until it's a neat loop. Another Christmas without the lights. An extravagance too far while the war staggered into another year.

Tidying the lights away into a cardboard box, Ellie sits back on her heels and frowns at the space she's cleared in the corner for the Christmas tree. The metal tree stand is ready. She's had to banish her father's footstool to the hallway to make room. He'll grumble, like he always does. Another Christmas tradition.

She reaches into her apron pocket and takes out the one-page letter, the last one she'd received back in June. She unfolds it again, for the hundredth time, and rereads the scrawling handwriting.

*166th (Newfoundland) Field Regiment*
*c/o APS Algiers, Tunisia*
*May 6th, 1943*

*My darling Ellie Mae,*
*I must keep this short, darling, as we're on the move. All is well in XXXXXXXX. Thanks so much for the package. Socks were just the ticket. It's cold enough to skin you at night, and hot enough to poison you in the day. All the fellows enjoyed the chocolate. Where'd you get that from, maid? Did you wheedle it out of George?*

*I think of you all the time, my darling. Can't tell you much more than they're keeping us busy here. May be heading to XXXXXXX next. Don't know when we'll be back in England again. Guess that depends on old Hitler.*

*I've learnt a new word. Habibati. It means darling in Arabic.*
*I'll see you in my dreams, habibati.*
*Your loving Thomas*

She refolds the letter and tucks it back into her apron pocket. Not a word from him since then, despite the letters she'd written him every week. *Where are you, Thomas? Are you safe? Are you even alive? Why don't you write? It's so hard, Thomas. The not knowing. Sometimes I— You don't know what it's like, the not knowing. It's so very, very hard.*

Over a year now since she'd last seen him, at the Cow Tower by the riverside that September when he'd given her the beautiful Art Deco engagement ring. Where he'd got it from, or how he'd afforded it, she couldn't begin to imagine. She'd thought it best to keep the engagement secret, with Thomas away. How do you tell your Catholic father that you're marrying a Protestant foreigner and moving to a place thousands of miles away? How do you tell your ex-fiancé, who mopes around you like a sad dog, that you're engaged to someone else? It had just seemed best to carry on as normal. As if nothing had changed.

She hadn't accounted for Dottie poking through her things and stealing the ring. And not only the ring. Thomas's telegram too! What had got in to Dottie? Why had she done these horrible things?

She unsticks a needle from her sleeve and takes a spool of white thread from her apron pocket. Threading the needle, she picks a fat white piece of popcorn from a bowl on the coffee table and sticks the needle through its spongy skin. At least Dottie's kept her promise. She hasn't told Poppy about the engagement. And Ellie hasn't revealed Dottie's thievery to Poppy. It is an uneasy truce.

She closes her eyes and tries to paint the picture of Thomas's face in her mind's eye, but it's like water has been spilled over the painting, washing out the colours and lines.

Nothing to do but to keep going. Wake up in the morning, wash, put on her uniform, ride to the fire station on the bicycle Poppy gave her for her birthday, type and file and make sandwiches and tea and deliver them to the firemen in the staff car, ride her bike home, cook supper, sleep. Then do it all again the next day. She was sleepwalking through her life, but was that so bad when so many others had lost everything? She still had the memory of Thomas, and she clung to it like it was a life preserver.

At night she'd tuck herself around her spare pillow and imagine it was Thomas; bury her face into the soft feather pillow and pretend it was the rough wool of his uniform, that its scent was Thomas's scent of musk and soap. She closes her eyes. *Be safe, my darling. Come back to me. Come back to me soon.*

The front door swings open and Dottie rushes into the sitting room, like a colt bolting from its stable. Ellie looks up. When did her sister become so tall? Fourteen now. How had she not noticed?

'Ellie! George found us the biggest tree! Bonds had a stack of them brought down from Scotland.'

'George helped you?'

'We bumped into him in the market.' Dottie smiles slyly at Ellie as she unwinds her scarf. 'I think he was buying you a present. He hid it when he saw us.'

Henry Burgess stomps into the hallway, dragging an enormous fir tree. 'Lift it up, George,' he calls over his shoulder. 'Careful of the telephone stand.'

He veers through the archway into the sitting room, George shuffling after him as he grapples with the bulk of evergreen fronds. 'Out of the way, Dottie, pet. Find an old blanket for us to lay this on till we put it up.'

Ellie springs to her feet and pushes her father's chair out of the way. 'Good heavens, Poppy. We're going to have to cut off the base to make it fit.'

'Dottie insisted George find us the biggest one.' Henry coughs into his handkerchief. 'You know she has him wound around her little finger.'

Dottie gallops back into the room, the cat dashing ahead, and tosses an end of the blanket to Ellie. They arrange it over the carpet as Henry and George manoeuvre the tree into place. They lay it down, its branches fanning out and creeping under the sofa and coffee table. The cat jumps on top, kneading the green bulk before it settles down purring.

Ellie sets her hands on her hips. 'Right. Dottie, show George where the saw is in the cellar. This is going to take some planning.'

Henry rises out of his armchair and yawns as he stretches. He sets his sherry glass on the coffee table and stands in front of the tree. 'You've done a grand job, girls.'

Ellie glares at her sister. 'No thanks to Dottie.'

Dottie grimaces at Ellie from the carpet, where she's curled up petting the cat. 'Stringing popcorn is boring. And you always move where I put the baubles anyway.'

'The colours need to balance. You can't put all the red decorations together. It doesn't look right.'

'Spoken like a true artist.' Henry taps Dottie's foot with his slipper. 'Time for bed, pet. We'll be up early for Christmas Mass.'

Dottie groans. 'Oh, Poppy, do we have to? Can't we just open presents and have a nice breakfast, play charades and listen to the king? Why do we always have to go to boring old mass?'

'Because we're good Catholics and we have to set an example for the boys who are boarding at St Bart's over Christmas.'

'Best listen to your father, Dottie,' George says as he collects the last of the sawn-off branches.

Rising to her feet, Dottie picks up the cat and buries her face into its patchwork fur. 'I guess we better go, Berkeley.' Dottie smiles at George. 'Thanks for helping with the tree, George, even if you did have to saw off three feet.'

George makes an exaggerated bow. 'Always at your service, Dottie.'

Dottie glances at a box wrapped in brown paper under the tree with a tag: *To Dottie From George*. 'What did you get me, George?'

'You'll find that out in the morning, pet,' Henry says as he heads towards the hallway. He waves his rolled-up newspaper in the air. 'Goodnight, all. Happy Christmas. Come along, Dottie. Thank George for the present.'

Dottie waves Berkeley Square's paw at George. 'Goodnight. Thank you for the present. I'm sure I'll love it.'

Ellie collects the empty sherry glass. 'Can I get you anything else, George? I should be getting to bed too.'

George clears his throat. Reaching into his pocket, he takes out a small box wrapped in the same brown paper. 'I ... I just wanted to give you this, El.'

'Oh, George, you really didn't have to. I haven't anything for you.'

'That's all right.' He holds out the box. 'Please, open it.'

Sighing, she takes the box. She tears off the paper and lifts off the cardboard cover. 'Oh, my word.'

George removes the ring with its tiny diamond from the box. Kneeling on one knee, he holds it up to Ellie. 'Will you marry me, Ellie? I've been an idiot. I'll never forgive myself for taking you for granted. I've got to thank Thomas, because it took that ... that situation to knock some sense into me. I love you, Ellie.' He clears his throat again. 'Will you be my wife?'

Ellie's stares at George's earnest face, at the neatly combed black hair with its slick of hair oil, at the solemn brown eyes behind his tortoiseshell glasses. 'George, I—'

'Looks like I got here in the nick of time.' Thomas stands under the archway, tall as ever, but his long, handsome face is leaner and shadowed with the need for a shave.

'Thomas!' Ellie rushes past the tree and throws herself into his embrace.

'I'm sorry, George,' Thomas says over Ellie's shoulder. 'I'm cutting in.' He looks back at Ellie. 'Have you got the marriage licence, maid? I've only wangled a few days' leave.'

'I have! I've had it a year. I've been waiting for you, Thomas.'

George rises to his feet. 'You made me think I had a chance, Ellie. All this time, I thought it was over between you two.'

'I'm awfully sorry, George. I didn't mean— We're just friends, George. I love Thomas. We're getting married. We've been planning to for over a year.'

George sets the ring into the box and replaces the lid. 'Just friends? You were never just a friend to me, Ellie. I thought you knew that.'

Walking past the lovers, he enters the hall and picks his coat off the coat hook. He steps outside onto the stone stoop. A fog sits like a veil over the garden, obscuring all but the tallest Gothic spires of the boys' school next door. Closing the heavy door quietly behind him, he heads down the steps into the ghostly night.

On the top step of the staircase landing, Dottie clings to the banisters as she spies on Ellie and Thomas through the open door of the living room. Berkeley Square steps delicately into her lap. She grabs it by the fur on its neck and pushes it away.

*You promised me, Ellie. You promised me you wouldn't leave me and Poppy. You cheated on George and you're a liar too. You're mean and selfish. I don't care if you are my sister. I hate you, Ellie. I hate you. I hate you. I hate you.*

# *Chapter 41*

## Tippy's Tickle – 16 September 2001

'Happy birthday to you! Happy birthday to you! Happy birthday, dear Ellieeeee! Happy birthday to you!'

Florie parades through the kitchen, the four dachshunds scampering through her legs, carrying Sophie's and Becca's towering chocolate cake aflame with tiny candles. She sets the cake on the table.

'There you goes, Ellie. Created by the fair hands of your niece and your granddaughter. I couldn't get seventy-nine candles on the cake. You'll just have to pretend.' She frowns down at the barking dachshunds. 'Oh, me nerves, girls. You'll be the death of me yet. Face down in a chocolate cake on the kitchen floor.'

Jumping up from her chair, Becca signs excitedly at Ellie.

*'Of course, Becca,'* Ellie says, signing back. *'Help me blow out the candles. Hurry! They're melting into the cake, and it's such a lovely cake. You and Sophie did a wonderful job.'*

The girl and her grandmother lean over the cake and blow into the flames, extinguishing all but two. Becca signs at her father.

Sam looks over at Sophie. 'She wants you to blow those out, Princess Grace.'

'Oh. Okay.' Sucking in an exaggerated breath, she blows out the two sputtering candles.

Ellie picks up a knife and holds it, poised, over the creamy chocolate icing. 'Help me cut the cake, Becca. None for Rupert or the doxxies. Chocolate's not good for dogs.'

'None for me, Florie,' Sophie says, patting her stomach. 'I could barely zip up my skirt this morning.'

At the sound of his name, Rupert raises his great black head up from where he's been snoozing by the door. Turning his head towards the door, he emits a husky *woof*. The door swings open and Emmett enters, carrying a cloth bag and a guitar.

'There you are, b'y!' Florie says as she licks icing off her bottom lip. 'We thought you'd fallen off the wharf. Come in and have some birthday cake. Good, you've brought your guitar. We're all set for a right good kitchen party now.'

Emmett shuts the door and pulls up a chair next to Sam. He thrusts the cloth bag across the table at Ellie. 'Happy Birthday, Mam.'

'Oh, thank you, Emmy!' Ellie holds up the bag and shakes it beside her ear. 'What is it?'

Emmett frowns. 'You has to open it.'

'Of course I do. Silly me.' Opening the bag, she pulls out something wrapped in a red bandana. Untying the bandana, she holds up a spherical vase the size of a basketball, constructed of an intricate design of dark and light wood polished to a soft gleam. 'Oh, Emmy, it's lovely!'

'I used bits of wood from Silas Feltham's old boat and some lobster traps.' Emmett shrugs. Was just rotting down by the tickle. Figured no one would miss it. Didn't cost me anything to do.'

Ellie hands the vase to Sophie who runs her hand over the smooth surface. 'It must have taken you hours to do this, Emmett. It's stunning.'

'I gots time.'

'Have you ever thought of making things like this to sell?' Sophie asks. 'You could make beautiful objects like this for Sam's business. People in places like London and New York would spend a lot of money on this kind of quality.'

Emmett grunts. 'Why would I wants to do that? I has my own business already. I don't needs to work for Sam.'

'Well, you could make more money.'

'Where am I gonna spend money here? I gots everything I need.'

Sam takes the vase from Sophie. 'There's more to life than working all hours of the day just to have a bigger house or a fancy car.'

'Everyone needs to earn a living.'

'We manage just fine.'

'But there must be things you want. Things you'd like to be able to afford.'

'Sure.' Sam turns the vase around in his hands. 'I'd like a boat like the one we went out in today. I'd like a new pickup truck.' He shrugs. 'But I can live without them. They're not what's important. I've got plenty of work putting in kitchens and bathrooms in Wesleyville and Musgrave Harbour when Emmett doesn't need help on the boats. And the furniture sells at a fair price when someone buys it. We're good.'

He sets the vase on the table and reaches over to hug Becca against his side. She holds out a fork with a large piece of her cake to her father and he takes a bite. He swallows the cake and smiles at Sophie, chocolate crumbs around his mouth. 'Now, birthday cake is important. Especially if it's chocolate.' He picks up a slice of cake and holds it out to Sophie. 'Go on, Princess Grace. Live a little. Have some of your cake. He takes a bite, icing spreading onto his nose. 'It's delicious.'

Sophie waves her hand at him. 'No, really. I'm fine.'

Becca claps her hands and signs to her.

'Becca insists,' Sam says, approaching her.

'No, Sam. Really ...'

Too late.

'Sam!' She glares at Sam as she wipes at the icing smeared across her face and licks cake and icing off her lips.

'Ooh, Sam,' Florie says, sucking the air in between her teeth. 'You're playing with fire, there, b'y.'

Becca jumps around the kitchen clapping her hands, setting the dachshunds off into a chorus of yapping.

Sophie licks her finger and nods. 'Wow. You're absolutely right, Sam. That really is very good chocolate cake. Cut me another piece, will you, Florie?'

Emmett picks up the guitar and begins to strum a jig, his long fingers flying over the strings.

'Doxxies are all tucked up in the kennel,' Florie says as she enters the kitchen through the screen door. 'Well, now, looks like the party's started! C'mon, Rupert, out you go, you big lump. We needs space to stomp about.' She beckons to Becca. 'C'mon, duckie. Music's started. That's our cue.'

Becca runs ahead of Florie out into the hallway. A few minutes later, the reedy bellowing of an accordion and a tinny jangling announce their return. They march into the room and around the table, Florie pounding out a harmony to Emmett's jig on the accordion. Becca jabs what looks like a rubber-booted mop hung with bottle caps onto the floor while she hits the caps with a drumstick.

Sophie points to the stick. 'What on earth is that?'

'It's an Ugly Stick,' Sam says as he pulls a harmonica out of the pocket of his jean jacket. 'It's not a kitchen party without one.' He joins in on the harmonica as Ellie drums out the rhythm on the table top with her hands.

Emmett segues into another spirited tune, similar to the Irish music Sophie had heard once in a Dublin pub, when she'd been entertained by an Irish client who'd had more on his mind than the design of his restaurant. Becca thrusts the Ugly Stick and drumstick at her.

'Have a go, Sophie,' Ellie says. 'Go on.'

Sophie stares at the disfigured mop. 'Oh, I couldn't possibly. I don't know how.'

Becca brushes her right hand twice against the back of her left.

'It's easy, Princess Grace,' Sam says as he gets up to get some more beer from the fridge. 'Just bash at it.'

'Thump it on the floor, duck, and whack it with the drumstick,' Florie says as she squeezes a tune out of the accordion.

Sophie jabs the Ugly Stick's rubber boot onto the linoleum. She whacks at the bottle caps, releasing a tinny jangle.

'There you goes, duckie,' Florie says as taps her foot to the music. 'You're a natural. You don't needs any talent at all to plays the Stick.'

Ellie taps Becca's shoulder. 'Come on, sweetie. Let's go dance.'

Becca sits on the floor and pulls off her running shoes. Soon, the two of them are stamping their feet and twirling around the kitchen floor as Rupert adds a baseline of *woofs* from outside on the porch.

Florie picks up the dozing child. 'Time for bed, duckie. School day tomorrow.'

Sam glances at his watch. 'Sorry, Florie. Lost track of time. We should be going.'

'Don't be silly, Sam,' Ellie says as she pours out several cups of tea. 'It's not that late. We'll put her in the attic room. She loves it up there.'

'If you're sure.'

'Yes, don't be silly.' Ellie looks over at Emmett who is tightening the guitar strings. 'Emmy, play the 'St John's Waltz'. I love that one.'

Emmett nods and, strumming out the first lilting chords, begins to sing the ballad in a strong, melodic voice.

Sam holds out his hand to Sophie. 'Let's have a go, then, maid.'

Sophie stares at his hand. Nodding, she slips her hand into his. 'All right.'

He leads her onto the floor and takes her into his embrace. She closes her eyes and leans into him, letting the warmth of his body and the lilting song dissolve her hesitation.

'Are you having a good time, Princess Grace?'

'Yes. Yes, I am. I'm having a wonderful time.'

'Best kind.' Pulling her closer, he leans his cheek against hers as they dance to Emmett's warm tenor singing out the words of the waltz.

# *Chapter 42*

## London, England – 28 December 1943

The thunder of the ack-ack guns on Clapham Common fills the night air, like the harbinger of a storm encroaching on the city. Ellie and Thomas turn left under the rail bridge and head down Balham High Road. At the greengrocer's they dodge across the street and hurry between the tall brick pillars flanking the driveway into Du Cane Court. The hulking shape of the Art Deco building obliterates the sky, its presence only hinted at by the clouds reflected in the moonlit windows.

Ellie follows Thomas through the revolving doors into an elegant marble-tiled lobby. They skirt around the fat black columns uplighting the white ceiling and head towards the lift. The building manager, looking dapper in a brown double-breasted suit, lurks behind the sweeping black lacquered reception desk. A microphone is in his left hand and his face is puckered with annoyance.

'Excuse me?' he says, covering the microphone with his hand. 'May I help you?'

Thomas heads over to the desk and extends his hand. 'Hello, there. Is Reg off tonight, then?'

The building manager raises an arched eyebrow. 'Am I meant to know who you are?' He sweeps his eyes over Ellie's feathered fedora and the tweed coat she has obviously remade from a man's overcoat.

'I'm Frank Edwards's cousin. Twice removed, or somethin' like that. Over from Newfoundland.' Thomas holds up a key. 'He's lettin' us use his flat for a couple of days while I'm on leave.'

Ellie peels off a leather glove and holds up her left hand. A thin gold band shines on her ring finger on top of her engagement ring. 'It's our honeymoon.'

The manager holds up a slender finger and leans into the microphone, which is connected by a thin wire cord to the building's integrated wireless system. 'Du Cane Court calling! Du Cane Court calling! A flat on the second floor in H block has the light on, and the blackout curtains are not drawn.'

The lift dings and the door slides open. A young, dark-haired woman in a black raincoat and a headscarf tied under her chin steps out into the lobby.

'Good evening, Miss Freeman,' the manager says as the young woman walks by, her shoes clicking on the terrazzo floor. 'Isn't it rather late to be going out?'

'Good evening, Mr Jackson,' she calls over her shoulder as she heads out the revolving door. 'I shouldn't think so.'

The manager clears his throat and looks at Thomas. 'You have a marriage licence, I assume?'

'Why's it I knew you'd ask me that?' Thomas unzips his leather satchel and removes a folded piece of paper. 'Here you goes. Signed, sealed and delivered, fresh from Wandsworth Registry Office.'

The man scans the document and sniffs. 'Indeed,' he says, handing back the document. He waves Thomas and Ellie to the lift and leans into the microphone. 'A reminder that Mrs Waring will be reading from her new book of poetry, *Tea Leaves Tell the*

*Tale*, tomorrow night at eight o'clock in the dining room. Please be prompt as latecomers will not be accommodated.'

Thomas unlocks the door and Ellie follows him into the dark apartment. He feels his way around the sofa and pulls the blackout curtains across the large window. Ellie switches on the ceiling light and removes her hat, throwing her coat over the fat arm of a salmon-coloured velvet sofa. She watches Thomas fiddle between the two wireless stations until the strains of 'I'll Never Smile Again' filter out of the wooden box.

She stands on the blue carpet, twisting her wedding band and engagement ring around her finger. 'Tea?'

Walking over to her, Thomas takes her in his arms, leading her in a slow foxtrot. 'I'm not thirsty.' He leans his cheek against her hair. 'I've dreamed about this moment. I'd lie awake in the tent in the desert, freezin'—'

'You said in one of your letters it's freezing in the desert at night. It's hard to imagine.'

'As cold as the North Atlantic in December.'

'Oh, Thomas, you're exaggerating.'

Thomas laughs. 'Maybe a little. But I needs to paint you a picture. I was lyin' there in the tent in the desert, listenin' to Charlie snorin' to beat the band. Night after night. Chasin' the Germans about durin' the day, freezin' at night. So, I'd close my eyes and draw the picture of your face in my mind.' He runs his fingers over a blonde curl. The corner of his mouth lifts in his crooked smile.

'You kept me goin', Ellie Mae. When we shipped out to Italy in October I was like a flea in a dog's ear till they gave me leave. They let me come back with some of the poor fellas who'd been shot up so I could get as many as I could onto a hospital ship back to Halifax once they got patched up in London. They knew if anyone could swing it, I could.'

Ellie frowns. 'Those poor men. What have we done with this world?' She looks at Thomas. 'I'm so glad you came back, Thomas.'

'I had to. I told them I had a beautiful maid to marry.' Thomas grabs her in a bear hug, lifting her up as he kisses her. 'I missed you, m'darling.' Setting her down, his eyes cloud over. 'I've gots to get back on the hospital ship in Southampton day after tomorrow. Headin' back to Italy, but don't tell anyone. It's top secret, but I trusts you.'

'So soon? When will I see you again?'

'As soon as I can, Ellie Mae.' Thomas presses his cheek against hers as they sway to the music. 'Did you miss me, just a mite?'

'Nothing was the same in Norwich when I knew I wouldn't bump into you somewhere. I'd go to Plantation Garden or Cow Tower, even in the market where you stole the hat from me, and I'd imagine you there. I'd imagine us there, together.'

'And at the dances?'

'At the dances, too.'

Thomas laughs. 'So, you went out to all the dances, did you? While I was freezin' my arse off in the desert! There's love for you!'

'It was just George.'

'Poor old George. I swears if I'd been gone longer he would have gotten that ring on your finger. They say it's those quiet ones you've gotta watch.' Thomas taps his eyebrow. 'George gots his eye on you, even if it's a blind one.'

'Don't be ridiculous.'

A deep laugh rumbles from Thomas's throat. 'Oh, no? He was down on one knee the other night.'

Ellie expels an exaggerated sigh. 'He had a ring and everything. I feel quite bad about it, actually.'

'All's fair in love and war.' Thomas slips his hand under Ellie's knees and lifts her into his arms. Laughing, she wraps her hands around his neck.

'What do think you're doing, Mr Parsons?'

'Carryin' you over the threshold, Mrs Parsons.'

'But we're already inside.'

Thomas crosses to the door and pulls it open. He steps into the hallway. Ellie squeals as he adjusts his grip on her.

The door to Number 23 across the hall jerks open and a stout woman in her fifties, in a flowered housecoat and a hairnet, glares at the giggling pair.

Thomas reaches up to tip his beret, prompting another squeal from Ellie.

'Don't mind us, Missus. It's our honeymoon. We'll be quiet as mice.'

# Chapter 43

## Tippy's Tickle – 16 September 2001

Sophie follows Sam and Rupert down a path winding between the spruce trees swaying wildly in the wind being blown across the island by tropical storm Maria. Nestled in a clearing at the bottom of the path, the white clapboard siding of the cottage is a soft grey in the night light, and its angled roof, split to accommodate clerestory windows, juts into the dark sky like a tectonic plate pushing its way skywards.

Pausing on a slate stepping stone, Sophie examines the building as the wind plasters Florie's jumper against her body. 'This looks a lot different from the other houses around here.'

Sam comes up behind her and leans his chin on her shoulder. 'That's because I built it.'

Sophie's heart thrums in her chest. 'You built it?'

'Welcome to Bufflehead Cottage.'

'Bufflehead?'

'It's a small sea duck that puffs out the feathers on its head to make it look bigger. Becca chose the name from a picture book of Newfoundland birds.' Taking hold of Sophie's hand, Sam leads her down the final steps to the front door. He twists the doorknob and then pushes the door open.

'You don't lock your door?'

'No. Why should I?'

'Ellie doesn't lock hers either.'

'Welcome to Tippy's Tickle. Come on, I'll show you around.'

They walk through the enclosed porch and under an archway, Rupert lumbering on ahead, into a large open-plan room with floor-to-ceiling windows on three sides and a wall with four green doors on the fourth. Sam flicks on a switch and light washes over the room from fixtures hidden amongst the exposed beams. A small hand-built kitchen with cupboards painted bright yellow nestles in a corner of the room, separated from the living area by a large fishing net draped from the ceiling, hung with a collection of seashells and driftwood.

Rupert flops onto a large braided rug as Sam strides over to a black wood-burning stove in a corner of the living room. After stuffing in logs and kindling, he lights the wood with a match. He gestures to the room. 'Welcome to our humble abode.'

Sophie surveys the wood-clad walls and the soaring angled ceiling with its row of high-level windows. The furniture is an eclectic mix of comfortable sofas, old antiques and Sam's hand-made furniture pieces: a long dining table with edges following the tree's natural contours; benches almost austere in their simplicity; a rocking chair with slender rockers like curved skis; an armchair with wide flat armrests and a frame similar to a barrel with seat cushions in woven wool; a chair like a large basket hanging from a beam in the corner. She walks over to the windows facing the seaside, but the night is moonless and the sky heavy with cloud, although the sweep and wash of the waves hums through an open window. She notices a framed photograph on a table near the window; Sam, beardless and younger, with an attractive, long-haired blonde woman who is cradling a baby.

'Would you like some wine?' Sam says as he heads into the kitchen. 'I've got some white. Or a beer? I think there's some cranberry juice there too.'

'Wine's good.' She glances over at Sam as he grabs a bottle of Blue Star lager from the fridge and a bottle of white wine. His dark hair is tousled by the wind, and he brushes it back with an unconscious gesture. It's been a long time since she's been in this kind of situation: alone with a man on a night like this. When the warm wind and the humidity thickens blood to a lazy torpidity. When a veil lifts and guards fall.

*What are you doing here, Sophie? You know you're playing with fire. That kiss at the lighthouse was a silly mistake. What on earth came over you? Acting like a bloody teenager. Don't be an idiot. Go! Go, now!*

She's been so careful. All those years in Manchester and London. Careful not to get side-tracked. Careful to keep her eye on the prize: a position at the pinnacle of her profession. She has no room for a man in her life. Certainly not a man like Sam, stuck in a backwater in Newfoundland. He's sacrificed everything for Becca. She could never do that. Not for anyone. But then, she has no one to sacrifice everything for.

Maybe she wants that. Maybe she wants someone to care about. Someone to care about her.

*Stop it, Sophie! Pull yourself together. You don't need anyone. Say your goodbyes.*

She sits on the thick white cotton cushion of the hanging chair and leans back against its curved woven-cane back. The chair swings gently, and she tucks her feet up underneath her.

*No, Mum. I'm not going anywhere.*

'Here you go,' Sam says as he offers her the wine glass. 'Pinot Grigio. Hope that's okay. We eat a lot of Italian food in this house when we're not up at Ellie's. Becca loves pasta. She doesn't drink the wine, though. That's just me.'

He sets down the beer bottle on the coffee table, and, grasping the sides of the hanging chair, gives it a gentle push. 'You found the chair.'

'I did indeed. I've always wanted to sit in a hanging chair.'

Sam gives it another push. 'I put it in for Becca. I used to sit in it when she was smaller and rock her to sleep in it. Now, she calls it her chair. She reads in it for hours with Tigger and Barbie.'

Sophie shifts in the chair. Reaching under the cushion, she pulls out a striped stuffed toy. 'I think I found Tigger.'

Sam laughs and takes the toy. He sits down on the sofa, propping Tigger against a pillow beside him.

'What's all that stuff in the net over there?'

Sam looks over at the net with its tangle of objects. 'That's our Net of Diverse Objects. Ellie named it. Just things Becca and I pick up on the beach. Mostly shells and driftwood, a couple of squid jigs. No plastic yet. They get that down on the south coast. More each year.'

Sophie unfolds one of her legs and pushes at the floor with the toe of Florie's borrowed socks, sending the chair into a gentle swing. 'Sam? You know with all the music tonight ... Can Becca hear it? She seemed to be able to keep the beat.'

'No, she can't hear it, but she's told me she feels the vibrations in the air and coming from the floor. That's why she took off her shoes. So she could feel the vibrations better. She says they're buzzy.'

'Ellie told me Becca can read lips.'

'Yes. Winny thought it would be good for Becca to learn to read lips. Not many people sign, especially hearing people. She thought it would help Becca in school. Life. She's pretty good at it.' Picking up his beer, he takes a drink. 'So, why don't you tell me all about the Millennium Pavilion?'

Sophie's eyes widen. 'You know about that?'

'The internet can be quite useful.'

'You searched my name?'

'You were easy to find. There were—' he counts silently on his fingers '—about twenty pages referencing you. Congratulations. That's quite an achievement.'

Sophie rests a foot on the wooden floor and gives the chair a spin. 'It was. I hired on some fantastic graduates and we pulled out all the stops developing the proposal. It was a long shot for a small practice like mine, but we got it. Then we had to do it. That was terrifying. It's been my life for the past few years.'

'And what about New York?'

'Yes. New York. Well, I was headhunted. I've already had a phone interview. Now I have a second interview and a presentation to do. I'm up against two other candidates. Richard Niven is going to Japan on the nineteenth for two weeks. If I don't make it there by Tuesday, I miss my chance. The other two have already been interviewed.'

'What are you going to do? That's the day after tomorrow.'

What is she going to do? Four days ago all she wanted was to get to New York for the interview. Now, part of her wants nothing more than to stay in Tippy's Tickle and start over. Reboot. She likes herself better here. She laughs more. Feels more. She's picked up Ellie's charcoal drawing pencils and rediscovered something that she'd thought she'd lost. And there's Sam and sweet Becca. Maybe she could care about them and they could care about her. But ... part of her still wants the big job in the big city. It's everything she's ever worked for. It's so close. A hand's reach away. All she needs to do is decide.

'You're not tempted to stay here in beautiful Tippy's Tickle?'

She shoots a look at Sam. Can he read her mind?

She laughs, though it sounds more nervous than she intends. 'What? No, no. Of course not. I'm going to Gander tomorrow. I'll call a taxi. If my plane isn't leaving, I'll find another way. There's a plane leaving from St John's tomorrow night. I'll catch that if I have to.'

Sam's looks at her, his eyes clouding over, and her skin prickles under his gaze. Setting down his beer, he gets up and walks over to the hanging chair. Grabbing hold of the chair frame, he kisses her.

He steps back, his hands on the chair frame. 'I've been wanting to kiss you since last night, when you waited for me and Becca in the rain.'

'Sam, I—'

He kisses her again; long, and slow, taking his time. Taking all the time in the world. He stands back and gives the chair a gentle push.

*Oh, my God. Oh, my God.* Sophie clears her throat, her mind full of the feel of Sam's lips on hers. 'Anybody would have done that.'

'Anybody didn't do that. You did that. The princess with the heart of ice.'

Sophie rubs her lips with her fingers. 'Sam, I shouldn't have kissed you at the lighthouse. I'm going tomorrow ... Our lives are too different—'

'Did anyone ever teach you how to play cribbage?'

'What?'

Sam walks over to a Victorian sidetable and pulls out a drawer. 'Cribbage. I warn you, I take no prisoners.'

'You want me to play cribbage with you?'

'It's either that or Settlers of Catan, but we're missing some pieces. I think Rupert ate them.'

'You're not serious.'

Sam sets out the cribbage board on the coffee table with a stack of playing cards. 'There you go. Red or blue?'

'You want me to play cribbage with you?' she repeats.

'Look, Sophie. You're right. You're leaving tomorrow. I was ... I thought ... Well, never mind. Cribbage is much better than sex, anyway.'

*I like him. I like him a lot.*

Sliding off the hanging chair, Sophie steps over the snoring dog and sits on the sofa. 'I'll be red.'

Sophie turns to Sam at the porch door. 'Thanks, Sam. That was fun.'

'Ah, to think you'll always think of me as the man who introduced you to cribbage.'

She laughs. 'It was fun. Really. I never have a chance to just ... to just be easy. It was easy tonight, with you.'

'That's me. I'm easy.' The corners of his eyes crinkle as he smiles. 'Or, I could be if you'd let me.'

Sophie laughs. 'Be careful what you wish for.'

They stand for a moment, the silence broken only by the thundering waves on the beach below. 'So, I'll call a taxi in the morning.'

'No, I'll drive you.'

'On the bike?'

Sam raises his eyebrows in mock offence. 'Don't you like *Miss Julie*? There's always the old pickup truck, but she could go at any minute.'

'*Miss Julie* is fine.'

'Are you sure you don't want me to walk you back to Ellie's?'

'No, she's just up the hill.'

'Okay. Watch out for those fairies.'

'I will.'

Sam shuts the door behind her. She turns towards the path. The waves crash on the beach below and the branches of the spruce trees whip around her in the growing wind.

She turns back to the cottage. The door opens before she's finished knocking.

'I don't have a heart of ice.'

'I never thought you did.'

# *Chapter 44*

## Monte Cassino, Italy – 19 March 1944

Thomas presses himself against the jagged limestone of the castle's remaining wall. The burnt-out shell of the great Benedictine monastery of Monte Cassino – immolated to sacrificial rubble in the Allied bombing of the previous month – lies ahead on the crest of Monte Cassino, now a nest for the German paratroopers who have dug in, allowing them eagle-eyed views of the smaller Hangman's Hill and Castle Hill below. The strains of a gramophone recording of 'Besame Mucho' drift down from the monastery, filtering through the barrage of Allied artillery guns.

He glances to the south towards Naples. The ink-black sky is washed with a glow of yellow and red where Vesuvius is throwing its innards into the sky. Too far away for them to worry about. There were other things to worry about. Like taking Hangman's Hill without ending up like one of the poor suckers rotting on the rocky hillsides, their bodies blackened by the creosote poured over them to cover the stench.

He fingers the cluster of wilted green weeds pinned to his uniform lapel. 'Italian shamrocks,' Father Ryan had said as he'd handed them out for St Patrick's Day. St Patrick's Day and his own birthday. *Happy Birthday to me. And not even a Catholic.*

He closes his eyes and tries to draw Ellie's face in his mind. Her hair the colour of the sandy beach at Lumsden, her eyes the blue-grey of an August sky over the North Atlantic shore. He breathes deeply, searching for the elusive lavender of her scent. The fingers of his right hand twitch, remembering the warmth of her skin and the hills and valleys of her body.

Machine gun fire blasts through the sharp pre-dawn air from the direction of Hangman's Hill, setting off a response from the Essex Regiment and the Newfoundlanders edging their way over the craters and rubble to the hill.

'You ready, Tommy?' Charlie Murphy adjusts the chinstrap of his helmet and picks up his rifle.

'It's madness, Charlie. They're gonna pick us off like ducks on a pond if we tries to attack the monastery from Hangman's Hill. They'll have a clear view of us from up there.'

'Don't I knows it, b'y. But you gotta do what they says. We're just soldiers.' A thick cloud of white smoke wafts through the rubble of the castle from the smoke bombs being lobbed at the hills from the divisions below. Charlie coughs and waves at the smoke. 'Holy Joe, how are we meant to see where we're goin' through this stuff? We won't be able to see the white tape the engineers laid out on the path.'

'I wouldn't worry about that, Charlie, the tape's blown to hell. We'll just have to try to figure out where to step. If you blows up, I'll knows not to step there.'

Thomas reaches into his tunic pocket and pulls out a metal flask. He unscrews the top and takes a long swig. He taps it on Charlie's rifle. 'Here you goes, b'y. Have some Dutch courage. You knows what they says, you gotta be a drunk or an idiot to be a soldier, and I knows I'm not an idiot.'

Thomas and Charlie follow the others down the side of Castle Hill, stumbling past bomb craters and the smashed mountain stone. The bodies of Allied and German soldiers killed in the battles of the previous week litter the hill like debris, and Thomas is glad of the black night and the thick smoke that cloaks them from view. They are a few metres up Hangman's Hill when a grenade crashes onto the hill above them, sending out shards of stone like daggers. A split second of silence, then the screams as men jolt back to consciousness. *It's true what they says. We all cries for our mothers and our lovers in the end.*

A blast of machine gun fire. Men falling through the smoke. Thomas grabs Charlie's arm and they run towards an opening in the mountain face. Bullets ricochet off the stone around them as they dodge into the crevice and flatten themselves against the ground.

'Holy, Jaysus, God,' Charlie says as he pants into the dust.

Outside, the air is a mash of the throbbing artillery guns, exploding grenades and blasts of machine gun fire. And the screams and cries of men.

'We'd best lie low, Charlie. Till things calm down.'

'Like I was ever gonna go out there, b'y. There's no way in hell. I intends to live a long, long life.' He lifts his head and yells towards the opening. 'You bloody bastards!'

A whizz. A ricochet. A gasp.

Charlie slumps against Thomas, his eyes wide in surprise, a trickle of blood tracing down his cheek from the neat hole in his forehead.

'Tommy? *Komm nach draussen*, Tommy.'

A stone rolls into the crevice. Thomas's heart beats a drum in his chest. Another stone hops along the ground, stopping an inch from his nose. His fingers turn white where they grip the barrel and trigger of his rifle. *So, this is how it ends. Tom Parsons and Charlie Murphy dead on Hangman's Hill.* They couldn't put that on their gravestones. His mam wouldn't have that, that's for sure. It would have to be something more ... heroic. The dawn is colouring the sky above the smoke pink. He has a clear view of Monte Cassino and the ruined monastery, sitting like a pink pearl above the fog. Maybe heaven looked like this. Maybe he was already halfway there.

Rising to his feet, he takes a deep breath. *I'm sorry, Ellie Mae. I'm sorry.*

He runs out of the crevice, just as a grenade explodes outside. His body is in the air. Then he hits the ground hard, his head smashing against a rock. He is falling. Falling. And then, nothing.

Thomas opens his eyes. He has landed amongst the branches of a long-dead bush on the hillside. His body is a map of pain, but none of it as bad as the fire emanating from his right boot. Raising his head, he sees his boot, bloated and distorted like a blown-out tyre. Above it his leg is a pulp of bone and shredded skin and wool. He falls back against the branches. His head throbs and he raises his hand to his forehead. When he looks at his hand it's like it's been dipped in a tin of red paint. Cold is seeping into his body. He shivers. He hopes it won't take long.

He drifts. He's in Cow Tower with Ellie. Moonlight streams in through the open roof, lighting her face in a silver glow. She takes his hand and guides it to her stomach. Her blue-grey eyes watch him as he cups the roundness.

'Our child,' she says. 'We're having a child.'

A flash of white light and his body is lifted as the explosion smashes into the hill beside him. His eyes fly open. The barrage goes off around him like an orchestra of war. Then, just as suddenly the guns stop.

He closes his eyes and lets his body float in the emptiness opening up to him. He is lying on a raft that is being pulled over the sea, bumping and dipping as the raft slides over the waves. He turns his head and sees the barnacled grey-black skin of a humpback whale slide into the sea. He'd had no idea there were whales in heaven. He turns his head to the other side and catches the dark eye of another whale before it disappears into the deep green waves.

When he wakes he is in a cave. There are others there, wounded, like him. They are moaning and crying out for their mothers and their lovers. In German.

A medical orderly leans over him. He removes Thomas's helmet and wraps newspaper around his head. He says something to another orderly when he looks at Thomas's leg. The word echoes around Thomas's head like a ricocheting bullet.

*Kaput. Kaput. Kaput.*

# Chapter 45

## Tippy's Tickle – 17 September 2001

'Good morning, Princess Grace.'

Sophie opens her eyes. She smiles. 'Good morning.'

Sam sits on the bed in a pair of jeans and a T-shirt, holding two mugs. 'Coffee? Milk, no sugar, right?'

Sophie stretches under the tangle of sheets and sits up against the pillows. The large bed almost fills the room, its wooden headboard further evidence of Sam's woodworking skills. Tucking a sheet around her body, she holds out a hand. 'Thanks. That's perfect.'

Sam watches her take a sip and smiles, fine lines fanning out from his dark eyes as his tanned, bearded face softens. He reaches out and brushes a strand of hair out of her eyes. 'I like you like this.'

Sophie runs her hand across her face. 'I must look a mess. Is my mascara all smudged?'

'Doesn't matter. You look cute.'

'Cute?' She hands him back the mug. 'I've never been accused of being cute before. Now I have to look.'

Sam sets the mugs down on a wooden chair beside the bed and reaches out for Sophie's arm as she kicks at the sheets. Clambering over the covers, he rolls on top of her.

'Sam. Sam, what are you doing?'

'Just looking.'

Sophie flops back on the bed and watches him as he spreads her hair across the pillow. His eyes are lit with something she's never seen in them before. Her stomach jolts, setting off the familiar anxiety in her solar plexus, like moths beating frantically for an escape. *Oh shit.*

He leans into her, pressing kisses, as light as a breath, along her neck.

She swallows. 'I'm leaving soon, Sam. Today. I'm leaving today.'

'I know,' he says as he traces kisses along her jaw.

'I'm ... I'm not sure this is a good idea.'

'Do you want me to stop?'

She shudders as a buzz runs up her body. 'No. No, I don't.'

Sophie stands at the window and sips her coffee as she rubs the flannel sleeve of one of Sam's plaid shirts. Outside, just visible beyond the wooden railings of a deck and over the tops of the spruces growing below the hill, a sandy beach curves along the shoreline, framed by a green-black backdrop of conifers. Tickle-aces duck and glide over the choppy water, peeling away like Spitfire pilots when a bald eagle spins into the cove, claws outstretched, and plucks a squirming fish from the water. *If only I could stay. But I can't. I just can't.*

'I see you found the coffee pot.'

She turns around. 'Yes. I had to step over Rupert in the kitchen to get to it. Much better than the coffee in the store.' She nods towards the wood burner. 'Fire's out.'

Sam walks barefoot out of the bedroom in his jeans and T-shirt, towelling his wet hair. He drops the towel onto the sofa and comes up behind Sophie, wrapping her in his embrace. The scent of soap lingers on his body as his warmth envelops her.

'How's that?'

'Better.' She turns around, and reaching her arms around his neck, pulls him into her kiss.

A crash of glass from the kitchen. Rupert's deep *woof*.

'Becca?'

Becca stands by the kitchen counter, her eyes wide, a river of orange juice snaking across the wooden floor between islands of shattered glass. Spinning around, she dashes towards the porch. The slam of the screen door.

'Becca! Becca, wait!' Sam races out of the room after his daughter, Rupert galloping behind barking.

Sophie stands on the braided rug, shivering as the chill of the unheated cottage filters through to her skin. Her stomach jolts and drops, like she is falling through air. *Bloody hell, Sophie. What have you done now?* She sets the mug down beside the photo of Sam and his family, and stumbles across the braided rug into the bedroom.

# Chapter 46

## Norwich, England – 11 August 1944

'Good heavens.'
Dottie spins around on the stool at Ellie's vanity table, the cardboard lipstick tube primed and ready in her fingers. 'I was just going to use a little bit.' Her eyes widen. A wet patch spreads out over the Persian rug between Ellie's slippered feet.

'I think my water just broke.'

Dropping the lipstick tube on the vanity, Dottie leaps to her feet. 'Is the baby coming?'

'Yes. Yes. It's coming.' Ellie picks at her wet dressing gown and holds it away from her body. 'You need to call the midwife. The number's by the phone.'

'The phone's not working. They still haven't fixed the line since the storm.'

Ellie cups her belly and shuffles over to the bed. 'Hand me a towel, Dottie. Then go over to the school and use their phone.'

Dottie eyes her sister as she tosses her a towel. 'Are you scared?'

'A little. I wish Thomas were here.'

'What if he—?'

'Don't even think it, Dottie. Thomas's fine. One of these days he's going to walk through our front door.'

'But you haven't had a letter for ages.'

Ellie presses her lips together. 'Which is a good sign.'

'You could always marry George instead, like you were supposed to.'

The fine line between Ellie's eyes deepens. 'Don't be ridiculous. I'm married to Thomas.'

'I mean if Thomas—'

Ellie's eyes widen and she clutches at her belly. 'Oh, my word.' She pants through the pain. 'Tell the midwife the contractions have started. Hurry, Dottie.'

George skirts the bicycle around an enormous pothole in the road outside St Bartholomew's School and brakes beside a telegraph boy on his black Post Office bike who is squinting at the headmaster's house behind the gate.

'Are you looking for the Burgesses?' he asks as he parks the bike by the flint wall.

The boy's pillboxed head shakes. 'No, M-M-Mrs P-P-Parsons.' He peers at the front of the telegram. 'Mrs T-Thomas P-P-Parsons.' He glances up at George. 'It's from the W-War Office. I h-hate these ones.'

'I'm going in there now. I can give it to her.'

'I-I'm supposed to w-wait for a r-r-reply.'

'Why don't you wait here by the gate, and I can let you know if there's a reply?'

The boy's pale face, coloured with a sprinkling of freckles across his nose, floods with relief. He thrusts the telegram at George. 'T-thank you.'

George takes the telegram and heads through the gate. Ignoring the broken doorbell, he knocks on the door and reads the address as he waits. *Mrs Thomas Parsons.* How did that happen? How did he ever let that happen? He'd always thought he and Ellie would be together, forever. He sighs and slips the telegram into his pocket. The War Office. My poor Ellie.

The door swings open. 'George!' Dottie throws her arms around George's neck and hugs him. 'You arrived fast! It's a boy!'

George disentangles himself. 'That's wonderful, Dottie. How are they? How's Ellie?'

'They're all fine. Nurse Blackmore said she'd never seen a firstborn in such a hurry to be born. He's a tiny little thing. She had to give him a really good spanking to get him to cry.' Dottie purses her lips. 'Ellie's called the baby Emmett Thomas. What kind of a name is Emmett?'

'Emmett? That's a perfectly nice name. It's my middle name, after Joseph.' Flipping open the flap of his satchel, he takes out a box of Mcklintock's chocolates. 'Give these to Ellie for me, would you, Dottie?'

Dottie takes the chocolates and grabs George's hand, tugging him across the polished brass threshold. 'Why don't you come in, George? I'll make some tea. Ellie and the baby are asleep but Poppy's out in the garden. I'll call him in.'

'No, don't disturb him. I just wanted to come by and give my regards. Make sure everyone was all right.' He reaches into his pocket. 'I bumped into the telegraph boy at the gate.' He hands Dottie the envelope. 'He's waiting for an answer. It's from the War Office.'

Dottie looks up at George. 'Thomas?'

George nods. 'I believe so. You might want to give it to your father.'

Dottie tears the telegram out of the envelope.

PRIORITY MRS T A PARSONS

THE WAR OFFICE REGRETS TO INFORM YOU THAT YOUR HUSBAND CORP THOMAS AUGUSTUS PARSONS HAS BEEN REPORTED WOUNDED AND HAS BEEN TAKEN AS A PRISONER OF WAR – LETTER TO FOLLOW

'Wounded? He's wounded? I thought he'd be d—' Dottie bites her lip.

'Dottie!'

'I'm sorry. I didn't mean it.'

George shakes his head. 'Poor chap. I hope they're decent to him.'

'Oh, George. I hate what Ellie did to you. She's just awful to have thrown you over for ...' Dottie spits out the name like a sour lemon pip '... that Thomas.'

'She was free to make her own choice, Dottie. The best man won.'

'The best man didn't win at all. She never appreciated you. I appreciate you.' Dottie loops her hands around George's neck and presses an impassioned kiss on his lips.

Grabbing her arms, George pushes her away. 'Dottie! Good grief. You're a child!'

'I'm almost sixteen, George. I'm old enough.'

'Good Lord, Dottie.' Spinning around, he rushes out of the door and down the path. The telegraph boy is waiting by the gate. George shakes his head as he grabs the handlebars of his bicycle.

'No reply.'

# Chapter 47

## Tippy's Tickle – 17 September 2001

Sophie pushes open the screen door to Kittiwake. Three heads turn in her direction.

She looks over at the tearful girl. 'How's Becca?'

Sam brushes his hand over Becca's blonde head. Her face is flushed pink and fine threads of her pale hair stick to her damp face. 'She's fine.'

Ellie rises from the table and turns on the burner under the kettle. 'Tea?'

Sophie nods and sits in a wooden chair opposite Sam and Becca.

A silence settles over the room, broken only by Ellie's shuffling and the clink of china as she makes the tea.

'I'm sorry, Sam.'

'It's not your fault.' He rubs his eyes. 'I should have been more careful.'

She sits back in her chair. 'You make it sound like it was an accident.'

He looks over at her. 'It kind of was, wasn't it?'

Sophie stares at him. *What on earth does he mean by that?*

Ellie glances at the two of them sitting opposite each other like two schoolchildren having a spat. She sets a couple of teacups and saucers on the table with the teapot. 'Let it steep for three minutes. Best to put the milk in last.' She tugs a yellow and orange tea cosy over the teapot, and sets a small jug of milk down beside it.

'You forget I'm English, Aunt Ellie.'

'Sorry, my dear. Force of habit. They drink it in mugs here. An abomination.'

'Milk in first, though.'

'On that we'll have to agree to disagree.' Leaning over Becca, Ellie kisses the girl's cheek. 'Come on, honey. Auntie Florie's over with Taffy in the kennels. She thinks the puppies are going to be born today. Let's go over and have a look.'

Nodding, Becca slides off her father's lap. She follows Ellie towards the door, turning to glare at Sophie as she walks by.

'I'm sorry, Becca. I didn't mean to upset you.' Sophie says as she reaches out her arms. 'Can I have a hug?'

Becca shakes her head, her braids swinging over her shoulders, and signs something to Sophie. She takes hold of Ellie's hand.

Sophie watches the door close behind them. She presses her fingers against her forehead. 'She seems quite upset.'

Sam reaches for the teapot. 'She'll be fine. It took her by surprise.' He pushes a teacup across the table towards Sophie. 'It's never happened before.'

Sophie pours in a splash of milk and watches it swirl through the clear brown tea. 'She's never seen you with a woman other than her mother?'

'No. I never brought anyone home before.'

Sophie sips the hot tea and sets the cup down in its floral saucer. 'I suppose I should feel honoured.'

She runs her finger around the rim of the teacup. 'Ellie said it was an accident. With Winny.'

'Yes. There was a fire.'

'Oh. I'm so sorry, Sam.'

Sam pushes away from the table. 'I guess we need to get you to Gander.'

Sophie nods. 'The plane's leaving at five. I checked when you were in the shower. I need to be there by two at the latest. It won't take me long to get ready. I don't have much.'

She pushes the teacup away. 'Look Sam, if you drop me at Wesleyville, I can get a taxi from there. You don't have to go all the way to Gander.'

'No. I'll take you. I promised, didn't I, Princess Grace? I'll meet you downstairs in an hour.'

'Sam, what did Becca sign to me?'

He pauses at the door. 'Oh, Sophie.'

'Please, what did she say?'

'She said, *You're not my mother*.'

'Fill her up, Wince. Taking Sophie down to Gander later to catch her plane.'

'Ah, b'y, she's finally on her way, then.'

Sam turns off the bike's engine and gets off the bike. 'Your coffee machine working?'

'Yes, b'y. Only tinned milk though.'

Sam takes off his helmet and runs his hand though his hair. 'No problem. Black's fine.'

'It'll take the hair off you, b'y, if you drinks it black. Throw in some milk.'

Inside the garage, Sam finds a paper cup and pours out the sludgy black coffee. He takes a sip, screwing up his face at the bitterness. He walks over to the garage opening and leans on the wall. 'What do you think of her?'

Wince peers at Sam from under his baseball cap. 'Of *Miss Julie?*'

'No, b'y. Sophie. What do you think of Sophie?'

Wince shrugs his thick shoulders as he waits for the gas nozzle to click off. 'Seems all right to me. Then again I only saw her the one time, so she could be an axe murderer for all I knows.'

Sam grunts. 'She's no axe murderer. I haven't met anyone quite like her, though. She gets right on my nerves, sometimes, some of the things she says.'

'What kinds of things?'

'Oh, about how I should think bigger about my work. Take the furniture-making more seriously. Find ways to earn more money. She has the idea that money defines success.'

'Don't see the problem there, b'y. Most people would agree with her. I makes some good money sellin' lottery tickets along with the gas. Everybody wants to be rich.'

'Yeah, well. Maybe I like the simple life.'

Wince hangs the gas nozzle back on the gas pump and wipes his hands on an oily rag. 'Sounds like she's got you twisted up like a boot in a net, b'y.'

'No. Nothing like that. There'd be no point. She doesn't even live here. And I've got Becca to think of.'

'Well, I don't knows about all that, b'y. Sounds to me like you've been caught, otherwise we'd be talkin' about baseball.'

Sam takes another sip of coffee then dumps the rest onto the gravel. He walks over to Wince and hands him the paper cup. 'Gotta tell you, Wince. Your coffee's no Tim Hortons.'

Sophie steps onto the potholed road at the bottom of Ellie's house. She sets her carry-on case on the dirt against a moss-covered rock and shifts her Longchamp bag on her shoulder. Turning to look up at the house, she raises her camera and takes a final shot.

'I wouldn't have thought a cutting-edge architect like you would be interested in an old house like this,' Ellie says as her feet crunch on the rocky path down from the shop.

Sophie turns and smiles at her aunt. 'It's a lovely house, Aunt Ellie. So much character. And what an amazing location. You have the best view on the coast.'

Ellie laughs. 'You should have seen it when I first arrived back in 1946. It hadn't seen a lick of paint in years.' She looks up at the house, its freshly painted turquoise trim and yellow and white clapboards shining cheerily against the blue sky. 'Florie's been a great help. I couldn't have managed it without her.' She looks at Sophie's luggage. 'So, you're off then.'

'Yes. My interview's tomorrow, then I'm flying back to London on Thursday. This time next week, I'll know whether I've got the job.'

'Well, good luck, sweetheart. It's been lovely having you here. Now that you know where I am, be sure to come back. Your room will be waiting for you.'

'Thanks, Aunt Ellie. Sorry to spring myself on you like this.'

Ellie waves her hand dismissively in the air. 'Don't be ridiculous. I only wish Dottie had made it over. It would have been nice to see her.'

'And my dad.'

'Yes, of course. And George. I would have liked to smooth things out with Dottie. It's one of the things I truly do regret. Misunderstandings are a terrible thing. They cause so much pain.' She squeezes Sophie's arm. 'Try not to have too many regrets, Sophie. They follow you around, you know. They cling to you like chewing gum.'

Sophie's laughs. 'Chewing gum? I'll remember that, Aunt Ellie. Anyway, I don't have any regrets. Everything is going just fine.'

'Is it?'

'Absolutely. I'm right on course.'

Ellie sweeps her eyes over Sophie and nods. 'You know, you could always come back, Sophie. Take up art again. I could teach you print-making. If you get bored of city life.'

Sophie smiles. *Chucking it all in and starting fresh. A new Sophie. A happier Sophie. Ellie can read her like a book. But she's closing that chapter.*

Ellie reaches out her arms. 'Oh, look at us being so very English. Give me a hug.'

The purr of a motorcycle engine grows louder and Sam rides into view, bouncing around the potholes towards them.

Ellie kisses Sophie on her cheek and whispers in her ear. 'Being on course is good, Sophie. But sometimes, a detour offers a richer view.'

# *Chapter 48*

## Gander, Newfoundland – 17 September 2001

Sam releases the rope securing Sophie's carry-on case to the back of the bike and sets it on the pavement in front of the airport terminal.

'So, this is it, then, Princess Grace.'

Sophie fiddles with the strap of her shoulder bag. 'Yes, I guess so. It's going to be strange being in New York. Everything's changed there. It's incredible to think how much life can change in just one day.'

Sam nods. 'Everything's changed everywhere.' He raises the handle of the case and hands it to Sophie. 'I guess it'll be a while before you find your way back here.'

She runs her fingers along the handle of her case. 'If I get this job, I'll be up to my eyeballs with work.'

'Sophie, I know I've teased you about being tied to your work. The fact is, I respect that. You deserve to go as far as you want to go in your career. I doubt you'll find what you're looking for in Tippy's Tickle.'

She sucks in a breath to squash the quivering in her stomach. To keep her hands from reaching out to him.

*No, you mustn't, Sophie. You can't just drop everything you've worked for to start over here as an artist. For a moment, it might have seemed possible. But it's a silly fantasy. And Sam is just part of that fantasy.*

Her mother was right. She can't let herself get distracted by a man. Especially now, when everything she's worked so hard for is within her grasp. *So why do I want him so much?*

'I'll call you, Sam. I'll keep in touch.'

'Becca would like that.'

'I thought Becca hated me.'

'Becca doesn't hate you, Princess Grace. She told Ellie this morning that she wants to have her hair cut just like yours.'

'Oh, no! Her hair is lovely. I'd have given anything to have long, blonde hair when I was a girl.'

Sam laughs. 'I've learned to choose my battles around here. I'm not sure that's a battle I want to have.'

Sophie smiles. 'No, probably not.'

He stands beside the bike, looking at the terminal building behind her as he rocks her case back and forth by its extended handle. 'Sophie, it wouldn't be fair to her for me to get involved with someone who lives in a different country.'

Her heart flops. *Here it is. Why didn't I see it coming? I should have seen it coming.*

She nods. 'Of course. I totally agree. It would never work. Timing's everything, isn't it?'

He looks at her as if he is trying to unravel a complex puzzle. 'Timing and geography.'

Sophie straightens her shoulders and tugs her jacket into place. 'Well, then, we can chalk up whatever it was that happened between us as a bit of harmless fun between two adults.'

'Is that what it was?'

Sophie looks at Sam. 'Wasn't it?'

'It seems so.'

Sophie swallows. 'Tell her goodbye for me.'

'I will.'

'No, like this.' Sophie signs *Goodbye, Becca*.

He signs *Goodbye, Sophie* and leans towards her. She closes her eyes. Not meaning to. Not expecting anything. The moment hangs in the air.

She opens her eyes to see Sam standing by the bike, watching her. Shaking his head, he puts on his helmet and throws his leg over the seat. He turns the key and the engine purrs into life. He taps his helmet in a salute. 'Good luck, Princess Grace. I hope life gives you everything you're looking for.'

The bike roars down the road to the intersection. Sam turns his head, checking traffic, then powers the bike out towards the highway.

A chilly wind buffets her on the airport concourse, and she brushes her hair out of her eyes. Over on the runway two planes sit, awaiting the final stranded passengers. A yellow and black school bus pulls into the parking lot. The door slams open, and a motley group of travellers files out, filling the air with chatter. She walks over to the queue and follows them through the doors into the terminal building.

# PART TWO

PART TWO

# *Chapter 49*

## Gander, Newfoundland – 11 September 2011

Sophie peers down at the grey tarmac, which is empty except for the articulated luggage cart snaking its way bumpily to the aeroplane. So different from ten years ago. Then, she'd watched a parade of school buses inch along the tarmac. Filing up to collect the thousands of confused and exhausted passengers from the thirty-eight aeroplanes that had been diverted to Gander on 9/11. If she'd known what the following few days would hold for her, she probably would've stayed in the legion hall in Gander with the other passengers from her flight. It would've been far less complicated.

She follows the other passengers – mostly Americans as far as she can tell from their accents and irritating friendliness – through the open glass doors into the terminal's cavernous 60s interior. The sweeping Modernist mural commands the room just as it had back then; it still surprises Sophie to see such a piece of art in a building so otherwise unremarkable. The bronze bird sculpture is there too, in the centre of the floor, but free of the handbags and jackets that had been hooked over the heads of the birds that day. On the far wall, the large brown letters spelling out CANADA – flanked by flags of Canada, the UK and Newfoundland – are still there, hovering over a portrait of the Queen.

New blue vinyl seating has been arranged in neat U-shaped islands clustered around wooden coffee tables on the polished beige and brown terrazzo floor. Ten years ago all the furniture had been shoved up against the walls to make room for tables of immigration officers. They'd worn short-sleeved white shirts and drunk bottle after bottle of water. Funny she should remember that, after all this time.

She glances over to where Mavis's tea table had been set up. Where she'd first met Sam. Just a plant there now, looking in need of a watering.

'Yes, m'dear. What can I do for you?'

Sophie smiles at the cheerful middle-aged woman with short permed orange hair. A pair of turquoise-rimmed bifocal glasses perches on her nose. A nametag is pinned to her white blouse, *Hello, I'm Phyllis* printed neatly in purple ink.

'I've reserved a car. Under Parry. Sophie Parry.'

'Oh, sure, duck. Gots your reservation right here.' Phyllis pushes a stack of paper across the orange Formica counter. 'Could you just fill out these forms?'

Scanning the documents, Sophie scribbles her signature and hands them back to Phyllis with her driving licence and a credit card.

'Would you like to designate any other drivers?'

'No. It's just me.'

'Just you goin' off all around the island on your own? You gots relatives here you're visitin'?'

'No. Yes. An aunt. Up the coast. In Tippy's Tickle.'

'Oh, that'll be lovely this time of year. Grab the last bit of summer sunshine. Snow'll be here before the end of the month. I can feel it in my knees.' Phyllis slides the credit card and licence across the counter, squinting at Sophie above her bifocals. 'You're not Ellie Parsons's niece, by any chance?'

Sophie raises her eyebrows. 'Yes, how do you know that?'

'You sounds just like her. From England, aren't you?' The woman nods at the portrait of the Queen on the far wall as she separates a copy of the contract for Sophie. 'We've gots the same queen.'

Sophie smiles weakly. 'Yes, we do. You know my aunt?'

'Oh, don't make me laugh, duckie.' Phyllis roots through a jumble of keys in a drawer behind the counter. 'Everyone in these parts knows Ellie and Florie. They're quite the pair, aren't they? They've been onto the news here and over in St John's all about the fish processin' factory closin' down in Heart's Wish. They tried to close it down ten years ago, but there was some fuss. Right shame they closed the factory. Consolidatin', the government said. Movin' things to a bigger place down the coast. Lots of people out of work in Tippy's Tickle now. They've been tryin' to gets the government to do somethin', but closures is happenin' all over the island. Hard to make a livin' out in the outports. Kids just end up movin' to Toronto or Alberta where the jobs is. Can't blame them, can you? We needs more people like your aunt. Trying to change things. And Ellie pushin' ninety! She's a right one, your aunt.'

Sophie folds her copy of the contract and shoves it into her shoulder bag. 'She is at that.'

Phyllis points at the exit doors with a set of keys. 'Derm'll meet you in the lot just outside the doors. He'll go over the car with you. Make sure it's all right. No dents so far. Just watch the moose on the highway. Don't worry though – there's lots of signs. They'll flash fit to blind you if they sense a moose in the area.' She waves to the left. 'Just to the left once you're out the door. Big Budget sign. Sign gots a crack so we can't light it up at night right now, which is a cryin' shame. How's people meant to knows where we are if they can't see the sign?' She hands Sophie the car keys. 'Got Derm's brother on the case. Should be fixed by the time you brings the car back. But in case it's not, you knows where to find us now, don't you, duck?'

Sophie grabs the handle of her suitcase. 'Thanks. I'll remember.'

'Your aunt'll be pleased as punch to see you. Tell her Phyllis from Budget sends her regards. She don't know me from Adam, but tell her we all loves her and Florie here.'

Sophie steers the car, a Volkswagen Golf in an alarming shade of red, along the bumpy asphalt of a two-lane highway along the coast from Gambo, through a landscape of grey rock and scrubby spruce. From time to time, as she crests a hill, a glimpse of steel-grey water glints below, undulating under the sharp blue sky, its ripples broken by the occasional crest of a wave or a spray of water like a fountain. Here and there a lone scraggy pine leans from a precarious foothold in a rock into the wind blowing in from the Arctic, like an old man fighting to keep upright on a blustery day. Sophie passes lonely clusters of clapboard houses and stores, the wooden sidings painted in vivid hues, the ones closest to the shore propped up on wooden stilts weathered silver grey by the elements. Neat stacks of wooden-slatted lobster traps and circular orange-net crab traps sit ready on the end of wooden piers, and an occasional lone motorboat bobs in a tickle or a cove, moored for the day.

Sophie slows, trying to remember the turn-off Sam had taken on that first drive from the airport. Her first time on a motorcycle. Her Escada velvet suit never recovered.

She indicates right and steers the car onto a narrow road,

pocked with potholes, leading through a knot of knobby pines. The road winds through the woods and breaks out onto a grassy meadow at the crest of a hill. Far along the coast to her left she glimpses the lighthouse, still keeping vigil over the steely ocean. Several clapboard buildings come into view near the shore as the car rounds the hill and bumps down the road. She stops beside the petrol pumps in front of a one-storey garage clad in yellow aluminium siding. A large blue and white illuminated IRVING sign shines like a beacon over the open garage door.

A stocky man with an impressive beer belly and a face that looks like it's been carved and cratered by a lifetime of wind ambles out of the garage, wiping his hands on an oily rag. 'Hey, there, b'y. How you getting on?'

'Fine, thanks. I don't need any gas, but could you check the oil?'

'Sure thing, duck.'

'Could I use your loo?'

He jabs behind him with a greasy thumb. 'Right round the building. Door's at the back.'

'I remember.' She opens the car door and gets out. 'You don't recognise me, do you, Wince?'

The man's blue eyes, almost as blue as the sky, peer at her between his hooded, red eyelids. 'Holy God. You're Sam's girl, as I live and breathe. What took you so long?'

'Oh, it's not like that. Sam and I ... we're just friends. Well, we were. I haven't seen him for ten years.'

'Oh, don't I just know that. He was a misery guts for ages after you left.' Wince props up the bonnet and unscrews the oil cap. 'Said you never called nor wrote.' He drills her with his blue eyes. 'But time heals and all that. Life goes on.' He checks the oil gauge and grunts as he wipes it clean with the rag. 'Them car people in St John's never checks the oil. Good thing you stopped.'

'Sam's still there? In Tippy's Tickle?'

'Still there. Doing what he does.'

Sophie swallows down the questions that are rushing up her throat. *Is he with someone? Is he married?* 'I'm staying with my aunt there for a couple of weeks.'

'Well, I expects Sam'll know you're comin' then. Just don't expects him to be doin' a jig about it.'

Wince wipes his hands on the oily rag as he watches Sophie crunch across the gravel path and disappear around the back of the building.

'Misery guts?'

Wince squints over at the tall man in motorcycle leathers leaning against the garage opening bouncing a can of oil from one hand to the other.

'Well, you were a misery guts for an awful long time, Sam, b'y.'

'How's she looking?'

'Some good, b'y. She was askin' about you.'

'So I heard.' Sam tosses the oilcan over to Wince. 'Doesn't mean anything.'

Wince catches the oilcan. 'All I knows about women, which, mind you, wouldn't fit on the end of a squid jig, is that if she's askin' about you, she's interested.'

Sam grunts. 'You don't know Sophie.'

'Not so sure you does either, b'y.' Wince stabs the oilcan with his penknife and leans over the engine, pouring the thick black oil into the car's oil tank. 'Why doesn't you say hello?'

'Bike's fixed,' Sam says as he heads back into the garage. 'I'll see her soon enough.'

Wince shrugs and tosses the empty oilcan into a rusty rubbish bin. The motorcycle engine roars to life inside the garage and Sam rides out on the gleaming black and red Kawasaki. Pausing at the road as he checks for traffic, he waves at Wince before turning right towards Tippy's Tickle.

A crunch on the gravel. Wince looks over to see Sophie pulling a wallet out of her shoulder bag as she approaches. 'All done? How much do I owe you?'

'It's twenty-two, but if you gives me a twenty, and we'll call it square.'

A car door slams and Ellie glances up from the watercolour she's working on and out of the shop's bay window. She drops her paintbrush into a jar of water and wipes her hands on her apron.

'She's here!'

Florie emerges from the back room wearing a red T-shirt, jeans and a checked lumberjack shirt with the sleeves pushed up past her elbows. She balances a mixing bowl full of icing sugar and butter against her left hip and clutches a wooden spoon in her right hand. She joins Ellie at the window.

'Took her long enough.'

Ellie glances at her wristwatch. 'What do you mean? She rang only two hours ago from Gander.'

Florie grunts. 'Ten years, Ellie. Not two hours.'

Ellie looks at Florie over the top of her horn-rimmed bifocals. 'Don't be like that, Florie. She's a busy woman. She's practically running that architecture firm in New York.'

'A phone call more than a couple of times a year would'a

been nice, even if she couldn't haul her arse up here. We didn't even gets a Christmas card last year.'

'Yes, well. People don't always act the way you expect. If there's anything I've learned in all my eighty-odd years, it's a waste of time to feel disappointed about things like that. I'm just delighted she's here now. That's the important thing. She's come for my birthday, and I think that's lovely.'

Florie shrugs. 'Just seems funny after all this time, her comin' up here like this at the last minute. You'd think she'd be plannin' her life a year ahead if she's so busy. Don't people like her have diaries and PAs and all that?'

'Florie. Be nice. She's my only niece.'

'Well, you could'a knocked me over with a feather when she said she was comin', that's for sure.' She frowns at the icing bowl. 'Where do you suppose Sam is with that cream cheese? Carrot cake's just not the same without it.'

The screen door squeaks open and Sophie looks up to see Ellie step out onto the landing at the top of the steps to the general store. She wears a purple embroidered smock top and jeans rolled up over red plimsolls, and her dark green apron is spattered with colourful blotches of paint. A pair of horn-rimmed bifocals sits on the tip of her nose. Her aunt holds out her arms, which shake with a slight tremor.

'Sophie! There you are! What a treat this is! My favourite niece here for my birthday.'

Sophie smiles up at her aunt and waves. *She's so tiny. So much smaller than I remember.* A flutter of nerves travels up Sophie's body. *I should have kept in touch. Why did I stop writing, for heaven's sake? Why didn't I just pick up the phone? She's family. My family. And she's so frail. What was so bloody important that I didn't even call until I needed something? Until I needed Kittiwake?*

Sophie runs up the steps and embraces her aunt. 'Your only niece, Auntie Ellie, unless there's something you haven't told me.'

Ellie squeezes Sophie tight and kisses her on the cheek. 'Come inside. Florie's making a carrot cake in the shop kitchen. If Sam gets back in time with the cream cheese, we'll have cream-cheese icing. Becca insisted that ordinary icing just wouldn't do.'

Inside, the store looks exactly the same as the day Sophie left Tippy's Tickle back in 2001 – the walls and shelving the same sage green, the wooden floor polished to a bright shine, the two long wooden counters either side of the narrow room still painted white, with the wooden tops laden with boxes of Ellie's art cards, jars of partridgeberry and bakeapple jam, and red paper bags of Purity hard tack bread for the stewed brewis everyone up here liked to eat with cod and fried pork-fat scrunchions, and for which she had yet to develop a taste.

A huge black Newfoundland dog with a red kerchief tied around its neck bounds towards them from the back room and rushes past Sophie out the screen door.

'That can't be Rupert.'

Ellie shakes her head. 'No, no. Rupert passed away some years ago. He's buried under the old tree up past the house. That's Rupert's son, Rupert Bear II. We call him Bear.'

Florie walks away from the bay window, carrying a large yellow bowl with a wooden spoon sticking out of what looks like vanilla icing. 'Well, would you look what the cat dragged in? You gots fed up with New York finally? Decided to make your way back to Paradise?'

Sophie kisses Florie on her cheek. 'Lovely to see you, Florie. How are the dachshunds?'

'Best kind, duck. I've got people comin' all the way from Halifax for my dogs now. Even had a fella email me the other day from Toronto, can you imagine that? Comin' all the way from Toronto to Tippy's Tickle for a dog?' She looks over her shoulder at Ellie. 'You'll have to be printin' up some more of your art cards, Ellie, for all these CFAs coming into town. Getting lots of publicity since Hildegarde won Best of Breed for dachshunds last year.'

Sophie raises her eyebrows in a question. 'CFAs? I've forgotten what that stands for.'

'Come From Aways.' A man's voice from the doorway.

Sophie spins around. Bear thunders back into the store, his tail wagging like a flag. Sam stands in the doorway, a silhouette against the late summer light streaming in from outside. The same leather jacket. Still lean in jeans and a white T-shirt.

*Oh, God.* Her stomach flutters and she takes a breath to calm her nerves. No man she'd met in the past ten years had stood a chance. She'd measured them all against Sam. Every single one of them had come up short. So, why hadn't she done anything about it? She should have returned his calls, but there didn't seem to be any point. She could have visited. People have long-distance relationships all the time. She'd thought Sam would just fade away. But he never did. *Bloody hell, Sophie, you've been sleeping for ten years.*

He sets a plastic Foodland bag on the counter beside the sign advertising hot chocolate for a toonie. Folding his arms, he leans against the counter. The stubble is flecked with grey, now, and threads of silver pepper his black hair. His brown eyes sweep over Sophie.

'It's anyone not from around here. You're a CFA until you get Screeched in.'

'Screeched in?'

Ellie grabs Sophie's arm and leads her towards the battered wooden table and mismatched chairs in front of the bay window. 'It's a silly thing they started doing in St John's some years ago for the tourists. It's a bit of fun, really.'

'Well, I don't know about that, Ellie girl,' Florie says, wrinkling her nose. 'Kissin' a cod! Whoever heard of such a thing? Eatin' them, yes. Kissin' them, not on your life.'

'You'll find out soon enough for yourself, Sophie. It's my eighty-ninth birthday on Friday and I'm having a party. We'll have a Screech-in then.' Ellie sits down in an old wooden chair painted purple. A web of lines fans out from the corners of her eyes as she smiles at Sam. 'You can play the Ugly Stick this time, Sam.'

'That'll be the day, Ellie.'

Sophie sits beside Ellie at the table, which is covered with stacks of art cards and jars of watery paints. 'Where's Becca? I have a surprise for her.'

'She went off with Toby Molloy after lunch,' Florie says as she peeks into the Foodland bag. 'Said they were goin' to check out the iceberg over by Seal Point. Don't usually see them this time of year, but they're coming around more often now. Breakin' off from the glaciers up in Greenland. Said she'd bring back some ice to make some ice cream with. Betcha that'd cost a bomb in New York, wouldn't it, Sophie? Imagine eatin' iceberg ice cream in Central Park. Purest ice cream you'd ever hope to eat.'

Sam sits on a red-painted chair, leaning back until it tilts precariously against the wall. 'I hope he knows what he's doing. It's choppy out there today. She should be studying for her university entrance exams.'

'Oh, Sam, don't be an old fuddy-duddy. They're eighteen,' Ellie says. 'They're young. Let them enjoy themselves.'

'That's just what I'm worried about.'

'Toby's a responsible boy, and Becca's always been a good student here at home,' Ellie says. 'She'll do fine on those tests, though I'm still surprised she wants to go to medical school. She's such an artistic girl. And the clothes she makes!' Ellie holds up an embroidered purple sleeve. 'Just look at that embroidery, Sophie. It's beautiful.'

Sam tips the legs of the chair back onto the wooden floor. 'It's hard to pay bills with art, Ellie. You know that for a fact. Being a doctor will give her some security.'

Florie sets the icing bowl on the table and pulls up a blue chair. 'Honestly, these universities all seems to think home-schooled kids are a bunch of illiterate streels. Makin' her sit these tests when she should be enjoyin' her youth, it's a sin.'

Sam sweeps his finger along the edge of Florie's bowl and licks the icing. 'From what I can see, Toby's just been hanging around on unemployment insurance doing not much of anything all summer since the plant closed. Nothing except getting under my feet in the store. He'll be off to the Alberta oil fields like all the others before you know it, and that'll break Becca's heart.'

He gets up and heads towards the door, grabbing a bag of hard tack bread off the counter on his way out. 'I don't like Becca wasting her time with him.'

'Ellie's right, b'y. You're soundin' like a right old fogey,' Florie says as she dips her finger into the icing bowl. 'You comin' for supper? I'm makin' Jiggs dinner.' Sticking her finger in her mouth, she sucks off the sweet icing.

'Yes, come, Sam,' Ellie says as she collects the shopping bag and hands it to Florie. 'We're giving Sophie a proper Newfoundland welcome.'

Sam glances at Sophie. 'Don't see why you're going to so much trouble. She'll be off and gone for another ten years soon enough.'

Sophie glances from Sam to Ellie and back. 'I'm sorry. My job is so busy ... Time just flew.'

Sam nods at Sophie as he stands with his hand on the screen door. 'Too busy to return a phone call? Last I heard they still had phones in New York.'

The door slams shut behind him, rousing Bear from a doze in front of the cash till. The dog lumbers to his feet. He lopes past the three women, his shiny black coat of hair swishing in the air, and pushes out through the screen door after Sam.

# *Chapter 50*

## Tippy's Tickle – 12 February 1946

Ellie leans over the child, who is asleep on the seat opposite them, and tucks the white blanket she'd spent the winter so carefully crocheting snugly around Emmett's sleeping face. She brushes his soft cheek lightly with her fingertip. Such a good boy. He'd barely made a squeak the five days the *Mauritania* had spent climbing and plunging over the angry Atlantic waves. When he was awake he'd sit on her lap and survey the chaotic goings-on with an expression of world-weary resignation. "E's the spit of that ol' geezer, Winston,' Mona had said when Emmett had fixed his steely blue eye on her. 'Butter wouldn't melt.'

She glances at Thomas who is deep into the *Fisherman's Advocate* newspaper. Her eyes stray to the pinned-up trouser leg before she hastily sits down and turns her head to the dirty window and the view trundling past at a moderate jog. View is too grand a word, Ellie thinks, for the barren wasteland of snowdrifts, wet rock, wind-slapped firs, and the occasional lonely clapboard house with its ubiquitous peeling paint and thread of smoke trailing from the chimney.

She feels like she's been travelling for years. From Halifax there'd been a bone-rattling nine-hour train journey up through Nova Scotia to North Sydney. Then, after an uncomfortable night in a hotel room shared with another couple who'd made no effort to hide their amorous fumblings, they'd taken the overnight ferry to Porte aux Basques. A horrible journey, almost worse than the *Mauritania*. She'd had to abandon the baby to Thomas's anxious care, as she spent the night being sick in the stinking communal toilet.

They were on the penultimate leg now, on the Caribou train – or the Newfie Bullet as Thomas told her the American GIs had ironically dubbed it because of its dawdling progress across the island. Heading to some place called Gambo, where Thomas's father, Ephraim, would meet them with his fishing boat and take them up the coast to Tippy's Tickle.

With every frantic transfer, juggling Emmett, and the luggage, and Thomas's frequent stumbles, her past slipped further and further away, until her life in Norwich with her father and Dottie and George seemed like something she'd once dreamed.

She'd feel disheartened if her body hadn't succumbed to the numbness that had taken hold on the Halifax dockside. When Thomas had kissed her, the kiss she'd spent hours imagining, it'd been like kissing a stranger. But that was to be expected, wasn't it? They hadn't seen each other for over two years. She was a mother now, and Thomas was ...

Ellie licks her chapped lips. She's made her bed and now she has to lie in it. Isn't that what Dottie had said to her that last night in the house? Dottie was furious with her. Yes, they'd always had their squabbles growing up, but sisters do. But then things had become so much worse after she'd met Thomas. Stealing a lipstick was one thing, but stealing her engagement ring and hiding Thomas's telegram were really beyond understanding.

Why was Dottie so upset that she'd married Thomas instead of George? Was it because she was jealous of Ellie's imagined life on the other side of the ocean? Maybe it was just that Dottie was caught in that awkward age between childhood and adulthood. Almost seventeen. About the same age she'd been when she'd met Thomas.

Ellie glances at her husband. At the shock of ash-blond hair grown darker now in the winter gloom. At the thin white scar on his left cheek and the fan of fine lines etched into his skin either side of his eyes. What had happened to him to leave these marks on the handsome, youthful man she'd fallen in love with? Why had he told her so little in his letters from Newfoundland? Why hadn't he told her about—?

She glances at the pinned-up trouser leg. Maybe it was better that she hadn't known.

Reaching into the net bag of oranges, she takes out a fat round fruit. She runs her thumbnail along the dimpled skin and pulls away the rind. Splitting the orange into segments, she holds one out to Thomas.

'An orange for your thoughts.'

Thomas glances at the orange and back at Ellie. A smile tugs at the corner of his mouth. 'Don't mind if I does.'

She smiles at him as they eat the sweet orange. They'll find their way back to each other. One segment of orange at a time.

'Well, here it is. Tippy's Tickle. Home sweet home.'

Ellie jiggles Emmett in her arms as her thin-soled English boots sink into the wet snow. She shivers as the damp, cold air rolls over her face and stockinged legs. In front of her, a tall wooden house with two round turrets perches on a snow-covered hill overlooking the ice-strewn, grey Atlantic. The clapboard house, like all the others she'd seen on her journey, is wind-battered, and its yellow paint is a ghost of its original incarnation. An ancient grey wooden fence missing several pickets separates the property from the roadside.

'It's ... it's larger than the other houses I've seen.'

'Belonged to my fadder,' Thomas's father, Ephraim, says, setting Ellie's trunk in the snow. Ellie looks at the tall, wiry man, still handsome in the weathered way a man who's led a physical life can be.

'Da' ran a good business with the fisheries back in the day, but times isn't whats they used to be. He wasn't much of one for pushin' paper around, not like his fadder who was captain of a sealer – that's why we has the big house. It's called Kittiwake after the sea birds round here. My da' started fishin' when he was a b'y. I joined him on the boat when I was fifteen.' He nods at his son. 'Just like Tommy joined me.'

'Dad closed off the top floors years ago,' Thomas says as he points at the house with his crutch. 'Too dear to heat. We just lives on the ground floor now.' He looks over at his shivering wife. 'Let's get the baby inside. It's cold enough to freeze the arse off the devil out here.'

Ellie frowns at her pile of luggage, which is accumulating a light dusting of snow. 'What about the luggage?'

'Don't worry, Ellie Mae. I'll come back for it.'

'But your—'

The warmth in Thomas's gaze turns frosty. 'I still gots my two arms.'

'Yes. Yes, of course. I'm sorry, Thomas. I didn't mean—'

Ephraim picks up Ellie's suitcase and several bags of provisions they'd bought in Halifax. 'Don't you worry, maid,' he says as he heads up the steps. 'Tommy and I'll manage. We'll gets the trunk up to the house together.'

Thomas scans the grey water and lets out an exhausted sigh.

'I'm sorry, Ellie Mae. I should've told you.' He looks at her, his eyes the colour of the winter sky. 'I was afraid if I did, you'd not come.'

'Of course, I would have come, Thomas. It doesn't matter. Really, it doesn't matter at all.'

Thomas shakes his head. 'It matters to me.'

'So, here she is, then. The English wife.'

'Yes, Mam. This is Ellie Mae. My wife.'

A short, broad, grey-haired woman moves away from the wood stove and reaches for the baby. 'Are you expectin' to give the baby pneumonia? What kind of a blanket does you call this?' She tugs Emmett out of Ellie's arms and swaddles him in a heavy wool blanket she picks off a wooden rocking chair. 'There you goes, sweetheart,' she says to the baby as she starts rocking. 'You'll be right fine now Nanny's got you. Will you look at you? You've got the mark of the fairies on your eyes. I's never seen the likes of it.' She squints at Ellie through her frameless glass and wrinkles her nose. 'Catholic girl, I hears, is it?'

'Yes.'

'Hmmph.' She looks over at Thomas. 'Told you to stay away from those Catholic girls, Thomas. You can't trusts them as far as you can throws them. Then you goes and gets one in England.' She frowns at Ellie. 'Thought everyone was Protestant over there.'

Ellie shakes her head. 'No. No, not everyone.'

'Now, don't you be giving Ellie Mae a hard time, Mam.'

Thomas's mother peers at Ellie over the top of her glasses. 'We only gots the Church of England here. No Catholics in these parts. You should'a married a fella down the South Coast where all the Irish is.'

Ellie glances over at Thomas. 'Oh. No Catholic church? I—I guess I'll manage.'

Thomas lifts the rattling lid off the pot on the stove. 'Where you putting us, Mam?'

'Your room, of course.' Thomas's mother nods towards Ellie. 'The Queen of Sheba wants the main room, I expects?'

'Her name's Ellie Mae, Mam. We needs a large bed for the two of us. Mine's only a small one.'

'Dad's dragged down the big bed from the attic. Probably has bedbugs.'

Ellie jerks her head around to Thomas. 'Bedbugs?'

'Mam's only pulling your leg. It's a brass bed. Anyway, bedbugs would freeze to death this far north.'

Ellie edges towards Thomas and whispers in his ear.

'Out the back door. I'll takes you.'

She looks out through the dirt-streaked glass of the door to the stony cliff beyond. 'Out the back door?'

Thomas's mother chuckles. 'She's gonna be a fun one to have around, Thomas. Wait till you shows her the piss pot.'

Ellie sets the candle on a chair beside the brass bed and tucks the pink nylon nightie she'd bought at Buntings with hoarded clothes ration cards around her. She shuffles under the stack of sheets and blankets.

'Jaysus wept, girl. Your feets are like ice.'

'I'm sorry. I didn't realise it'd be so cold here.' Lifting a foot, she rubs it under the covers.

Thomas takes hold of her hand. 'Your hands is freezing too.' He sandwiches her hands between his warm palms and rubs them until she feels the blood run back into her fingers. 'Give us your foot, maid.'

Thomas's face glows golden in the warm candlelight. 'How do you manage here without electricity or plumbing?' Ellie asks.

Thomas takes hold of Ellie's left foot and rests it across his jersey undershirt, rubbing it like it's kindling for a fire. 'You don't miss what you don't has.'

'But, you've had it in England, so you must miss it now.'

Thomas nods. 'Too right, maid. I'd give up a lifetime of Jiggs dinners to have an indoor toilet. But the government won't bring plumbin' out to the outports because it's too dear. They're starting to get electricity poles up though. They're as far as Gambo now. They'll get to us in another couple of years or so.' He releases her foot. 'Give us the other one, maid.'

Ellie swings her right foot over and hits the stump of Thomas's leg. He groans. She sits up in the bed. 'I'm so sorry, Thomas. I didn't mean to.'

'I knows it, Ellie Mae.' He rubs the scar on his cheek. 'I'm not much of a specimen, am I? He grunts. 'You half expects to die, but you don't expects to come back half a man.'

Pressing her body against Thomas's, Ellie tucks her head against his chest. 'I don't care. I'm just so glad we're together again. We're a family now. Emmy's such a good baby. I'll wager you've already forgotten he's in here with us. He hardly makes a sound.'

'He must take after you, Ellie Mae. Mam said I howled like a banshee till I was five.'

'I don't think your mother likes me.'

'I'd say you're right.'

Ellie's head bolts up. 'Thomas! You're supposed to say something like *"She'll come round"*. Or, *"She's just having an off day"*.'

'Mam's a hard case. She's lived in Tippy's Tickle since the day she was born. Saw her mam and her four brothers die of TB.

Lots of people die of that up here. Then my brothers and sister with the Spanish Flu in 'Eighteen.'

'That's awful. At least she has you and your father.'

'And look what the war's done to me.'

'Your father seems nice.'

'Best kind.'

'Where did he go tonight?'

'Rod Fizzard's stage down on the tickle. It's crib night. He's the best cribbage player in Tippy's Tickle.'

'Cribbage?'

'Well, that's what he tells Mam. Mostly, they goes there to drink Rod's rum.'

Thomas slides his fingers under the pink nylon strap of Ellie's negligee. 'What's this get-up you're wearin', maid?'

Ellie runs her hand over the shiny pink fabric. 'It's the nicest negligee I could find in Norwich.'

He hooks his finger around the thin strap and slides it down her arm. 'You've gots too many clothes on.'

'But, Thomas. It's freezing.'

Thomas raises the sheets and blankets over their heads. 'Not under here it isn't, maid. Come under here with me.'

# *Chapter 51*

Tippy's Tickle – 12 September 2011

Emmett's store is how she remembered it. The paint the colour of meat that's been left to age. The four small windows painted white. The wharf leading down to it from the rocky beach a salt-blasted silver.

Sophie stands on top of a slab of grey rock and watches Sam as he leans over the white wooden hull of a small boat, sanding it by hand to what Sophie can only imagine will be a pristine smoothness. *If a job's worth doing at all, it's worth doing right.* She smiles. Sam didn't believe in shortcuts. The old way is the best way, he'd once told her. Just mix the method with modern design.

It's why his furniture has been selling so well in New York. Whenever she'd missed him, when she'd wondered what he was doing right then at that minute when she was thinking about him, she'd stop by The Future Perfect and run her hands over his sculptural tables and chairs. Everything fashioned out of the silver, salt-cured wood of old Newfoundland wharves and abandoned outport houses. She'd feel its contours, its lines, as smooth and cool as satin under her fingertips, and imagine herself back in Sam's cottage. But then she'd close down the thought like a shutter over a beautiful view that she knew she'd never see again.

He'd called, just after she'd emailed Ellie with her new contact details after she'd started the job in New York.

She'd been rushing up Madison Avenue to a meeting at TBWA to pitch for the redesign of their offices. She'd had her laptop case and the huge portfolio with the presentation boards and she'd been trying to drink a Starbucks skinny latte without spilling it over herself. Then her phone had rung.

She'd meant to call him back later. He'd called a few more times, sent some texts. She'd never answered those either. She'd meant to, but she'd been so busy.

The last time she'd seen him, in front of the airport terminal, he'd said it would never work. That it wouldn't be fair to Becca to get involved with someone who lives in a different country. He was just doing that ping-pong thing men do. When you want them, they don't want you. Then when you don't want them, they can't leave you alone. She wasn't going to play those kinds of games.

For about a year he'd tried to keep in touch, the messages thinning out until one day she realised she hadn't heard from him for several months. Then, about a year and a half after her detour to Newfoundland, she'd walked by The Future Perfect furniture shop. Sam's picture was in the window.

### Introducing the exclusive Bufflehead collection of hand-crafted furniture

#### by Sam Byrne.

*A collaboration between an artisan furniture maker and nature, from the north shore of Newfoundland. Meet Sam Byrne on Friday evening at 6.30pm on a rare visit to New York.*

*By appointment only. Inquire inside.*

She'd gone into the shop and had her name put on the guest list. But when the day came, she'd bottled out. What was it that Sam had said? *Timing and geography.* They were two people on two different paths that had crossed, but now they were travelling in different directions. It was just one of those things.

He didn't call her when he was in New York. She'd been expecting the call. Her heart jumping every time her phone had rung. But it was done. A boat missed. A ship passed in the night. The possibility of a relationship with Sam had slipped away, like a memory of a dream that dissolves when you open your eyes to the morning. She'd drunk two bottles of wine and cried in the bathtub. Then she'd got on with life. And life was work.

A tall man with a shock of wiry, grey hair emerges from the store, carrying two mugs. Emmett. He must be about sixty-five or so now. Emmett hadn't thought much of her, back in 2001. Couldn't have said more than two sentences to her. Sometimes he'd scrutinise her like she'd caused him some great wrong. She'd never had a chance to find out why. He'd avoided her like she was carrying the flu. If Newfoundlanders were known for their friendliness and hospitality, Emmett Parsons was certainly the exception that proved the rule.

He joins Sam by the boat and hands him a mug. *It'll be coffee. Black. Sam's a coffee man.* The two men lean their elbows on the boat's hull and talk. Sam shakes his head and rubs his forehead. She wishes she could read his lips. To know if he was speaking about her.

'Sam.'

Sam and Emmett look up. Sophie picks her way down the rocky slope onto the wharf.

'Hi, Emmett.' Sophie holds out her hand. 'Nice to see you again.'

Emmett screws his lips together and stares at her with his odd blue and brown eyes. He gives her a quick nod. He takes Sam's empty mug and heads back into the store.

'That wasn't very friendly.'

'Why do you suppose that is?' Sam picks up the sandpaper and drags it across the wooden hull.

'He never liked me. He's always been like that with me.'

'Maybe he's a good judge of character.'

Sophie bites her lip. He's just needling her. Trying to get a rise out of her. She runs her hand along the boat's hull.

'Why didn't you tell him his jumper is inside out?'

Sam shrugs. 'I'm not his mother.'

'No, that you're not.' She leans against the wall. 'I've seen your furniture in New York. I specified it for a restaurant we designed in Tribeca.'

'That was you?'

'I had a colleague in our interior design practice place the order. I didn't want you to think I was doing you any favours.'

'And were you?'

'No, of course not. If your furniture was rubbish, I'd never order it. I take my work very seriously.' She glances at the store. 'You're not still making it in there, are you? I ordered over a hundred chairs.'

'No.' Sam nods towards the shore. 'I've got a bigger place down by the shore now.'

Sophie squints at the shore. 'You've got people working for you now?'

'Emmett helps on the bigger orders when I need it. I still help him on the boats when he needs it. Becca's boyfriend, Toby, has been getting underfoot there, too, since the fish processing plant closed in Heart's Wish. I've had him turning out the table and chair legs on the new lathe.'

'Why don't you expand? The lead-time was quite long.'

Sam grunts. 'Why would I want to do that?'

'Well, to make more money. Be successful.'

Sam pulls a chamois cloth from his back pocket and rubs it along the sanded hull. 'That's it, then? In order to be successful, you need to earn a lot of money?'

Sophie crosses her arms. 'It's what capitalism is all about.'

'Right. And money plus success equals happiness?'

'Yes, of course.'

'Are you happy?'

'Why wouldn't I be? I've got everything I've ever wanted.'

'That wasn't what I asked.'

Sophie frowns at Sam. 'Why are you so angry with me?'

Sam folds the cloth and stuffs it back into the pocket of his jeans. 'Because I haven't been able to forget you. And it tees me off.'

Sophie feels the blood rising in her cheeks. *He hasn't been able to forget me?*

'Sam, look, I'm sorry. Life just … the past ten years just went so fast. I never intended to lose touch.' She kicks at a small orange buoy on the wharf. 'I concentrated on my career and it's been wonderful. I'm a lead architect at the firm. Up for a partnership. I design buildings all around the world. It's everything I've ever wanted.'

'Great. That's great. I'm happy for you.'

Raising her hands, she signs the words she's been practising: *How's Becca? Is she well?*

Sam signs back: *She's beautiful.*

Sophie folds her right hand and moves it over her chest in a circle, then she spells out Sam's name with her fingers. *'I'm sorry about what happened.'*

Sam nods. 'It wasn't your fault. I think she's forgotten all about it. She was just a kid.'

He looks out over the tickle's rippled blue water. 'So, Princess Grace, what brings you back after all these years? I wouldn't flatter myself that you've come to see me, and, knowing you, I don't imagine it's a holiday.'

Her stomach jolts. *How does he know? Can he read me that easily?* She can't tell him about the hotel. At least, not yet. She needs to handle this carefully. It affects everyone in the town, not just Sam. Say the wrong thing, to the wrong person, and the locals will dig their heels in and refuse to budge. A luxury hotel in the centre of Tippy's Tickle is an idea that she needs to introduce when she's warmed them up, planted some seeds. The closure of the fish processing plant is a windfall of good luck. The hotel will bring jobs, she'll tell them; she'll get the consortium on board with that somehow. Jobs bring money. And money, despite what they say, can definitely bring happiness. Or, at least something close to it.

'Well, you're wrong, Sam. I needed a break and I know Aunt Ellie's birthday is coming up. I know I've been rubbish keeping in contact with her, so I thought it was time to come to see you all.' She glances towards the store. 'Though not particularly Emmett.' She rests her elbow on the boat hull. 'I've done nothing but work for the past ten years. I love my job, but I want more balance in my life. Otherwise someday my headstone will say *"Here lies Sophie Parry. She worked herself to death".'*

'So you figured you'd get some balance by coming here.'

'Why not? I used to draw and paint when I was younger. My

mother said I was like Aunt Ellie that way. I really enjoyed picking it up again with Aunt Ellie the last time I was here. I've actually kept it up since I've been in New York. I've just signed up for a painting class, too. I thought I'd spend some time working on some sketches up here. Maybe one day I'll be good enough to have an exhibition.' She waves her hand over the view of the tickle and the rocky shoreline with its spattering of colourful houses and wind-bent trees. 'If I can't find inspiration here, I'm a lost cause.'

Sam rubs his forehead. 'Well, you can do what you like, but don't distract Becca. She's studying for her entrance exams for med school. She wants to study at Memorial next year.'

'Oh, I'd never do that, Sam. I know how important it is to be focused.'

Sam looks at Sophie and shakes his head. 'You know, I thought there was something between us.'

Sophie's heart jumps. *You thought there was something between us? Why didn't you say anything at the airport? Why didn't you say anything?*

'Sam, you said you couldn't get involved with someone who lived in a different country because it wouldn't be fair on Becca. At the airport, when I left. You said something about timings and geography. Remember? I remember.'

Sam sucks in a breath of air between his teeth. 'I was an idiot, Sophie. Wince said as much.'

'You told Wince? The guy at the garage?'

He tugs the cloth out of his pocket and starts buffing the boat's paintwork again. 'You get in a garage, and you talk.' He shrugs. 'I thought you'd come back at some point and I could make it right.'

Sophie reaches across and rests her hand on Sam's. 'But Sam, I have.'

# *Chapter 52*

## Tippy's Tickle – 11 August 1947

Ellie shuts the flimsy wooden door of the outhouse and skirts under a line of washing as she hurries back to the house. She stops to pick several stems of the wild fireweed that shoots up in bright purple banks around the scrubby yard, and swats at the mosquitoes that whine persistently around her head.

Agnes looks up at her from her knitting as the screen door slams. 'Don't be bringin' those weeds in here, girl! We'll have bugs all over the kitchen. Was you born on a raft?'

Ellie looks down at the flowers, her heart sinking. 'I thought they'd be pretty for Emmy's birthday.'

'Weeds belongs outside. I'm not havin' them in my house. Honestly, you're as stunned as a dead cat sometimes, girl.'

Ellie feels the heat rise in her cheeks. Nothing she did was right. She couldn't sew a seam straight enough, or make dumplings plump enough, or find berries ripe enough when they were out berry picking in the marshes.

'I always had flowers in the house at home in England. My father loves them.'

'There's no accounting for people's ignorance. You wants the place crawlin' with ants or worse?'

'That never happened in England.'

'There we goes again about England. England this and England that. Why don't you do us a favour and go back there where you belongs?'

Ellie blinks back the tears that threaten to spill over her hot cheeks. She was doing her best. But nothing she did was good enough for Agnes. 'I'm sorry, Agnes. I thought they'd be nice.'

'Well, I'm not chancin' any bugs in here. Throw them out.'

Her shoulders slumping in defeat, Ellie wipes the back of her hand across her eyes and opens the screen door. Out on the porch she closes her eyes and raises her face to the cool breeze blowing in from the ocean. If only she could go back to England. Persuade Thomas to pack up and leave this wretched place. But that would never happen. Not least because they'd never be able to afford to.

She's lost herself. She doesn't know who she is anymore. Where's the Ellie who'd dodged bombs and who'd driven through the devastation left by the Baedeker raids with supplies for the firemen in the Auxiliary Fire Service? Where's the Ellie who used to giggle with Ruthie at the latest Marx Brothers film or swing around the dance floors of the Samson or the Lido? Where's the artist? The daughter? The sister? *Who am I?*

She swats at a mosquito with the bouquet of purple fireweed and heads slowly down the wooden steps. On the final step, she stops.

*This isn't right. This is my home, too. I'm Ellie Parsons. I'm the wife of your son, Agnes. I'm a mother to Emmett. I'm Eleanor Mary Burgess Parsons. I'm a woman and I intend to live my best life, Agnes Parsons. I live here now. You'll just have to get used to the idea, because I'm not going anywhere.*

She juts out her jaw and pulls back her shoulders. *There's nothing wrong with bringing some flowers into the house. Into my house.*

Ellie stomps up the steps and pulls open the screen door. Tossing the flowers onto the table, she heads over to the cupboard, shoving the pots and pans aside until she finds what she's looking for.

'What kind of racket do you think you're makin', girl? My teeth are fit to rattle out of my head.'

*If you had any teeth left, you old bat.* Ellie dips the metal pitcher into the bucket of water by the stove and sets it on the table. Picking up the flowers she sticks them into the pitcher.

Agnes sets down her knitting and glares at Ellie over the top of her glasses. 'What are you, deaf as a cod, maid? Didn't I tells you to throw them out?'

'You did, indeed.' She takes a deep breath. 'But I fancy them, and I truly don't see the harm in having a few flowers in the house.'

Agnes shoves the knitting aside and pushes herself out of the armchair. 'Are you givin' me lip, girl?'

Ellie folds her fingers around the back of a wooden chair to steady herself. 'I am not. This is my home, too, and I'd like to have a few flowers for Emmy's birthday.'

Agnes's mouth falls open. 'You ... you—'

The thud of footsteps on the back porch. The screen door flies open and Ephraim strides into the kitchen, scratching his neck. 'Jaysus God, those skeeters are some thick.' He throws a stack of dried cod onto the table. 'Well, look at that.' He bends over and sniffs at the flowers. 'Aren't those lovely. Cheers the place right up.'

A smile tugs at the corners of Ellie's mouth as she glances

over at Agnes. 'Yes, don't they? Now, if you'll excuse me, I must go check on Emmy.'

Ellie roots through the baking sheets and muffin tins in the cupboard beside the stove. 'Have you seen the cake tins, Agnes? I'm sure I saw them here just the other day.'

The kitchen is silent except for the click of Agnes's knitting needles.

Ellie rises to her feet. 'Agnes? Have you seen the cake tins? I need to bake Emmy's birthday cake.'

Agnes peers over at Ellie, her pale eyes as hard as the ice of a ballycatter along the shore. 'Hasn't seen them.'

'Martha Fizzard hasn't borrowed them?'

'Martha Fizzard's gots her own.'

Ellie kneels down on the faded green linoleum and pulls the contents out of the cupboard until they're stacked around her like a fortress. 'They're not here.'

'You must'a put them somewhere else last time you used them. If it wasn't for your lack of sense, you'd have no sense at all.'

'I put them back here. I know I did.'

'Looks like there'll be no birthday cake today.'

'But Emmy'll be so disappointed.'

Agnes holds up a knitted needle with half a toddler's pink wool jumper. 'The baby's only three. He doesn't knows what he doesn't know.'

'You hid them, didn't you, Agnes.'

'Never did any such thing.'

Rising to her feet, Ellie steps over the piles of pots and pans and pulls open the screen door.

'Where'd you think you're goin', miss? You left a mess there in the kitchen.'

'It's Emmy's birthday, and he's going to have a birthday cake.' The screen door slams behind her as she hurries across the yard and down the steps to the Fizzards' house by the tickle.

*That spiteful old woman! First the flowers and now the cake tins.*

She says the words over and over again in her head as she makes her way to the Fizzards': *This is my home, too. This is my home, too. This is my home, too.*

# *Chapter 53*

Tippy's Tickle – 12 September 2011

'Have you spoken to them?'

Sophie glances at her bedroom door and turns down the volume on her laptop. 'Give me some time. I've only just arrived, Richard. I have to find the right way to do this. Most of the people in Tippy's Tickle have been living here all their lives. It's their home.'

Richard removes his round, black-framed glasses. He huffs on the glass and wipes the lenses with a white handkerchief. 'Sophie, we don't have time. You know what we can offer. It's more than generous. I don't know why you're making this so complicated. We only need the land around that big house on the cliff and access to the water for the marina. For a start, anyway. What's that? Three, four properties? Everyone else can stay in their shacks, for all I care. Believe me, those folks will think they've won the lottery. They'll be lining up once we start handing out the money.'

He picks up a tiny white china espresso cup in a thick-fingered hand and sips the coffee. He sets down the cup in its saucer, the chink of china resonating over the Skype connection. 'I've got a meeting with the consortium Friday afternoon here in the board-room at two. I want to give them some good news, Sophie.'

'I'll do my best.'

Richard slides his glasses up the bridge of his large Roman nose. 'Failure isn't an option.'

'What do you mean by that?'

Richard shrugs, the neck of his black turtleneck sweater swamping his chin. 'If you don't get every one of those people signing up to sell by Friday, don't bother coming back to New York.'

Becca runs up the road from the cottage towards Sam's pickup truck, Bear loping at her heels, a stuffed dinosaur, frayed and faded, in his mouth. Standing with her hand on the pickup's door handle, Sophie watches the girl approach; tall, like Sam, and so pretty in the loose floral cotton dress and oversized blue sweater embroidered with fabric flowers, her fine blonde hair pulled back into a messy ponytail. Sophie waves at her, signing, 'Hello, Becca.'

Becca nods politely at Sophie, her eyes behind her wire-rimmed glasses the steely blue of a winter sea. *Hello, Sophie. How are you?* she signs.

*I'm well. It's nice to see you.*

A shadow of a smile flicks across Becca's face, then she climbs into the back of the pickup truck with Bear, making a nest for herself amongst the easels and blankets.

Florie hands Sophie a wicker picnic basket and a yapping dachshund. 'Here you goes, maid. Make sure Hildy doesn't get into the food. She almost had my finger off this morning when I was makin' the cheese sandwiches.'

Sam turns the key in the ignition. The engine sputters and chokes. He tries again, and the engine engages with a gritty whine. He leans out of the window. 'Get in or we'll miss the sun. It's going to rain later.'

'Sit in the front with Sam,' Ellie says, coming up beside Sophie. 'I get nervous when we're driving along the coast. I'll sit in the back with Florie.'

Sophie glances through the window at Sam, who is twisting the radio knob through a range of static. When she'd put her hand on his earlier, he'd pulled away.

*What did you expect, Sophie? That he'd declare his love for you and you'd live happily ever after?*

'Are you sure, Aunt Ellie?'

'Absolutely.' She nudges Sophie's shoulder. 'Go.'

Sophie climbs into the passenger seat beside Sam. Glancing into the rear-view mirror, she catches Becca's eye and smiles, but the girl turns away.

# *Chapter 54*

## Tippy's Tickle – 24 July 1948

'You sees how I'm doin' it, Emmy? You takes the penknife and you just skims the wood a bit at a time till it's smooth as margarine.' Thomas hands the small carving to his son. 'Does that feels like margarine to you, son?'

'Yes, Da'.'

'What does you think it looks like?'

Emmett runs his fingers over the curves and something that looks like a beak. 'A bird?'

Thomas tousles Emmett hair. 'It is a bird, b'y. Aren't you a clever clogs? We'll gets your mam to paint it up for you, so it looks one of the puffins we saw down the coast.'

Emmett's round face crumples into a frown. 'There's no wings.' He sticks a finger into a hole on the side of the carving. 'What's that?'

'That's where the wings goes. See? There's a hole on each side.' Thomas picks up two thin, tapered batons, and hands one to Emmett. 'Here, son, put the narrow ends in the holes.' Holding the bird's round body steady, he helps Emmett slot the batons into the holes. He sets the tall wooden stand he's carved on the table.

'You sees how the bird has a nice round base likes a ball?'

Emmett nods.

'And you sees how the stand has a curve in it like a saucer? Now, you puts the bird on top. Don't knock off those wings.'

Emmett carefully sets the bird on top of the stand until the long baton wings splay out either side. He clutches the bird's round body. 'It'll fall off, Da'.'

'Let go, son. It won't fall, I promises you.'

Emmett releases the wooden bird. Thomas taps the bird's plump body, setting it teetering wildly on top of the stand.

'It'll fall!'

'It won't, Emmy. See these wings? They're balancing the body. It'll just roll around and go back and forth, but it won't fall off.'

A knock on the store's door. A waft of hot baking. Ellie walks in with a basket covered in a tea towel. 'How are my boys? I brought you some tea buns fresh out of the oven.' She sets down the basket on the battered wooden table. 'Well, look at that. Isn't that clever?'

'You needs to paint it likes a puffin, Mammy.'

'I can do that, Emmy. Daddy will just need to find me some paint.' She unwraps the tea towel and sets out the tea buns on a plate with a pat of margarine, a jar of home-made partridge-berry jam and a knife.

'That smells good enough to tempt a saint, maid.'

'I thought you might like a snack,' Ellie says, slicing open a tea bun. She slathers it with margarine and jam and hands one half to Emmett and the other to Thomas. 'You've been in here for hours.'

Thomas lifts the tea towel and peeks into the basket. 'You didn't bring any beer, did you, maid?'

'You and Ephraim drank the last of it last night. All eight bottles.'

'Fishing's thirsty work.'

'Yes, but every night, Thomas? If you're not drinking up Agnes's beer, you're off down at Rod Fizzard's or Jim Boyd's.'

'Don't be getting on at me, Ellie Mae. It helps me with the pain in my leg. It's part of life here, anyway. Keeps us cheerful.'

'The women don't drink.'

'Women don't needs to drink.'

'Thomas—'

The door swings open and Ephraim enters the store. 'You can smell those buns all the way to Jim Boyd's.' He pulls up a chair to the table. 'Is it good, Emmy, b'y?'

Emmett nods as he licks jam off his lip. 'Looks what Da' made.'

'Well, isn't that a lovely thing.'

'Push it, Grandpa.'

'I can't do that, Emmy, b'y. It'll fall right off.'

'It won't, Grandpa. Look.' Emmett pokes at the carved bird, setting it teetering around the stand.

Ephraim whistles. 'Well, isn't that a clever thing?'

Ellie hands her father-in-law a buttered tea bun. 'Have you heard anything about the referendum results? I heard Archbishop Roche was dead against Newfoundland joining Canada.'

'Jim had the radio goin' in the shop. Big crowd there listenin'. Most of the Catholics on the Avalon Peninsula listened to that old fella. They mostly all voted for independence, though some of them was upset they couldn't vote to join the States like's been talked up these past months.'

Ellie licks a dollop of jam off her finger. 'Newfoundland could have joined the United States?'

'There was some talk about it, maid, yes,' Ephraim says, 'but it never gots onto the ballot.'

Thomas wipes a crumb off his chin as he chews on a tea bun. 'So, we're independent, then? Is that whats you're sayin'?'

'No, b'y. Smallwood's lot won the day. We're joinin' Canada next year. Agnes's got a face like a can of worms. I stopped in to tell her on the way here.'

'Joining Canada will be a good thing, don't you think?' Ellie says as she scoops jam onto a tea bun. 'I read in the paper that they're going to pay an annual baby bonus to parents for every child. They'll send us money for Emmy. We can start a college fund for him.'

Thomas laughs. 'I doubts our Emmy'll be heading off to college. It's not for the likes of us around here.'

Ellie sets down the tea bun. 'What do you mean by that, Thomas? Our son can go to college. All he needs is a proper education here first.'

Ephraim reaches into his pocket and takes out an envelope. 'Hold on. I just remembered. This came for you yesterday at Jim Boyd's, Ellie.'

Ellie rips open the envelope and slides out the telegram.

10.45 NORWICH

DEAR ELLIE – POPPY DIED 16 JULY – FUNERAL YESTERDAY
– LEAVING FOR LONDON – DOTTIE

She clutches the telegram against her chest. 'Poppy's died, Thomas. Poppy's died and I never got to say goodbye.'

# *Chapter 55*

## Tippy's Tickle – 12 September 2011

Sam slams the door of his pickup truck and kicks the front tyre as the others clamber out with the dogs, and onto the gravel parking lot beneath the lighthouse.

'Looks like the tyre's got a slow leak. I'm going to have to head over to Wince's place and get him to look at it.'

Sophie eyes the once-black truck, which is now patchy with rust and faded to a dirty grey from years of salty rain. 'You might ask him if he can fix the hole in the floor on the passenger side, too. I think the only thing holding this truck together is rust, Sam. Don't you think it's time to buy a new one?'

Sam holds up a hand and rubs his thumb and forefinger together. 'Money.'

'But your furniture's selling for a bomb in New York.'

He shrugs. 'Retailers charge what they want. I make a fraction of what the stuff sells for in New York. It's enough to pay the bills, but there's no gravy.'

'There's always credit.'

Sam shakes his head. 'That means the bank owns you.'

Ellie hands Sophie a burlap bag full of paint tubes, brushes and palettes. 'Enough chit-chat, you two. Florie, give Becca the lunch hamper and take the easels. We've got a painting lesson to get on with.'

Standing back from her easel, Sophie lifts her face up to the soft warmth of the September sun. It feels so good to be back. She'd forgotten how this place seemed to wrap her in possibilities – the possibility of being an artist, the possibility of being part of a family, the possibility, maybe, of love. She could almost pretend that the New York Sophie didn't exist. Almost.

She scrutinises her painting. The white lighthouse with its red beacon sits resolutely on the grey rock of the headland, puffs of white clouds floating above it in the whisper blue of the sky. Cocking her head, she squints at the white house on the cliff, and screws up her mouth.

She's made the roof too large. She needs to work on her technique. When is she supposed to find the time? She'd already missed two life-drawing classes this month. Maybe it's just a silly dream. She dabs her brush into the blue paint, mixing it with white, and works at obliterating the roofline.

Ellie wipes her brush on a cotton rag and dabs at her palette, blending grey paint into the pale blue sky. 'You're worrying too much about making a pretty picture, Sophie. Don't overthink it. Art has to come from within. How does the lighthouse make you *feel*?'

'It's a building on a cliff, Aunt Ellie.'

'That's where you're wrong.' Ellie points at the lighthouse with her brush. 'Does the lighthouse make you feel secure? Reassured, maybe? Or does it make you think of sea storms and danger? Is it romantic, or solid? The way the lighthouse and the cliff make you feel is what you need to express in your painting.'

Sophie glances over at Ellie's painting. The lighthouse is a blend of mauves and whites, and in the greyed sky of a hazy morning, the cliff's sharp edges disappear into a soft mist. A place of promise and dreams.

'How did you learn all this?'

'I was at art school in Norwich during the war. I studied under Dame Edith Spink.'

'Dame Edith Spink? Seriously? She's an icon! There's a fantastic painting of hers in the Imperial War Museum in London of a WAAF who saved a pilot. My dad showed it to me once. He said it was his favourite painting. I have a postcard of it on my refrigerator.'

Ellie smiles. 'Corporal Deirdre Cross. She wanted me to join the WAAF.'

'You knew her?'

'I worked for Dame Edith for a short while, before ... Well, the war changed everything. I joined the Auxiliary Fire Service, met Thomas, moved here, and that was that for my art until Florie came along.'

Sophie looks over at Florie and Becca who are playing with the dogs on a patch of yellowing grass nearby. 'How long have you been together?'

'Forty-four years this summer. I only knew Thomas for fourteen.'

Florie bangs a tin pot lid with a metal spoon. 'Lunchtime! I'm that hungry I could eat a pig fish.'

Ellie's thin face breaks into a grin. 'I don't know what I would have done without her. Money was always tight after Thomas died. She bought the old store from the Boyd family for a song with money she'd saved when she was teaching. She convinced some of the fishermen to do whale tours and iceberg tours. She put Tippy's Tickle on the tourist map. She got me teaching art classes and selling art. She started her kennels. Florie's a force of nature.'

'She certainly is.'

'We seem to manage, somehow. I own Kittiwake outright, which is a great help. The bank threatened to repossess it for years. Emmy helped when he could, bless him. He made good money fishing out of Fogo before he got into boat-building, and he gave me what he could. Thank goodness those days are over. It was very hard after Thomas died. I can't imagine ever wanting to live anywhere else now, though.'

'It's lovely here, Aunt Ellie.' Sophie runs her tongue over her lips. How can she broach the subject of selling Kittiwake to the consortium? She's got to start somewhere.

'Kittiwake is a beautiful house, but the winters must be freezing up there on the cliff.'

'Oh, you can't imagine, Sophie! The wind whips across the ocean down from the Arctic. I don't think I was warm for fifty years. But since Sam put in the radiators we're snug as bugs in a rug. No, I'm not going anywhere. I'll be in that house till the day I die.'

Florie flakes out on the Hudson's Bay blanket, throwing her legs wide, and pats her stomach. 'That was some good, Ellie. I do loves your salmon loaf.'

Ellie jiggles Florie's denim-clad leg with a bare foot. 'Well, you did eat half of it, honey.'

Sophie closes her eyes and lifts her face to the sun. A gust of fresh air wafts across her skin, spiked with the salty tang of the ocean below. Opening her eyes, she tucks her hands around her knees and looks over at Becca. She's playing a tug of war with Bear with the stuffed dinosaur as Florie's dachshund, Hildegarde, runs and yaps around her feet.

Sophie chews her lip. *I'm still unforgiven, aren't I, Becca? How can I fix it? How can I make it better between us?*

The mobile phone buzzes in her jeans pocket. She pulls it out and looks at the caller's name. No surprise there. 'Hi, Richard. Just a second.'

She looks over at Ellie. 'Sorry. Work call. I'll just be a minute.'

'That's fine, dear. We're not going anywhere.'

She strolls past Becca towards a line of mangled spruce trees. 'What is it, Richard? No, not yet. Yes, I know. Friday. I know. Yes, I've had a walk around the cliff. My aunt's house is definitely the perfect location for the hotel. There's a nearby cottage, too, with access to a sandy beach. Yes, Bufflehead Cottage. Yes, I thought so too. The one I sent you a picture of. No, I don't think that one will be a problem. He needs money. I have to work on my aunt, though. Yes. Yes. Friday. I'll have everything you need for the meeting, Richard. Don't worry.'

Switching off the call, Sophie pockets the phone and jogs across the grass towards Becca. She grabs the dinosaur from Bear and tosses it to the girl. The great black dog leaps into the air, barking as the dinosaur soars overhead. The toy falls at Becca's feet, and the dachshund dashes in and scoops it up. The dogs spin across the grass in an explosion of joy.

'Becca?'

Becca stares at Sophie. Turning, she heads back to join the others.

# *Chapter 56*

## Tippy's Tickle – 1 April 1949

'At the confederation celebrations in St John's today, Joseph R. Smallwood was called upon to form an interim government—'

'That's right, my son,' Ephraim says as he chews on a piece of boiled cabbage. 'You go on there.'

'*Sssh*, Dad. I wants to hear McSwain.'

'Cryin' shame,' Agnes says as she pours tinned milk into her tea. 'I'm a Newfoundlander no matter what that Smallwood says.'

'You looks like you're goin' to a funeral, woman, in all your black.' Ephraim opens another bottle of beer. ''Tis the best thing that's happened to us here on The Rock since the Americans built their bases here in the war.'

Thomas rolls his eyes. '*Ssh*, will you both. You're as nattery as noddies after cod heads.'

Ellie leans back from her chair and turns up the dial on the new radio, which Thomas has set, pride of place, on the centre of the hutch. Monthly payments for two years to Jim Boyd, he'd said. They'll need to find the money from somewhere. Still, she's glad. It's a connection to the outside world. A world she can barely imagine still exists.

'*… The effects of confederation have already been felt widely in*

*Newfoundland. Prices for many commodities have dropped drastically, such as clothing and food—'*

'That's a good thing, Mam. Food and clothes'll be cheaper now.'

'… *Railway passenger and freight rates also were slashed—'*

'Does you hears that?' Ephraim says. 'We might be able to get to the Regatta in St John's this year if the train's cheaper.'

Agnes dabs at a drop of gravy on her black wool dress. 'I'm not takin' that train anywhere. Tippy's Tickle's all I needs. Can't be doin' with all those Catholics prancin' about St John's.'

Ellie sets down her teacup. 'The Catholics mostly voted for independence, Agnes. Just like you.'

Agnes shoots a glare at her daughter-in-law. 'That's as may be. Doesn't mean I'd shake the hand of the Pope on a cold day.'

'… *Perhaps the predominant feeling was expressed by a seal hunter who returned from the northern ice flows last night on the* Terra Nova. *This man, who voted anti-confederation—'*

'There's a Catholic for you, Mam.'

'… *said, "We're in this now and we're going to be good Canadians, but whatever they want to call me, I'll still be a Newfoundlander at heart."'*

'Man after my own heart,' Agnes says as she pours another cup of tea.

Ellie collects the supper plates. 'Maybe they'll find the money to build a school here now.'

'Don't hold your breath it'll be any time soon, Ellie Mae.' Thomas takes a swig of beer. 'Towns'll be lined up for Canadian money all the way to Cape Spear.'

'Well, we need to do something, Thomas,' Ellie says. 'Emmy will be five this summer. He needs to start his schooling and there's no way to get him to the school all the way down in Wesleyville.'

'We could set him to board with my cousin Edna in Badger's Quay,' Ephraim says, stuffing his pipe with tobacco. 'The school's only a couple of miles from her place. A good walk for a young lad.'

'That's very nice, Ephraim, but I'm not having Emmy board at his age. And two miles is too far for him to be walking to school on his own.'

Agnes places a plate of molasses cookies on the table. 'Ellie's right.'

Ellie's head snaps around to face her mother-in-law.

'Slap me in the face with a cod, Mam,' Thomas says, laughing. 'Did you just agree with Ellie Mae?'

Agnes picks out three of the cookies and puts them on her dessert plate. 'Pains me, for sure, but Emmy's too young for that lot out there. No tellin' who'll get his hands on him.'

'You gotta stop dressin' him likes a girl, Mam. He's a boy. He'll start gettin' ribbed for it.'

Ellie reaches over for a cookie. 'Maybe we can find someone to teach the children over in the church basement. I can speak to the vicar. He might know where we can find a teacher.'

'You're gettin' awfully tight with Father Gill, there, maid,' Thomas says. 'You thinkin' of becomin' a Protestant?'

'No, of course not, Thomas. It's just I don't have much choice if I want to worship. The closest Catholic church is in Gambo.'

Agnes crunches on a cookie with her new set of dentures. 'I imagines your God's gonna put a black mark against your immortal soul for steppin' into a Protestant church.'

Ellie dunks her cookie into her tea. 'We actually have the same God, Agnes. I think He understands. It's not ideal, but *"Needs must"* as a friend of mine used to say.'

# Chapter 57

## Tippy's Tickle – 13 September 2011

Sophie taps HOTMAIL into the search bar on her laptop, but the screen goes blank except for the message: No Internet Connection.

She groans and flops back against the wooden spindles of the desk chair. *Bloody hell. No Wi-Fi connection again!* She has to get these pictures and a report on the site to Richard today, or she'll never hear the end of it. She can't use the connection over in Florie's shop. There just isn't enough privacy. She glances out at the view from her bedroom window at the top of Kittiwake. Her eyes travel over the horizon, with its base of deep blue abutting the bright blue sky. Tufts of clouds hover high in the sky above the ocean, blowing in from the east. She looks towards the right, where the triangular tops of firs and spruce trees obscure the view of Sam's cottage and the sandy cove beyond.

Sam. He has a computer. She's seen his furniture website. He must have a decent connection. She could ask to use his Wi-Fi. Pushing the chair away from the desk, she switches off the laptop and slides it into her computer bag.

Sam pokes the kindling in the wood burner with an iron poker, stirring up the flames. 'Do you have everything you need?'

'Thanks again, Sam. You're a lifesaver.'

'Tell your boss I charge a hundred dollars a half-hour.'

Sophie laughs. 'Sure.'

Sam raises an eyebrow. 'You don't believe me?' He points to the router. 'This is an ultra-deluxe range-extending router brought all the way from St John's on the back of Thor's bike.'

'How is Thor, anyway? And his brother ... Ace, wasn't it?'

'They're good. Ace's remarried. A Brazilian physiotherapist from St John's. Thor's had twins since you were here. Ruby and Pearl.'

'You still go biking with them?'

'Sure.'

'How about you?'

'What about me?'

'Are you ... involved with anybody?'

Sam snorts. 'Would it matter if I was?'

'Well, uh, she might not like me being here ... using your Wi-Fi.'

Sam hangs the poker on a hook and joins Sophie at the table where she's set up her laptop. He shifts aside a pile of drawings. 'Anything else you need?'

'No, no, I'm good.'

'You're sure? More coffee, tea?'

'She doesn't live with you, does she?'

Sam grins. 'It's just me and Becca. And Bear, of course.'

Sophie taps a drawing with her pencil. 'What are you drawing?'

Sam unrolls the drawing and sets Sophie's coffee mug on one corner while he holds the other down with his left hand. 'I had an idea for retreat cabins. We've got all sorts of artists finding their way up here in the summer. Painters, writers, textile artists, photographers ... you name it. They see some pictures online, and the next thing you know, they're showing up at Florie's asking where they can stay for a few months. Some of the locals rent out rooms, but there's no place for them to do their art except around Ellie's art table in the store or on someone's kitchen table. So, I came up with an idea for these cabins.'

Sophie leans over the plan drawings. A simple square room clad in plywood, with a tiny toilet and kitchenette, and a log burner in the open-plan main room.

'This looks great, Sam. Could I ... would you mind if I made a few suggestions?'

'Sure.'

Sophie slides a blank piece of paper across the table and draws a truncated cube, its far wall replaced by a plane of glass, with a deck protruding from the side wall like a platform.

Standing back from the table, she cocks her head and tucks a stray strand of hair behind her ear. 'What do you think? We could keep the interior simple, play with a mix of plywood and cladding painted white, and paint the exterior in the colour of the stores I've seen – red, white, some blue, you know. Let the deck go silver like the wharves.'

'Looks good. I like it.'

'I just tweaked it a bit, that's all. We could play with the shapes. Maybe make one triangular, even a circle. I can do some drawings while I'm here. They won't take me long.'

Sam laughs.

'What?'

'You said *we*. Twice.'

'Did I? I meant you. Or me. Drawing. You know.' Sophie feels the blood rise in her face. *Bloody, bloody, bloody hell*.

'I like it. I like that you said that.'

'Yes, well.' She clears her throat. 'Where were you thinking of putting them?'

'Thought I'd put a couple down along the coast the other side of the beach, and one on the cliff the other side of Kittiwake.

'On the cliff?'

'Yes, it's a great spot. I haven't found better along the coast here. I've been looking for the past year. I bought the land six months ago.'

'You bought the land?'

'Yes. Down by the beach too. Ellie and Florie wouldn't sell to anyone else. That's why I've still got the old pickup and Florie has new kennels.' He grins. 'Priorities. Thought I'd snatch up the land before some CFA speculator put a hotel or a condo up there.' He laughs. 'Can you imagine it?'

Sophie laughs. 'No. That would be ridiculous.' She clears her throat again. 'So, you're planning to build these artists' retreats there. Won't they be ... intrusive?'

'No. Look at the size of these. They're small, and I'm using local materials. Compost toilets. That sort of thing. They're not going to affect the landscape like a huge development would.'

Sophie rolls up her sketch and hands it to Sam. 'How are you going to build these when you barely have staff to fill your furniture orders, let alone the time it takes you to do your construction work?'

He shrugs. 'I'll find a way.'

'What about just moving to St John's? You could make your furniture just as easily there, and have a showroom. A lot more people will see your work. You'd be close to Becca, too, when she's at university.'

'I'm sure Becca will be thrilled not to have her old dad hanging around. Besides, I like it here. It's grown on me.'

'So, you do have a girlfriend.'

Sam laughs. 'I don't think Bear would appreciate being called my girlfriend.'

He reaches out, his fingers hovering near Sophie's cheek. She leans away from his hand. 'Sam, I—'

He drops his hand. 'Right. Take it easy, Princess Grace.' Turning to the big dog who is lying on the floor like a black rug, he claps his hands. 'Bear! C'mon, Bear!' He heads out past the kitchen and into the porch. The door slams.

Sophie stares at the flashing cursor. *What am I doing? It's just like last time. It'll never go anywhere with Sam. So, why do I want it to such much?*

And now Sam owns half the land the consortium wants. And Ellie and Florie own Kittiwake and the shop.

Maybe she can convince her aunt to sell – the stairs up to the house can't be that easy for her to climb anymore. Especially in the winter with the snow and ice. And if Ellie went, so would Florie, that was a given. But, where would they go? She could suggest Florida. Lots of Canadians retire down there. She could talk up the weather. But Sam would never move, no matter how much money Richard and the consortium waved in front of him.

Sam is a problem.

# Chapter 58

### Tippy's Tickle – 24 October 1949

'Mrs Parsons! This is a surprise.'

Agnes Parsons eyes the new schoolteacher. *Sensible-looking enough. Good shoes, plain dress. Wool cardigan, which you'd expect this time of year. Short dark hair in the permanent wave everyone's doing now. Odd-shaped glasses, though. Like cats' eyes. Town woman, that's for sure.*

'Why should it be a surprise? Emmy here's my grandson. I've come to fetch him home from school.'

'Is Ellie not well?' Bertha Perkins asks as she buttons the last button on Emmett's pink jumper. 'She always picks up Emmett.' She pulls the matching pink wool cap over his wavy brown hair and pats his head.

'She's brewed a cold. Took to her bed.'

'Oh, I'm sorry to hear that. Please give her my best wishes.'

'English, you see. Weak as a bent branch in a storm.'

'Oh dear. Is there anything I can do? Bring over some soup?'

Agnes screws her face into a frown. 'You sayin' my soup's not good enough?'

'No, no, of course not. I'm sure your soup is very good, Mrs Parsons. I just thought to be helpful.'

Agnes huffs. 'We don't needs charity. We can takes care of our own.' She takes hold of Emmett's hand. 'Come on, b'y. Let's go.'

Bertha Perkins watches the older woman pull the small boy along the path from the church's basement hall. 'Lovely to see you, Mrs Parsons! Give my best to Ellie!'

No response. She pulls her blue cardigan close around her body and closes the door.

Ellie rolls over under the covers and reaches for the handkerchief on the bedside table. She blows into the handkerchief and coughs hoarsely. Flopping back against the pillows, she pulls the covers up to her chin.

She should get up. There was supper still to make, and Thomas's trousers to mend for tomorrow. At least Agnes had gone to collect Emmy. Agnes would never admit it, of course, but she had a soft spot for her grandson. If only she'd stop knitting Emmy girls' clothes. Thomas was right. He'd start getting ribbed, now that he was in school.

She closes her eyes and succumbs to the aches throbbing through her body. The last time she'd been this sick she'd been back home in Norwich, tucked up in bed in her old room, Poppy filling her hot water bottles and Dottie bringing her hot lemon and honey for her throat. Before Thomas. Another life.

Why didn't Dottie answer her letters? Nothing. Not a word since that telegram about Poppy. If only she could speak with her. Apologise for leaving, if that's still what was upsetting Dottie so much.

*Things change, Dottie. Don't blame me for that. I have to live my life. And my life is with my family here in Newfoundland. My Emmy and my Thomas. I hope you find what you're looking for, Dottie. I hope one day you'll forgive me.*

Agnes sets a glass of milk and a plate with a date square on the kitchen table in front of Emmett. 'There you goes, Emmy. Don't tell your mam, for it'll spoil your supper.'

'I won't, Nanny.'

'Say grace, Emmy. You must always thank Holy God for what you're given or it's a black mark against your immortal soul and you'll go to Hell with the Devil. You don't wants that, do you?'

Emmett's eyes widen. 'No, Nanny.' He presses his hands together and squeezes his eyes shut. 'ForwhatImabouttoreceive throughthybountyChristaLordAmen.'

'Good b'y.'

Agnes takes up her knitting and sits in a chair across from Emmett. 'How's the little Chaffey girl? She back at school now?'

Emmett chews on the date square. 'Yes.'

'She have anything to say about when she was gone?'

'No.'

'Ah, well. That's normal, Emmy. It's just like what happened to the girl down in Colinet back in 1915.'

'What girl, Nanny?'

'I don't know her name, son. But the fairies took her.'

Emmett's odd eyes widen. 'Fairies?'

'Yes, Emmy. I heard about it myself. I was visiting my sister down in Gambo and a neighbour came over for tea. She told us she'd been on the train from Brigus just the week before and a man got on who she recognised from Colinet – that's down south, Emmy. He told her he'd been there helping to look for a little girl who'd gone missing.'

'Did she run away?'

'No, she was only a year old. She'd been crawling around the floor when her parents were havin' their tea one day and she crawled out onto the porch. Her mam went out to get her but she wasn't there.'

'She was gone?'

'Yes, b'y. Sure as ice melts, she was gone. So, the parents looks around all over the yard and the neighbours' but they don't find her. They searched high and low for twelve days. They tried every lake and river, thinkin' the baby had fallen in.'

'Did she, Nanny? Did she fall in the water?'

'No, Emmy. They looked and looked and the parents were very sad because they couldn't find her. Then after twelve days the father looks out the window and he sees a man walkin' down an old path from the woods carryin' a bundle. The father and the mother went out to meet him and he had the baby girl in his arms. He said he'd found her six miles away sittin' under a tree playin' with the dead leaves, happy as can be. He gave her some hard tack to chew on and picked her up and brought her back to Colinet.'

'Was she hurt?'

'No, she was fine. Just a bit of sunburn on her neck.'

'How did she get so far away, Nanny?'

'It was the fairies, Emmy. They're angels that Holy God shut out of Heaven in the war with the Devil. You don't wants to mix with fairies, Emmy. They took the child and they kept it alive, but you can be sure they were plannin' some mischief. The baby was lucky to be found. Sometimes the fairies takes a child and you never sees it again. You don't wants that to happen to you, do you, b'y?'

Emmett shakes his head, his eyes wide.

'That's right. You're lucky 'cause the fairies gave you different coloured eyes for protection. But just in case, always wears a piece of your clothes inside out and carry a bun. That way, they'll leave you alone. Will you do that for Nanny?'

Emmett nods. 'Yes, Nanny.'

'There's a good b'y, Emmy. Now, don't tell your Mam which I told you. This is our secret. You gots that, son?'

'Yes, Nanny.'

Agnes smiles and pulls another ball of wool out of her knitting bag. 'There's a good boy. Those fairies will never come after you. Not so long as your Nanny's around.'

# Chapter 59

## Tippy's Tickle – 13 September 2011

Sam waves at Wince as he powers *Miss Julie* out onto the highway, turning left towards Wesleyville. The sun is high in the sky. Twenty degrees, going up to twenty-two the next few days. And icebergs off the coast in September. Unheard of. It'd hardly ever got this hot in September when he'd first come back to Newfoundland. He used to have to wear his winter jacket to school this time of year when he was a boy in Grand Falls. Maybe there was something to this climate change stuff he'd been reading about in the papers.

He glances at his watch. Just gone eleven. Nine-thirty New York time. Nine-thirty and she was already working and emailing New York. Didn't she say she was here on holiday? For someone on holiday, she had a hard time tearing herself away from her phone and her laptop. But then, she'd always been a workaholic. She hasn't changed that much. Maybe she hasn't changed at all.

*So, why can't I get her out of my mind?*

There hadn't been anyone else. Not seriously. He'd been careful. He had Becca to think of. He didn't want a repeat of what had happened with Sophie. It wasn't fair on Becca. Bringing somebody new in, not when she loved Winny so much. Winny was still her mother. Winny would always be her mother.

*But, Winny. It's hard sometimes. Lonely. I miss you. I miss you, but you're gone. I love you, Winny, but maybe I need to start over. You'd understand that, wouldn't you?*

Sophie wasn't a stranger to Becca, and she was Ellie's niece. That was a bit strange, Sophie being Winny's cousin, but it wasn't like he was related to her. *Maybe that's why I like her, Winny. Because there's something about her that reminds me of you.*

An image of Sophie sitting at his table in jeans and a Billy Idol T-shirt sketching out her ideas for the artists' retreats floats into his mind. The habit she had of biting her lip when she concentrates; of tucking her hair behind her ear when it falls out of her ponytail. When she did that it just got him. His fingers itched to tuck that hair behind her ear. To kiss that lip.

*Maybe it's time, Winny.*

Sam parks the bike and stamps up the steps into Florie's shop.

'Florie! You got any canned tomatoes? They were fresh out at Foodland.'

Florie emerges from the back room, two of her dachshunds at her feet. 'Jaysus, Hildy and Mamie. Get outta my feet, girls. Sure thing, Sam. It's over there on the top shelf. Just grab yourself what you needs.'

The screen door swings open and Becca enters, a look of urgency on her face.

'Becca, maid, thought you were at home studyin',' Florie says. 'Does Ellie need somethin'?'

Becca shakes her head, her pink pompom earrings swinging against her neck.

Sam sets two cans of tomatoes on the counter. 'Becca? Where

were you till all hours last night? It was past three when I heard you come in.'

She signs to her father.

'You want to speak to me outside? Sure, all right, honey. Just let me pay Florie. I'll meet you outside in a minute.'

# *Chapter 60*

## Tippy's Tickle – 25 September 1952

'I's the b'y that builds the boat—' There's a crash of tin as the empty milk can by the picket fence tumbles onto the dirt road.

'Jaysus God, b'y! Watch where you're goin'. Your mam will fry us up with scrunchions for supper.'

Thomas grasps a picket and steadies himself. 'Do you figure Mam's cooked up cod and scrunchions tonight? I'm gut-foundered.'

'You gots a hollow leg, b'y.'

Thomas stares at his father. Grinning, he slaps him on his shoulder. 'Well, you're not blind there, Dad.' He lifts his face to the darkening sky and belts out the next line of the ditty. *'And I's the b'y that sails her—'*

Throwing his arm around his son, Ephraim bellows out the song with Thomas. *'And I's the b'y that catches the fish and brings them home to Liza!'*

Ellie slides up the sash window in the kitchen. 'They're back, Agnes.'

Thomas's mother wipes her floury hands on her apron. 'I'm not deaf as a cod, girl. My sister could hear that racket all the way to Salvage.' She picks up the old metal kettle and thrusts it at Emmett, who is sitting at the kitchen table assembling a set of thumb-sized stone bricks into a lopsided house. 'Fetch some water down the pump, Emmy. I'll need to be pourin' tea down the likes of them when they gets in.'

Eight-year-old Emmett slides off the wooden chair and silently takes the handle of the kettle, exiting through the back screen-door.

Ellie opens the pantry and takes out two tin pails, setting them on the floor in front of the stove. Agnes eyes her as she lifts the lid off the pot of soaking hard tack and pokes at the softening bread with a wooden spoon.

'Where're you off to with those?'

'To get water to heat up for a bath for Thomas. It helps him sober up.'

'He'll have to make do without the bath tonight. I's got beer stewin' in the tub. 'Course you'd knows that if you wasn't off dilly-dallyin' all the live-long day with your pencils. I can't have Rod Fizzard takin' all Ephraim's money.'

'I wasn't dilly-dallying. I brought you bakeapples for the crumble. They were even ripe this time.'

'It took you six years to finds me ripe bakeapples when the marsh I showed you is full of them. You're as blind as a snow-blind Canadian in a blizzard. I'll hardly give you a prize.'

The front door slams open and the men stumble down the hallway into the kitchen. Ephraim grabs his wife and plants a sloppy kiss on her plump cheek. He drags over a pressback wooden chair and slumps into it, shrugging out of his pea jacket. 'What you got for the scoff, maid? I'm that hungry I could eat the arse off a low-flyin' duck.'

'You think I lives my life at your beck and call, old man? Maybe I was out with my fancy man in Gambo.'

'Don't you be teasin' a hungry man like that, Nessie, or I'll be back off to Rod Fizzard's. His wife's cookin' up flipper pie.'

Thomas slides into a chair and leans his crutch against the freshly painted yellow wall. 'I'd stop there, Dad. Mam's gots a face on her like a burnt boiled boot.'

'It's fish and brewis tonight with scrunchions,' Ellie says as she peels the papery brown skin off an onion. 'We were waitin' for you to get home before we fried up the fat and onions. The cod's been soakin' since last night.'

The screen door swings open and Emmett enters with the kettle. After handing it to his grandmother, he slips silently onto his chair and takes up the construction of the tiny house.

Ephraim pats his grandson on his head. 'You're a good boy, Emmy.' He ruffles Emmett's dark hair and tweaks his nose. Emmett fixes his steady blue/brown gaze on his grandfather and wrinkles his nose.

'You're a funny one with your brown hair and that brown eye, b'y.' Ephraim bends over with a grunt and tugs at the laces of his boot. 'You must get those from your mudder's side. The Parsons and Mam's Inkpen side are all blond and blue-eyed. It's those Vikings hittin' up the Brits all those years ago.'

'He gets his dark hair from my mother,' Ellie says as she chops up the onion. 'She had dark eyes, too.' Probably best not to tell them she was a half-French Catholic. Agnes would have a field day with that.

'It's a fairy blast,' Agnes says as she hands out mugs of steaming tea to the men.

Ellie looks up from the pork fat she's begun to cut into chunks. 'A fairy blast?'

'He must've got touched by a fairy when he was a baby. Some around here takes it as a bad sign, but I thinks it makes our

Emmy special. The fairies gave him a brown eye to leave their
mark on him, so the other fairies knows to leave him be.'

Ellie laughs. 'Surely you don't believe—'

'There was that little girl went missin' in Colinet back in
'Fifteen,' Ephraim interrupts as he eases his feet out of his boots.
'A year old or so. Disappeared out of the kitchen when her
mudder's back was turned. Showed up twelve days later six miles
away sittin' under a tree in the forest, not a mark on her. Happy
as a duck on a fresh pond.'

Ellie shakes her head. 'Someone must have brought her
there.'

Agnes's eyes narrow behind her wire-rimmed glasses. 'T'was
the fairies. They took the child and kept it alive. It couldn't
happen any other way.'

Ellie turns over in the bed and pulls the covers up to her neck.

'Aren't you getting into bed, Thomas?'

Thomas sits on the edge of the bed in his undershirt and his
long johns, contemplating the dark room. 'You didn't believe the
fairy story, did you, Ellie Mae?'

'Of course not. It's silly superstition.'

He looks at her over his shoulder. 'The Rock's a funny place
sometimes. The fog rolls in, and the whale song drifts in on the
breeze. It's an odd sound, that. Clicks and groans. They say you
can only hear it properly under the water, but I swears I've heard
it out on the boat. Clear as a baby's cry. Sometimes, something
shifts out on the water. I can't explain it. Then you hears it. The
clickin' and the groanin'. It's like you drop through time into a
different place.'

'But you know that can't happen. You're just hearing sounds.'

'It can happen, Ellie Mae. It happened to me once. I was out on the boat by myself. It's before I signed up for the infantry. I had to tell Mam and Dad, but I didn't know how to do it. I took the boat out and floated around the coast for a bit. It was September, just like now. There was a full moon and the stars shone like diamonds in the black sky.' He leans back onto his pillow and looks over at Ellie. 'Not that I knows what diamonds looks like, mind you. But you can imagine.'

'Of course you know what diamonds look like.' Ellie wiggles her finger with her engagement ring.

'Oh, maid. That's not a real diamond. Where would I gets the money for that? Think they called it ... what was it? A zircon, that's it.'

Ellie looks at the large square-cut zircon. 'Oh.'

'Pretty like a diamond, though, don't you think? I promised you a beautiful ring, didn't I? It's the best I could find with the money I had.'

'It's lovely, Thomas. Really.'

'So, anyways, I was bobbin' along on the water – I could see the lighthouse up by the cape. It was a clear night and the light reached far out over the sea as it spun around in the lighthouse. Suddenly a fog rose up off the water like steam. Like someone put on the kettle to boil. And the sea went flat as glass and the light disappeared. Then this sound filled the air like somethin' from another world. Like singin' and cryin' at the same time. If fairies sang that would be the sound they'd make, Ellie Mae.

'I'm sittin' in the boat and don't know what to think about what's goin' on. Then I feels like I'm not alone. And I sees him. The great head risin' up beside my boat. And the eye lookin' at me. And he just rose out of that water higher and higher until he fell back through the fog and it was the most thunderous crash. And just likes that the fog rolled away and the boat started bobbin' along, and the lighthouse light appeared again. Just like nothin' had happened. But somethin' happened out there. It's like we're sittin' on the edge of the world here. And sometimes, when somethin' shifts, we see things that are normally hidden from us. There's a kind of magic here on The Rock, but I'm not always sure it's a good thing.'

'You'd probably just fallen asleep and had a dream.'

Thomas's eyes sweep over Ellie's face. 'How'd you suppose Emmy really got his brown eye?'

Ellie sits up against her pillow. 'What?'

'I was away a long time, Ellie Mae.'

'Thomas, what are you saying?'

'Emmy's birthday's in August. He should have been born in September.'

'That's not so unusual. He was early. I hadn't heard from you in months, and the war was going on and on. I started to think something had happened to you. That you were missing, or wounded, or—'

'I wrote you, Ellie Mae. I swears it. But the mail boats got hit a lot on the run up to England. Maybe that's why you didn't get my letters. I didn't get many of yours, and you said you wrote every week.'

'You have no idea what it was like, Thomas. The pressure, the worry ... It's no surprise the baby came early.' Ellie reaches for Thomas's face and brushes her hand along his cheek, tracing the thin scar with her thumb. 'Don't ever doubt that, Thomas. Emmy's our son. Our lovely son. And, God willing, we'll have more children. A little girl next time, maybe.'

'It's been over six years, Ellie Mae. Maybe there's somethin' wrong with me. Maybe I can't father a child.'

'But it was only your leg that was injured.'

Thomas takes hold of Ellie's hand and looks at her intensely. 'Maybe I've never been able to father a child.'

Ellie looks deep into Thomas's agitated grey eyes. 'You have a son, Thomas. A fine son. And one day he'll grow up into a fine man, just like his father.'

# Chapter 61

## Tippy's Tickle – 13 September 2011

Sophie leans over the white porcelain pedestal sink and blinks into the mirror. She wipes at the sweat beading on her forehead and pulls at the skin on her cheeks, tugging it towards her ears. Releasing her fingers, she watches her skin settle back into its softening contours.

When did that happen? Forty-eight. She was still thirty-five in her head. The mirror was a liar. Or maybe she just hadn't looked at herself closely for a long time. And the sweating. She wasn't even fifty yet.

She opens the door into Sam's living room and spies Sam in the kitchen.

'Sam! I didn't hear you come in.' She glances at the laptop, the email to Richard open on the screen.

Sam smiles at her as he unloads two Foodland bags. Bear sits on the floor beside him, his black head poised in expectation. 'Hope you like eggplant. I do a great eggplant pasta.'

'Sure, I like eggplant.' She quickly saves the emails and shuts off the laptop. 'It sounds a lot nicer when you call it aubergine pasta, though. Eggplant makes it sound like it's made of eggs.'

He begins singing 'Let's Call the Whole Thing Off' and Sophie joins in, singing the other part.

'Well, you can carry a tune, Sam. Another one of your hidden talents.'

'Newfoundlander, you see. We're a musical bunch.' He unscrews the top of a bottle of red wine and pours out two glasses. 'I hope you like Valpolicella. It's the best Italian Wesleyville can offer.'

'Valpolicella's perfect.' She accepts the glass from Sam, relieved that the awkwardness before he left appears to have been forgotten. 'I designed a winery in Verona a few years ago.'

'Well, I can't trump that.' He clinks her class. 'Chin-chin.'

'Chin-chin.'

He sets down his glass and hands Sophie a fat purple eggplant. 'Right, so, Princess Grace. Slice this up, will you? I'll get the pasta on.'

'Is Becca joining us for supper?'

'No, she's out with Toby again. Just bumped into them in Florie's store. Said they were going to a time over in Badger's Quay.' He frowns as he pours water into a cooking pot. 'That boy's a real distraction. Becca needs to study for her exams. She promised me she'd get down to it next week if I let her go.'

'A time?'

'A party. I think I need to get you a Newfoundland dictionary.'

Sophie dabs the napkin against her lips. 'That was delicious, Sam.'

He picks up the wine bottle. 'More wine?'

'Sure. I'm not driving.'

Sam takes a sip of wine. 'When were you going to tell me?'

'Tell you what?'

'Becca told me about your phone call yesterday.'

'What phone call?'

'You got a phone call at the picnic. She reads lips, remember?'
Sophie stares at Sam. 'Oh, Sam.'

He sets down his wine glass and shakes his head. 'I didn't want to believe her. I mean, she doesn't always get it right. You've got an accent. It makes it harder for her.'

'Sam, I—'

'Then, I read your email, and I knew she hadn't misunderstood anything. Let me see if I remember the subject line right. *Luxury Eco Golf Hotel in Tippy's Tickle.* Is that right?'

Sophie folds her napkin and sets it on the table. 'What do you want me to say?'

'A golf course? Seriously? The wind will hurl their golf balls all the way to Greenland!'

'I've told them the golf course is a bad idea—'

'It's Ellie's home.' He thumps his chest. '*My* home.'

Sophie presses her fingers against her eyes. 'I know. I know.' She reaches for her glass and takes a large gulp of wine, willing the alcohol to steady her nerves. 'Look, Sam, the biggest thing Tippy's Tickle has going for it right now is the dole. This is a great opportunity for the town. The hotel will bring in employment. The economy here will boom. You can get involved on the build, make the built-in units, the furniture. You said yourself all the kids are moving to the cities because there's no work.'

'These kinds of places aren't interested in spreading the wealth. The investors want a good return on their investment. It's all about money. *Their* money.'

'That's not it at all, Sam. They want to make this an eco-friendly hotel.'

Sam's huffs. 'With a golf course? Where are the superyachts going to berth? Have you seen how narrow the tickle is? Or are they going to dredge that and blast away the rocks to make room?' He points out towards the ocean. 'We have harp seals just off shore. Whales. Puffins just down the coast. What's going to happen to them? Where's the helicopter going to land, because they'll want that for all their VIPs flying into St John's. They'll have to blast rock away for that too. So much for our ecosystem. Open your eyes, Sophie. They're taking you for a ride.'

'I think you're exaggerating. They want to build here *because* of the ecology. They don't want to destroy it. They're offering good packages. You'll have all the money you need to expand your business.'

'I won't take a cent from them, and I'd like to be a fly on the wall when you tell Florie. That'll be colourful.'

'They'll play dirty, Sam. These kinds of people always get what they want.'

'Nice company you keep, Princess Grace.'

'You've heard of requisitioned property?'

'They'd just take the land away from me? Only the government can do that.'

'They have friends everywhere, Sam.'

'Is that a threat?'

A clatter of shells, stones and tin echoes around the room as the fishing net hurtles to the floor. Becca stands under the ragged pieces of net, her face pale with rage.

'Becca?'

Running at Sophie, Becca flails at her as strangled sobs tear from her body. Sophie throws up her arms. 'Becca, stop. I'm sorry. I'm sorry.'

Sam grabs hold of his daughter, hugging her against him. The girl's body shakes, and her wails infiltrate the core of Sophie's being.

Sophie picks up her laptop and walks past Sam and Becca

and out to the porch. Outside the cottage, the first drops of a night shower splatter against her body. Tucking her laptop against her body, she raises her face to the rain and lets it run over her. Willing it to purify her. Willing it to make everything better.

# Chapter 62

## Norwich, England – 21 November 1952

'George!' Dottie smiles at George in the dressing room mirror and waves for him to enter the cluttered room. Bouquets of roses and lilies spill over every surface, their fragrance sitting on the stale air like perfume on sweaty clothes. 'Come in! I had no idea you were coming to the performance tonight. My goodness, don't you look dashing.'

George edges past discarded dresses towards the glamorous woman seated in front of the mirror, ashamed now of his meagre bouquet.

'I brought you some flowers, Dottie. It's lovely to see you again. You look ... you look smashing.'

Setting down her lipstick, Dottie reaches out for the bouquet of carnations. 'They're lovely, George. That's very sweet of you.'

George pushes his glasses up his nose. 'You were marvellous tonight, Dottie. I was watching you and kept thinking to myself, *There's little Dottie! Up on stage at the Norwich Philharmonic! I knew her when!*'

'You certainly did. I'll defy anyone to say you didn't.'

George straightens the bow tie on his rented dinner suit. 'It's been ages, Dottie. I wouldn't have recognised you if I'd seen you in the street.'

'Is that a good thing or a bad thing, George?'

'Oh, a good thing. No, I mean, it was always lovely to see you when you were younger, too.'

Smiling at George in the mirror, Dottie picks up a bottle of Shalimar and dabs behind her ears. 'I was just a silly girl back then. You only had eyes for Ellie, anybody could see that.'

'That was a long time ago.'

Dottie glances over at George from the corner of her eye. 'Have you been in touch with her?'

'I've had some Christmas cards from her. I ... I always send her one, too.'

'Oh, isn't that nice.'

'Well, we've known each other since we were children.'

'Just like me.'

'Yes, I suppose so. I've known you since you were a baby.'

Dottie, pushes out of the chair and tugs at the décolleté of her blue satin dress. 'Well, I'm not a baby, now.' She takes hold of George's arm. 'Where was it you were taking me to dinner?

'Oh, uh. I haven't ... I haven't—'

She collects her fur stole from the back of a chair and picks up her clutch purse. 'Don't worry, George. I have a table booked at the Royal Hotel. Their dover sole is to die for.'

Dottie watches George exit the hotel as she waits for the lift up to her floor. He was miles older than she, of course, but what did that matter? Elizabeth Taylor had just married her second husband and he was thirty-six to her twenty. George was only nine years older. It was nothing.

The lift bell rings and the doors open. A young attendant in grey uniform and white gloves pulls aside the polished brass grill doors. 'Which floor, please?'

'Fifth.'

He pulls the doors shut and the lift jerks to life. George had looked quite handsome tonight in the dinner suit, with his hair slicked down, just like the men in London. The suit was a little too large for him – rented, obviously – but, still, he'd been a worthy dinner companion. So very polite. Not fawning like the London men. It was all too easy with them. She'd had to pull out her full flirtatious arsenal for George. Well, perhaps not the full arsenal. That would come later.

If only Ellie could see them now. She shivers with the thrill of it. Her little sister, Dottie, on her ex-fiancé's arm at the best restaurant in Norwich. She'd felt the eyes of the other diners on them all night. This was what it was like to fly. Soon Norwich would be nothing but a long-forgotten memory. She was off on a tour of the great cities of Europe with the London Philharmonic Orchestra next year. Featured soloist. Look at me now, Ellie. Look at me now.

First, though, she had some unfinished business here in Norwich.

George.

# *Chapter 63*

### Tippy's Tickle – 14 September 2011

Sophie hurries down the wooden steps from Kittiwake and heads across the road and past a row of the colourful houses towards the shop. She takes the note out of the pocket of her jeans and scans the scrawling blue ink. Frowning, she refolds it twice and slips it back into her pocket.

She mounts the steps to the store. A hum of loud chatter wafts through the screen door. Pulling it open, she walks past the white counters and into the large room with the bay window. Instead of finding Ellie bending over her printing press, or hosting an art class at the wooden table while Florie packages up purchases, she's met with a bank of angry faces as the room falls into a tense silence.

Ellie rises. Crescents the colour of prunes sit under her eyes and she takes an additional step to steady herself as she waves away Florie's extended hand. 'Come in, Sophie.' She gestures to a chair that has been centred in the bay window. 'Please, sit.'

Sophie scans the faces – her aunt, Florie, Sam leaning against the back wall, Becca and a good-looking boy she can only imagine is Becca's boyfriend Toby Molloy, Emmett, Wince – and other faces, some of whom she's seen on her walks around the village, and others she doesn't recognise. About forty people. All of them looking at her like cats about to pounce on a mouse.

Sophie sits on the chair. 'What's going on?

'Oh, I thinks you have a good idea about that, my girl,' Florie says. 'Nice to have a spy livin' under our roof.' She glances at Ellie. 'Told you it was odd, her visitin' at the last minute, didn't I, Ellie?'

'I'm not a spy, Florie. I don't know what Sam's told you, but ... but, really, it's not ... it's not ...' She closes her mouth. She feels sweat bead on her forehead as her cheeks flush.

There's a scrape of the wooden chair legs against the floorboards as Emmett stands. 'What is it then? Where do you wants me to live when they builds the hotel?'

Sophie's mouth drops open. 'You can live anywhere, Emmett. The investors are offering an excellent package—'

'I don't owns anything to sell but for the stage on the tickle. I lives with me mam in my Da's house. If Mam sells the house, where do you expects me to live?'

Sophie glances at Ellie. 'Well, I'm sure that can be worked out. I ... I wouldn't worry about it, Emmett.'

Emmett frowns, hooding his strange eyes into a squint. 'I's worried about it. I's worried about it a lot.'

A murmur rumbles through the room. Another man stands. 'I'm worried too, b'y! I heard they're gonna chase out all our boats to makes way for them superyachts.'

Sophie shakes her head. 'No. No. Where did you hear that?'

Florie jumps to her feet and waggles a sturdy finger at Sophie. 'The nerve of you, girl. We opens up our arms to you, and look what you does to us. Boots us out of our homes. I don't know how you looks in the mirror.'

Sophie leaps to her feet. 'That's not fair, Florie,' she says, her voice rising. 'You're the one being selfish.'

'Oh, am I? How do you figger that?'

'How many steps is it to get up to Kittiwake? Thirty-four. And two of them are so rotten you have to watch where you step or you'd go right through. Thirty-four steps is a lot for someone who's about to turn eighty-nine. Have you ever thought about that?'

'Ellie's tough as old boots. Isn't that right, Ellie?'

Ellie looks at Florie. She shakes her head, her fine white hair fanning across her thin cheeks. 'No. No, Sophie's right. It's not as easy as it used to be.'

Florie's eyes widen. 'What're you saying, love? You never said a word before.'

Ellie shrugs. 'I know. Sophie's right, Florie. It isn't that easy anymore.'

'I'd make sure they'd pay you over market value for your house, Aunt Ellie,' Sophie says. 'You and Florie could buy a lovely place wherever you like.'

Florie crosses her arms. 'I likes it fine enough here.' Another murmur ripples through the crowd. Someone stamps their feet.

Sophie scans the faces, resting her gaze on Sam. 'Look, I don't know what you've heard.' She looks back at the crowd of locals. 'Please, let me tell you what's being proposed. Then, why don't you go away tonight and think about it? We can meet here again tomorrow at the same time and put it to a vote. If you decide you don't want the hotel here, I'll tell that to the consortium. And that's the last you'll hear from me.'

The room erupts into life. Sophie watches Sam shake his head. He skirts around the chairs and heads out the door.

Sophie flops onto the large iron bed in the attic room. She pulls the quilt, one of Becca's hand-made designs – a triumph of orange and pink floral pieces arranged in an intricate knot design

– over her head, and shuts her eyes. The swoosh of waves surging against the rocky cliff below the house beats a rhythm outside her open window, like a symphony building to a climax. The first wave piano, washing softly against the cliff; diminuendo as the water quietens as it recedes; then the second wave, crescendo, growing louder; followed by another diminuendo, lingering as the ocean pulls itself into the final thundering wave; fortissimo.

Sophie laughs to herself. The legacy of a pianist mother. The flip-top piano bench in their Norwich home had been stuffed with yellowing musical scores, annotated in her mother's impatient hand. *Piano. Diminuendo. Crescendo. Fortissimo.* Funny how she remembered that after all these years. Funny the things that bury themselves in your mind.

She tosses off the quilt and kicks it to the floor. She fans her face with her hand. The air is heavy with humidity, pressing down on her chest like a weight. She sits up and walks over to the small desk in front of the window. Switching on the old brass desk lamp, she opens her laptop and switches it on. She opens a Word document. Her fingers hover over the keyboard as she stares at the flashing cursor. Bending her head over the keyboard, she writes.

# Chapter 64

## Tippy's Tickle – 14 June 1953

The iceberg sits like a moored boat at the mouth of the tickle, its triangular shape like a clipper ship in full sail. The wooden houses along the shore look as small as boxes from the cliff, and as the sun rises and sets, the iceberg's shadow spreads democratically over the outport, first darkening the wooden turrets on the Parsons' house on the cliff, then moving over Jim Boyd's general store and Rod Fizzard's stage with its wharf and store, and the one-storey fishermen's houses clustered along the tickle. Then, if it's a rare cloudless day, the berg swallows its shadow until the late afternoon, when the triangular greyness once again reaches out over the tickle to the aluminium steeple of St Stephen's Church on its rocky spit of land, until the shadow settles on the round hill of the cemetery.

On this day, there is the suggestion that summer has finally arrived for its brief stay on the island. The sky is a vivid blue and the sun sits high above the floating clouds. Ellie sets down her charcoal drawing pencil on a spongy mound of moss under the twisted fir near the house, and lifts her face up to the sun. The warmth tickles her skin and turns the world underneath her eyelids red. The baby bounces in her stomach and she rests her hand over her blossoming belly.

*Not long now, little one. Clever you to come in the summer-*

*time. We'll go for walks amongst the summer flowers – the wild
lupins and buttercups, the tiny blue irises and cloudbanks of the
purple-pink fireweed – and in the autumn we'll pick blueberries
and partridgeberries and bakeapples for all the cobblers and
crumbles I'll make. I'll take you down to the beach and we'll
search for winkles in the shallow tide pools to steam up for
Daddy's supper.*

A movement from the direction of the house draws her eye,
and she sees Emmett heading through the tufts of long grass
sprinkled with yellow buttercups in her direction. He's grown
so tall. Nine years old in August, and already up to her shoulders
and as skinny as a reed no matter how much she feeds him.

Emmett flops down on the grass, and she runs her hand over
his newly cut hair. 'You finished your chores, Emmy?'

He nods and reaches into the pocket of his corduroys, pulling
out a white envelope. 'Mr Boyd brought it over. Came in the
post from St John's.'

'From St John's? Whoever could that be?'

'It's not a Newfoundland stamp.'

'It isn't?'

'Could I have it, Mam?'

Ellie looks at the careful vertical handwriting. She's knows
that hand. An English stamp. She turns over the letter. An address
in Norwich.

'Could I have the stamp, Mam? I can add it to the others from
Mr Boyd.'

'Of course, Emmy. Hold on a minute.' Ellie runs her finger
under the envelope flap and carefully tears off the stamp. 'Here
you go. Ask Nanny to soak it in some warm water for you so
you can stick it in your scrapbook.'

Emmett holds the stamp between his thumb and forefinger

like it's a delicate butterfly. 'Thank you, Mam.' He rises to his feet, unfolding his lanky frame like an expanding accordion, and makes his way back down the slope to the house.

Ellie pulls out the letter.

*Pleasantview*
*Newmarket Road*
*Norwich*

*15th May, 1953*
*Dear Ellie,*

*I hope you and Thomas are well, and I expect Emmett is quite a young man by now. You're probably surprised to receive this letter, after all this time, but I do want to thank you for the Christmas cards and the yearly update on your life over in Newfoundland. I'm sorry I have been such a poor correspondent, but it was difficult for me after you married Thomas. I have thought of you often, though, and hope you have found the life you were looking for.*

*I'm still at Mcklintock's, but I was made assistant manager last year and I've just overseen the reopening of the factory after the bomb damage from the Baedeker raids. It's nice to have it up and running properly again. We're launching a whole range of new sweets – Bingos, Whippets and Choccos. It seems everyone wants chocolate now after all the war years with so little.*

*But I don't imagine you're all that interested in the state of chocolate in Norwich. Since your father passed away, I know your sister hasn't kept in touch. She still seems to harbour some kind of grudge over some imagined slight, though I'm sure she'll come around one day. You are sisters after all.*

*There have been developments and I felt someone should let you know what has been happening.*

*After your father died, Dottie took a place at the Royal Academy of Music in London. She said there was no reason for her to stay in Norwich with everyone gone, and she was quite right too. She's done so very well with her career as a pianist, and I saw her in Norwich recently when she was here as the guest pianist with the Norwich Philharmonic Orchestra for the winter season.*

*We ended up spending a great deal of time together. You wouldn't recognise Dottie, Ellie. London turned her into quite a sophisticated young woman. She's so self-assured and—*

*Ellie, we've married. It seems I was meant to be part of your family one way or another! Your sister is now Dottie Burgess. She prefers Dorothy now. And there's more news. Dottie's expecting. Emmett will soon have cousins! Yes, cousins plural. Dottie's expecting twins in November. I'm only sorry your parents aren't here to be a part of this.*

*There it is. The news from Norwich. Do take care. I can't think of anyone else I'd rather have as a sister-in-law.*

*Fondly,*
*George*

*PS: I've often wondered why you gave Emmett my middle name. You would have told me, wouldn't you, Ellie? Wouldn't you?*

Ellie folds the letter and slips it back in its envelope. There was nothing to tell. Yes, she'd known Emmett was George's middle name. She liked the name. And it connected her to the life she was leaving behind in Norwich. Emmett was Thomas's boy. Hers and Thomas's.

Her eyes scan over the blue-inked writing. *Dottie and George.* She couldn't quite believe it. Of course, Dottie had had a crush on George for as long as she could remember. But a schoolgirl crush and a marriage were entirely different things. How on earth had that happened?

Is she so shocked because she'd always seen George as hers? She'd been engaged to him for ages before she'd met Thomas. But that's ridiculous. She's a happily married woman now. At least as happy as one could reasonably expect to be, considering ... Well, all the men drank in Tippy's Tickle.

The life she'd found herself living in this remote corner of the world was so much harder than she'd imagined. The fishing money only went so far, and when the sea froze over in the long winter, the men turned to the seal hunt. She hated that. The ice floes were dangerous – men drowned every year. Agnes thought she was a fool when she'd refuse to cook the bloody seal flippers Ephraim and Thomas brought home. *Would you have us starve?* Agnes would admonish her. So, she'd cook them, but she refused to eat them. She'd had more than one supper of bread and margarine.

They'd only just got the electricity connected in the spring, though indoor plumbing was still a distant dream. And finding a book to read in Tippy's Tickle was like searching for a diamond in a mountain of coal. It'd been a shock when she'd discovered that most of the locals were illiterate. Though, now that money was coming in from the Canadian government there was talk of a new regional high school down the coast in Wesleyville. Ellie had managed to lobby the village council to ask for Canadian money to sponsor Bertha Perkins, up from Grand

Falls, to teach the younger children in the church hall basement, though, admittedly, she'd done that more for Emmett's benefit than from any altruistic impulse. So, things were improving, but it was a slow road. Newfoundland was hardly the romantic idyll she'd imagined.

And now Dottie had married George. She should be happy for them. She *would* be happy for them. She'd made her choice. Her life was in Newfoundland with Thomas and Emmy and the new baby. She'd likely never see Norwich or her sister or George again.

# *Chapter 65*

### Tippy's Tickle – 15 September 2011

They turned up in the middle of the night, beaching themselves on the sandy shore below Bufflehead Cottage. Over
one hundred of them. Pilot whales. All female. Most of them
pregnant.

'Grab the flukes, Becca! Pull them with me!'

Becca looks at Sophie, hesitating as the blood-laced waves
beat against her rubber boots.

'Please, Becca! Please!'

Becca splashes into the water between the whales' writhing,
sleek grey bodies, and grabs hold of the flailing flukes with
Sophie. They tug, grinding their booted feet into the shifting
sand, but every centimetre of success is countered by the whale
thrusting its huge body back onto the shore.

'Again! Again, Becca!'

'Over here, Sophie!' Toby Molloy, his too-long hair plastered
back over his head with saltwater, throws Sophie the end of a
rope he's tied to the seat of the rowboat he and Thor are rowing
in the pinkening water. 'Tie this to the flukes. We'll haul it out
into the sea.'

Sophie ties the rope into the slipknot her father had taught
her for her school tie and pulls the loop wide. She tosses the

looped rope to Becca. 'Take hold of it, Becca. We'll loop it over her flukes together.' She pulls the knot tight and gives Toby a thumbs up. He and Thor thrust the oars into the churning ocean and drag the whale away from the beach.

A roar of motorcycles. Sophie looks up to see the bikes of the Chrome Warriors bounce down the rocky path towards the beach. After parking the bikes in the scrubby grass along the sand, the bikers charge like a leather-clad army down the beach to the floundering whales. Sam splashes through the pink foam towards them.

'It's awful, Sam. I've never seen anything like it.'

'I know. I've called the whale release group over in Portugal Cove. They're sending a team to help. They'll be here this afternoon. I put a call out to the Warriors in the meantime.'

'Emmett's out there in the motorboat with Florie. Everyone's here. The fishermen have been hauling the whales out into the ocean all morning. We've managed to get about half of the whales back out there.'

Ace stamps through the water and claps Sam on his shoulder. 'What next, b'y?'

'Grab as many of their flukes as you can, and haul them out. Get one of the guys to help Becca.'

'Right, b'y.' Ace tips his hand to his forehead in a salute. 'Consider it done.' He turns and strides down the beach to the others. 'Get your hands outta your trousers, b'ys, and grab yourself some tail. Show us what you're made of.'

Sophie holds up her phone and records the scene, spotting Becca on the screen cradling the bull-like head of a whale in her lap further down the beach. 'Why are they doing this?'

Sam surveys the writhing bodies of the exhausted whales. 'Some say it's radar affecting their homing abilities, some say it's pollution, oil in the water ... How would your hotel guests like waking up to see this out of their windows? Not quite what the consortium has in mind, is it?' He runs his hand through his hair. 'Sorry. Thanks for coming out.'

Sophie pockets her phone. 'I'm not all bad.'

Sam nods. 'Come on, Princess Grace. Let's do this.'

Sophie stands on top of a rock by the beach and wipes her wet face with her hand. 'We're getting there, Sam. There's only thirty-five still on the beach.'

Sam leaps onto the rock beside her, waving at Becca who is in the boat with Toby and Thor. 'I saw you and Becca working with each other earlier.'

'Yeah. The whales, you know. I don't imagine she's forgiven me.' Sophie waves at the boat. 'Toby's been doing a great job. He's been back and forth all day pulling the whales away from the beach.'

Sam holds up a hand to shield his eyes from the sun and squints at the boat. 'He's still a distraction for Becca if she wants to pass her exams.'

'Sam, have you ever thought that maybe she's only taking these exams to please you? Maybe that's why she's procrastinating. Maybe she doesn't want to be a doctor. Maybe she wants to do something more creative. She does amazing work with textiles and she can embroider like a dream.'

'Are you saying I don't know my own daughter?'

'No, of course not. But why not just talk to her? You keep blaming Toby, but maybe it's not all his fault. Just communicate.'

Sam's eyes cloud over. 'Look who's talking. You should have been honest about the hotel.'

Sophie bites her lip. 'I know.'

'Look, Sophie, I know we have to move with the times. There's a lot of people out of work. The outports are dying. Kids moving out to the cities. But, you know, we've got something special here in this place. It's harsh and it's wild, and things like this ...' he waves towards the beach '... things like this happen sometimes. But it's beautiful here. I've never been anywhere like it. I don't want to see Tippy's Tickle ruined by people who just want to exploit it for their own profit.' Sam frowns. 'I can't support you. I'll do everything I can to stop it.'

Sophie nods. 'I guess that makes us enemies.'

'Not enemies. Adversaries, maybe.' Sam wipes a trail of salt water from his face with the back of his hand. 'You need to figure out want you want, Sophie.'

'I'm not the only one, Sam.' She shivers as a gust of wind whips across the shore. 'Do you remember when you dropped me off at the airport last time?'

'I remember.'

'I wanted ... I wanted you to say something, do something, to make me think we might have a chance together. I wanted it more than anything.'

Sam stares at Sophie. 'You could have fooled me. I thought you couldn't wait to see the back of me.'

Sophie looks out at the boats bobbing in the waves. Her heart judders. She'd been an idiot. They both had. Now, it was too late.

Something catches her eye out in the water. Dorsal fins. But they were pointing in the wrong direction, skimming through the sea towards the shore. Two, four, five, then more of the sleek grey bodies of the whales plough through the waves towards the beach.

'They're swimming back! Oh, my God. Sam, they're swimming back!'

The whales thrust themselves onto the beach, one after the other, churning up the sand with their flippers and their flukes as they attempt to swim forwards in a waterless ocean.

That evening, later than planned, after the marine biologists of the whale release group have confirmed the deaths of one hundred and thirty-seven female pilot whales on the beach at Tippy's Tickle, the villagers reconvene in Florie's store. The mood is sombre, the vote unanimous.

'Sam? There you are.'

Sam turns away from the view of the beach below Bufflehead Cottage. 'Ellie?'

She joins him out on the deck of the cottage, sipping from a *World's Greatest Dad* mug. 'I made myself a cup of tea. I hope you don't mind.'

Sam chuckles. 'Not at all. *Mi casa es tu casa.*'

'I came to see how Becca is doing. I know she's been very upset about Sophie and this hotel.'

'Yes. She's not the only one.' He takes a drink from the bottle of Blue Star beer he's holding. He looks over at his mother-in-law. The breeze catches her fine white hair and blows it around her face. She brushes it out of her eyes with a thin hand. She'd lost weight. She seemed … smaller. When had that happened?

'She's gone off with Toby again.'

'Florie said he was a great help out there today.'

Sam nods. 'Yes, he was.'

'She said Sophie was too. She said that Sophie was even working with Becca to pull the whales out into the water.'

'Yeah. That's true, too.'

'Sam, it's none of my business …'

He smiles. 'But ...'

'You know, I remember when you arrived here with Becca thirteen years ago. It was a terrible time. Such a shock for all of us.'

'Yes.'

'I'd spent days over in the cemetery, talking to Winny. Telling her not to be afraid. Telling her you and Becca ould be fine.'

Sam sucks in a ragged breath. 'I didn't know that. I couldn't— I couldn't go there. I was a mess. I barely remember anything about that time. I'm glad you were there to pick up the pieces, Ellie.'

'For years I'd visit Winny every day. Every day, Sam. Without fail.'

Sam nods.

'Then, three years ago, on her birthday, I went to the cemetery, and, instead of walking to her grave, I sat on the bench. You know the one. Near the gate. With the view over the ocean.'

'Uh-huh.'

'I sat there and I said goodbye to my precious girl. I told her she'd always be in my heart. And anytime I wanted to see her, I'd just close my eyes and she'd be there. Laughing. Happy. My lovely Winny.' Ellie takes a sip of the tea and cups the mug in her hands. 'I didn't visit her grave that day. I just sat on the bench and listened to the birds and the waves. I felt a release. She was with Thomas and it was ... okay.

'I only go twice a year now. On her birthday and on Thomas's. And, it's okay. They understand, Sam. They're in us. They'll always be a part of us. But it's right to say goodbye. Otherwise, we lose ourselves. Unable to move forward, nor step backward. We're here to move forward, Sam. Believe me, Winny understands. Winny wants you to.'

He finds her standing by the tickle, her slight figure wrapped up in several of Florie's jumpers. He watches her as she looks up at the waning moon revealing itself from behind a bank of thick grey clouds.

'Sophie.' I know what it feels like, Princess Grace. To be ostracised. To be reviled. To be misunderstood.

Sophie turns. 'Sam?'

He walks towards her.

'What are you doing here, Sam? I thought—'

Then she is in his arms, and it is like all their differences melt away in the rightness of it.

# Chapter 66

## Norwich – 2 August 1953

Dottie slides Ellie's card with the birth announcement back into the envelope and sets it down on the green leather blotter on George's desk where he'd left it that morning. Winnifred Agnes Mary Parsons. She purses her red lipsticked lips. Quite the mouthful for a baby. Still, their mother would be pleased to have a namesake, though why Ellie had thought Agnes was a good choice for a name was beyond her. She wrinkles her nose. The girl will end up being called Winny or Aggy. She wouldn't make that mistake with her babies.

She runs her hand over the round bump under her navy and white polka-dot maternity smock. So much for her career as a concert pianist. Those tedious hours of lessons and practice, the auditions and the recitals. She'd wanted fame and success. She'd been well on her way, too. Now, look at the state of her. She didn't even have a baby grand to play, let alone the Steinway grand piano she'd become so used to in the London practice rooms and the concert halls. All she had was her mother's old upright. Right back where she started.

She'd almost got away from Norwich. From provincial life. A European tour with the London Philharmonic had been booked for the autumn. But she'd had to go and sleep with George, hadn't she? He'd resisted at first, of course. He still seemed to nurse some misplaced affection for Ellie. George was really quite wet sometimes.

She'd had to make him want her. If she were honest with herself, it was possibly because he was the only man she'd met who hadn't fallen at her feet. She'd learned a lot of things in London. How to wind a man around her finger was one of them. She'd had to pull out all the stops with George, but she'd got him in the end.

Dottie flicks her swollen belly with a sharp, red-painted finger-nail. *Now I'm stuck, aren't I? I'm a good little Catholic so I've got to have you.* Of course, George insisted on the marriage as soon as he knew. Good old reliable George. Boring, earnest, dull George. *What choice did I have? None, that's what.* She wished Ellie could have been there. She would have loved to have seen Ellie's face when George placed the wedding ring on her finger.

She takes a pack of cigarettes and a lighter out of the pocket of her maternity top. Sticking a cigarette between her lips she lights it and inhales deeply, blowing out the smoke in a long stream. She peers down at her belly, already swollen so large that the women at the hospital auxiliary have been telling her how lucky she is to be having summer babies.

*Ha! Summer babies my arse! I've got three more months of swollen feet and an aching back and breasts that hang like two balloons from my chest. You two are going to make it to the top of Norwich society, if it kills me. If I couldn't get there myself, I'll make sure you get there and pull me up with you. And I'll kiss every girdle-constrained backside of every Norwich grand dame to help George become the husband I deserve. Then, I'll swan over to Newfoundland and rub Ellie's nose in our success. With George on my arm.*

*Serves her right for abandoning me and Poppy, and dumping*

*poor, love-sodden George for that Newfoundlander with his ridic-*
*ulous accent. Running off to be a free spirit with not a care in the*
*world. Leaving me all on my own. Everybody leaves, eventually,*
*don't they? Mummy, then you, Ellie, then Poppy. You're not dead,*
*Ellie, but you may as well be to me. Well, I hope for your sake*
*leaving us all behind was worth it. At least you got to make a*
*choice.*

Stabbing out the cigarette on George's green blotter, she grabs
the card off the desk. She tears it and lets the pieces fall until
they litter George's desk like white confetti.

# *Chapter 67*

### Tippy's Tickle – 16 September 2011

A door slams. Sophie opens her eyes and turns over in the bed. The white curtain flutters in front of the window, settling back into stillness before it is caught again in a gust of wind. Outside the window, a veil of fog obscures the sky, though a soft light glows behind it, promising a sunny day.

'Good morning.'

She looks over her shoulder. 'Good morning to you, too. I heard a door slam.'

Sam smiles back at her, his dark eyes shining with warmth. 'Becca. She likes to go for a run first thing.'

'She's not going to be happy if she finds me here. You'd better hide anything breakable.'

'I'll talk to her later.' He reaches across Sophie's body and pulls her against him, trapping her with his leg. 'I hope you're not intending to go anywhere this morning.'

'Hardly. I think I'll hide out here for the day. I don't think anyone in Tippy's Tickle's speaking to me since the vote yesterday.'

Sam kisses her neck, trailing soft kisses along Sophie's nape. 'I have absolutely no objection to that, Princess Grace.'

Sophie reaches behind her head and brushes her hand over Sam's cropped hair. 'Come here. I want to see you.'

He rolls on top of her. 'Hmm, you're comfy.'

Sophie pokes at his shoulder. 'You're crushing me, you big oaf.'

He props himself onto his elbows and examines her face. 'Your eyes are the same colour as a stormy sea. The same as Winny's.'

Sophie's smile fades. *My divine, beautiful cousin Winny. Is Sam only interested in me because I connect him to Winny?*

She squirms out from underneath him. 'Look, Sam, I actually should go. I've got to email Richard my report before his meeting this afternoon. He's been hounding me for it. He's not going to like what I'm going to tell him.'

'Hold on, Sophie. Just a minute ago, you were saying you'd like to hide out here all day.'

'I know.' She pulls her T-shirt over her head. 'That was just … you know. Early morning chit-chat.'

Sam laughs, his voice husky with sleep. 'Chit-chat? Do people still say that?'

Sophie pulls on her jeans and zips the zipper. 'Well, I do.' She glances at her watch. 'Oh, God. It's nine already. The consortium's meeting in New York at two.'

Sam takes hold of Sophie's wrist, covering the watch with his hand. 'Hold on. Sit down. Please.'

Sophie sits on the bundled sheets with a huff. 'Yes?'

'You've got plenty of time. We're an hour and a half ahead of New York, remember?' Sam turns over her hand in his. He traces his finger along her palm. Sophie swallows, willing the shocks snapping in her body to stop.

'It's Winny, isn't it?' he says.

Sophie's shoulders slump. *How can he read me so well?*

'I'm not Winny, Sam.'

His finger runs up the side of her ring finger, cresting the tip, sliding down the other side like a skier on a steep slope. 'I never said you were.'

'You did. You just said my eyes were like Winny's.'

'Well, they are. And they're like Ellie's too. And Becca's.' The swooping finger, sliding up her index finger and down to the base of her thumb.

'I'm not Winny.'

'I know. Believe me, I know. You're Sophie and you're ...' he chuckles '... you're impossible.'

Sophie tugs to free her hand but he holds fast. 'I'm impossible? What about you? Stomping around the place like some ... like some bloody biker in the middle of nowhere? You had a successful business in Boston. Why are you even here?'

'I like it here.' He shakes his head. 'Impossible.' He takes her ring finger into his mouth.

Sophie closes her eyes. 'Oh, God.'

'Stay here as long as you like. I've set up my laptop for you and lit the fire.'

Sophie slides onto the bench. 'Are you sure? You know you're sleeping with the enemy?'

'Can't be the first time that's happened in the history of the world. And I'm still not going to sell. Even if you do that thing you did last night again.'

'Sam!'

Sam ducks as Tigger shoots across the room into the kitchen. He takes a quick sip of coffee from the *World's Greatest Dad* mug and sets it on the kitchen counter as Bear lumbers across the living room rug to join him. 'I'll pick up something for dinner. Try to pull Becca away from Toby to join us. I'll tell Ellie you're eating here tonight.'

'No, it's Aunt Ellie's birthday. Florie's throwing a surprise party, remember?' Sophie drops her head into her hands. 'I probably shouldn't go. Everybody in Tippy's Tickle hates me.'

'That's no reason not to go.'

Sophie jerks her head up. 'You agree with me?'

Sam shrugs. 'I've got to agree with you sometimes.'

'Yes, but not when I don't want you to.'

'I'll come by before the party,' he says, grinning. 'We can go over together. That'll give them all something to talk about.' He grabs his jean jacket off a peg and heads towards the porch.

'I'll need to go over earlier to change and spruce myself up. I'll see you there later.'

Spinning around, Sam strides back to Sophie and plants a kiss on her lips.

'I don't think you need any sprucing up.'

Sophie smiles. 'Oh, do you have phone charger I could borrow? I've got an iPhone like yours and my battery's run out.'

'Sure. In the drawer by the sink. You'll find one in there.'

Sophie watches him as he walks towards the porch, the dog at his heels. She is still smiling when the door slams.

Sophie rubs her bare arms and snuggles deeper into the sofa cushions. She glances over at the wood burner, but there's no sign of the fire Sam had set that morning. She sniffs; the acrid, smoky smell of something burning hangs in the air.

Setting Sam's laptop on the coffee table, she pads across the braided rug to the kitchen and pulls open the cupboard doors. She checks the plugs and the appliances, but there's no sign of anything burning. Probably just some lingering smoke from the morning's fire.

She heats up a mug of coffee in the microwave and meanders

back into the living room. The picture of Sam, Winny and Becca catches her eye and she walks over to the table and picks it up. She's nothing like Winny, with her slim, blonde beauty. She'd inherited her father's brown hair and modest stature. But she did have the Burgess blue-grey eyes. *They're your best feature,* her mother used to say. *In fact, your only good feature, Sophie. Otherwise, you're fairly ordinary, but beauty isn't everything. It didn't do your aunt any good. Look at the trouble she caused your grandfather.*

Settling back on the sofa, she sets the laptop on her lap and rereads the document she's been working on for Richard. In response to her morning email about the villagers' unanimous vote not to sell, Richard had emailed her back to say the consortium were determined to "plough forward". *It's nothing that adding a few more zeros won't solve,* he'd said. *Everybody's got their price. Everybody.*

She glances at her watch, which is still on New York time. One fifty-five. Just in time for Richard's two o'clock meeting with the consortium. He's probably flapping around his office like the buzzard he's starting to look like, cursing her for taking so long to send him her report. But it's a delicate situation, what with her aunt and Sam being involved, and she'd wanted to get it right.

Taking a deep breath, she presses *Send*.

# *Chapter 68*

## Norwich – 3 September 1953

'Oh, my God.'

George turns over in the bed. 'What? What is it, darling?'

Groaning, Dottie throws off the bedcovers and clutches her belly. 'Something's wrong.' She turns on her side and curls into a foetal position, panting between whimpers.

George tries to speak, but his eyes are locked on to the spreading red stain on the bed where Dottie has been lying. He stumbles out of the bed, knocking over the table lamp, which crashes to the floor, exploding into shards of pink glass.

'You're bleeding, Dottie.'

Another groan. 'I can't be.'

'I'll call the doctor.'

'The babies are coming, George. They're coming.'

'No, Dottie. Not yet. I'll call the midwife.'

'The doctor, George. Call the doctor. I need to get to the hospital.' Dottie begins to pant, and her red face drips with rivulets of sweat. 'Promise me they'll be okay, George.' She reaches out and clasps George's arm. 'Promise me.'

'I promise, Dottie.'

Dottie smiles weakly and sinks back on the bed. 'Hurry George. Save the babies. Please, save them.'

'I will. Don't worry. I won't let anything happen to the babies or to you. Everything will be fine, Dottie. I promise.'

The doctor turns away from the sleeping woman and nods at George to follow him into the corridor. Outside the ward, the fluorescent lighting throws a garish shine over the worn blue linoleum floor.

'Mr Parry, I'm afraid your wife has had a very bad time of it. She was quite far along in her term. There was ... I'm very sorry. There was considerable damage. We've had to perform a hysterectomy.'

'A hysterectomy?' George stares at the doctor. The man's dark hair has threads of silver running through its careful combing, and there's a smudge of grease – a thumbprint – on his round glasses. A pin on the white lapel of his lab coat. *Dr F.J. Fry* 'You mean ...?'

Dr Fry shakes his head. 'She won't be able to have any more children.' He reaches out and pats George's shoulder. 'I'm very sorry.'

George's eyes widen. 'What will I tell my wife?'

'You'll find a way. She'll come to accept it eventually. You'll just need to give her time.'

George rubs his forehead. 'You don't know my wife. I promised, you see. I promised the babies would be fine.'

'Of course you did. Any husband would have done the same.'

George draws his eyebrows together in a frown above the rim of his glasses. 'You don't understand. I promised her. She'll never forgive me. She'll never forgive me for stealing her life from her, not just once, but twice.'

# Chapter 69

## Tippy's Tickle – 16 September 2011

She wakes with a start, pulled out of a dream where she's drifting on a boat with Sam, black-eyed whales swimming and breaching around them in a steel-blue sea. She opens her eyes. Blue smoke hangs in the air like fog. She coughs, but every intake of breath draws the smoke deeper into her lungs. Pressing her hand to her mouth, she leaps off the sofa and stumbles to the bedroom where she'd left her phone charging on the bed.

She pushes open the bedroom door. Hot air and smoke blast from the room, sending her staggering back as she throws up her arm to shield her face. The bed is ablaze and yellow flames crawl up the curtains and eat at the wooden panelling.

She makes it as far as the kitchen before the smoke brings her to her knees. Gasping for breath, she claws at the floorboards as she crawls towards the porch. She pushes her body against the floor, tears streaming down her cheeks from the heat and smoke. The thick fog of smoke presses on her back like a boulder, squeezing the breath out of her lungs. Reaching through the smoke, she grasps the leg of a wicker chair in the porch.

*This can't be happening. This can't be happening.*

She gasps as the smoke burns into her lungs, choking her. Then nothing.

A tongue laps at her face. Something pushes at her chest. She chokes and coughs, gasping for air. Cool air. A drop of water on her face. Then another. A dog barks.

'Oh, my Jaysus God! She's okay, Ellie! Get away, Bear. Let the maid breathe.' Florie's voice.

Sophie opens her eyes. Above her the sky is white like a blank page. A face looms into view, the blue-grey eyes hooded with worry. 'Are you all right, darling?' Ellie brushes a hand along Sophie's cheek.

Sophie moves to sit up, but coughs rack her body. Someone shoves a water bottle into her hand. 'Drink this.'

She raises her eyebrows as she takes the bottle. 'Thank you, Emmett.' She drinks the water, the coolness lubricating her dry throat.

'Jaysus God, duck,' Florie says as she and Emmett help Sophie to her feet. 'You gave us some fright. I didn't know whether to shit or go blind when Bear started barkin' to beat the band.' She rubs the dog's huge head and kisses its forehead. 'If it wasn't for him, you'd be cooked to a crisp.'

Sophie looks around the clearing beside Sam's cottage. 'Where's Sam?'

'I'm here.'

Sophie turns her head. He is standing in the doorway of the cottage, his relieved face streaked with soot. But there was something else. Something about the way he looked at her. Shock? Panic? Fear?

'I'm so sorry, Sam. The phone charger must have overheated on the bedcovers.'

'Don't worry. I'm just glad you're safe.'

'Is the damage bad?'

'Just the bedroom and smoke damage in the rest. I'll manage.'

'It's my fault. I should never have left the phone charging on the bed.'

'Don't worry. It was an accident.'

'Accidents seems to follow you around, Sam.'

Sophie jerks her head around to Emmett.

Ellie squeezes Sophie's arm. 'Are you all right for walking back to the house, sweetheart? Let's get you back and get you some tea. Florie's cooking roast beef and Yorkshire pudding for my birthday dinner, just like I used to eat in England.'

Florie takes hold of Sophie's arm. 'Tea's your ruddy answer for everything, Ellie. The poor maid needs a shower and a lie-down.'

'The war in England was won on tea, Florie. Don't underestimate it.'

Sophie looks back at the cottage, but Sam and the dog are nowhere to be seen.

# *Chapter 70*

## Tippy's Tickle – 19 June 1954

'Oh, look, Winny!' Ellie points across the kitchen table to Emmett who balances the plate with the birthday cake in his hands as he shuffles across the green linoleum floor. 'Nanny and Emmy have made you a cake.'

Emmett lays it gingerly on Agnes's best linen tablecloth. 'It's chocolate.'

Ellie buries her nose into Winny's soft blonde hair and jiggles the baby's chubby feet, which are clad in the pink booties Agnes has knitted as a birthday present. 'Oooh, chocolate, Winnybel! Your favourite.'

'Chocolate's *your* favourite, Mam,' Emmett says as he slides onto a wooden chair. 'Winny never had cake before, so she can't have a favourite.'

Thomas sets down his beer beside the other empty bottles and, picking up a knife, winks at his son as he leans over to cut the cake. 'He's got you there, Ellie Mae.'

Agnes sets a stack of her late mother-in-law's best Royal Winton dessert plates on the table with several silver forks. 'And what do you think you're doing, Thomas? We haven't sung 'Happy Birthday' yet.'

Staring at his mother, he places a hand on her forehead. Agnes pushes his hand away. 'What in the name of all that's holy do you think you're doing?'

'You don't have a fever, so it's not that. Did you fall, Mam? A cake and 'Happy Birthday'? You never made me a cake, nor even Emmy here. Ellie always has to go over to Martha Fizzard's to bake Emmy's cake 'cause you hide the cake tins on her.'

Agnes glares at Ellie. 'She said that, did she? She couldn't find a fly if it was on her nose. I never hid anything.'

'You gots more lip than a coal bucket, b'y,' Ephraim says as he twists the top off his fourth bottle of Agnes's beer. 'You're goin' to make her right binicky.'

'Boys don't needs cake. Spoils them for no reason.' Agnes leans over and chucks Winny under her chin. 'Little girls is different, isn't that right, Winny?'

'I knows the words to 'Happy Birthday',' Emmett says as he hands the forks out to the others. 'Mrs Perkins taught us. She makes marshmallow squares when it's someone's birthday at school. She lets us choose the colour. I always chooses blue 'cause no one else'll eats them 'cept me.' Emmett eyes the double-height cake with its glistening icing and licks his lips. 'Mam, I has a present for Winny.'

'Do you, Emmy?'

Emmett roots around in his trouser pocket and pulls out a wood carving of a long-coated dog the size of his hand. He pushes it along the table to his mother. 'It's a Newfoundland dog. Like Mr Boyd's.'

Ellie picks up the wooden dog. 'That's really an excellent carving, Emmy. It looks just like Thumper.' She holds it out to Thomas. 'Doesn't it, Thomas? Look like Jim Boyd's dog?'

Thomas takes the carving and squints as he inspects it. 'Where'd you learn to do this, son?'

The boy shrugs. 'Dunno. I just does it.'

Thomas whistles. 'Well, aren't you the clever clogs.'

'Don't you be fillin' his head with slop, Thomas,' Agnes says as she fishes the stub of a pink candle out of her apron pocket. 'Put that on the cake, Emmy, then we'll all sing 'Happy Birthday' and you can cuts the cake. You can pretends it's your birthday cake, too.'

Thomas pulls on his yellow oilskin jacket, grabs his crutch and heads for the screen door.

Ellie sets the dirty dishes in the soapy sink water. 'Where are you going? It's getting late.'

'Just going down to the store to check the boat. She had a slow leak the other day that I fixed up with some pitch.'

'You're not taking her out now, are you?'

'Just for a quick run down to the lighthouse to check she's tight. We've gots to get out early tomorrow before the big factory trawlers turns up. They sucks up more fish in a day then all of us b'ys here does in a month. Sun won't be down till close to ten. There's a good couple of hours yet.'

Emmett takes his yellow rain jacket off the coat hook by the door. 'Can I come too, Da'?'

'Sure, son. High time you learned about boats.'

'But Thomas, it's almost his bedtime. He's only nine.'

'I was on the boat with my dad when I was eight. Time for him to learn the family business.' Thomas grabs a couple of beer bottles out of the new refrigerator, and stuffs them into his jacket pockets.

'My son isn't going to be a fisherman.'

'Something wrong with being a fisherman, maid? Maybe you wished you'd married a chocolate salesman instead?'

'Thomas!'

'It's the truth, isn't it, Ellie Mae? Don't I knows you fell in love with a solider in a sharp uniform, and ended up the wife of a piss-poor fisherman at the back of beyond? Don't I knows you should have had better? Don't you knows I've been tryin' to make it better for you?'

'Thomas? What's got into you?'

He taps his forehead with his hand. 'I'm up to here in debt to Jim Boyd and Rod Fizzard. How'd you think you gots the fridge? And all the paint in from St John's so I could paint you the colourful house you wanted? We has to get out fishin' longer hours, and Dad's not so young anymore. It's all I can thinks to do is to get Emmy helpin'.'

'Thomas—'

Thomas gestures to Emmett. 'C'mon, son.'

'Our son's not going to be a fisherman, Thomas.'

The screen door slams, bouncing on its sprung hinges until it slowly settles back into its frame.

Thomas peers through the window of the bridge of the small boat and steers through the water towards the silhouette of the lighthouse on the cliff. The darkening sky is shot with streaks of yellow, red and orange, which reflect off the tops of the waves. Just like Ellie's bakeapple and partridgeberry cobbler when she pulls it steaming hot from the oven, Thomas thinks.

He twists the cap off the second beer and takes a long gulp. He shouldn't have set on to Ellie like that. He was lucky to have a woman like her. A lot of women would have hightailed it back to England before they learned what a scrunchion was. Jim Boyd's cousin up in Baie Verte had just that happen to him. His Bristol bride had refused to get off the boat in Halifax when she saw the sight of it and headed straight back to England.

Still, when he looked at Ellie, in her plain dresses and her sturdy brown shoes, and her blueberry-stained aprons that never came clean no matter how much he saw her scrub at them in the sink, she was as lovely as he remembered that first time he'd laid eyes on her at the Samson and Hercules. More lovely, if that were possible. Her figure fuller, but firmed by the physical life on The Rock. Her face slimmer, her hair a deeper blonde that spun threads of gold in the summer months. Her beautiful eyes, as stormy and blue as the north Atlantic. How did he deserve this woman? How could he show her how much he loved her? How much he hated himself for giving her such a hard life, so far away from her family.

He shakes his head. One day he'd get her a proper diamond ring. He would have done, if he could have. But, the diamond rings he could afford had been so small. Not right at all for Ellie. He was lucky to have found that old pawn shop down on Elm Hill. Maybe it was only a cheap zircon, but it had the right look. One of these days, he'd get her a proper diamond ring, that's for sure. She'd like that. He'd put her through a lot; it was the least he could do.

His mother had never taken to her, no matter how much he'd seen Ellie try with her. '*That English wife of yours,*' Agnes would call her, not to Ellie's face, of course. '*Fancies herself an artist, like that'll do a fat lot of good gettin' food on the table out here.*' The two of them existed in an uneasy truce, he could see that, like two prisoners forced to share a cell. His mam was a hard case. He knew it'd been hard for Ellie, all these years.

Still, he'd given Ellie two beautiful children. Well, Winny, at least. But Emmy was his son, no matter how he'd come into the world. Even if George was Emmy's real father, no matter what Ellie said. He had to let go of his jealousy. It was a small man who'd take such a thing out on a child. The war was a different world. Who was he to judge Ellie, when she hadn't heard from him in months. When she'd thought he'd been killed in North Africa?

The boat lurches over a large swell and Thomas staggers against the wheel. His crutch and the beer bottle crash to the floor. Thomas grabs for the wheel, blinking hard as the cabin spins.

'What was that, Da'?'

'Nothing, son,' Thomas calls over his shoulder. 'How's it holding out back there, Emmy? Any leaks?'

'Nothing inside.'

'That's good. We'll turn back at the lighthouse. We'll be home before the sun sets. That'll please your mam.'

'Okay.'

Thomas picks up his crutch and secures it under his armpit as he steadies himself in front of the wheel. Focusing on the horizon, the spinning eases. He begins humming, and the random notes form into an old song he'd learned as a boy.

*'Jack was every inch a sailor,*
*Five and twenty years a whaler,*
*Jack was every inch a sailor,*
*He was born upon the bright blue sea.'*

He shouts over his shoulder. 'How was that, Emmy? Shall I teach you the words? Emmy?'

'I'm checkin' the outside for leaks, Da'.'

Thomas glances to the stern, his heart leaping into his throat.

The boy teeters on his stomach over the side of the boat. Forward and back with each dip and swell of the sea. Forward and back. Forward and back.

'Emmy! Get off there, b'y! My God! Get your life jacket back on!'

A large wave slams the boat. The boy teeters forward, hovering like a baby bird on the edge of a nest.

'Emmy!' Thomas lurches towards his son, hobbling over the fishing net and coiled ropes with his crutch.

Too late.

The next minutes last hours, days, years. The sea, which had looked so benign in its bakeapple colours just moments before, has turned black, its glistening inkiness broken only by the whitecaps of the swelling waves and the small dark head bobbing in the water.

Thomas staggers back into the bridge and shuts off the ignition. Grabbing the life preserver, he heads starboard and launches the orange ring out to the flailing boy. 'Grab it, Emmy! Swim to it son. It's just a stroke away.' Thomas gathers up the fishing net and throws it over the side so that it hangs from its fastenings down the side of the boat.

'Da'!' Emmett takes a mouthful of water. 'Da'!' He coughs just as another wave splashes over his head.

Throwing the crutch aside, Thomas plunges into the water. It sucks him down into a deathly quiet until he can no longer sense where the surface is. A large dark body slides past him, its belly gleaming white, and the barnacles on its huge mouth glowing an iridescent green in the murky water. The creature's black eye watches him as it glides past. Its body rises in a graceful arc to the surface to breathe through its blowhole.

Following the humpback's lead, Thomas musters every iota

of strength as he breaks through the surface and crashes through the water towards his son.

Emmett raises his hand out towards his father. Then he's hit by another wave, and he's gone.

Thomas dives into the freezing black water. His hand brushes the hood of Emmett's yellow jacket. Grabbing it, he twists the fabric into his grasp and pulls his son up to the surface. Emmett gasps and grapples for Thomas's arm.

'Calm down, Emmy. Breathe, son. Just calm down.' He reaches around Emmett's shoulders and swims towards the orange life preserver, thrusting it over his son's head. 'Grab hold of this, son. You won't goes anywhere. You're fine now.'

The fishing boat is about sixty feet away, bobbing like a dull white cork on the black ocean, the fishing net draped like a web over the side. The lighthouse has awakened, and the white light flashes from the top of the cliff about a mile away. Thomas reaches through the water and takes hold of the rope connecting the life preserver to the boat. He sidestrokes awkwardly towards the boat, cursing the German grenade for stealing his leg as he pulls Emmett and the life preserver along behind him.

The cold Atlantic tugs at Thomas's body. He can no longer feel his hands, and his boot drags at his foot as he splashes towards the boat. His mind, fuzzy at the edges from the many beers, focuses on the boat. There is nothing but the boat. *You must get to the boat.*

After an eternity, his hand brushes the wooden hull. 'We're here, Emmy.'

'Don't go, Da'.'

'I'm not goin' anywhere. Now, you has to be brave, son. Grab hold of the net. You knows how you liked to climb the riggin' when that American fella's schooner came into Rod Fizzard's last summer? It's just like that. Pretends the net's the riggin' on that schooner.'

Emmett grabs hold of the net. 'I gots it, Da'.'

'Good fella. Now, I'll lifts off this life preserver so you can scamper up the riggin', just like last summer.'

Emmett slowly climbs up the net. When he reaches the top he turns around, his face lit by a bright smile. 'I did it, Da'!'

Thomas smiles up at his son. 'Good boy, Emmy. Be careful now. Just gets in the boat and I'll be right up after you.'

A thud as Emmett slips and falls into the boat.

'Emmy?' Thomas thrusts the life preserver away and swims to the net. 'Emmy!'

The net swirls around Thomas as he grapples for a hold. Twisting around his leg, it tangles through his boot and around his body, dragging him down into the sea.

The large grey body with its white belly slides by, the barnacles that ghostly green. The black eye watches him as the creature glides past. The whale rises in a graceful arc to the surface, where all that exists is light and the memory of Ellie's smile.

Emmett reaches for the side of the boat and pulls himself to his feet, his head throbbing. He peers out into the inky blackness.

'Da'! Where you at, Da'?' He scans the surface of the water. Fear stabs at his belly.

'Da'! Da'!'

His voice breaks into a sob as he slides to the floor of the boat. 'I'm sorry, Da'. I'm sorry. I didn't wear my jacket inside out. The fairies gots you, Da'. I'm sorry.'

# *Chapter 71*

## Tippy's Tickle – 16 September 2011

Ace levers himself onto one of the long counters in Florie's store, and jabs an Ugly Stick against the wooden countertop, setting the bottle tops jingling as he pounds at the tin can head with a drumstick.

'Here ye, here ye, we is gathered here tonight to celebrate two ...' he holds up two fingers '... what's that, Thor? Three, not two ...' he holds up three chunky fingers '... three important events in the life of this hidden paradise of Tippy's Tickle.'

'Get on with it, b'y! The cod's thawin'!'

Ace winks at Thor who is holding a glistening frozen codfish above his head. 'Right you are, b'y.' Ace bangs the tin can head. 'Firstly, we gots to pay homage to the Queen of Tippy's Tickle, who's all of eighty-nine years on this earth today. Now, I's been told she landed on this here rock back in nineteen forty-six, which actually makes her ...' he screws up his face as he counts on his fingers '... a young maid of sixty-five 'cause your life starts when you comes to The Rock. Florie, take some candles off the cake, girl!'

Florie gives Ace a thumbs up. 'Right you are, b'y!'

'I thought you didn't approve of all this tourist stuff, Florie,' Ellie says.

'Well, if you can't beat them, you joins them, right? And we could all use a knees up.'

'The cod's startin' to whiff, son!'

'Holy God, he's not jokin'!'

Ace thumps the Ugly Stick. 'Hold your horses, I'm just about there, b'ys.' He motions to Thor who is wiping a hand on his Rush T-shirt. 'Bring up the fish, b'y. We're gonna need her in a minute.' Ace surveys the room. 'Now, I hears we gots some Come From Aways here today.'

'Gotta change that, son! Can't have CFAs here!'

'Screech 'em in, b'y!'

Holding the dripping cod above his head, Thor weaves his way through the throng towards the counter. Ace bangs the Ugly Stick until the crowd quietens. 'Now, we's got to fix this situation 'cause we all knows what happens to CFAs if they'd don't gets Screeched in, don't we?'

Emmett cups his hands around his mouth. 'They stays CFAs!'

'Right you are, Emmett Parsons! We can't have that happen. So, will the followin' CFAs approach the Ugly Stick – Miss Becca Byrne, Miss Sophie Parry and Miss Ellie Parsons!'

'That's three Screech-ins and the birthday, Ace! That's four events, not three!'

Ace's thick grey eyebrows draw together. 'You gots more tongue than a logan, Toby Molloy!'

Sophie glances at Sam in panic. 'What do they want me to do?'

He prods her forward. 'There's no getting out of this one, Princess Grace. Just do what he says.'

Becca walks over to Sophie. Smiling shyly, she grabs Sophie's hand and pulls her to the front as Florie pushes Ellie forward.

'Right you are, ladies! Give us the Screech bottle, Toby, and three glasses. What am I sayin'? Glasses all round!'

The room erupts in a cheer.

Ace splashes the dark rum into three shot glasses for the women and one for himself and hands the bottle to Toby. 'Pass it around, b'y. We're all gonna Screech them in. But first we needs some ceremony.' He clears his throat and stamps the Ugly Stick.

*Here's to your health, and here's to your gullet,*
*Drinks up the Screech, b'y; hangs on to your wallet.*
*Then when you're done, don't goes, m' duck,*
*The cod's here to kiss, and we all gives a—*' he waggles his bushy eyebrows '*—buck.*'

He waves at Emmett. 'Emmett, b'y! Pass the hat. Pops your loonies and your toonies in the hat, b'ys and maids. We're collectin' for the cancer charity today.' He taps Sophie on her shoulder with the stick. 'Now, m'dear, you gots to kiss the cod.'

'I have to what?'

'Kiss the cod, girl. G'wan. Best to do it before she thaws out all the way. Give her a right smack on the kisser.'

Thor holds the dripping fish up to Sophie. Screwing up her nose, she puckers up and gives the mouth a quick peck. The crowd erupts with whoops.

'There you goes, maid. That's how it's done.' Thor moves along to Becca who pinches her nose and kisses the fish. Ellie pushes the sleeves of her pink turtleneck sweater up her arms and plants a kiss smack on its mouth. The room thunders with cheers.

Ace holds up his shot glass of rum. 'Now, they says that one day a fella gave an American GI here a glass of Newfoundland rum back in the war. The GI gulped it down and let out an almighty screech. And that, so they say, is how Screech gots its name. Up to the lips and over the gums, watch out gullet, here she comes!'

An accordion wheezes into a lively tune. Sophie sets her empty glass on the counter and holds her hand up to Ace. 'Pull me up.'

'What's that, maid?'

Sophie steps onto a chair. 'Pull me up.'

Ace grabs her hand and hauls Sophie onto the wooden counter. She takes the Ugly Stick and pounds it on the countertop. 'Excuse me! Excuse me!'

Sam stands on a chair and whistles. 'Oi! Quiet!' The room settles into a low buzz.

Sophie licks her lips and glances at Ellie. 'I've got news about the hotel and the golf course.'

The room hums with *boos*.

'They turfin' us out, maid?'

'They'll have to drag me out by my boots!'

She clears her throat. 'As you know, the consortium for the hotel development met with Richard Niven Architects in New York this afternoon. I'd advised Richard this morning of your unanimous decision not to sell, but the consortium didn't consider that an impediment to pursuing the project. They felt,' she clears her throat, 'they felt they could, well, they could pay you more money.' She glances at Ellie. 'A lot more money.'

'Ten million, you gots yourself a deal!'

'Start practisin' your golf swings, b'ys!'

Sophie glances at Sam. 'I know the golf course is controversial, but the consortium believes that the development would benefit Tippy's Tickle by bringing employment into the area and by rebranding the town with a new name.'

'A new name? What's wrong with Tippy's Tickle?'

'Old Tippy's turnin' down in Davy Jones' Locker, b'y!'

She raises her voice. 'They've decided on ... They've decided on Walrus Heights for the new name.'

'Walruses? There's no walruses in Tippy's Tickle!'

''Cept for old Thor, there! He's the spit of a walrus!'

Sophie clears her throat again. 'Anyway, this was the state of play until—' she takes a deep breath '—I'm afraid I accidentally attached the video I took of the whales beaching themselves to my feasibility report for the consortium.' She glances at Sam. A smile slowly forms on his face.

'I've been informed that the investors found it most distressing – which, of course, it was for all of us. They feel, very strongly, that they can't risk any incidents like this happening to the Walrus Heights Golf Resort and Spa. Consequently, they've decided not to proceed further with this project in Tippy's Tickle.'

The room thunders into cheers. Sophie stamps the Ugly Stick, setting the bottle caps jingling. 'I also want to say that I've tendered my resignation from Richard Niven Architects effective—' she looks at her watch '—effective today at two o'clock New York time. Three-thirty Newfoundland time.'

'You go there, Sophie, girl!'

'She's a right Newfoundlander now!'

Becca climbs onto the counter beside Sophie. *'I have something to say,'* she signs to the crowd. Toby Molloy steps onto a chair to translate her signs, his clear green eyes exposed by a recent haircut. Becca looks over at Toby, her face luminous. She holds up her hand, a gold band circling her ring finger. *'Toby and I are married!'* She pats her flat stomach. *'And we're expecting a baby!'*

# *Chapter 72*

## Norwich – 1 December 1961

Dottie leans over to air kiss Marion Humphrey's jowly, over-powdered face. A whiff of musky perfume assaults her nose, and she pushes her tongue against her teeth to suppress a sneeze.

'That was a lovely luncheon, Marion. It looks like everything is on course for the hospital auxiliary Christmas Fair. Your husband has been so generous sponsoring the event.'

'Oh, heavens, Dorothy. He's happy to do it. He says it's good advertising for Firman's Mustard. Community spirit and all that.' The older woman grasps Dottie's gloved hand through the window of the Wolseley. 'Do try to persuade your husband to come to our New Year's Eve do this year. Walter has some business he wants to discuss with him. We've all been so impressed with what George has achieved at Mcklintock's since he became manager. Walter said he was on the train out of Liverpool Street just last week, and the first thing he saw was a huge billboard for the new Space Bubble chocolate bars.'

Dottie smiles. If Walter only knew how many of the new ideas came from her. 'Don't worry, Marion. I'll do my best to pull George away from his desk, though it won't be easy. He's so committed to Mcklintock's, as you know.'

'Oh, yes, dear. We all know.' Marion Humphrey adjusts the

mink stole around her bulky shoulders. She leans closer to the window. 'You don't suppose George can send me over a few boxes of Mckintock's Dark Chocolate Fantasy Selection? For guests, you understand.'

'Of course. Consider it done.'

Marion Humphrey smiles, revealing a streak of fuchsia pink lipstick across her teeth. 'Lovely. I'll see you on Saturday at the fair.'

'Yes, absolutely.'

Dottie watches the polished navy Wolseley glide down Newmarket Road past the handsome Victorian and Georgian homes until it disappears from sight. She breathes out an exhausted sigh and heads through the gate and up the paved footpath to the white-painted porch of the modest yellow-brick Georgian house. She frowns as she sweeps her eyes over the large sash windows and elegant proportions. They'll be out of here by the summer, if her plan comes off. If it weren't for her, they'd still be living in George's flat above the fish shop on Duke Street. The manager of Mcklintock's Chocolates had to live in a house equal to his status. She had her eye set on a perfect pink-brick Queen Anne house hidden behind a gated wall further down Newmarket Road away from the city. Not for sale yet, but soon. She had her sources.

In the hallway, she unpins her hat and tosses it on the telephone table on top of her handbag and white kid gloves. Reaching into her handbag, she takes out the cigarette packet, grimacing when she finds it empty. She leans into the mirror and examines her face, pursing her lipsticked lips and pressing at the fine lines that have begun to form at the corners of her eyes. Thirty-three and still in Norwich. Aside from one disastrous April holiday in Paris five years ago, when George had taken a resolute dislike to French food and the Impressionists, and it had rained for four days, she's never set foot outside of Britain. This wasn't the life she'd planned.

She reaches down and rests her hands on her girdled stomach. No babies. She hadn't wanted any, not when she was younger. Certainly not when she'd fallen pregnant with the twins. She'd hated them for snatching her dreams away, for forcing her into this life of torpid provincialism. But then, as the pregnancy had lumbered on, she'd come to see their usefulness. How they could be the key to the closed doors of Norfolk society. She'd get the twins into the best schools – Church of England if she had to; the best clubs; they'd play cricket with the Earl of Leicester's team at Holkham; learn to ride and shoot. They'd be her golden ticket to a better life.

Then they'd died. Two little boys. She hadn't let George touch her after that. What was the point? Her womb had been stripped out of her. Why put up with George's inept fumblings?

He'd suggested adoption. After her initial tantrums, she'd even become excited about the possibility. She could steer the child through the same course she'd planned for her twins. Another chance at the golden ticket. But then, George's age and his blind eye had scuppered that idea. NOT SUITABLE FOR ADOPTION. The red stamp across their adoption application. It was George's fault. Again. Her miserable life of pushing and grappling for the wealth and status, and, yes, the freedom, she deserved was all George's fault.

George was like a distant and irritating brother to her now. She had her room and he had his. He'd buried himself in his work, and she'd negotiated her way onto the boards of the Women's Institute, the Norfolk and Norwich Hospital Auxiliary, the Norwich Philharmonic Society where she was now Vice

President, and slowly and tactically climbed the social ladder. She and George had reached an accord. He was useful to her in his position at Mcklintock's, but she wasn't satisfied with that. Oh no. George was going to buy the business, but for that he needed a partner with money. This is where Norwich's wealthiest industrialist, Walter Humphrey, owner of Firman's Mustard, came in. How her arduously cultivated friendship with his wife, Marion, would finally bear fruit. Walter wanted to talk business with George. Finally, she was on her way.

Dottie wanders into George's study. The panelled shutters are drawn closed. She walks over to the tall sash windows and throws them open. The dull grey light of the December day filters into the wood-panelled room. She sits in the antique green leather chair and sifts through the stack of documents under the Maltese glass paperweight she'd found in a Holt flea market. The envelope has been torn open with George's brass letter-opener. She'd recognise the hand-writing anywhere. She slips the letter out of the envelope and reads.

Dottie sits in the large brown leather wingback chair in the shadows in front of the book-lined walls. She has closed the shutters. She wants to take him by surprise.

She hears the key in the front door, the squeak as the heavy panelled door swings open, the soft thunk as it closes. The keys rattling onto the telephone table. The pause as George hangs up his hat and bends down to remove the rubber covers of his Church's shoes.

The study door opens. A pause. A hesitation. The flick of the light switch.

'Dottie?'

Dottie holds out Ellie's letter. 'You've been sending her money? *Our* money?'

George's cheeks, flushed from walking home from the factory in the chilly winter – a habit she was going to have to put a stop to as soon as he finished his driving lessons – drain of colour. He pushes up the bridge of his glasses in the habit she finds so irritating.

'You found the letter.'

'Of course I found the letter. It was on your desk, for all the world to see.'

'It was under my work pile.'

Dottie raises a finely pencilled eyebrow. 'How long has this been going on? How much of our money ...' she stabs a finger against her chest '... how much of *my* money have you sent her?'

George crosses over to the desk and slumps into the chair. He rubs his forehead and sighs. 'I had to, Dottie. After Thomas died, Ellie was in a bad way. She has two children to support. Her mother-in-law was threatening to throw them out. She's your sister, Dottie. I had to do something. She has no one else to turn to. She's family.'

'Emmett's your son, isn't he?'

'Dottie!'

'I'm not an idiot, George. I've done the maths. Ellie and Thomas married at Christmas. Emmett should have been born in September, not August. I saw you and Ellie in the Cow Tower that night in November. I saw everything. I followed you.'

George stares over at his wife, at her carefully made-up face stiff with rage. 'You saw us?'

'Don't be such a dolt. I knew you loved Ellie. She told me she thought Thomas might be dead. She hadn't heard from him in months. Trust a man to go in for the kill.' Dottie glares at George, spitting out the words like a snake spitting venom. 'You still love her, don't you, George?'

George shakes his head. 'Dottie, you're my wife. I love you.'

'Don't be ridiculous, George. You've never loved me. I was always the amusing little sister, wasn't I? The little sister with the enormous crush on her older sister's boyfriend. Or should I say fiancé? Then *he* came along. Tell me, George. Did you and Ellie laugh at me behind my back? Did you think I was a silly little girl with my first crush?'

'Of course not, Dottie. I've always been extremely fond of you.'

'Fond of me? Isn't that lovely. You're fond of me. Your wife. Aren't I lucky?' Dottie leaps from her chair and crosses to the desk, throwing the letter at George. 'You have to stop it. No more money to Ellie. Do you understand me? I honestly don't care if you are Emmett's father. You're not to say a word about that to anyone. He's Ellie's problem. She made her bed and now she's got to lie in it. And if you ever, ever cross me again, I'll tell everyone you're an adulterer. I'll take you for every penny, and your career and your status as a fine, upstanding Catholic pillar of the community here in Norwich will be ruined.'

George sits back in the chair. A silence, as heavy as a theatre curtain, settles over the room. 'You're right. You're right, Dottie. I still love Ellie. I've always loved Ellie.'

'I knew it! I knew it!'

'I've tried to be a good husband to you, Dottie. I've done everything you've wanted me to do. Given you everything you've asked for.'

Dottie spins around and sweeps the papers off George's desk. 'I never wanted this! None of it, don't you understand, George? I wanted freedom. I wanted what Ellie had. I wanted to choose my life. Instead, I'm dead. Dead! Condemned to life in this dull, boring, mediocre backwater!'

'I see.' George adjusts his glasses on his nose. 'I can see why you've taken against me. But why do you hate Ellie so much? That's always been a mystery to me.'

Dottie straightens up, and George sees her beautiful face harden, as if she is Galatea returning to stone. 'Because she had a chance at the life she wanted, and I didn't. And that's just not fair. I worked hard practising on that blasted piano night and day while she doodled around with her art and went out dancing even when the bombs were being dropped on us. Then she had to go and run off with some foreigner.' Dottie slaps her chest. 'She abandoned me, George! Just like Mummy did!'

'Your mother didn't abandon you, Dottie. She was killed in a car accident.'

'It was my fault, George! My fault Mummy was hit by that car. She'd told me not to ride my tricycle into the road.'

'You were only four years old. You're not to blame.'

'I knew better, George. I did. I wanted her attention. She was playing Cat's Cradle in the garden with Ellie and I wanted her attention.' She drops her head into her hands. 'I saw her run across the garden, screaming at me to get off the road. I just sat there on my little tricycle and clapped my hands. I'd won, you see. I'd made her notice me.' A sob wrenches out of Dottie's throat. 'And then, there was blood. Blood everywhere.'

'Dottie, it was an accident. It wasn't your fault.'

Dottie looks over at George. She wipes her eyes, leaving a streak of black mascara across her cheek. 'She left me, George. Ellie was only seven years older than me, but she became like a mother to me. I loved Ellie. You were always around too. You were part of the family. Everything was perfect.' Her jaw tightens.

'Until *he* came. He was another car accident, don't you see, George? He took Ellie from me, just like that car took Mummy.'

'Oh, Dottie. What can I do? What do you want me to do to make you happy?'

I did everything right, George. The only mistake I made was to sleep with you and fall pregnant. That was the end of everything for me. You owe me for taking my career away from me, George. For stealing the life I was supposed to have.'

# Chapter 73

## Tippy's Tickle – 16 September 2011

Sophie watches Sam, Becca, and Toby, lit yellow by a street light out by the road, through the shop's bay window. Their hands fly at each other like birds attacking. Silent angry words.

Emmett joins her at the window, his tall, lean figure looming above her. Behind them the party is in full swing, with Thor thumping the Ugly Stick as Rod Fizzard's grandson squeezes out a folky tune on an accordion. Emmett brushes back his untidy grey fringe with his fingers. 'Might be he'll listen to her now.'

Sophie looks up at him. His face is a craggy profile against the white venetian blind that's been pulled closed over the bay's side window. 'What do you mean?'

Emmett shrugs, his shoulders rising and falling under his inside-out plaid shirt. He stares down at Sophie, his two-coloured eyes hard and cold as marbles. 'Seems like he's been distracted.'

'What? By me?'

'Sooner you're gone, the better for us all. Better yet—' he nods towards Sam '—take him with you. We don't needs his type here. Things was better before.'

Sophie stares at him. 'What have we done?'

'What hasn't you done? You almost sold the place to the devil. That fella—' his eyebrows draw together as he nods at Sam '—that fella *is* the devil.'

She frowns out the window. 'You're talking rubbish.'

'I'll pays you to go.'

She jerks her head around. 'You'll what?'

He shrugs again. 'It's your money, anyway.'

'My money? What are you talking about?'

'The money your fadder gave me mam after Da' died. Blood money. I saved up to pay it back. Now he's dead, I'll gives it to you and you can gets back to wherever you came from.'

Ellie places a hand on Emmett's arm. 'That's enough, Emmy.'

Emmett looks at his mother, his face softening. 'I has to give her the money, Mam. I saved up to pay it back. I has to do it to save your immortal soul. You shouldn'ta taken it, Mam.'

Sophie stares at Emmett. Saving Ellie's soul? Blood money? Was he mad?

'My soul is for God to judge, Emmy. The money—'

The front door slams against a counter. Becca runs into the shop and through the crowd towards the kitchen, her face flushed as red as the ribbons she's threaded through her dress.

The door swings open. 'Becca, wait!' Toby flies into the store after her, his Dr Martens thumping on the floorboards. 'He didn't mean it!'

Florie emerges from the kitchen, a large chocolate cake ablaze with candles in her hands. 'Jaysus, kids!' she says, looking over her shoulder while the kitchen door swings to a stop. She proceeds into the room singing 'Happy Birthday'. The crowd joins in, filling the room with robust song as Florie makes her way towards Ellie.

Sophie feels Ellie's fingers clutch her arm. She looks over at her aunt in time to see Ellie's knees buckle as she slides to the floor like a wilting flower.

'Aunt Ellie!' Sophie drops to her knees. Ellie's face is as white as a winter sky, and the lines that were a thin tracery just the day before are etched deeply into her cheeks. Sophie looks around the room. 'Sam! Somebody! Call a doctor!'

The cake crashes to the floor.

# Chapter 74

## Tippy's Tickle – 24 June 1967

Ellie raises the sash on the attic window and leans her elbows on the sill. The breeze off the ocean brushes against her face, and the sun sits high in the pale blue sky, throbbing with the promise of another warm day. Unseasonable, the weather man has been saying on the new television. One of the coldest springs on record across Canada, fog sitting over Nova Scotia like a soggy blanket, but the sun shining up here on The Rock.

The rhythmic swoosh of the waves against the rocks below the cliff is broken by the scrape of furniture across the floor in the bedroom below. Ellie winces. She'd been on her hands and knees for days sanding and waxing the wooden floor until it gleamed a warm golden brown. Polished Agnes and Ephraim's Victorian four-poster mahogany bed until the dull white foxing of the years of built-up wax had burnished to a high sheen. It had been her bed after Agnes had followed Ephraim – dead from cirrhosis of the liver back in '55 – to a plot beside him in St Stephen's Cemetery four years ago. Ephraim on one side and Thomas on the other. Her mother-in-law's stubborn, intransigent spirit finally squashed by the cancer that had slowly eaten a hole through her colon as she'd refused to see a doctor in favour of hot mustard plasters and juniper tonic. Until she'd died crying out to Jaysus, God and all the apostles in the back seat of

Emmett's pickup truck on the way to the hospital down in Gander.

The new lodger had arrived the day before. Hitching her way around the island, she'd said. Up from Placentia originally where she'd taught elementary school for a few years, then via a Master's degree in Education from Memorial in St John's. She'd turned down a teaching place at Sacred Heart in Halifax to hitchhike her way across Canada 'for the Centennial', she'd said. This Florie was a free spirit if ever she'd met one. Ellie smiles. Like she'd once been herself, as an art student all those years ago in Norwich. Before the war. Before Thomas.

Ellie pads across the round rug she braided from clothing scraps, past the brass bed, and over to her easel. She frowns at the painted landscape of the shore, squinting at the sharp yellow dots of the buttercups and the purple crowns of the Blue Flag irises prising their way through the long grass on the cliff, the white bulk of an iceberg in the distance in the blue-green water. The lighthouse is in the distance, the lines of its white tower and red beacon hazy in the incoming fog.

Tucking the painting under her arm, she picks up a folder stuffed with drawings from the top of the old Art Deco walnut bureau. With any luck, the weather will have enticed people up to the north coast from St John's and Grand Falls for the holiday weekend. She and Bertha Perkins had managed to get an ad at half price into the local papers and one in the St John's *Telegram* for a third off, advertising the Tippy's Tickle Centennial Jamboree. Hopefully, she'd sell some of her artwork. George's money was long gone. If it weren't for Emmy's boat-building ... No, she wasn't going to think about money today. Today was a holiday.

She shakes her head. She'd hated herself for writing the letter to George after Thomas died. But she'd had no choice. Thomas's war pension had barely covered the essentials, let alone gone anywhere near to paying off all the debt he'd left behind. If it weren't for the monthly baby-bonus cheque from the federal government, Agnes would have had them all out on their ears after Ephraim's death.

Sometimes, on the worst of the days just after Thomas's drowning, when she'd lain in bed stuffing her hands against her ears to muffle the roar of the wind and the crashing of the ocean against the cliff, when the worry of debt collectors, and the constant battle with Agnes over every household expense had dropped her into a well of despair, George's face would materialise behind her eyes, and she'd wonder what her life would have been life if she'd married him instead. But then, that would never have happened. Not after she'd met Thomas. The man who brought her to this lonely place away from all the people she loved. The man who'd caused the rift with her sister. The man who, when he died, she knew was the only man she would ever truly love. For better or for worse.

George had come good, as she'd hoped – no, she'd known he would – the cheque arriving four times a year. Slowly, month by month, year by year, she'd paid off Thomas's debt and the interest the scrounging banks and loan sharks had demanded. She'd managed to clear everything except the mortgage. Then, one day, the cheques stopped coming. Just dried up, like a plant she'd forgotten to water. When three months passed with no money, and the mortgage falling behind, she'd written to George. But she didn't hear from him again, until …

No, it was best not to think of that. She'd go mad if she thought about that.

Taking in lodgers and giving art lessons at the high school down in Wesleyville, with the amount of money Emmy gave her when he could, had helped keep her and Winny afloat after that. Someday she'd pay that final mortgage payment, and the house would be theirs. No one would ever take it away from her. It would be her legacy to her children.

The bedroom door moans on its hinges as it opens. A blonde head, the wheat-gold hair tied into a long braid, pops around the door.

'Are you ready, Mom? Emmy's worried we're going to be late.'

'Just coming now, honey. What on earth is that on your face?'

Winny lopes across the room with the uneven grace of a colt and gazes into the mirror on the wall above the bureau. She twists her mouth to get a better view of the peace sign painted in bright blue on her cheek. 'Florie did it. She's got one too.' Winny spins around and raises her right fingers in a V. 'Peace, Mom.'

Ellie rolls her eyes. 'I'm going to have to have a word with her. I can't have her turning you into a flower child just because she's one.'

'Oh, Mom. She's groovy. She's got a guitar – did you know that? She's bringing it to the jamboree.'

'Oh, for heaven's sake, Winny. Everyone in Tippy's Tickle is going to think I've turned this place into a hippy commune. I'll get called up in front of the town council, just you watch.'

'Hey, there, m'dear!'

Ellie glances up from the table where she's laid out her artwork to the athletic woman of about thirty striding across the field towards the craft tent. She wears a long-sleeved pink T-shirt and dungarees decorated with psychedelic flowers and peace signs. One of the straps on the dungarees is undone, and it flaps across her belly as she approaches.

'Hi, Florie. You found me.'

'I certainly did. Winny told me where to find you.' She holds out a hot dog dripping with mustard. 'She sent you this. She's doin' a grand job over there on the barbecue.'

Ellie leaps up from her stool to catch a drip of mustard leaking from the hot dog. 'Don't let it drip on the drawings. Wait a minute, I'll come around the table.'

'How're the sales goin'?' Florie asks as she watches Ellie bite into the hot dog.

Ellie shrugs. 'Sold one to Bertha Perkins, but I think she felt sorry for me. The day trippers don't seem to be much into art.' She nods towards the cliff where a cluster of about twenty people hover like gulls, their cameras pointed out towards the ocean. 'It's all about the whales and icebergs. Someone up from Toronto asked me if the berg out at the mouth of the tickle is the same one that sank the *Titanic*.'

Florie chuckles and wrinkles her nose. A scattering of faint freckles sits across her nose like flecks of dust. 'Bless them CFAs. You gots to laugh. What did you tells them?'

'I said yes, of course.'

'Ha! Good goin'.' Florie tosses her long brown hair over her shoulder and picks up a drawing, blowing at her overgrown fringe as she scrutinises the charcoal view of Tippy's Tickle. Setting it down, she picks up another, a view of the lighthouse down the coast. She looks at Ellie, squinting as she cocks her head. 'You did these? Seriously?'

'Yes. Why are you so surprised?'

'Oh, don't mine me, duck. Sometimes I talks outta my arse. These are great. You definitely knows what you're doin'.' She sets the drawing down and steps back, frowning at the display. 'But you wouldn't know how to sell a flea to a dog, m'dear. Not a one can see what you gots on the table. You gots to hang them up. Your paintin' has to be right smack in the middle for all to see.'

Ellie purses her lips. 'That's all very well and good, but if you notice, I don't have a wall to hang anything on. I'm under a tent.'

'Oh, m'dear. You might be an artist, but you lacks imagination. I'll be back before you knows it.'

Florie returns fifteen minutes later with a roll of string and a bag of wooden clothes pegs. Ellie watches as she ties the string between two tent poles and clips the drawings to the line with the pegs. She ducks behind the tent and returns with two small orange buoys, which she uses to prop the painting against on the table.

Standing back from the display, she nods. 'There you goes, m'dear. That's better, don't you thinks?'

Ellie nods. 'You're right. It is better.'

'It's better, but we needs one more thing.' Florie pulls the stool out from behind the table and plops down on it. 'Now, draw my picture.'

'What?'

'Don't you likes my face? Draw my picture.' She nods to the tourists on the hill and the queue over by the barbecue. 'Mark my words, once they see you drawin', they'll all be clamourin' for one. How much you gonna charge?'

# Chapter 75

## Tippy's Tickle – 17 September 2011

Propping herself up against the pillows, Ellie reaches for the plastic cup of water on the bedside table, her body shaking with the effort.

'Wait, Aunt Ellie.' Sophie takes the cup and holds it to Ellie's parched white lips. She watches her aunt, who had only two days before buzzed with vigour, but who was now as pale and frail as an aged swan in her white nest of hospital sheets and pillows.

Ellie lies back against the pillows with a sigh. 'Thank you, Sophie.' She looks at Sophie, at the pale, heart-shaped face, so like her mother's, now clouded with confusion. She reaches out a hand and takes hold of Sophie's. 'There's something I need to tell you.'

'What do you mean?'

Ellie runs her tongue over her parched lips. 'Your father ... George was Emmy's father.'

Sophie stares at her aunt. 'Emmett's my brother?'

The old woman nods. 'Thomas always suspected it, but I told him Emmy was born a month early. The war was a different time, Sophie. Thomas had been away for over a year, and I'd barely heard from him. I thought ...' She shakes her head, the fine strands of grey hair clinging to her damp face. 'I don't know what I thought. I was young. I was lonely and frightened. People were being killed in the bombing raids every day. My best friend Ruthie was killed—'

Sophie raises a hand. 'Stop. Please. I get the picture.'

'Your father was a good man. He asked me to marry him. But I was already engaged to Thomas. No one knew. He'd proposed to me just before he was shipped out to North Africa. George didn't even know I was pregnant when he proposed. I didn't either. It had only been the one time. I never thought ...' She drops Sophie's hand and rubs her thin fingers along her forehead. 'Then Thomas showed up on leave at Christmas and we ... we eloped. We married in London.'

She sighs, her breath shallow and ragged. 'Thomas left for Italy a few days later on a hospital ship, and I went back to Norwich and told everyone we'd married. My father was furious. Thomas wasn't Catholic, you see. And Dottie ... Dottie wouldn't speak to me at all. Poor George, I think he was in shock. It was an awful time, Sophie. I felt very alone.'

Ellie closes her eyes, and for a moment Sophie thinks she's fallen asleep from the effort. Her aunt coughs delicately and opens her eyes, the deep stormy blue undiluted by age. 'I found out I was pregnant. I only realised that the baby was George's when the doctor said I was a month further along than I should have been.'

Sophie flops into the blue vinyl chair, her heart jolting in her chest. 'Does Emmett know?'

Propping herself on a thin arm, Ellie reaches across the sheets and grasps hold of Sophie's hand. 'Don't tell him, Sophie. It would break his heart. He adored Thomas.'

'I'm meant to keep your secret now?'

'What does it matter? Emmy has no children. It won't make

any difference to anyone. You needed to know, but no one else does.'

Whipping her hand from Ellie's hold, Sophie rises and stands at the window. 'It makes a difference to me. I'm his half-sister and I can't even tell him?' She turns and faces her aunt, her arms folded across her chest. 'Emmett hates me. I've no idea why. If I tell him I'm his sister, it might change things.'

Ellie sinks back into the pillows. She sighs heavily, her breath rattling.

Sophie picks up the plastic cup and offers it to Ellie. 'Are you okay? Should I get the nurse?'

Ellie shakes her head wearily across the pillow and waves away the cup. 'There's something else.'

'There's more?'

'Sit down, Sophie. I need to tell you a story.'

# Chapter 76

## Tippy's Tickle – 10 July 1962

The visitor locks the door on the rental car and pockets the keys. He looks up at the big house on the cliff, which sits sturdy and proud against the breezy blue July sky, though the yellow paint has fought a losing battle against the salt and wind coming off the North Atlantic. The grass has been left to grow long beside the grey wooden steps up to the house, but clumps of wild lupins in all their tints and shades of pink, mauve and deep purple crowd over the simple banister rail. Sighing heavily, he adjusts his brown felt fedora and heads up the steps.

Ellie moves away from the window and stands in the middle of the room, waiting for the knock on the front door. For her name to be called out. Emmy is down at Rod Fizzard's working on the boats, and Winny is out in the fields with Jim Boyd's granddaughter, Nancy, foraging in the marsh for early bakeapples for the jam they were hoping to sell in Jim's shop to scrape a few extra pennies together.

The knock. Ellie sets down the latest demand letter from the bank. She turns her ear to the sound. Another knock. Then his voice, tentative. 'Hello? Ellie? Is there anyone home?'

Ellie unties her apron and tosses it onto the bed's patchwork quilt. She pats her hair, tied into a messy bun, and clears her throat.

'I'm coming.'

Ellie hurries down the staircase, pausing for breath on the final step. Crossing the small foyer, she opens the door.

'George! Good heavens, this is a surprise.'

George takes off his hat and holds it awkwardly against his chest. 'Ellie. It's so lovely to see you.'

Ellie leans forward and gives him a quick kiss on his cheek. 'Come in. Come in. Where are my manners?' She looks over his shoulder. 'Where's Dottie? Is she in the car?'

'No, Dottie didn't come. She doesn't like the idea of flying.'

Ellie frowns. 'Is everything all right?'

'Oh, everything's fine. I—I thought it was time for a visit. I'm Vice President of Mcklintock's now, Ellie. I just told them I was taking some leave. And, here I am.'

'And, Dottie ... didn't mind? You coming out to see me?'

'Actually, it was her idea.'

Suddenly, it's like a weight she's been carrying for years is lifted from her shoulders. *Dottie's come around? Forgiven me for whatever it is she felt I did to her?*

She takes hold of George's arm. 'That's wonderful, George. You have no idea how happy that makes me. Come in. You must tell me everything. We have so much to catch up on.'

Ellie reaches for the teapot. 'More tea, George?'

George shakes his head. 'Thank you. I'm fine.'

His face is fuller, Ellie notes, and tired. Dark marks like thumbprints dent the skin under his glasses, and his black hair, still carefully combed and shiny with brilliantine, is thinning, and grey threads the hair at his temples.

'It's lovely to see you, George. Though, it's such a surprise. Why didn't you write to say you were coming?'

'I know.' He takes off his glasses and, removing his handkerchief from his trouser pocket, rubs the lenses. He puts the glasses back on and looks back at Ellie.

'I need to talk to you about something.'

'Is it about the cheques?' She reaches over and squeezes his arm. 'It's fine. It really was presumptuous of me to ask you for money after Thomas died, and you've been so good. The money got me on my feet, though the past few months have been ... challenging. But, I'll manage. Don't worry at all about that.'

She looks down at her teacup, at the tea leaves clumping on the bottom of the china cup. 'I had no one else to turn to after Thomas died. You don't know what it was like. I would have gone back to England, if I could have.' She presses her lips together into a sad smile. 'But that was impossible.'

Shifting in the wooden chair, George pulls his arm away. He rubs his forehead and clears his throat. 'I was happy to do it, Ellie. I was ... I was so pleased you came to me. I've always ... I've always loved you. You have to know that.'

'George—'

'No, please. Let me say what I've come here to say.'

Ellie sits back in her chair, surprised by the note of urgency in his voice. 'All right.'

'The money stopped because Dottie found out about it.'

Ellie holds her hand up to her mouth. 'She didn't know? You didn't tell her? Oh, George.'

'I couldn't. Dottie's changed a great deal since you last knew her. She's ... I was careless. She found one of your letters on my desk. She didn't take it well.'

'But you said it was her idea for you to come here.'

He leans his elbows on the table and presses his fingers into his forehead. 'You know she can't have children?'

Ellie shakes her head. 'No, I didn't know. I'm sorry, George. But, there's been no communication. She's never answered any of my letters or cards. The only time I heard from her was a short telegram when Poppy died. And you never said anything, either, in your letters, though I did wonder why you never mentioned the twins to me over all those years.'

'Nothing would make her happier than to have a child.'

'I'm so sorry, George. If only there were something I could do.'

George looks over at Ellie. 'There is, Ellie.'

Emmett stands behind the screen door. He watches his mother bury her face in her hands. Watches the man with the shiny hair reach over to touch his mother's shoulder. Watches her bat the hand away.

Slipping off his rubber boots, he pads down the porch steps, careful to avoid the creaking step. When he reaches the dirt road at the bottom of the hill, he stuffs his feet back into the boots and heads back down to Rod Fizzard's. Just last month there'd been a notice up for fisherman up in the Change Islands. He was too late for that, but he'd keep an eye out. The government was finally throwing some money at the outports. It wouldn't be long before something else'd come along. When it did, he'd take that money from Ottawa. It might take him a dozen years or so fishing cod, but he didn't need much to live. He'd save every penny he could. Then he'd buy the boat-building business from Rod Fizzard and he'd provide for his mother. He'd never let her be brought this low again. One day he'd pay back the man with the shiny hair. Every cent. He'd save his mother's immortal soul, free her from this black debt, and set her free.

# Chapter 77

## Tippy's Tickle – 17 September 2011

'What did my father mean when he said you could do something?'

Ellie reaches out a thin hand, the veins like blue rivers against the white, age-mottled skin. 'I'm your mother, Sophie.'

Sophie pulls her hand away. 'Dottie was my mother.'

'Yes, of course, she was. She raised you and loved you. But I gave birth to you.'

Sophie steps away from the bed and stares at the old woman, her mind a rollercoaster of confusion. 'How can you be my mother? That's impossible. I was born in England.'

'Yes, you were born in Peterborough, England, just like your birth certificate says. George and I had to go to a hospital where no one would know me. He said I was Dottie. I had her identity papers. He paid for me to fly back to England for the birth. Emmy had gone up to Fogo to join a fishing crew for a few months before I started showing and I left Winny with Agnes. I told her Dottie was ill, and I needed to be with her for a while. I told her George was buying the aeroplane tickets for me.'

'Why on earth did you do such a thing?'

'I did it for Emmy's and Winny's futures. I did it because I thought it might heal the terrible rift between Dottie and me.

I was desperate, Sophie. The bank, the creditors ... you have no idea what it was like.'

Sophie presses her fingers against her forehead where a throbbing headache is taking hold. 'I don't understand.'

'Dottie agreed for your father to pay me a substantial amount of money if I had their baby. I'd have enough money to go back to England with the children, like I'd dreamt about all those years after Thomas died. All those years when I'd felt like a prisoner in that house. Thomas's war pension was hardly enough to live on, and Agnes ...' Ellie shakes her head. 'After you were born, I flew back to Gander. George promised to transfer the money to my account.'

'I can't believe this.'

'The money never arrived, Sophie. I wrote to your father, I tried ringing ...' Ellie licks her dry lips. 'After that, the only place I wanted to be was here in Tippy's Tickle. My relationship with your parents ...' She grimaces. 'Well, that was finished. There was nothing left for me in England.'

She looks at Sophie, a weak smile playing on her pale lips. 'Somehow I managed. Emmy helped me when he could with money from his fishing. He knew nothing about you. I've never told anyone, not even Florie.

'I began teaching art at the school and started selling my work. When Florie arrived, she persuaded me to make postcards and prints for the tourists. Florie bought the shop with some money she'd saved up. Things slowly got better.'

She reaches over to the table for the plastic cup of water, her body shaking with the effort. Sophie holds the cup to Ellie's mouth, watching her take a long sip.

Ellie settles back against the pillows with a sigh. 'I was furious with your parents for a long time, Sophie. Furious with myself.

Then, as the years passed, I often wondered about you. I sent a few Christmas cards, a few letters, but I never heard back from George or Dottie.' Her thin shoulders rise and fall under the hospital gown. 'Then you showed up on my doorstep ten years ago, and all of the anger I'd been harbouring for years dissolved.' She smiles weakly. 'You were a lovely baby, Sophie, but you weren't mine. You were Dottie's and George's.'

'But why did my mother hate you so much, if you did that for her? Because she did. She really did.'

'I don't know, Sophie. Perhaps she was just a very, very unhappy woman. She had a terrible fear of abandonment. She felt that she was responsible for our mother's death, which was ridiculous. It was an accident, a terrible, unfortunate accident.'

'What happened?'

'Dottie had been playing on the road on her tricycle, even though she knew it was forbidden. When Mummy ran out to get her, she was hit by a car. Dottie saw everything. She was only four.'

'That's awful.'

'Yes, it was. But it was an accident. I think Dottie may have felt guilty about what she'd asked of me and George. We'd all committed a terrible sin. We're Catholics, Sophie, or I was then. We're very good at guilt.'

Sophie's eyes burn as the tears finally come. She brushes her hand across her wet cheeks.

'Why do you want to ruin my life like this?'

'I don't want to ruin anything. There've been too many secrets in this family. Years of secrets. It's time for you to know the truth. For Sam to know the truth. That Winny was your half-sister. That you're Becca's aunt.'

'But you want me to keep the secret from Emmett that we have the same father.'

'Please, Sophie. If you feel you have to tell him, please wait until ... I can't bear to see his face.'

Sophie fights back a sob. 'What do you want me to say? That I love you because you're my mother?'

'Sophie, my darling girl, you don't owe me anything. I just wanted you to know who you are, before it's too late.'

# *Chapter 78*

## Tippy's Tickle – 17 September 2011

Aside from black streaks of soot on the white clapboard around the bedroom window, Sophie sees little evidence of the fire as she follows the path down to Bufflehead Cottage. She spies Sam's motorcycle beside the porch door. As she approaches, voices filter into the garden, but the words are carried away on the cold breeze. Tugging Florie's sweater up to her chin, she rubs her cold nose with the rough wool and steps into the porch.

'... another fire. Just like the last time. Did you set this one too?'

'What are you talking about, Emmett?'

Sophie steps back against the porch wall and turns her ear to the agitated voices coming from Sam's living room.

'Boston. The one in Boston, Sam, b'y. The fire that took my poor sister. There was some big whisperin' about that when you came here all those years ago. Not a penny on you, and me havin' to take you into the business. I didn't wants to do it, b'y, but poor Mam was beside herself, losin' Winny like that in the fire, and Becca only a young thing.'

'That fire ...' Sam's voice cracks. 'That fire was an accident.'

'So, why did you hightail it up here, broke as a tinker when you'd had a big business down in Boston? Smelled like rotten cod to me.' A rattle of paper. 'Where there's a stink, there's a reason.'

A long pause. 'Where did you get this?'

'In the desk drawer in your furniture workshop. Had to jimmy the lock on the tin case. Figured there'd be something interestin' in there, it being all locked up. I should'a looked a long time ago. When the fire happened yesterday, it got me wonderin' all over again.'

'I know what the report says.'

'You're a murderer.'

There is the crash of objects hitting the floor, something decelerating as it spins to a stop. 'Get out of here, Emmett.'

'Heard you had a temper, Sam. Did a good job of hidin' it. Is that what happened, Sam? You had a fight with Winny and you set fire to the place to cover it up?'

'Get out of here!' Something slamming against a wall. 'Get out!'

Footsteps thud towards the porch. Sophie presses herself against the wall, nothing to conceal her but the late afternoon shadow. Emmett stumbles past her and out of the door, his hand over his left eye.

Sophie treads quietly across the threshold into Sam's kitchen. Sam stands by the wood burner staring out of the window, a white document rolled up in his hand.

She steps over the broken crockery and pot lids. 'Sam? What's going on?'

Sam turns to look at her, his face shadowed with turmoil. 'Nothing.'

'He called you a murderer.'

'You believe him?'

Sophie hesitates at the dining table.

'I guess you do.'

'Don't make this about me, Sam. What's going on? What's that paper?'

Sam strides over to Sophie and hands it to her. 'I'll be outside cleaning the soot off the wall. Come and talk to me after you read it ... if you still want to.'

Ellie opens her eyes. She must have dozed off. The sun is so lovely. So warm on her face. She takes a deep breath. Such fresh air. She loves this spot. Just under the fir tree on the hill by the house. Her spot.

She reaches for her sketchpad and her pencil.

'You've made me look quite nice.'

She laughs. 'What an odd thing to say, Winny. Quite nice. You sound like a little English girl.'

Winny leans over the drawing, her long blonde braids hanging over the sketch like two tassels. She smiles at her mother, her blue-grey eyes shining. 'C'mon, Mummy. I want to show you something.'

'Not right now, pet. Mummy wants to rest for a bit. Sit down and I'll draw another picture.'

Winny holds out her hand. 'Please, Mummy. You'll like this. I promise.'

Ellie looks at her daughter's eager face. Someone's drawn a Peace sign on her cheek. 'Where did that come from?'

Winny laughs. 'Florie. She has one too.' She beckons to her mother. 'C'mon, Mummy.'

Ellie sighs. 'All right then.' She sets her sketchbook on a velvety clump of moss. 'But we can't be long. Your sister's coming later, all the way from New York. We need to make supper.'

'Can we have spaghetti and meatballs?'

'If you like.'

'And chocolate cake? It's my favourite.'

'We can have chocolate cake too. Just don't let the dogs get at it. Chocolate's not good for them.' Ellie threads her fingers through her daughter's. 'So, where are we off to?'

'You'll see.'

They start along the crest of the cliff, through the scrub woods and past the old grey piebald horse in Joe Gill's field. When they reach the marshland, they stop to pick handfuls of fat, ripe red partridgeberries, and then they climb, higher and higher, up the grey rocky hills until they reach a thick mass of bushes heavy with blueberries. Someone is bent over one of the bushes, intent on filling a fedora hat with loot. He turns around.

'Thomas?'

'There you are, maid. You took your time. Blueberries are some good, but there's a limit to how many a body can eat.'

He picks up the hat and walks over to them. 'Go on. Help yourself, m' darlins'. They're the best you'll ever eat.' He pops a fat blueberry into his mouth. 'Purple heaven.'

Far below, the ocean glimmers blue under the summer sun, the water broken only by spouts like fountains. Far down the coast, the red roof of the lighthouse is a dot of colour against the blue sky.

They stand on the cliff, eating blueberries from Thomas's hat. Winny points out towards the horizon, which shines silver in the distance. 'See, Mummy. I told you.'

'It's lovely, Winny. You were right.'

Thomas holds out his hand. 'C'mon, maid. Let's have a dance.'

Winny squeezes Ellie's hand. 'Let's go, Mummy.'

Sophie takes another sip of coffee. 'So, the fire in Boston was caused by faulty wiring?'

'We'd been renovating an old Victorian house in Dedham. It was pretty much a wreck when we bought it, but we could see the potential. Our money was tied up in my construction business. I figured if I did most of the work myself, we'd save money.'

'So you did the wiring.'

Sam nods. 'The night of the fire I was out of town managing a project upstate. Becca was in the hospital having some tests. Winny ...' He shakes his head. 'Winny never had a chance.' He presses his fingers against his eyes.

He shakes his head. 'There was an inquiry. I was found to be culpable. I lost my business. I had a deaf five-year-old daughter to support. It was a disaster. Ellie offered me a lifeline.'

'A job working for Emmett.'

Sam shrugs. 'We moved into Kittiwake with Ellie and Florie. I had to swallow my pride and get on with it. I knew how to build things, and Emmett taught me how to turn wood. I built the cottage in my spare time, then I started making furniture. I set up my own joinery company a few years ago. I've been helping Emmett with the boat-building when he needs it. He does some work for me. That's over now.'

Sophie pushes the coffee mug away from her and taps her fingers on the table. 'My mother always believed that you could control your destiny by the decisions you make and the actions you take. If you don't choose your path, your path will be chosen for you. Random things would occur, and you'd be like a plastic duck bobbing in a swirling current, getting tossed around with nothing to ground you. My mother hated that idea. She was all about control.'

She looks across the table at Sam. 'Maybe she felt that way because she grew up in England during the war, when everything was so chaotic. She and Aunt Ellie lost their mother in a car accident when they were young. That's pretty destabilising. Maybe that's why she pushed me to take control of my future from an early age. Then, one day, a plane got diverted and I found myself here. Something totally out of my control.'

'And everything changed.'

'It should have, shouldn't it? But nothing really changed for me. I didn't let it. Nothing changed until I came back.'

'What's changed this time?'

'Me. I've changed.'

The screen door slams and Toby Molloy bolts into the room with Becca, her cheeks flushed as she chokes on sobs.

'It's Ellie! Mr Byrne, she's dead!'

# *Chapter 79*

## Tippy's Tickle – 24 September 2011

On the hill of St Stephen's Cemetery, the crowd slowly files past the weather-beaten headstones on its way to Kittiwake. In the distance, the aluminium spire of St Stephen's Church shines on its spit of land, pale grey against the blue September sky. Clouds scuttle like seed tufts across the vast blue, and, here and there, black-legged tickle-aces keen and dive for fish in the undulating ocean beyond the village. Sophie wanders over to the stone cross beside the newly dug grave and rubs her hand along the top as she reads the inscription.

*Thomas Augustus Parsons*
*17th March 1915 – 19th June 1954*
*Always loved*

'I always knew they'd end up together in the end.'

Sophie looks over at Florie. 'She loved you too, Florie.'

Florie adjusts the black felt fedora that Becca had decorated with purple ribbon and seashells for the funeral. 'Oh, I knows it, maid.' She looks out at the ocean, its water glistening a deep blue under the September sky. 'She was the love of my life, just like Thomas here was hers.' She shrugs. 'It goes like that some-times.'

'You made her happy. Isn't that what's important, in the end?'

'Well, Sophie duck, you've changed your tune. I thought you were all about work, work, work. Didn't you once tell Ellie that relationships were a distraction? What's happened to you?'

Sophie glances over to Sam, Becca and Toby at the far end of the cemetery.

Florie nods. 'Ah, say no more. Sam Byrne.'

Sophie smiles. 'I didn't come back here to rekindle anything with Sam. It was all about my career, Florie. I tried to convince the consortium to find another spot along the coast, but they loved the pictures I'd taken of Tippy's Tickle and Kittiwake the last time I was here. This was the place they wanted. I sold my soul to the devil, all because I wanted to be a partner in the firm.'

'You're not paintin' yourself a good picture, duck.'

'I know.'

'So, what changed?'

'Ellie got me drawing again. I loved that when I was a child, but my mother always considered it a waste of time.' She nods towards Becca. 'Becca changed me too. Her zest for life. Her boundless creativity. Her independent spirit.' She shrugs. 'I wish she liked me more. It's better than it was, but ...'

'She just has to get used to the idea of sharin' her dad with another woman. She'll come around.'

'I've got a lot to think about, Florie. Sam. And ... and Ellie told me some things I need to get my head around. I'm going back to New York in a few days.'

Florie digs into the pocket of her black pea-jacket and takes out a small blue box.

'What's this?'

'Ellie wanted you to have it, duck. Open it later, when you're on your own.' She nods towards Becca who is walking between the headstones towards them. 'I think someone wants to have a natter with you.' She turns to leave. 'You haven't seen Emmy, have you? Haven't seen him since the service.'

'No, afraid not.'

'All right, then. I'll sees you at the house. I've got bakeapple cheesecake at the house. I knows you likes it.'

'Best kind, Florie.'

Florie laughs. 'We'll makes a Newfoundlander out of you yet, duck.'

Sophie watches Becca approach, a slender sprite in a 50s navy polka-dot dress that she'd obviously liberated from one of Ellie's old trunks in the attic. She places a posy of wildflowers on Ellie's grave.

'Is everything okay with your father?' Sophie asks, fumbling with the sign language.

Rising, Becca signs. 'Dad's going to take on Toby in the workshop. He's going to teach him how to make furniture.'

'That's wonderful, Becca!'

Becca nods. 'We're moving in with Florie. I'm going to make clothes for the shop.'

'That's just brilliant, Becca. I'm so happy for you.'

Becca looks at Sophie, chewing her lip. 'I'm sorry I was awful to you,' she signs. 'I didn't want Dad to forget Mom.'

'He won't forget her.' Sophie looks over at Sam, who's in a deep discussion with Toby. 'I have to go back to New York, anyway.'

'Don't do that,' Becca signs, her hands flying. 'This is your home. We're your home.'

Sophie shakes her head. 'Thank you, Becca,' she signs. 'I appreciate that, but I still have to go.'

Sophie takes the blue box out of her pocket and walks over to a window in Emmett's store. She wiggles the lid off the box. Inside, a gold locket sits on a cushion of white satin, its fine chain curled around the gold heart. Setting the box on the worktable, she lifts out the locket and holds it up to the window. A fine filigree of tendrils decorates the dull gold. She opens the locket. There's no mistaking the pretty girl on the left: Winny, her perfect oval face framed by hair the colour of wheat in golden morning light.

She squints at the face looking back at her from the right side of the locket. A little girl of about five, her face sweet but ordinary, her brown hair cut into a blunt Dutch-boy bob. She holds the locket up closer, her eyes widening. It's her. On her fifth birthday.

Setting the locket on the table, she lifts the cushion out of the box. A small piece of paper is folded into a neat square. She opens it up and reads.

*Dearest Sophie,*
   *This was your grandmother Winnifred's locket.*
   *I can't think of anyone to whom I'd rather give it than you.*
   *All my love, always.*
   *Your mother, Ellie*

'So this is where you escaped to, Princess Grace.' Sam stands in the doorway, silhouetted against the sharp white light of the late September afternoon.

'It was too noisy at the house. I thought I'd come look for Emmett. He's missing Florie's bakeapple cheesecake.'

Sam enters the room. For the second time that day, Sophie blinks at his transformation. The dark grey suit shows the skill of a tailor in its perfect fit, and Sam has shaved off the stubble. He smiles, and the Sam she knows is there in the warmth of his deep brown eyes and the teasing grin.

'Looks like most of the peninsula came out for the service today. The Warriors are on their second run to Wesleyville for more supplies.' Sam leans against the windowsill and folds his arms. 'Becca told me you're heading back to New York.'

'I have to. I have an apartment to sort out.'

'Sort out?'

Sophie shrugs. 'I haven't got a job anymore. I'll have to move.' She rolls her eyes. 'You wouldn't believe the rent on my place. I'll run through my savings in no time if I'm not working.'

'You'll land on your feet. Just not in those awful shoes you were wearing the first time I met you.'

'I'll have you know they were very expensive Jimmy Choos. Totally ruined, just like my green velvet suit. I made scatter cushions out of it. Did I ever tell you that?'

Sam chuckles. 'A fitting end.'

'Sam, there's something I need to tell you. Something Aunt Ellie told me before she died. I've been trying to tell you, but it's been so crazy around here this week.'

'You don't need to tell me.'

'What?'

'You're Winny's half-sister.'

'How long have you known that?'

'Emmett. He told me everything after the fire. I think he thought it'd put me off.'

'Emmett knew? How could he possibly know that Ellie was my mother? She told me she'd never told anyone, not even Florie.'

'I have no idea.'

'Did he say anything else? About me? About my father?'

Sam shakes his head. 'No. Why?'

*So, Emmett doesn't know everything, it seems. Doesn't know that George was also his father. But how did he know about Ellie's pregnancy? I'll find out. I'll talk to him and find out. I'm sorry, Ellie, but I'm not going to keep your secrets. It's time everything was out in the open.*

'It's a bit strange, isn't it? You and me? Winny being my half-sister?'

'Yes, maybe a bit. But, it's not like *we're* blood relatives.' Sam opens out his hands. 'As far as I'm concerned, it's all fine by me. Ellie was a wonderful woman. I wish you'd known her longer. You shouldn't have stayed away so long.'

Sophie sighs. 'I know. I was wrapped up in my career. But, the last couple of years ... I don't know. I was starting to feel ... unbalanced. I was never much good at relationships. My parents' marriage wasn't exactly a great example. I was good at choosing the wrong people. I guess because I expected things to end. It was easier if things ended with someone I didn't really care about that much. It kept me from getting hurt.'

'Love hurts, haven't you heard that, Princess Grace?'

'That's what I'm afraid of, Sam.'

'You know, Sophie, it's been hard for me to move on—' his voice catches '—to move on from Winny. I loved her. She was my wife. I thought we'd be together forever.'

*Here it comes. The gentle let-down.* 'I know, Sam. I understand.'

'When Becca took such a shine to you when you were here last time, that was hard too. I felt like her liking you was somehow betraying Winny.' He sighs. 'Sorry, it's crazy, I know.'

*We may as well get to the point.* She leans against the desk. 'And now? How do you feel about things now? How do you feel about me? About us?'

He reaches out and runs a fingertip along her cheek. 'Ellie wasn't only beautiful, she was wise. She told me it was time to appreciate everything I had with Winny, and give myself permission to move on. Winny's a part of me and a part of Becca. She always will be. But, Ellie was right. It's time to move on. And, Princess Grace. I'd like to move on with you.'

Sophie blinks. 'Really?'

'Yes, really.'

'You sure you don't just want to play cribbage instead?'

Sam laughs. 'Oh, there'll be plenty of cribbage, don't you worry.' He picks up the locket from the table. 'What's this?'

'It was Ellie's. She's given it to me.'

'Turn around.'

'What?'

He rolls his eyes. 'Nothing's ever easy with you, is it? Turn around, Princess Grace.'

Sophie turns her back to Sam. She feels his breath on her neck as he fastens the locket around her neck.

'I'm not going to hurt you, Sophie.'

Then, she is in his arms, her hands pressing his head to hers, kissing him like it's a gift she's only now learnt how to give.

She steps back and puts her hand to her mouth. 'I'm sorry. I don't know what came over me.'

Sam smiles. 'I'm not. Not one bit. I've got you a present, too. Something to remember me by in the Big Apple.'

'You didn't have to do that.'

'I know.'

'I mean you didn't have to do that because I'll be back in a few weeks. As soon as I can tie everything up in New York.'

'You'll be back? In a few weeks? Are you sure? I can always fly to see you in New York.'

'Florie cornered me in the house over the cheesecake. She had it all figured out. I'm moving into Kittiwake with her and Becca and Toby, and the baby, when it comes. We're going to be a proper commune. I'm going to become an artist, Sam. I'll sell my work online and in Florie's shop. I can help you design the art retreats, too, if you like.'

He slides his arms around Sophie's waist. 'It's pretty quiet up here, Princess Grace. Not much to do here, except this.' He nuzzles her neck. 'And this.' He slides his hand to the small of her back as he kisses her ear. 'And this ...' He presses his forehead to hers. 'You might hate it here. You haven't been in Tippy's Tickle in winter. Did anyone tell you we've got seven seasons?'

'Seven seasons?'

He counts the seasons off his fingers. 'Spring – that's snow and icebergs; trap berth – fog and rains mostly and we call it mauzy; summer – a bit of sun, and fog, of course; berry – that's berry-picking time to you and me; late fall – snow; winter – more snow; and pack ice – snow, fog, ice, rain. Party time.'

Sophie grimaces. 'You're not selling it to me, Sam. Have you ever thought about Florida?'

Laughing, Sam opens a drawer under the table and takes out a package of Jam Jams, wiggling them at Sophie. 'Consider them a bribe to stay.'

Sophie's smile dissolves into a frown.

'What's the matter? I had Ace bring these back from Wesleyville especially.'

Reaching into the drawer, Sophie removes a white envelope. *Sophie* is scrawled across the envelope in blue ink. 'What's this?'

'I don't know.'

Sophie turns over the envelope. Through the white paper she

can feel something hard. She tears open the side and tips a key into her hand. 'A key? What am I supposed to do with this?'

'There must be a note.'

Sophie peers into the envelope. At the bottom, a piece of blue paper is folded in two. Taking it out, she reads. She looks at Sam. 'It's the key to a safety deposit box in St John's. It's from Emmett.'

# *Chapter 80*

## Seal Point Lighthouse – 24 September 2011

Emmett pulls in the oars and rubs the calluses at the base of each of his thumbs. He raises his face to the sky. It'd been a fine day. Another hour or so left before the chilly autumn night draws in. He'd thought summer was done for sure after the rain yesterday. It'd been right mauzy and cold enough to skin you. But, there you goes. Just when you thought things were what you expected, something came along to change everything. Something or someone.

He bobs on the waves, letting the rowboat drift. He squints up at the lighthouse on the cliff, the jab of white like a flag against the blue sky and grey cliff. Leaning over, he picks up an old leather satchel with a frayed strap held on by uneven stitches of green twine. He nods as he feels inside the bag. Still there.

He looks up at the clouds hovering in the sky like wads of cotton. *Are you there, Mam? Up in Heaven? It's where you belongs. I saved you, Mam. You knows that now, don't you? I knows it was hard for you after you came back from England. After the baby. You didn't think I knew, did you? I was away up in Fogo. You fixed that up for me, didn't you, Mam? Got Jim Boyd's brother-in-law to get me the job on the boat so I wouldn't see the baby growing in you.*

A spray of water shoots through the waves about fifty feet

starboard. A grey-black hump curves through the water and disappears. Emmett scratches his nose. He pulls out the stack of papers from the satchel, sifting through them until he finds the one he's searching for.

*Alder Lodge*
*Newmarket Road*
*Norwich*

*5th May, 1963*
*My dearest Ellie,*
*I hope this finds you well, and that the trip back to Newfoundland wasn't too onerous. The baby is a delight. We've named her Sophie Mary and she has your eyes. Dottie is delighted to have a little project to keep her busy. I must confess I'm happy to have her divert her attention from me! I feel I've always come up short whenever she's attempted to 'improve' me.*

*I've enclosed the first cheque of eight as promised. I'm sorry it's taken a few weeks, but it's a large amount, so the bank took some time to make the proper arrangements. All you need to do is countersign it and present it to your bank over there. I'll send the subsequent cheques quarterly over the next two years, as we agreed.*

*There, that's enough of all that, though I hope you find your situation eased with the additional funds. I hadn't realised it had been so difficult since ... Well, since the awkward business with Dottie a few years ago after Thomas's passing.*

*You mentioned you'd buy a camera with some of the money and send me a picture of Emmett and Winny. I would love to see them. I will do the same with Sophie so you can see*

*how she grows over the years. Dottie and I will do our very*
*best for her, of course. You have no worries on that score.*
　　*Do take care of yourself, and please know how very much*
*we appreciate what you've done for us.*

　　　　　　　　　　　　*With sincere fondness and gratitude,*
　　　　　　　　　　　　　　　　　　　　　　　　*George*

He folds the letter and slides it back into the satchel with the
others. Eight letters in all and eight cheques. Mam hadn't needed
to see those. Poison letters. Letters about her shame. It'd been
one of his chores to collect the post from Jim Boyd's store when
it came in. It'd been easy to take the letters. As soon as he had
all eight, he was back up to Fogo to fish on one of the new
boats up there. Another government initiative. You could say
what you wanted about that Smallwood fella over in St John's,
but he sure knew how to spread Ottawa's money around.

He needed to put the letters in a safe place. He didn't want
*her* finding them, with her snooping around. It had to be the
cave. No one would ever find them there.

She'd probably found the envelope by now. Or maybe Sam
had. He was in and out of that drawer ten times a day when he
was using the old lathe in the store. Said he liked it better.
'Course he would. It'd been Marsh Puddester's down in Windsor.
Best wood lathe in central Newfoundland.

Maybe that woman was reading the note at this very minute.
*Soon, Mam. Soon, you'll be free. The poison money will be back*
*where it came from. Heaven'll open its doors to you and you'll be*
*the angel you always were to me here on this earth. A real angel,*
*Mam. You'll be where you belongs.*

It hadn't been hard to put that man's cheques into his account
instead of his mam's. He'd practised copying his mam's signature

off the food orders from Jim Boyd's a hundred times a day. Everyone at the Wesleyville bank knew he was Ellie's son. No one had batted an eye when he'd said his mam had signed the cheques over to him.

There was a lot of money in the safety deposit box now. All that poison money from those twelve cheques, and all this stuff called interest. And then there was the money he'd saved up from his fishing and boat-building to repay all the money Mam had started getting from England after Da' died – the cheques he'd seen his mam hide in the Fry's cocoa tin on the top shelf till she'd get a lift into Wesleyville the last Thursday of the month with Jim Boyd to bank it. All this poison money was going back where it belonged. To the daughter of the man who'd blackened his dear mam's soul.

Take the money and leave Tippy's Tickle, that's all she needed to do, and take that murderer, Sam Byrne, with her. Then, everything would be back to normal. He looks up at the clouded sky. *I'm just sorry you won't be here to see it, Mam.*

He reaches the giant shards of rock that thrust up through the ocean at the base of the lighthouse. Cutting off the motor, he steers the boat through a crevice with an oar until he is underneath the cave opening. Dropping anchor, he grabs hold of a slice of rock. He tosses a rope over it and secures the boat to it with a bowline.

Tucking the leather satchel under his arm he jumps onto a flat rock sleek with water. He stumbles but catches himself on the bobbing boat. The tide is coming in. He doesn't have much time.

Grabbing a crack in the cliff face, Emmett jabs his boot onto a jutting rock and slowly makes his way up the rock face to the cave. Another toehold, another fingerhold. Then another. *No one'll ever find the box up here. That's for sure.* The wind whips a spray of saltwater against his face and he blinks to clear his eyes.

*Not far, now, b'y. Just a few more—*

The rubber sole of his boot slips against the wet rock. He hovers in the air in a millisecond that lasts an eternity. Then he crashes against the rocks and through the waves and down, down, down, sliding like an anchor into the deep, cold water.

The whale breaches, its huge body soaring out of the ocean like a missile. It slides under the water, the white foam of the waves from the breach slowly settling. Around the base of the cliff, George's letters float like white waterlilies, until they slowly sink into the blue-grey water of the North Atlantic.

# Epilogue

## Wesleyville, Newfoundland – 5 October 2011

'Bloody Nora. There's thousands here, Sam. Where on earth did Emmett get this money?'

'I haven't a clue.'

Sophie hands him a stack of hundred-dollar bills wrapped into neat piles of a thousand dollars. 'Help me count, will you?'

'Sure thing, Princess Grace.' He reaches into the safety deposit box and takes out a stack of money.

'You don't think he stole it, do you? Do you think it had anything to do with the accident over by the lighthouse? Why on earth would he have been out there?'

Sam shakes his head as he silently counts out the money. 'Emmett was a closed book, Sophie. He pretty much kept to himself. I don't think even Ellie knew what went on in his head.'

'Wait, there's something else in the box.' Sophie takes out a small white satin bag and an envelope that has yellowed with age. She slides a card out of the envelope. 'Look at this, Sam. An old Valentine's card. Looks like it's from the war, judging by the uniforms.'

Sam flips over the card. Glancing at Sophie, he clears his voice. '*Cupid is the victor o'er many a heart today. He's made me love you, sweetest, far more than words can say. One little kiss would be such bliss, oh, don't refuse me, pray!*'

Sophie smiles. 'Do you suppose Thomas gave that to Ellie when he was courting her?'

'Were you listening, maid?'

'What do you mean?'

He leans over the table. 'One little kiss would be such bliss, oh, don't refuse me, pray!' He reaches out and plants a kiss on her lips.

'Sam. Sam!' she says, giggling. 'They've probably got a camera on us in here.'

He sits back in his chair and licks his lips. 'Is that cherry?'

'Lip gloss. Becca gave it to me.' She opens the drawstring on the satin bag and shakes out two rings, a thin gold wedding band and a silver ring with a large square-cut stone. She picks up the silver ring. 'I think this was Aunt Ellie's engagement ring. She mentioned it to me once when we were drawing. This must be her wedding ring. She said she'd lost them years ago.'

'That's some diamond.'

'It's not a diamond. Ellie said it was a zircon.'

'Let me have a look at that.' He holds up the ring and squints at the silver band. 'I don't think this is silver. It's got a maker's mark. Look, a dog's head.'

Sophie takes the ring and looks at the mark on the inner rim. 'What do you think that means?'

'I've seen that mark before on a ring my mother had. It's platinum.'

'Platinum? It can't be. That's expensive.'

'Uh-huh.'

Sophie rolls the ring around her fingers. 'Do you think this really is a diamond? I've never seen one this big.'

'If the ring's platinum, that's not going to be a zircon.'

'Ellie thought it was a cheap zircon all these years.' Sophie slides the rings back into the satin bag and hands it to Sam. 'Give these to Toby for Becca. She doesn't have an engagement ring. Ellie would have liked her to have it.'

'Are you sure? If that's a diamond, that ring is going to be worth a lot of money.'

'Sam, look at the table. I have plenty of money.'

Sam surveys the ordered stacks of thousands. 'You don't have to give up your apartment now. You can stay in New York if you want to. You won't have to join Florie's commune.'

Sophie nods. 'Sam, I wanted to talk to you about that.'

He sits back in the chair. 'Uh-huh.'

'I've had an email from one of Richard's partners. Baxter T. Randall. He's not as stuffy as his name makes him sound. He's a real visionary. He has a great sense of humour, too. He's jumping ship and opening up his own practice. He's invited me to join him as a founding partner. Randall and Parry Architects.'

'Has a nice ring to it.'

'He wants me to head up the London office.'

Sam nods. 'London, eh? Just your cup of tea, Princess Grace. You'd be great.'

'I would, I know. It's a fantastic opportunity.'

'It sure is.'

'For someone else.'

Sam shakes his head. 'What do you mean?'

'The thing is, I've taken another job.'

'Right. Listen, I understand—'

'Smaller company, but big ideas. I insisted on a partnership, of course. I want a place where I can grow. If I partner up with Baxter, it'll be all about his vision. I've been through all that with Richard.'

'I get that.'

She holds out her hand across the table.

Sam stares at her hand. 'What?'

'Shake my hand.'

'What?'

'Just shake my hand.'

Sam reaches across the table and gives Sophie a firm hand-shake.

She smiles. 'Hello, partner.'


THE END

If you enjoyed *The English Wife*, be sure to follow Adrienne Chinn on Twitter @adriennechinn and on Facebook @AdrienneChinnAuthor for all the updates on their latest work.

You can also find us at @0neMoreChapter_, where we'll be shouting about all our new releases.

# *Acknowledgements*

O ne day, back in 1940, my Aunt Stephanie, then still a
teenager, met my uncle Gus Edwards, a Newfoundlander
stationed with the 57th Newfoundland Heavy Regiment (later
renamed the 166th Newfoundland Field Regiment), at Sunday
lunch at her grandparents' house in Filby, Norfolk, England.
Stephanie's grandfather was the local vicar, and he'd thought
it only right and proper to invite one of the new soldiers, so
far away from their home, to Sunday lunch each week. So, I
must thank my Aunt Stephanie's grandfather for his generosity
of spirit, without which this story may never have been
written.

The stories of Ellie and Thomas, and Sophie and Sam, were
born during a city break in Seville with my sister Carolyn
Chinn. Between visits to the Alcazar, the Cathedral, and
flamenco shows, we'd drink sherry over tapas and I'd throw
out my ideas for the novel. After five days (and a lot of excellent sherry and tapas), I had the shape of the novel, and an
idea of the main characters. Thank you, Carolyn, for listening
to my jumbled thoughts and helping me put them into some
kind of order.

Shortly after that, my friend, Mandy Sinclair, kindly lent me
the use of her flat in Marrakech while she was back in Canada,

and I spent a productive week drafting out the outline and character biographies, fortified by supportive outings around my favourite city with another friend, Aine Marsland. Many thanks to you both!

A few months later I visited Norwich, where novelist Melvyn Fickling, a Norfolk boy through and through, and another great friend, walked with me through the twisting medieval streets, seeking out the landmarks and old bomb sites that helped me recreate Norwich during the years of World War II. Thank you, Melvyn.

I spent a month during iceberg season (May), writing in St John's and Eastport, Newfoundland, as the guest of my cousin, Jennifer Edwards Gill (Aunt Stephanie's daughter), and her husband, Rob Gill. I benefited enormously from Jennifer's insight into her mother's experiences as a war bride, as well as evenings playing killer games of Settlers of Catan. Jennifer and Rob, I am indebted to you. Thank you!

In Newfoundland, I also spent writing time at my cousin, Glen Edwards's, in my home town of Grand Falls-Windsor, where I enjoyed the company and stories of my uncles, John and Reg Edwards. I rented a car and explored Fogo Island and the Kittiwake Peninsula, with a stop in lovely Trinity, all of which provided inspiration for the locations in *The English Wife*.

After Newfoundland, I availed myself of the hospitality and writing tables of my brother, Geoff Chinn, and his partner, Wendy Buckingham, and many people in Quebec and Ontario whom I'm fortunate to call my friends: Claire Delisle, Cate Creede, Craig Ryan and J-P Talb, Vicky Seton and Pierre Cardinale, Lori Legault Lorenzo and Danny Lorenzo, Krista Fidler and Greg Sayer. Thank you all.

Thank you, too, to Laurence Daren King, for being one of the guides on my writing road; to my wonderful editors, Hannah Todd, Bethan Morgan, Helena Newton, and Lydia Mason at One More Chapter; and to my agent, Jo Swainson, for keeping the faith.